BLOOD FROM A STONE

BLOOD FROM A STONE

A Jack Haldean Mystery

Dolores Gordon-Smith

This first world edition published 2013
in Great Britain and in the USA by
SEVERN HOUSE PUBLISHERS LTD of
19 Cedar Road, Sutton, Surrey, England, SM2 5DA.

British Library Cataloguing in Publication Data

Gordon-Smith, Dolores.
   Blood from a stone. – (The Jack Haldean mysteries; 7)
   1. Haldean, Jack (Fictitious character)--Fiction.
   2. Murder–Investigation–Fiction. 3. Novelists,
   English–Fiction. 4. World War, 1914–1918–Veterans–
   Fiction. 5. Detective and mystery stories.
   I. Title II. Series
   823.9'2-dc23

ISBN-13: 978-0-7278-8263-9 (cased)

Except where actual historical events and characters are being
described for the storyline of this novel, all situations in this
publication are fictitious and any resemblance to living persons
is purely coincidental.

All Severn House titles are printed on acid-free paper.

Severn House Publishers support the Forest Stewardship Council [FSC], the
leading international forest certification organisation. All our titles that are printed
on Greenpeace-approved FSC-certified paper carry the FSC logo.

Typeset by Palimpsest Book Production Ltd.,
Falkirk, Stirlingshire, Scotland.
Printed and bound in Great Britain by
MPG Books Ltd., Bodmin, Cornwall.

Dedicated to my friend, Jane Finnis,
who knows stacks about ancient Roman curse tablets!

ONE

I n *Lamont's Rambles in Sussex and Hampshire Byways*, published by Rynox and West, 1922, price one shilling and threepence, the following entry may be read:

Breagan Grange, Breagan Hollow, near Madlow Regis, Sussex: the property and chief residence of Francis Leigh, Esquire. The house, a neo-classical edifice on a mediaeval foundation, was extensively remodelled c.1728 under the influence of John Vanbrugh and little of the original structure now remains.

The gardens are particularly noteworthy, boasting a classical Arcadian temple ascribed to Vanbrugh. The temple, built into the hillside of Breagan Stump, acts as the portico or entrance to a cave housing a Roman altar and carvings dating from the latter period of Roman occupation.

The altar has been ascribed to the worship of the British-Romano god, Euthius, to whom one other dedication in Tidepit, Dorset, has been found.

A Roman urn, of native manufacture, was discovered buried beneath the altar, which, when opened, was found to contain the treasure which came to be known as The Breagan Bounty. Part of this treasure is now in the British Museum. The Bounty, dated to the late Third Century, consisted of Roman coins, jewellery and a golden box of exquisite workmanship containing a collection of uncut sapphires.

A series of excavations in the cave were carried out in 1834 when the grisly discovery of ancient human remains led to speculation (fuelled in part by a possible interpretation of the carvings on the altar and walls) that the cave could have been the scene of human sacrifice.

Nearest Railway Station: (approx. 2 miles) Madlow Regis.

Admission: by application.

Mary Hawker shielded her eyes from the August sunshine, looking at the man standing beside the wooden bench. 'I don't like the thought of digging in the cave, Frank. Whose idea was it?'

Frank stuck his hands in his pockets, hesitating before he answered. 'It's Evie's, as a matter of fact.' He grinned. 'I think what she's really hoping for is some more treasure.'

Mary nodded unenthusiastically. She'd had a good idea that it was Frank's wife, Evie, who was responsible. She didn't like Evie, a fact of which Frank was completely oblivious. Mary chose her words carefully. She always did when talking about Evie.

'I don't like it,' she said. 'Perhaps Evie doesn't understand but you grew up here, Frank. You know – you *must* know – there are forces in the cave which shouldn't be disturbed. No good will come of it.'

Frank turned and glanced up the gentle slope of Breagan Stump to where the white stone of classical pillars gleamed through the surrounding trees. His mouth twisted.

Mary Hawker, who was usually such a nice, sensible woman with no nonsense about her, had an obstinate belief in what his wife, Evie, roundly dismissed as stupid rubbish. Mary Hawker had even, Frank knew, gone in for séances after her husband, Charlie, had died.

Mary saw how his shoulders went back as he unconsciously braced himself. 'Nonsense,' he said with false heartiness. 'Absolute nonsense. It's about time the temple and the caves were properly looked in to. It might put a stop to some of these silly local superstitions.'

'You can't dismiss the stories about Breagan Stump as silly local superstitions, Frank. It's a place that must be treated warily.'

Frank, stuck for a reply, scuffed his foot awkwardly.

'What about Terry's painting of the temple?' asked Mary, knowing she was onto a winner. Although it was years since Terry and Frank had met, she knew the depth of Frank's affection for Terry. He was Frank's cousin but, after his parents had died, Terry had lived with the Leighs and been more like a brother than a cousin to Frank. 'You've always said it's one of the best paintings he ever did and yet you don't like it, do you?'

Frank shrugged. 'There's something about the shadows,

that's all. I've got it on display,' he added defiantly. 'It's in the hall for all to see.'

'I remember talking to him about it,' said Mary reminiscently. 'It's years ago now, of course, but Terry was very dubious about having it framed. I remember him saying that when you paint a scene, even if it's somewhere you know well, you get under the skin of a place. There was something about the temple that he didn't care for at all. You must have sensed a presence there at times.'

Frank ran his hand through his grey hair. 'I suppose I have,' he admitted with a rueful grin. 'But dash it, Mary, that has to be nothing more than a flight of fancy or a trick of the light. It's different for Terry. He's an artist and a damn good one. He has to have a lively imagination. I haven't got any imagination. I'm no artist.'

No, Frank wasn't an artist, thought Mary. He was something far better, a kindly, honest man with a capacity for hard work. Evie didn't appreciate him . . .

I appreciate him, she thought savagely. I care for him much more than Evie, with her fashionable clothes, her holidays and her trips to Town ever could.

Mary was in love with Frank. She didn't know how long she'd been in love with him, but she knew to the minute when she'd first admitted it to herself.

It was sixteen months and three days ago, the second anniversary of Charlie's death. Frank had called with a bunch of flowers for her. 'Something and nothing,' he'd said awkwardly. 'Celia sends her love. She picked the flowers for you. Sad occasion and all that, but we wanted to mark it in some way.' He coughed awkwardly. 'Charles was a grand chap. You must miss him. It's been tough for you.'

Frank really did understand how tough it had been. She knew that. His wife, Diana, had died years before, leaving him with baby Celia.

Celia was a young woman now, engaged to be married. Frank had been a good father. She'd always liked that, and it had been kind of Celia to think of her. She remembered thanking him – she'd said something about Celia – and reaching out for the flowers. Their hands touched and she suddenly noticed how strong and capable his hands were.

It was like a dam bursting. In that instant, with shattering force, her world turned upside down. She loved Frank.

She hadn't said anything, of course. But Frank knew. He *must* know. The world, which had been grey, drab and everyday was suddenly shot through with blinding light and glorious possibilities. She didn't have to say anything. They were such old friends it could surely only be a matter of time.

Frank sat down on the bench beside her, took his pipe from his pocket and filled it thoughtfully. 'Evie's going to dig up an expert to investigate the cave. I'll be interested to hear what he has to say.'

'When's she expected back?' asked Mary.

'Soon, I hope,' said Frank. 'The holiday will have done her good.' He brought out his tobacco pouch and pipe and stuffed tobacco into the bowl. 'I wish there was more for her here. She gets bored with the country.'

Evie had no right to be bored, thought Mary waspishly. What on earth was wrong with the country?

'I can't really blame her for being bored,' Frank said with his shy, rather boyish smile. 'I'm so tied up with the estate it's difficult to come and go as I please.'

'Only because you work so hard.'

'Yes . . .' His brow furrowed in a frown. 'I can't afford to be away.'

Mary looked at him sharply. It sounded as if Frank couldn't afford the time, but she was fairly sure he couldn't afford the money, either. He had to be careful. Evie, she guessed, resented it. She probably, thought Mary, resented it very much . . . Had Frank guessed? Maybe not. He had never guessed how she felt, after all.

Sudden, bitter hatred clutched deep inside. If only Evie would stay away and never return! Without Evie she could pretend that her dearest dream, that the enticing future that leaned out and beckoned to her sixteen months and three days ago was still possible.

Frank was an idiot. A very dear idiot, but still an idiot. That was another date she would never forget, the day ten months ago when he broke the ghastly news to her. *'Mary, I know you'll be pleased. I'm getting married again.'*

God knows what she'd said or done. Nothing out of place. Nothing to make him guess that all the colour had been drained from her world. Conventional, dowdy and dull. That's what she was and that's what she seemed. Not, she thought bitterly, like Evie, with her wonderful clothes and her perfectly made-up face.

Frank was completely bowled over by Evie. They had met at a cocktail party, and had fallen into conversation when it turned out that Evie knew an old aunt of Frank's, a Mrs Constance Paxton. Evie had, in Mary's opinion, played the connection for all it was worth, and Frank was caught, hook, line and sinker.

Frank clearly thought that Evie was the bee's knees. He really was, thought Mary, this time without a warm glow of affection, an idiot.

'I think we'd better be getting back,' said Frank. He stood up, offering her his arm, and together they walked across the grounds to the house.

Frank, pipe in mouth, stopped beside the painting in the hall. Terry's painting, the painting of the temple.

On the grass in front of the temple sat a younger Frank, his hair dark, sharing a picnic with little Celia. The chequered blue and white picnic cloth at the centre of the painting, the white of the classical columns and the blue of the sky picked up the colours of Celia's white frock tied with blue ribbons.

'I dunno,' he said, between puffs of smoke. 'There's something about it. I don't know what.'

It should have been, Mary thought, a delightful picture but there was something unsettling about it, as if something was hiding in the shadows, hidden by the bright glare of the sun. She looked at the signature. *Terence Napier. 1914.* Very soon after the painting was completed, the war had gathered him up and carried him off.

She shivered. That summer of 1914 had been wonderful, the last in a line of wonderful summers. It was as if the old world, the world before the war, had wanted to end in one last blaze of sun-soaked glory before the black clouds rolled in and darkness shrouded the earth.

'Mary?' asked Frank. 'What's wrong?'

'It's nothing.' Incredibly, her voice nearly broke. 'Nothing much, that is.'

There was lots more she could have said: in 1914 Charlie was alive, Frank was young and unworried and, most of all, there was no Evie lurking in the shadows, draining her happiness away.

'Before the war,' Frank said softly. He sighed. 'Nothing was ever the same again.' He reached out and touched the painted signature. 'Good old Terry. I haven't heard from him for ages.'

Mary shook herself. 'Didn't he go to the South Seas or something?' she asked in a consciously bright voice. 'I know it was somewhere frightfully exotic.'

'Absolutely he did,' said Frank with a laugh. 'The last time I saw Terry he said he wanted to get as far away from the war as he possibly could. I had a postcard from him in Tahiti. He was painting and beach-combing, poor as a church mouse, but as happy as a sandboy, without a care in the world.'

For all her belief in the supernatural, Mary had a strong practical streak. 'What on earth did he live on?'

'Terry never bothered about money.'

Mary found that unsatisfactory. Everyone had to bother about money. The painting was very, very good. Surely someone with that amount of talent would amount to something? 'I wonder,' she said thoughtfully, 'what Terry's doing now?'

In the village of Topfordham, twenty-two miles from Breagan Grange, Dr James Mountford could have answered Mary Hawker's question.

'Terence Napier?' said Dr James Mountford with a frown. He picked up the note from the tray of coffee and biscuits his wife had brought in to the surgery.

Mrs Mountford always brought in coffee and biscuits into the surgery after the morning patients had departed. It was part of Dr Mountford's invariable routine and Dr Mountford, a solidly built, middle-aged, well-scrubbed-looking man with the healthy complexion of one who enjoyed country air and country food, liked routine.

Urgent visits first – they weren't that common, thank goodness – then down to business in the front room of the Mountfords' house in Fiddler Street which was kitted out as a surgery.

Mildred Mountford, who, with the help of a girl, acted as both secretary and dispenser, used the adjacent room to make up the medicines her husband prescribed. Elevenses, as Mrs Mountford called their morning coffee, was followed by visits to those patients who were either ill enough or well-off enough to warrant a call from the doctor.

'That's right. Terence Napier,' said Mrs Mountford, as she crunched her way through a custard cream. 'Mrs Paxton's nephew. Mrs Paxton sent the note round with her maid, Florence. I imagine she wants to discuss him with you.'

Dr Mountford's eyebrows rose slightly. Mrs Constance Paxton of The Larches definitely came into the category of the well-off. If she requested a visit, he would certainly call, but he was still puzzled as to why.

'Mrs Paxton doesn't say anything about any nephew in her note, Milly. I didn't know she had a nephew.'

'That's just it, James. Nobody did, but he's there, all the same. Just turned up out of the blue. Naturally Mrs Paxton wouldn't say anything about it in a note. Apart from anything else, Florence would be bound to read it, but I'm certain Mrs Paxton wants to talk to you about Terence Napier. I questioned Florence and she said her mistress was perfectly well. As far as I'm concerned,' she added with an air of finality as she brushed crumbs from her dress, 'that settles it. I'm surprised you haven't heard Terence Napier spoken of.'

'I never listen to gossip,' grunted her husband, reaching for his coffee.

'No, dear,' said Mrs Mountford, looking at her husband affectionately. 'I hope Mrs Paxton's not going to keep you long. It's liver for lunch and it doesn't like being kept waiting. You'd think, wouldn't you, that an old lady like that would go to the vicar if she wanted to talk things over.'

'Douglas Billington's too young,' said Dr Mountford absently. 'Tell me about this nephew.'

Mrs Mountford pulled a face. 'He hasn't made a very good impression. He's tall, with fair hair, a pointed beard and spectacles with those very thick rims which always make me think of motoring goggles. He's just arrived from Paris, would you believe. He's about thirty-five or so, isn't married, seems a bit down at heel and is very off-hand and superior in his manner. Heaven knows why, because he doesn't sound anything special. His clothes are very well worn – scruffy, even – and *not* the best quality. He sleeps with the window open, had hardly any luggage and doesn't like haddock.'

James Mountford blinked. Mrs Mountford laughed at her husband's expression. 'Cook heard as much from Redditch, the fishmonger, and young Wilf, the butcher's boy. She wanted to know more, but that's all Mrs Welbeck, Mrs Paxton's house-keeper, would say. She isn't very forthcoming.'

'Heaven forbid what she'd let slip if she was chatty,' said the doctor with a grin. He put the list of calls in the pocket of his tweed jacket and picked up his bag. 'Keep my lunch hot for me if I'm late.'

Although Dr Mountford had laughed at his wife's interest in Mrs Paxton's nephew, he was curious enough to feel a twinge of expectation as he rang the bell of The Larches later that morning.

The Larches was a monument of Victorian gothic, and was, in Dr Mountford's opinion, far too big for one old lady and a couple of servants to run. However, he could hardly criticise Mrs Paxton for living in the house. Mr Paxton had been dead a long time and, as far as he could gather, Mrs Paxton had eked out her subsequent life of genteel poverty in boarding houses in London and on the South coast before the Burwells, distant relatives of the deceased Mr Paxton had died, leaving her The Larches together with, so it was rumoured, a fair amount of money, some eight years ago.

The door was opened not, as he had expected, by Mrs Welbeck, the housekeeper, or Florence, the maid, but by a tall, languid man with lank, grubby-looking fair hair curling over his collar, a pointed beard, heavy-rimmed glasses and an ill-fitting jacket. The nephew. He looked Dr Mountford up and down and seemed uninspired by what he saw.

'Hello. You must be the doctor, I presume.' He spoke in an affected, tired voice. 'My name's Napier, don't cher know. My aunt said you'd be calling. Come in, won't you?'

Dr Mountford felt he'd been judged and found wanting. He couldn't help taking a dislike to Terence Napier on the spot.

'God knows what she wants to see you for,' continued Napier. 'She's not ill or anything.'

Dr Mountford handed Napier his hat. Napier gazed at it vaguely before shrugging and putting it on the hall sideboard.

'She's frantically old, so it might be some medical thingamajig or other.'

Dr Mountford cleared his throat in a non-committal manner as he followed Napier down the hall.

Terence Napier smiled in sly understanding. 'You wouldn't tell me if there was, eh? It could be nerves, I suppose. Living here would be enough to put anyone in a looney-bin. The house is a perfect scream but there's enough Victorian gloom in it to get anyone down. My aunt's in the parlour. She likes it in there. God knows why.'

'Perfectly decent room,' muttered the doctor.

'My dear man!' said Napier in horror. 'It's like a museum. Those button-backed horrors of armchairs are positive instruments of torture, and as for the *colour* . . . All those muddy greens and browns and chintzes. I ask you! Watch out for the horsehair sofa, by the way. It's like sitting on thistles.'

He opened the door of the parlour and ushered Dr Mountford into the room.

Mrs Paxton, a redoubtable woman with a high forehead and iron-grey hair was sitting in the fireside chair, her walking stick beside her.

'Here we are, Aunt Constance,' said Terence Napier. 'One doctor, as prescribed, to be taken regularly before lunch.'

'There's no need to be facetious,' reproved Mrs Paxton. Despite the words, her expression softened as she looked at Napier. 'Come in, doctor. Please sit down.'

As Dr Mountford took a seat, he felt the itchy prickle of horsehair through the material of his trousers. He reflected that, although he didn't like Terence Napier's manner, he did have a point about the sofa.

It was an old-fashioned room. Indeed, he didn't think it had been altered since the Burwells' time. The massive gilt-framed and highly ornamented mirror over the massive and highly orna-mented mantelpiece reflected a welter of draped occasional tables, whatnots, plant-stands and ferns under glass domes. The room was dotted with silver-framed photographs, mainly of exuberantly moustached men and rigidly corseted women. A grand piano, its brass candleholders brilliantly polished, stood in one corner. Everything in the room was repressively polished and cleaned, regimented into its place and yet this gloomy grandeur made him feel oddly at home. It was like the parlours of his youth, the sort of room that went with stability and success, and he guessed for Mrs Paxton, with her history of boarding-house life, it represented security.

Mrs Paxton turned to her nephew. 'Off you go, dear, and leave us in peace for a few moments.'

'Just as you like, Aunt Constance.' Napier shrugged and left the room.

'He's a dear boy,' said Mrs Paxton, looking fondly after him as the door closed. 'What do you think of him?'

Dr Mountford, a tactful but honest man, coloured slightly. The real answer was *not much*, but the expectant look on Mrs Paxton's face warned him to be careful. 'It's a little difficult to say,' he said diplomatically. 'I've only just met him. He seems a little – er – unconventional.'

'He's an artist.'

Dr Mountford's face lengthened. He didn't know anything about artists.

'He was brought up, if you can call it that, by my cousins, the Leighs. You might have heard of them.'

Dr Mountford nodded. He might not listen to gossip, but everyone knew Mrs Paxton was connected to the Leighs of Breagan Grange.

'There's bad blood in that family,' said Mrs Paxton severely. 'Francis Leigh has very poor judgement and his father, Matthew, was a *gambler*.' Dr Mountford grunted in agreement. He had heard Mrs Paxton on the subject of the Leighs before. 'How Francis Leigh keeps the place going I do not know, with the pittance his father left.'

She brooded quietly for a few moments, then shook herself. 'Still, I didn't ask you here to talk about the Leighs. There is quite another matter I wish to discuss. I know in the past you have been concerned about my heart and I know I am obliged to be careful of my chest, but would you, doctor, say I am in reasonably good health?'

'Absolutely, dear lady,' agreed Dr Mountford, happy to drop

the thorny subjects of artists and families and return to familiar ground. 'Let me see . . . You were suffering from bouts of sleeplessness, but I think we've cured that, haven't we? The sleeping draught I prescribed does the trick, eh?'

'Indeed it does. I find it very beneficial. I know I'm getting older –' She was, as Dr Mountford knew, in her mid-sixties – 'and my knee gives me trouble, but I'm not *old*, am I, doctor?'

'Of course not. Mind you,' said the doctor with a smile, 'I won't see fifty again myself. But why do you ask? You're not worried about your health, are you?'

She shook her head. 'No, it's not that. I want to go abroad. I wanted your reassurance that I was fit to travel.'

'Abroad, eh? Jolly nice, too. It'll do you good to have a change of air, as long as you don't attempt anything too strenuous. I'd prescribe it for all my patients if I could.' He stroked his moustache, looking at her curiously. There was an expression on her face that he found hard to pin down, a sort of pleased excitement mixed with wariness. She was itching to talk but something was holding her back. 'Where are you off to?'

She leaned forward in her chair, her eyes alight. 'I'm going to Paris.'

'Paris!' repeated the doctor, startled. 'What, with your nephew, you mean?'

She nodded in suppressed excitement.

'But why, dear lady?'

He was right about her mixed emotions. He could see the struggle on her face. She was silent for at least a minute, then she reached a decision. 'If I tell you, doctor, you will promise to keep it to yourself, won't you?'

'You can be assured of that,' said Dr Mountford.

She took a deep breath and Dr Mountford looked at her alertly. She seemed to be nerving herself.

'My nephew – a dear boy – thinks I should say nothing but I have managed my own affairs for years. I prefer to take advice from someone I can trust.' She looked at him appraisingly. 'Dr Mountford, I trust you.'

Doctor Mountford muttered deprecatingly, but he couldn't help feeling flattered. Mrs Paxton was a sharp old lady. Very sharp indeed.

For a few moments she didn't speak. She was obviously turning something over in her mind. Then she raised her chin and looked him straight in the eye. 'Doctor, you're a man of the world. Tell me, is it true there is a general amnesty for deserters from the war?'

This was so unexpected that Dr Mountford was totally taken aback.

'An amnesty for deserters?' he said in complete astonishment. 'Whatever . . .' He stopped abruptly, covering his confusion with an artificial-sounding cough.

Her voice trembled. 'Is there, doctor?' She put a hand to her face, her eyes fixed on him.

Dr Mountford picked his words carefully. 'A deserter certainly can apply for amnesty. That's perfectly true.' He put his head to one side. 'Excuse me, Mrs Paxton, but have you got someone particular in mind?' He coughed once more. 'Your nephew, perhaps?'

To his surprise, she shook her head vigorously. 'No, not my nephew. Certainly not. Is there an amnesty, doctor?'

The doctor ran his hand round his chin. 'It's been discussed in Parliament a few times, as you probably know. During the war, a deserter would be shot –' Mrs Paxton winced – 'but now? They should be safe enough. There isn't a general amnesty, although it's often referred to as such. Each case is treated on its merits. The man has to report to the correct authorities and establish who he is, then his case is gone into. If he's not guilty of any other crime, apart from desertion, the War Office won't prosecute.'

Mrs Paxton swallowed hard and looked at him sharply. 'No other crime?' She bit her lip. 'That might be awkward,' she muttered. 'People are always so ready to judge, aren't they? It's only natural that a young man should want to enjoy himself but there was never any vice in him. He just wanted to enjoy himself. He was basically a good boy but very easily led and got into bad company. I hoped, at one time, that he would consider the church. I know he had a friend who was a minister – a vicar – but that came to nothing.' She scrunched a fold of her dress in her hand. 'I've read of explanations – medical explanations – where the boy in question was excused after he'd deserted. Especially if he had a . . .' She paused. 'A trusting nature? There really isn't any blame in those circumstances, is there?'

'Excuse me, Mrs Paxton,' said Dr Mountford. 'Who are you talking about?'

The Topfordham Poor Person's Clothing Aid Society and Ladies' Sewing Circle met every Thursday evening in the Vicarage. The Reverend Douglas Billington was dubious about the circle, referring to it, in private, as The Coven. He characterised it as nothing more than a gossip shop.

His wife disagreed. 'It's all very well, Douglas, saying it's a gossip shop but you can't expect the ladies to sit and sew in absolute silence. They do some very good work, you know. There's plenty of mothers and old people in the parish who rely on what the sewing circle provides.'

'I still say it's a hotbed of gossip,' grumbled the Reverend Billington.

And, on this particular Thursday evening, his wife had to agree that her husband might have a point.

'A nephew,' said Winifred Bilborough, her eyes bright with excitement as she crocheted the trim for a baby's dress. She glanced around the room. It was a great pity, she thought, that Mrs Henderson hadn't arrived. Mrs Henderson's Mavis was a great friend of Mrs Paxton's Florence and could be relied upon as an authoritative source of news. 'A nephew,' she repeated. 'From nowhere!'

'Hardly from nowhere,' countered Edith Henshaw. 'I understand he's a connection of the Leighs.'

'The Leighs,' repeated Agnes Beeding in a rumbling undertone, looking up from the grey woolly hat she was knitting. 'Mrs Paxton has always disapproved of *that* family.'

'I don't see why,' said Violet Sutton, her mild blue eyes circling. She was a good deal younger than Agnes Beeding. 'I mean, they're landed gentry, aren't they?'

Mrs Beeding pursed her lips and gathered herself for a rebuke, when she was pipped at the post by Susan Cunningham.

'You are too young to have heard the stories, my dear, but Matthew Leigh was an old reprobate.' She dropped her voice to a low whisper. 'He was a *gambler.*' Her voice became nearly inaudible. 'Horses! Fallen women! Nameless vice! Do I have to say more?'

Gwyneth Williams, who prided herself on being up to date with modern thought, tossed her head in disapproval. 'I imagine the stories lost nothing in the telling. All those Victorian types were far too bound by outworn shibboleths.' She pronounced this word with some satisfaction. 'I know it's difficult for older people to adjust,' she added, ignoring the disapproving snorts from Agnes Beeding and Susan Cunningham, 'but we have to move with the times. Terence Napier,' she added, glancing up to see the reaction, 'is an artist.'

'An *artist*?' repeated Agnes Beeding, aghast. 'What? Here in Topfordham? You don't mean . . .' Her soundless lips framed the words. '*Nudes?*'

Gwyneth Williams nodded in delight. 'I believe he paints from life. In Paris! And,' she added, dropping her voice to a breathy whisper, 'I did hear that he's taking Mrs Paxton to Paris with him. They leave tomorrow.'

Susan Cunningham was so agitated she jabbed the needle into her thumb. 'To Paris? At Mrs Paxton's time of life? Whatever for?'

No one knew the answer to that.

'No good will come of it, Mrs Williams,' said Susan Cunningham, sucking her thumb. 'I shall tell my girls they must steer well clear of him. An artist! You know what they're like.' She struggled with the word and dropped her voice. '*Nudes.* And Paris! Whatever does he want to carry poor Mrs Paxton off to Paris for? He can't wish to paint her, surely?'

The collected ladies blinked, shuddered and shied away from this association of ideas.

'Hardly,' boomed Agnes Beeding. 'The reason's staring you in the face, if you ask me. He's after money. Mrs Paxton,' she said, dropping her voice portentously, 'has been left very comfortably situated.'

'But he's well-off, isn't he?' said Violet Sutton wistfully, letting her mind dwell on a romantic bohemian world she knew solely from magazines. 'He must be if he's really a Leigh. Even if he is an artist.'

Edith Henshaw shook her head decisively. 'The Leigh family

are not as blessed with the world's goods as you may think, Mrs Sutton. Besides that, money in the family is not at all the same as having money oneself.'

'Exactly,' agreed Winifred Bilborough. 'I'm glad to say that Mrs Paxton's jewellery is not kept in the house. That would be *most* ill advised. Horace insists that I keep my jewellery in the bank.'

Mrs Bilborough's jewellery, consisting of an opal necklace and a pair of earrings, had long since ceased to be of any interest to the Topfordham ladies. Mrs Paxton's jewellery, on the other hand, a sapphire necklace with matching sapphire drops, rumoured to be worth many thousands of pounds, had assumed almost mythic proportions, partly because it had never been seen.

'How on earth do you know where Mrs Paxton keeps her jewellery?' asked Edith Henshaw. 'Oh, I was forgetting. Your Sally is very friendly with Mrs Paxton's John Bright, isn't she?'

Now this was something of a social brick. As a matter of course, all the women relied on their servants for news but it wasn't really done to say so quite so baldly.

'*Not* the most reliable source,' sniffed Agnes Beeding. 'And I, for one, would positively forbid any dalliance with John Bright. *Most* undesirable. I know it is the fashion to allow servants to come and go as they please, but we have an *obligation* to supervise the girls under our roof. Although there might be two views on the subject –' Mrs Beeding's tone informed her listeners precisely what she thought of anyone holding the second view – 'I would be failing in my duty if I did not warn my servants against, or, indeed, *prohibit* what I cannot but regard as a most undesirable association.'

'Some people's attitudes,' remarked Gwyneth Williams, 'are positively Victorian.'

'And no bad thing too,' said Mrs Beeding, swelling visibly. 'John Bright should have settled down long since. He must be at least forty, if not older. A man of his age should be married. It would, in my opinion, be a great deal *safer.*'

'He spends far too much time in the Malt and Shovel for my liking,' said Susan Cunningham. 'A very low establishment. If I were Mrs Paxton, I would have something to say about it.'

'He's only the outdoor man,' remarked Winifred Bilborough.

'And really, in this day and age, what can one expect? Mrs Paxton's Florence is, in my opinion, inclined to insolence but I understand her new housekeeper is an excellent cook and a most *managing* woman.'

'I know nothing about her,' said Edith Henshaw. 'She's not local, is she?'

'She's from Leeds, I believe,' said Mrs Bilborough, 'but she has excellent references.'

Violet Sutton sighed deeply. She wasn't remotely interested in servants. 'An artist sounds terribly romantic. I wonder if he was cast off by his family? Maybe they wanted him to marry against his will. Perhaps he's eloping to Paris.'

'He'd hardly elope with Mrs Paxton,' said Edith Henshaw dryly.

'Maybe his true love lives in Paris,' said Violet Sutton dreamily. 'Just like *La Bohème,* you know, where the poor singer was desperately ill. Perhaps she needs money for an operation and Terence Napier has promised to get it for her. You did say, Mrs Bilborough, didn't you,' she said, resuming hemming a blanket, 'that you knew he needed money?'

'Indeed I do,' said Winifred Bilborough. 'Shameless! You mark my words, this young man's scented some rich pickings.' She looked up as Mrs Dorothy Henderson joined the group. 'Ah, Mrs Henderson.' She leaned forward confidentially. 'We were discussing this nephew of Mrs Paxton's. He's whisking Mrs Paxton off to Paris, would you believe!'

'I certainly would,' said Mrs Henderson, opening her work-bag and taking out her knitting needles and a ball of navy-blue wool. Her eyes were bright with excitement. 'What's more, I know why.'

There was a collective gasp and the ladies craned forward.

'She's going,' said Dorothy Henderson, with the pleasurable anticipation of one about to drop a bombshell, '*to find her son.*'

She couldn't complain about the lack of reaction. There was a stunned silence as the ladies froze in their seats.

Agnes Beeding was the first to recover. 'But Mrs Paxton hasn't *got* a son,' she said blankly.

'Oh yes, she has,' said Dorothy Henderson, lowering her voice still further. 'But I'm not surprised she kept it quiet. In the circumstances she would.'

Winifred Bilborough's eyes bulged at the possible implications of this remark. '*What* circumstances?' she demanded, horrified. 'Surely you cannot mean –' her voice became virtually inaudible – '*immorality!*'

'Really, Mrs Bilborough,' said Edith Henshaw, shocked. 'How can you imagine such a thing? I must say, Mrs Henderson, I think you have been misinformed. Mrs Paxton's son died on the Somme. She told me as much. And,' she added grimly, 'sad as it was for Mrs Paxton, he doesn't sound any great loss. He was a little too free with other people's possessions, if you see what I mean. A great friend of my sister-in-law's came across him, years ago. Pleasant enough, but, to call a spade a spade, he never ran straight. That's why Mrs Paxton's never talked about him.'

'He didn't die in the war,' said Dorothy Henderson. 'He went missing. And why?' The ladies waited in breathless anticipation. 'He was a deserter!'

A pool of silence widened round Dorothy Henderson.

'Are you sure?' demanded Agnes Beeding eventually.

Dorothy Henderson nodded vigorously. 'Absolutely. She said as much to Dr Mountford. She swore him to secrecy and I'm not surprised. This Terence Napier came across him in Paris and he's taking Mrs Paxton over there to find him.'

'Stuff and nonsense,' boomed Winifred Bilborough. She was feeling very put out that the most red-hot piece of news ever voiced at the sewing circle had not fallen to her to announce. 'A likely tale! I don't believe a word of it! You mark my words, Mrs Henderson, there's more to this than meets the eye! If you want my opinion, Terence Napier has made up the whole story in order to ingratiate himself.'

The vicar's wife, who had caught snatches of the conversation, thought it was time to intervene. 'Why, you've nearly finished that crocheted trim, Mrs Bilborough! Well done! Those stitches are perfect. I want to put together a parcel of baby linen for Mrs Meddon. It's her fourth, you know, and it could be any time now. And Mrs Beeding, do you think that hat would be suitable for Wally Lightfoot? His mother would be very grateful for it.' And, much to the collective ladies' seething annoyance, she firmly steered the conversation towards clothing.

'I know what I said earlier, Douglas,' she remarked to her husband that evening, 'and I take it all back. Who on earth is this Terence Napier they were talking about?'

'I haven't a clue, my dear,' remarked the vicar absently. 'I've never heard of him.'

Two weeks later, everyone who bought that morning's newspaper had heard of Terence Napier. His name was headline news.

TWO

M rs Paxton and Terence Napier, much to Topfordham's collective disappointment, returned from Paris alone.

That evening, Mrs Welbeck, Mrs Paxton's housekeeper, called at Doctor Mountford's to request a bottle of her mistress' sleeping-draught and to ask the doctor to attend Mrs Paxton the following day.

Dr Mountford delicately enquired of Mrs Welbeck if Mrs Paxton's trip had been a success.

She looked at him blankly. 'I don't know,' she said in her flat Northern accent. 'She's not said nothing to me. I don't like to talk about other folk's affairs, especially them as pay me.'

Which was laudable, thought Dr Mountford, but frustrating all the same.

Mrs Welbeck, said Milly Mountford, who had heard the exchange, was as close as wax, adding, with a sniff, in her opinion, she gave herself airs.

That, Dr Mountford argued, had a lot to do with Mrs Welbeck's appearance. She was skinny, with sallow skin, rabbit teeth, goggling spectacles and a curiously colourless personality. In Dr Mountford's experience, everyone wanted to be recognised for *something*. If a woman wasn't good looking, intelligent or kindly, she would fall back on arrogance. It was her way of saying to the world that she simply didn't care what it thought.

Mrs Paxton's mysterious nephew and Mrs Paxton's still more mysterious son had, naturally enough, been the chief topic of conversation in the village for the last fortnight. Of all the inhabitants of Topfordham, Doctor Mountford was, as far as he knew, the only one who knew the reason for Mrs Paxton's trip to Paris.

It said a lot for his wife's tact that she let him continue in this state of blissful ignorance. She had, of course, raised the subject, but Dr Mountford had looked away, coloured, muttered *ethics, dear* and refused to discuss it.

The next morning, Dr Mountford rang the front doorbell of The Larches with a feeling of anticipation. He might not listen to gossip but he wasn't immune from curiosity, and he was looking forward to hearing Mrs Paxton's account of the search for her son.

There were footsteps in the hall in answer to his ring on the doorbell. Hurried footsteps, the doctor noted, with a feeling of surprise, then, with a rattle of bolts, the door was flung open by the housekeeper.

Dr Mountford took a step back in alarm. When Mrs Welbeck had called at the surgery the previous evening, she had been coldly reserved. Now she was a badly frightened woman and anything but reserved. Her face was flushed and her cap askew, with grizzled grey hair escaping in strands down her face. She clasped her hands together at the sight of him and sagged in such heartfelt relief that Dr Mountford couldn't help but warm to her.

'Doctor! I'm that glad you're here!' She nervously glanced up the stairs behind her. 'I . . . We . . . don't know what to do.'

'There, there, my good woman, don't take on so,' he said reassuringly. 'Whatever is it?' he asked, coming into the hallway.

She twisted her hands together once more. 'It's Mrs Paxton. I can't wake her and the door's locked. She never locks the door, doctor. Both me and Florence have knocked and called, but can't get any answer.' There was mounting panic in her voice. 'I've tried. We both have. Florence and I looked through the keyhole, but the curtains are drawn and the room's very dark. I thought of breaking the door down, but I didn't like to. It's Mrs Paxton's bedroom, after all and it doesn't seem right. Then I saw you coming up the path and I knew you'd know what to do.'

Dr Mountford, although his mind was on Mrs Paxton, couldn't help feeling flattered by Mrs Welbeck's complete confidence in him. He put his hat on the sideboard – Mrs Welbeck was too flustered to take it – and, unconsciously bracing himself, slipped into the language of the consulting-room. 'Never mind, my dear. Don't worry. We'll soon see what the problem appears to be.'

He strode up the stairs, Mrs Welbeck following in his footsteps.

Florence, the maid, a sharp-looking girl of about eighteen, was standing awkwardly outside the bedroom. 'I'm that glad to see you, sir. We haven't heard a peep from the mistress' room and we couldn't think what to do for the best. Mrs Welbeck said maybe we should force the door.' She clasped her hands together. 'I screamed at the idea. I did, true as I'm stood here.'

Florence's bulging eyes made Dr Mountford fearful she was about to repeat the performance. He hastily reached out a hand to comfort her. 'There, there. Don't upset yourself unduly. There's no need to panic, I'm quite sure.'

'But the notion of forcing the door worried me so!' Dr Mountford became aware that Florence was rather enjoying the drama. 'The mistress is always so particular. Terrible particular. She wouldn't like it if Mrs Welbeck or I took the law into our own hands, as you might say.'

'I knew you'd know what to do, sir,' said Mrs Welbeck.

Dr Mountford felt encouraged.

'Leave it to me,' he said. He rapped on the door, then, when there was no answer, knelt down and looked through the keyhole. 'I can't see a thing.' He stood up and dusted off the knees of his trousers, then put his shoulder to the door and pushed hard. Nothing happened. 'Is there another key to this room?'

Mrs Welbeck shook her head. 'No, sir.' She glanced nervously at the door. 'It . . . It doesn't seem right, does it?'

'No,' said Dr Mountford, stepping back. 'No, it doesn't seem right at all.' He stepped away from the door. 'I think I'll have to break the door down.'

Both Mrs Welbeck and Florence gave a little shriek in unison. Dr Mountford held his hand up sternly. 'Don't argue. It's all for the best.' He thought for a moment. Another man would be useful. 'Is Mr Napier here?'

Florence's eyes circled. 'No, sir. He's gone. Last night, it was. Packed his bags and gone, he has.'

Dr Mountford dismissed the disappearing Terence Napier and

eyed the door appraisingly. He'd been a keen rugby player in his youth and was still a powerful, well-built man. He braced himself and, taking a run up, thudded shoulder first, into the door. The door creaked but remained closed. That had nearly done it.

He gathered up all his strength and ran at the door once more. Under the force of the blow, the wood splintered and broke and the door was flung back.

Dr Mountford smacked his hands together in satisfaction. With Florence tagging along and Mrs Welbeck bringing up the rear, he stepped gingerly into the room.

'Mrs Paxton?' he called hesitantly. 'Mrs Paxton?' The curtains were closed and it was difficult to see in the velvet-induced gloom.

Mrs Welbeck walked to the window, drew back the curtains, then turned and gave a gasp, her hand to her mouth.

Constance Paxton was sitting in the chair by the fireplace in her nightclothes and dressing gown. Her mouth had fallen open and her arm dangled by the side of the chair.

Florence stared at her. 'She's a corpse,' she said with the unconscious brutality of a country-bred girl. 'My Gran looked like that when she passed on,' she added knowledgeably. 'She's a corpse.'

Dr Mountford swallowed. Mrs Paxton was indeed a corpse but he found Florence's willing acceptance of grim reality a little hard to take.

'There, there, don't upset yourself, my dear,' he said, knowing it was a completely redundant statement. Florence gazed at him and he looked back to Mrs Paxton, not knowing what to say.

More to reassert his authority than with any real purpose in mind, he walked to the body. He tried to lay Mrs Paxton's arm back on her knee, but she was stiff and unyielding. *'Rigor mortis,'* he muttered.

'She's stiff, isn't she?' said Florence. 'My Gran was stiff. We had to sit on her knees to straighten her out.'

'Yes, yes, yes,' said Dr Mountford hastily. Again, he looked for an excuse to show he was in charge. An empty brandy glass, a small jug, and a brown medicine bottle were on the table beside Mrs Paxton. Dr Mountford picked up the bottle. His face altered.

'Bless my soul!' He was struggling for words. 'God bless my soul! This is the bottle I prescribed yesterday. It's empty!'

'She must've drunk it all,' said Florence. 'Shouldn't she have done?'

Doctor Mountford had gone pale. 'Of course she shouldn't, girl!'

Mrs Welbeck gave a muffled cry and slumped against the wall. Dr Mountford quickly strode across the room, put his arm round her and sat her gently on the bed. 'Easy now. Easy.'

'What happened, doctor?' asked Mrs Welbeck fearfully.

Dr Mountford took a deep, ragged breath. 'I'm afraid she must have taken the entire bottle.'

There was a little whimper from Mrs Welbeck. 'The poor thing must've made a mistake.'

That was the kindest theory. For a brief moment Dr Mountford nearly agreed, but he simply couldn't bring himself to do it. He shook his head slowly. 'I don't think so. The dose is written on the bottle. One teaspoonful, that's all, not the entire bottle.'

'Could she have got it wrong?' whispered Mrs Welbeck.

'I'm afraid not. Facts are facts, and we must face them.' He turned to look at Constance Paxton and sighed deeply. 'The poor, silly woman. I'd have said she was the last person in the world to do such a thing.'

Mrs Welbeck covered her face with her apron and broke into hard, dry sobs. Dr Mountford squeezed her shoulder comfortingly.

'I'm sorry, doctor,' she said after a little while. 'I was dreading something like this, but this is worse than I thought. Poor lady! To see her there and in her night things, too! She'd have been absolutely mortified, at the thought of you seeing her like this. There doesn't seem to be any sense to it!' She gulped noisily, gathered up her apron in her hands once more and buried her face in the cloth.

Dr Mountford glanced up to see Florence staring at him.

'Did she do it herself? *Deliberate,* like? Are you saying she killed *herself*?' asked Florence with goggling eyes.

'That's enough from you, my girl,' said Mrs Welbeck with an attempt at sharpness. 'Can't it be a mistake, doctor?'

'I honestly can't see it can,' said Dr Mountford. 'Did you see her take the sleeping-draught?'

Mrs Welbeck shook her head slowly. 'I'm trying to remember. No, I don't think I did. As often as not, she liked me to get everything ready and then she'd sit for a while, reading or what have you. That's what happened last night.'

'Fancy her doing herself in,' said Florence with barely suppressed excitement.

'Will you be hushed, girl!' snapped Mrs Welbeck.

Florence tossed her head petulantly, then gave a little cry. 'Why! There's the key. It's on the floor, look!' She picked it up and handed it to the doctor. 'She must've locked herself in. She'd want some peace and quiet if she was going to do herself in. She shouldn't have done it, should she? It's wrong, that. She went to church regular, too. She should've known it was wrong.'

Dr Mountford had a sudden mental picture of Mrs Paxton in her Sunday best and off to communion service.

'It'll be in the *News of the World*,' said Florence. 'It always is when someone does themselves in.'

'It'll be nothing of the sort!' said Mrs Welbeck in a harried way. 'Tell, her, doctor.'

'As a matter of fact, she's right,' said Dr Mountford reluctantly. 'I'm afraid there will have to be an inquest.'

'An inquest?' repeated Mrs Welbeck, horrified. 'Surely not. Mrs Paxton wouldn't have approved of that *at all*.'

'It's necessary, my dear lady, I'm afraid. The coroner will have to be informed.'

Mrs Welbeck made a choking noise. 'Why? What's it got to do with him?'

Dr Mountford sighed. 'I have to inform the coroner so he can ascertain the cause of death. I can't possibly give a certificate in these circumstances.'

'It's none of his business,' muttered Mrs Welbeck.

'It's a matter of law. I am obliged to inform the coroner in all causes of violent or suspicious deaths, such as suicide or murder.'

'*Murder?*' echoed Florence. 'Cor! Was she *murdered*? That'll be in the papers for sure. Who did it? I bet it was that Mr Napier, weren't it? You said they'd had a right old barney, Mrs Welbeck, didn't you? And she sent him packing. I bet he sneaked back and seen her off. *Murder,*' she said happily.

'Don't be ridiculous, girl,' began Dr Mountford, then stopped.

As a matter of fact, despite the sensational nature of the word, there was nothing inherently improbable about murder.

In fact, he admitted to himself, granted Mrs Paxton's character, of the three possibilities of accident, murder or suicide, murder was actually the most probable. Mrs Paxton wasn't careless or given to emotional highs or lows and he couldn't honestly say that she had ever displayed the slightest suicidal tendency.

He bit his lip, worrying the thought to its conclusion. Murder meant the police and the police, in Topfordham, meant Constable George Upton. His heart sank.

Crime, as such, hardly occurred in Topfordham. Constable Upton was well versed in the various misdemeanours of village life, such as Drunk and Disorderly, poaching, kids scrumping apples, keeping an eye on any tramp or vagrant, infringement of livestock regulations and pulling up the odd speeding motorist, but he wasn't up to murder.

He had a good idea that Constable Upton would find the very idea of murder in Topfordham so utterly bizarre that he'd have to be bullied into taking it further. Dr Mountford was sensitive enough to shrink at the thought of Constable Upton's bovine incredulity. If he could assemble enough facts he could insist that Upton take the matter seriously from the start.

He looked at Florence thoughtfully. She was a bright girl. Maybe she'd put her finger on it right away.

'Mrs Welbeck,' he said questioningly. 'What was Mrs Paxton's quarrel with Napier about?'

She looked at him, startled. 'Why?'

'Just tell me what it was about.'

Mrs Welbeck shrugged. 'I couldn't follow properly. There were some foreign names I couldn't catch. I do remember one word though. Very distinct, it was.' She hesitated. '*Fraud.*'

Dr Mountford felt a thrill of discovery. 'Did you catch what was said about this fraud?'

Mrs Welbeck shook her head slowly. 'No, doctor. It was to do with money, I do know that. She was upset, though, I could tell. It must have been something that came up sudden, like. She was friendly enough with Mr Napier when they got back. She was never one for showing her feelings but she was all over him, as you might say, at first. I know that for a fact. Then they had words. The mistress mentioned her will but I couldn't follow what she was saying.'

'Her will, eh?' said Dr Mountford dubiously. That sounded complicated. 'Did she keep her will here, d'you know?'

Mrs Welbeck shrugged. 'I don't know, sir. If she did, it'll be in the walnut desk in the morning room. That's where she kept all her papers.'

Dr Mountford hesitated. He wanted to see the will but his curiosity was tempered by official caution.

'Mrs Paxton always kept the desk locked,' said Mrs Welbeck. 'The key's in her bedside drawer.'

That settled it. Medical matters were a proper subject for his enquiries but opening a locked desk to hunt for a will, however tempting the prospect, certainly wasn't. However, fraud was certainly a motive for murder. As to the murderer . . .

He had disliked the languid, long-haired Terence Napier on sight, despite Mrs Paxton's obvious affection for him. There really wasn't any doubt in Dr Mountford's mind that if Mrs Paxton had been murdered, Terence Napier was the guilty party. However, he reminded himself with strict fairness, no matter how affected Terence Napier's manner was, he wasn't a magician.

The locked door wasn't a problem; it would be easy enough to turn the lock from the outside and slip the key underneath the door but how on earth had he induced Mrs Paxton to drink a whole bottle of her sleeping-tonic?

Had Napier been in the room? There were no signs of a struggle. Mrs Paxton's sleeping-draught was, as he well knew, sulphonal. It was one of his favourite prescriptions, especially for elderly patients, as it had no effect on either the heart or lungs.

Sulphonal was odourless and tasteless and dissolved readily in warm water or alcohol. A teaspoonful in a glass of warm brandy and water, drunk as a nightcap, was a prescription most patients were perfectly happy to take. Looking at Mrs Paxton's peaceful pose, it looked as if that was exactly what she'd done. Maybe Napier had given her the tonic before she'd gone to bed.

'Mrs Welbeck,' he asked, 'when did Mr Napier leave the house?'

'After his quarrel with the mistress, sir, just like I told you.'

'Yes, but when? The time, I mean?'

Mrs Welbeck screwed up her face in memory. 'Seven o'clock or so, I'd say.'

'And what time did Mrs Paxton come up to bed?'

'About half past ten.'

Doctor Mountford clicked his tongue in irritation. Napier had left the house long before Mrs Paxton died. The action of any given drug on any given subject was very idiosyncratic, but if Mrs Paxton had taken a large dose of sulphonal before seven o'clock, she would have been incapable long before half ten.

He walked across to the bedside table and picked up the brown medicine bottle thoughtfully. He simply couldn't think how it had been done.

At that point Dr Mountford's belief Mrs Paxton had been murdered wavered. Then he looked once more at Mrs Paxton in her chair and his instincts revolted. He *knew* Mrs Paxton. Suicide was easier to explain than murder, but it was just as incredible.

'Mrs Welbeck,' he said. 'Tell me exactly what happened last night when Mrs Paxton came to bed. Did you give her the sleeping-draught?'

Mrs Welbeck swallowed convulsively. 'Yes, sir.' She looked nervously at the body. 'I didn't do anything I've not done a hundred times before. Mrs Paxton liked the same routine. Old ladies like to have things just so. I turned down the sheets and helped her into her night things. She didn't get into bed straight away but sat in the fireside chair with that shawl round her. She said she was going to read for a while.' Her lip quivered. 'Last night, I stayed for a little longer than usual, thinking she might want to say something about her trip to Paris and Mr Napier going off so sudden, but she didn't.' She looked appealingly at the doctor. 'She was never one for confidences, as you know, sir, unless it might be you, perhaps.'

'I don't know what she did in Paris,' said the doctor. 'I was hoping to learn more this morning. Tell me about the sleeping-draught.'

Mrs Welbeck gulped. 'I brought a small glass of brandy and a little jug of hot water upstairs and set it on the tray on the table by her chair. Then I measured out a spoonful from the medicine bottle and stirred it into the glass. She didn't drink it all right away. That's what usually happened. Often as not, she'd sip it while sitting in her chair.' Mrs Welbeck's mouth quivered once more. 'You'd told her she might as well enjoy it, poor old thing, and that's what she did.'

Dr Mountford shook his head. There didn't seem much to go on there. 'Was there anything out of the ordinary last night? Was there anything unusual about the jug, the bottle or the glass, say?'

To his intense satisfaction, Mrs Welbeck hesitated. There *was* something! 'Go on,' he encouraged. 'What was it?'

'Well, I don't know as you'd call it unusual, particularly, but I did think the bottle was very light. I used the last spoonful.'

'Very light?' questioned Dr Mountford sharply. He looked at the bottle in his hand. 'I gave you a new bottle when you came to the surgery last night. This is it.'

'I know, sir,' said Mrs Welbeck in distress. 'I was halfway down the stairs when it struck me I had a new bottle, but I didn't really think about it properly, if you follow me. I suppose, if I thought anything, I must've thought that I used the last of the old. I know I put one teaspoonful in her glass and that emptied it.'

Dr Mountford absently weighed the bottle in his hand. He was badly puzzled. 'You say the bottle was nearly empty *before* you gave Mrs Paxton her sleeping-draught?'

'Nearly empty. Yes, that's right.'

'But what happened to the rest of the medicine? Could Mrs Paxton have spilt it, perhaps?'

'She *could* have done, I suppose,' began Mrs Welbeck hesitantly, 'but . . .' She shook her head vigorously. 'No, that's not right. If she'd spilt it, she'd call for me or Florence to clean it up. Very particular, she was. She wouldn't have done it. I doubt if she could bend to do it and she wouldn't have the cloths or water to clean it up, nasty sticky stuff as it is.' Her bewilderment increased. 'But if it wasn't spilt, sir, what did happen to it?'

'That's the question,' muttered Doctor Mountford. 'If the bottle was empty, Mrs Paxton couldn't have added it to her brandy after you'd left the room. So if the sulphonal wasn't in the bottle, where was it?'

Mrs Welbeck looked at him blankly.

'It must've been in the bottle, the jug or the glass,' continued

Dr Mountford. 'It wasn't in the bottle, so that leaves the glass or the jug. Unless she drank it from the bottle before you came into the room,' he added.

'Drank it from the bottle?' cried Mrs Welbeck in astonishment. 'No! She'd never do such a low, common thing. Drink from the bottle, indeed!'

Dr Mountford glanced at Mrs Paxton. He might be mistaken about her committing suicide but he was certain Mrs Welbeck was right about her not drinking from the bottle. That really was incredible.

'In that case it must have been in the jug or the glass.'

'It most certainly was not,' said Mrs Welbeck indignantly. 'I filled that jug with water from the kettle and as for the glass, there was nothing in it but good brandy.'

Dr Mountford chewed his moustache again. 'Where's the brandy kept? In the kitchen?'

'Not the drinking brandy,' said Mrs Welbeck, bristling. 'The cooking brandy, yes, that's there, as you'd expect, but the drinking brandy is most certainly not kept in the kitchen. How can you suggest such a thing, doctor?' She dabbed at her eyes with the corner of her apron. 'It's bad enough with the mistress lying dead without you suggesting that I helped myself to her spirits. In the kitchen, indeed! It's on the sideboard in the dining room, as you'd expect.'

'There's no need to upset yourself,' said Dr Mountford pacifically. 'I'm just thinking something through. Can you show me the brandy decanter?'

Mrs Welbeck was only partially mollified. 'I suppose so, though what you're going to tell by looking at it, I don't know. If you come with me, I'll show you exactly where it is. Kept in the kitchen! I've never heard the like!' She stalked out of the room, her shoulders set in a defensive line.

On the dining-room sideboard was a soda siphon and five cut-glass decanters with silver labels. The whisky, sherry, port and Madeira decanters were half full, but the brandy decanter was nearly empty.

'Was the decanter nearly empty last night?' asked Dr Mountford.

'Yes, it was, since you ask. I should have filled it this morning,

but you can't blame me for not thinking of it, I've been so upset.'
Mrs Welbeck reached out as if to pick it up, and was stopped
by a quick exclamation from Dr Mountford.

'Leave it!'

She turned to him, startled. 'I'm very glad you didn't refill
the decanter,' he said. 'Have you got a key to this room?'

'Yes, of course.'

'In that case, I think we'd better lock the door and leave things
as they are until the police get here.'

Despite her evident bewilderment, he refused to say what
was in his mind. Mrs Welbeck was notoriously close-lipped,
but she was a woman after all. He didn't want the slightest
chance of his suspicions being bruited abroad until they could
be proved.

Terence Napier had left the house after a quarrel concerning
fraud. It would be easy enough for Napier to have slipped upstairs,
taken the sulphonal, put it in the brandy decanter then replace
the bottle in her bedroom and leave the house without anyone
being any the wiser. It would, thought the doctor, be a very easy
way to commit a murder.

The image of Constable Upton occurred to him once more
and he quailed. This was way beyond Upton. Who did he
know? He suddenly thought of the chief constable, Major-
General Flint.

Of course! Flint was a bit of a martinet and had rather too
great an idea of his own self-importance to be a genuinely like-
able soul, but at least he wouldn't boggle at the idea of murder.
Suddenly cheered, he turned to Mrs Welbeck with a reassuring
smile.

'Now don't distress yourself, my good woman. Florence went
to put the kettle on, didn't she? It should've boiled by now. Why
don't you go and make yourself a nice cup of tea? I have to
make a few telephone calls.'

'There's no telephone in the house, doctor,' said Mrs Welbeck.

'I know that. I'll go back to the Surgery and telephone from
there. I'll see everything's sorted out.'

It was an hour and a half later. The chief constable, Major-General
Flint, Inspector Sutton and Dr Mountford were in the morning

room of The Larches. Mrs Welbeck, who had been dispatched to bring the key to the walnut cabinet, obviously wanted to linger in the room, but was curtly dismissed by General Flint.

'There is a will in here, sir,' said Inspector Sutton, opening the desk and rifling quickly through the neatly arranged pigeon-holed contents.

'Is there, by George!' said the general in satisfaction.

'In fact,' said Inspector Sutton, looking at the collection of stiff cardboard envelopes he had spread out on the lid of the desk, 'there seem to be three.'

'Three?' barked General Flint in astonishment. 'Let me see those.'

Sutton stood out of the way as the chief constable picked up the envelopes. 'Why on earth would she keep all her previous wills?'

'A lot of people don't like to destroy official documents, sir,' said Sutton with a shrug.

'I suppose so,' said general Flint absently. 'All three wills are written on printed will forms. Did she have anyone to look after her legal affairs?' he asked, turning to Dr Mountford.

'I really don't know,' replied the doctor. 'She certainly didn't use the local man. She was badly off in her younger days, so she may not have had a solicitor at all.'

'I see,' said the general, slipping the first will out of the envelope. 'What have we got here?' He adjusted a pair of spectacles on his nose. '*Last Will and Testament of Constance Agnes Paxton. Eighth of March, 1913.* It all seems fairly clear. She leaves everything to her son, Alexander Robert Paxton, with the exception of the sapphire necklace and sapphire drops, currently in the safe-keeping of the Provincial and Counties Bank, Leadenhall Street, London EC1. They go to Francis Leigh of Breagan Grange, Madlow Regis, Sussex. She names the bank as the executor.' He looked over the top of his spectacles. 'Francis Leigh? Bless my soul! I know Mr Leigh!'

'She was related to the Leighs,' put in Dr Mountford.

'Well, well, well. Was she, by Jove! What's this second will? *Last Will and Testament of Constance Agnes Paxton, Second of January 1917.*'

He read it through, muttering to himself. 'The bank's the

executor again, but there's no mention of her son or Francis Leigh. I wonder why not?'

'As I understand it, she didn't get on with the Leighs,' said the doctor. 'And, of course, by 1917 she thought her son was dead. She believed he'd died on the Somme. It was only later she discovered he was still alive.'

'It's handy to be thought dead if you're a deserter,' said the general dryly. He turned his attention to the will once more. 'Apart from a bequest to the Red Cross, she leaves her entire property to a Mrs Evangeline Farley of Eleven, Rawling Road, Kensington. *In acknowledgement of my gratitude and an expression of fellow-feeling and sympathy for the grievous loss she has suffered in the war.*' He looked at the doctor enquiringly. 'I don't suppose you've any idea who this Mrs Farley is, have you?'

Dr Mountford shook his head, reaching out his hand for the will. 'I've never heard of her, but it sounds as if she might be a bereaved mother or a war widow,' he ventured. 'Mrs Paxton lived in a succession of boarding houses before she came into her money. She might be a friend from those days. It's witnessed by the Pollucks,' he added with a fleeting smile. 'I remember the Pollucks. They had the bakers-and-confectioners' shop on Shaw Street.'

'Hello!' said General Flint, taking the third will from its envelope. 'Listen to this! *Last Will and Testament of Constance Agnes Paxton, Twenty-third of June 1925.*'

'That's only a couple of weeks ago!' said the doctor, startled.

General Flint read the will through and turned to Dr Mountford with a curious expression. 'The bank's the executor again, but would you like to guess at who is named as the chief beneficiary? In fact,' he added, 'the only beneficiary?'

'I haven't a clue. Mrs Paxton never consulted me about her will.'

'Would it surprise you to learn she leaves everything to Terence Napier?'

'It most certainly would!' exclaimed Dr Mountford.

He took the will from General Flint's outstretched hand and read it through quickly. 'That's extraordinary. She was convinced her son was alive. I'm not surprised she drew up a new will, but surely she'd leave everything to him.'

Inspector Sutton coughed. 'I wouldn't be at all surprised, sir, if that will turned out to be a forgery.'

'It *looks* all right,' began Dr Mountford doubtfully, then stopped. 'Dash it, no it's not! Look who's witnessed it. *Albert Polluck, baker, and Jessie Polluck, married woman,* exactly the same as the previous will. Dammit, that's impossible!'

Inspector Sutton looked gratified at this support but as puzzled as Major-General Flint.

'Would you care to explain yourself, Mountford?' asked the general.

'I most certainly would. Albert Polluck's been dead these last three years and Jessie died last March! I should know. Both of them were my patients.'

general Flint snatched back the two wills and examined them closely. 'By George, I think you're right,' he muttered after a few moments' intense study. 'These signatures aren't bad likenesses of the originals, but they're too carefully done, if you know what I mean. I think they've been traced.' He looked up triumphantly. 'I'd say these signatures are definitely forgeries.'

As the witnesses had been dead before they apparently signed the will, it didn't need much reflection to conclude they were false, thought Dr Mountford, but he let Major-General Flint have his moment of self-congratulation.

The general put the will down on the desk and rubbed his hands together. 'There we are. Motive, suspect and, if your suspicions about the brandy decanter prove to be correct, doctor, the method as well.'

At the end of a very busy day, Major-General Flint put down the telephone in the tiny front room of Constable Upton's house that was Topfordham's police station.

Constable Upton, evicted by his superiors – not only Inspector Sutton from Lewes but the chief constable himself – was in the kitchen, feeling disgruntled and, at the same time, relieved, that the only major crime ever to have occurred in the living memory of Topfordham had been so imperiously taken out of his hands.

The chief constable turned to Dr Mountford with a satisfied

expression. 'That telephone call was the result of the analysis. You were right. There was sulphonal in the brandy decanter.'

Dr Mountford couldn't help but breath a sigh of relief. 'So it was murder, then?'

'No doubt about it,' said the chief constable decisively. 'Granted that Napier quarrelled with his aunt on their return from Paris, he had to act quickly. The only problem, as I see it, was that the bedroom door was locked and the key inside the room.'

Sutton shook his head. 'I reckon Napier waited outside the house, then sneaked back in, locked the door and pushed the key under the door.'

'To come back in the house seems quite a risk.'

Sutton shrugged. 'Not really, sir, and it did make it look like suicide. If Napier had been seen, it would have been awkward but he could have explained it easily enough. He could have left something, say, and wanted to get it back without disturbing the house – that sort of thing. He was at a big advantage from knowing the household routine. The outdoor man sleeps over the old stables, the housemaid was off out and Mrs Welbeck was in the housekeeper's room, listening to the radio. Who's going to stop him? After all,' he added, with a grudging acknowledgement of credit where it was due, 'it was only because Dr Mountford felt so certain Mrs Paxton wasn't the type to kill herself he went looking for another explanation.'

'You'd have said it was suicide, eh, Sutton?'

'Yes, sir,' agreed Sutton with reluctant honesty. 'Faced with that locked door, most would. Of course,' he added to the doctor, 'you were at an advantage, knowing the lady as you did.'

The chief constable took an arrest warrant from his briefcase and signed it. 'Here you are, inspector. You'd better make a statement to the Press. We could do with any publicity we can get to find Terence Napier. The sooner that gentleman is behind bars, the better for everyone.'

THREE

Some two months after the events in Topfordham, Mrs Isabelle Stanton, fresh from a fortnight spent with her parents, weaved her way through the crowds to the end of the platform at Market Albury station.

A pile of boxes, parcels and suitcases, five bicycles and four baskets of clucking hens, basking in the August sun, marked the pile of goods to be loaded into the Guard's van destined for London and stops en route. Behind Isabelle, the porter, delayed by his laden trolley, followed in her footsteps.

'This'll do, Miss,' said the porter, as he brought his trolley to a halt. As a matter of courtesy, all ladies were 'Misses' to him. 'I'll see the luggage onto the train.' He pushed his cap back and wiped his forehead as she tipped him the expected shilling. 'Thank you very much, Miss. You've got about quarter of an hour before the London train gets in.'

Isabelle retreated to the welcome shade outside the Ladies' Waiting Room. The bench was occupied by a stout woman who was evidently feeling the heat, holding the handle of a black umbrella in a deathly grip. She was darting dubious glances at a well-dressed, foreign-looking woman who was, not very effectively, attempting to control her two small boys with bursts of idiomatic French.

Beside the foreign-looking woman sat a little girl, very prettily dressed, who was, to Isabelle's eyes, consciously being good. The two small boys skittered in and out of the crowd of waiting passengers, calling to each other in shrill French voices. Beyond the station, the gold of the cornfields rose up the tree-crowned hills, hazy in the hot August air.

Market Albury, thought Isabelle idly. She wasn't very far from Celia's house, Breagan Grange in Madlow Regis.

She hadn't seen Celia for ages. Did she know anything about the murder in Topfordham?

Isabelle wouldn't have known there was any connection

between Mrs Paxton's murder and her old friend, if her father hadn't said as much the other day.

'I see they still haven't found Terence Napier,' he said, tapping the newspaper. 'Shocking business. Rackety bunch, the Leighs. Napier's a cousin of theirs, of course.'

'It's a little hard to dismiss the entire Leigh family as rackety, Philip,' said her mother in mild reproof. 'I know old Matthew Leigh was a real rip, but Francis Leigh is very well thought of and Celia is a very nice girl.'

'Terence Napier is Celia Leigh's cousin?' asked Isabelle in astonishment. 'What, you mean the man who murdered his aunt?'

'Terence Napier is Francis Leigh's first cousin, therefore he is first cousin once removed to Francis Leigh's daughter,' croaked Great-Aunt Clarissa from the winged chair in the corner.

Isabelle's parents were enduring Great-Aunt Clarissa's annual visit. Aunt Clarissa was, in fact, the reason why Isabelle had temporarily abandoned her husband to spend a fortnight at home. Her mother felt she needed the support. Arthur had said Isabelle was welcome to go. If he'd to face Aunt Clarissa, he'd need all the support he could get too. It was just too bad, he added with a mournful expression that didn't fool her for a moment, that he couldn't spare the time to come as well.

The various ramifications of County families were one of Great-Aunt Clarissa's abiding passions. 'Napier lost his parents as a boy and was brought up by Matthew Leigh. A very unfortunate influence, in my opinion. He became,' she added with a sniff, 'an artist. *Most* unsatisfactory.'

It was, thought Isabelle, difficult to say if Great-Aunt Clarissa disapproved of Terence Napier because he was an artist or because he'd bumped off his aunt. Both, by the sound of it.

'Celia's never mentioned him,' said Isabelle, looking over her father's shoulder at the newspaper. 'I say! I wonder if that means the Leighs have got the old lady's sapphires? They're worth a fortune.'

'They could certainly do with the money,' said her mother. 'Francis Leigh was left very badly off by old Matthew.'

A clank and a whoosh from the opposite platform recalled Isabelle to the present as a little local train puffed into the station and rumbled to a halt.

'Market Albury,' shouted a stentorian voice over the slam of doors. 'Change here for London.'

Eight minutes to go. She was glad to be on her way. She grinned as she remembered Great-Aunt Clarissa's horror at the notion she would be travelling up to London by herself. Once she had bowed to the inevitable, Aunt Clarissa had been unstinting with advice.

'Now do remember, dear, you have to change trains and it is inadvisable to be too familiar with your fellow passengers, however ladylike or gentlemanly they may seem.'

Aunt Clarissa was of a generation who believed unspecified danger lurked for any unaccompanied female traveller. Aunt Clarissa was surrounded by so many unspecified dangers, thought Isabelle, she must have quite an exciting life.

She would certainly feel a frisson at the sight of the man in a blue suit and trilby hat, for instance, walking down the steps from the bridge to the opposite platform as if he owned the place.

He was dressed in sturdy, inexpensive clothes but he radiated a sort of self-assured raffishness that gave him an air of importance. He was in his forties at a guess. He must have been quite good looking once, a big man with fair hair, tanned skin and blue eyes, thought Isabelle, idly. He'd let himself go, though, and run to fat. He wasn't, thought Isabelle, someone to trust. He seemed to become aware of her gaze and smiled in a satisfied way. Isabelle turned away quickly, rather embarrassed.

The two little French boys wormed their way through the waiting passengers, loudly pointing out the train on the opposite platform to each other. Although Aunt Clarissa would have classed mothers with children as being of undoubted respectability, foreign mothers with children would have merited a sharp intake of breath. *('No discipline, dear!')*

Isabelle watched with idle amusement as the mother in question launched a torrent of rapid French at the two bright-eyed boys. They reluctantly came away from the platform edge and started a game of hide-and-seek between the crowd and round the stack of milk churns. The little girl tugged at *Maman's* hand, wanting, as far as Isabelle could make out, to look at the wicker baskets of clucking hens piled at the end of the platform. Temporarily distracted, *Maman* raised her head just in time to see one of the boys dodge away from his brother and run slap into the blue-suited man.

Isabelle instinctively started forward as the little boy fell over with a wail but she was brought up sharp by the expression of fury on the man's face. Aunt Clarissa, thought Isabelle, with a sharp stab of apprehension, would have been quite right to be careful of him.

Then, almost as quickly, the expression was gone as *Maman* hurried over, full of apologies. The man shrank back from the crying child and waved away the Frenchwoman's protestations. 'It's all right,' he said gruffly, spreading his hands wide. The Frenchwoman continued to apologise, while alternatively scolding and comforting her son. 'Forget it.' He dug deep and added, in soldier's French, 'San fairy ann, eh? Napoo. Napoo, savez?'

The Frenchwoman looked bewildered and Isabelle, conquering her embarrassment and marshalling her command of French, stepped into the fray.

'He means it's all right,' she said, smiling at the woman. *'Ca ne fait rien,'* she said, translating. *'Il n'a pas d'importance.'*

The woman turned to Isabelle with a relieved smile. 'Ah, Madame! *Merci, trés merci!* Please,' she added, picking out the words carefully, 'I am sorry, yes? *Je suis désolé, vous comprenez?'*

'It's all right,' said the man, picking up the sense, if not the words, of what the woman had said. He smiled at Isabelle in a knowing sort of way. 'Foreigners, eh? I bet you know all about them, Miss.' He grinned at her with undisguised pleasure. 'Are you going to London?'

'My husband will be meeting me from the train,' said Isabelle stiffly. Aunt Clarissa, she thought with an agonised stab of insight, couldn't have been more repressively Victorian.

The man shrugged in a suit-yourself manner. 'Only asking.' He reached out and ruffled one of the boy's heads with an air of great indulgence. 'Kids, eh?' adding, with a rusty sort of laugh, 'Boys will be boys, eh?'

Despite his laugh, there was an angry gleam in his eyes that Isabelle didn't care for. With more apologies, she ushered mother and children up the platform. By the time she'd sacrificed a handkerchief to minister to *petit* Michel's grazed knee, distracted the small but insistent Agathe with the baskets of hens and agreed with young Jules that Michel had been very careless (*'négligent'*) she knew that Mme. Clouet and her family were travelling to meet M. Clouet, a man who, as Mme. Clouet put it, was of many affairs in *Londres,* and had more or less resigned herself to travelling with them.

The train pulled in, the blue-suited man strode down the platform and Isabelle, together with her newly adopted family, squashed in to a first-class compartment with an elderly lady wearing depressing amounts of jet and a comfortable-looking woman who liked children. Isabelle cheerfully relaxed into a corner as the comfortable woman entertained the junior Clouets with the contents of a bag of sweets. After forty minutes or thereabouts and a few stations later, little Agathe, Michel and Jules had, much to the jet-encrusted lady's disapproval, become distinctly travel-stained.

'I'll take Agathe to have a wash, shall I?' suggested Isabelle sometime after West Hassock. Her French had improved dramatically in the last half hour or so. She stood up and stretched out her hand to the little girl. 'Er . . . *faire sa toilette?'*

As she spoke, the train gave a terrific jolt, sending Isabelle staggering into the comfortable woman and hurling the contents of her bag of sweets around the compartment. With loud exclamations, Michel and Jules dived after the sweets like a pair of circus seals chasing fish. Grubbing round on the floor added nothing to their appearance.

'You take them all?' asked Mme. Clouet hopefully, regarding her sticky-faced sons, now liberally coated with sooty dust.

Isabelle looked at the two boys and drew the line with a shudder. One at a time perhaps, but all together? Not a chance.

Isabelle, with Agathe clinging to her hand, stepped out of the compartment into the corridor. The lavatory in their coach was occupied, so, much to little Agathe's evident enjoyment, Isabelle pressed on to the third-class coach at the rear of the train.

A thin, tall man in a shabby trench coat blocked the way. He was leaning out of the open window of the door, his hands braced on the window-frame, gulping in air.

'Excuse me,' said Isabelle politely.

The man turned slowly and looked at her. His face was ghastly. He looked as if he was going to be sick. He swallowed and made a great effort to speak. 'No,' he said, barring the way to the coach. 'No, you mustn't go along there.' His eyes slid to Agathe. 'Not with a child.'

'Why ever not?'

The man swallowed again. 'There's a man. There's been an accident, I think.'

'An accident?' repeated Isabelle.

The man nodded dumbly. He was older than she had assumed at first glance. He must be in his mid thirties at least and his voice, she thought, with a little stab of surprise, didn't match his clothes. It was precise and well bred, and made them, in an oddly indefinable way, equals.

A horrible possibility came into her mind. 'Is he . . . Is he . . .' she said slowly.

'He's got a string of jewels,' said the man unexpectedly. He nearly laughed. 'There's jewels at his feet.'

The door between the coaches opened and the ticket inspector came through. 'Tickets, please,' he said in a Sussex burr. He nodded affably at Isabelle. 'I've seen your ticket, Miss, I know. However,' he added, in mild reproof, 'you really shouldn't block the corridor like this.'

The man in the shabby coat turned to him eagerly. 'You'll know what to do! There's a man. A . . . A . . . Well, a man. He's had an accident.'

The ticket inspector pushed his cap back and scratched his head thoughtfully. 'An accident, sir? You'd better show me what's what. Where is he?'

'In the second compartment.' The shabby-coated man swallowed again. 'The blinds are down. I thought it was unfair that someone should try and bag a compartment all to themselves, so I looked in and . . . and . . .' He broke off. 'I couldn't think what to do.' He put a trembling hand to his mouth. 'He's got jewels. At his feet. Jewels.'

'Jewels?' The inspector raised his eyebrows meaningfully. 'Just as you say, sir.' He glanced at Isabelle and, in an unostentatious but significant gesture, tapped the side of his head. 'We'll soon see what the problem seems to be,' said the inspector easily. 'Lead the way, sir.' He looked meaningfully at Isabelle who was barring his way. 'After you, Mum.'

The shabby man looked at Agathe. 'It's not suitable,' he muttered, but Agathe pulled at Isabelle's hand.

'*Moi*,' she said insistently. '*Moi aussi.*'

'Come on, sir,' said the ticket inspector insistently.

The shabby man swallowed, shrugged and walked the few steps along the rumbling corridor where he stood outside a compartment.

What Isabelle should do, she knew, was take Agathe back to her mother but, not only would it be difficult to squeeze past the burly inspector who was clearly waiting for her to move, she very much wanted to know what had happened. *Jewels?*

'It'll be all right,' said the inspector reassuringly in a low voice to Isabelle. 'I know his sort. Nervy. It'll be something and nothing, I'll be bound. Someone took bad, you mark my words. Let's just have a look, shall we? Come on, Miss.'

Isabelle let herself be shepherded along the corridor towards the shabby man. As he said, the blinds were down. The inspector opened the door.

For a fraction of a second, Isabelle couldn't see anyone in the compartment, then she realised the window was wide open and a man in a blue suit was leaning out. Very far out, she thought. He'd bent double, leaning right over the edge of the window. He could hurt himself like that . . .

Her mind seemed to have slowed to a crawl, reality coming in little, jerky images. The hot little hand of Agathe's, holding hers, the way the man's hand knocked against the outside of the door as his arm swung carelessly, moved by the rattle of the train, the sturdy blue cloth of his trousers, the flash of some-thing very bright on the floor, his thick-soled brown shoes, the gasp the ticket inspector gave, the stuff that seemed to be splashed on the outside of the window.

'What's he done?' said the inspector stupidly, his red face growing blotchy as the colour drained out of it. 'He mustn't lean out of the window like that.' He shook himself as if denying what he saw and walked forward a couple of paces. He put his hand on the man's bent back. 'Up you come!'

'No!' yelled Isabelle. She couldn't see the man's head. It was hidden by his body. She very much didn't want to see the man's head.

There was stuff splashed on the outside of the window. *I'm looking at it!* she thought in horror.

The inspector still didn't seem to catch on but he paused with his hand on the man's back. 'Come on,' he said again, his voice wavering. He forced himself – Isabelle could see what an effort it cost him – to lean forward.

Then he understood. 'No. No,' he repeated. 'No.' He staggered away from the body by the window, his face mottled with grey patches. 'No.' He turned to Isabelle. 'He's dead,' he said wonderingly. 'His head's swiped clean off. Clean off, I tell you.'

The fact he'd actually said it seemed to make it real. 'Oh my God, he's dead!'

He lunged forward and making a wild grab, tugged at the communication cord. 'Get that kid out of here!' he called, raising his voice above the whoosh of air from the brakes. 'Get her out of it!' he shouted as the train rumbled to a halt.

But Agathe, excited by the noise, pulled away from Isabelle's hand and darted into the compartment. The ticket inspector vainly tried to stop her.

The train jerked to a halt with a series of sharp metallic clanks as the wheels jarred along the rails. All along the train came shouts as windows were pulled down and passengers leaned out, loudly demanding to know what was happening. Isabelle made a grab for Agathe who was crouched behind the inspector on the floor between the seats.

'Agathe!' she shouted, her voice shrill with anxiety. 'Agathe, come here!'

Agathe scrambled to her feet and peered round the inspector's legs. She had something in her hand. It was a string of beads, which, as she held them out to Isabelle, caught the light in a breathtaking flash of deep midnight blue. '*Joli!*' she squeaked excitedly. '*Joli, joli, joli!*'

'What's she say?' asked the inspector, bewildered, looking round and down. 'How does she mean, jolly?'

'She means pretty,' translated Isabelle mechanically. 'Agathe, come *here*!'

She made another grab for the little girl and this time succeeded in pulling her into the corridor, shutting the door on that nightmare compartment.

The shabby man followed them. 'He's dead.' His voice was high and nervous. 'He had to be dead, leaning out of the window like that.' He gave a little broken laugh. 'I was worried about the kid, but she's all right, isn't she?'

Isabelle stooped down to where Agathe was holding the string of beads, her face rapt with wonder. She held them out to Isabelle for inspection. '*Joli,*' she murmured reverently. '*Joli.*'

'But these are *beautiful,*' said Isabelle in bewilderment. She took the necklace in her hands and looked at the shimmering deep blue. The necklace consisted of sixteen stones, in an ornate heavy gold setting. The stones increased in size from the clasp, culminating in the principle stone, which hung by itself at the front. All the stones were beautiful but the principal stone was a deep, velvety blue. It was like looking into the ocean on a still, moonlit night. Almost instinctively, Isabelle ran her fingers over the stones.

'They're sapphires,' said the man in the trench coat in a dried-up voice. He was obviously finding it hard to speak. 'I saw them.' He swallowed. 'After I saw *him.*'

He held out his hand for the necklace and Isabelle noticed that, although his cuffs were frayed, his hands were clean and well cared for. He ran the sapphires through his hands, twisting them so they caught the light. 'They're worth a lot of money.' There was a catch in his voice, a longing, even reverent, note. 'A dickens of a lot of money.'

Isabelle suddenly understood. The glittering stones weren't just stones to this man, but a home and food and freedom from want.

I'd have been tempted to steal them, thought Isabelle, then saw the hungry look in his eyes. He *did* think of taking them, added Isabelle sympathetically to herself.

With a reluctant shudder, he thrust them into Isabelle's hand. 'Sapphires are meant to be unlucky. They were certainly unlucky for *him.*' His voice broke as he said it. 'Poor devil.' He glanced down at Agathe. 'She seems all right, doesn't she? I was worried about her seeing *that,*' he added, jerking his thumb in the direction of the compartment.

'I don't think she realised what had happened,' said Isabelle. 'She was more interested in the jewels. I'd better take her back to her mother.'

'Isn't she your little girl?' asked the man. He eyed up Isabelle's fashionable coat and wide-brimmed hat with a puzzled frown. 'You're not her governess or anything, are you?'

'Good heavens, no. She's French.' She indicated the compartment behind them with a tilt of her head. 'Little Agathe's brother ran slap into that poor man in there – at least, I think it was him – and Madame Clouet, Agathe's mother, couldn't apologise properly in English. That man obviously couldn't understand French, so I stepped in to help as best I could and got roped in for the rest of the journey.' She bent down to Agathe. 'Come on, sweetheart. Let's go back to Mummy. *Laisse le retour à la Maman, oui?*'

'Shouldn't you wait?' asked the man. 'I expect all sorts of people will want to ask us questions about what happened. I've never been caught up in this sort of thing before but I imagine that's the drill.'

'I'll be back. I'm Mrs Stanton, by the way. Isabelle Stanton.'

'My name's Duggleby. Leonard Duggleby.' He gave a humourless laugh. 'I'm a journalist, or, at least, I try to be.'

Isabelle nodded towards the compartment. 'You should find something to write about there.'

Leonard Duggleby closed his eyes and clapped his hand to his mouth. For a moment Isabelle thought he was going to be sick. 'I suppose so,' he said at last. 'It's beastly though, isn't it? I don't know if I can do it.' He grasped the window-frame for support. 'I don't think I *can* write about it. It's horrible.'

'Don't worry,' said Isabelle gently. 'You'll feel better once the shock's worn off. I'd better get Agathe back to her mother but I'll be back soon.'

In the event, it was a good ten minutes before Isabelle returned. The corridors were crowded with passengers in various degrees of irritation and she had to find enough French to give Mme. Clouet an idea of what had happened. She couldn't possibly describe what had happened. That was far too horrible, so she compromised by saying there'd been an accident – which was true enough – before threading her way back along the train.

She was greeted with frank relief by Leonard Duggleby who was besieged by the ticket inspector, guard and driver. He broke off with as she came into the coach. 'There you are, Mrs Stanton!'

'You didn't ought to have gone, Mum,' said the ticket inspector disapprovingly. 'The police will have to know about this and it didn't look right.'

'We were about to search the train for you,' added the guard. He looked grim and shaken. 'Have you told anyone about this?'

Isabelle shook her head. 'I said there'd been an accident, but I didn't give the details, of course.'

The guard, the driver and the inspector swapped looks. 'It's a bit more than an accident,' said the guard heavily. 'He was murdered.'

Isabelle gaped at him speechlessly.

The inspector shook his head. 'He can't have been, Sam. Not on *our* train.' His voice was pleading.

'He's got a knife through his ribs,' said the guard shortly. 'I saw it,' he added. 'I got him back inside and I saw it.'

There was silence for a few moments, then the driver sighed heavily. 'What next, Sam?' he asked the guard. 'You're officially in charge, but we can't keep the train stopped for much longer. It's blocking the line.'

The guard took off his cap and rubbed a hand through his sparse hair. 'I think you're right. I don't know what to do, and that's God's own truth. We'd better take her on to Turnhill Percy and telephone the police from there.'

'Turnhill Percy?' questioned the ticket inspector. 'We don't stop at Turnhill Percy, Sam. What about the timetable?'

'The timetable's up the spout good and proper, Arnold. You can't worry about timetables with a murder on our hands. That's gone west, good and proper.' He looked at Isabelle. 'The police will want to talk to you, Miss. To all of us, I suppose.'

'We'd better get on,' said the driver. 'The police will know what to do.'

He opened the door and, with a grunt, clambered down onto the track and crunched his way along the line back to his cab.

A few minutes later there was a shout from the driver's cab, a noisy whoosh of steam followed by a blast on the whistle, and the train chugged on its interrupted way to Turnhill Percy.

FOUR

F lanked by two uniformed police constables and a sergeant, Inspector William Rackham stood by the gate of platform four, Charing Cross station. He raised a hand in greeting as Arthur Stanton and Jack Haldean walked through the barrier.

'Thanks for meeting us, Bill,' said Jack, raising his voice above the noise of the station.

'It's a pleasure. It's a bit tough on your wife, Stanton, being caught up in something like this. Was she very upset?'

'She said she was all right in her telegram,' said Arthur, 'but you know what Isabelle's like. She doesn't like to make a fuss.'

Isabelle had telegrammed Arthur from the station master's office in Turnhill Percy. Arthur telephoned Jack and Jack immediately contacted his old friend, Bill Rackham, who, after talking to Sir Douglas Lynton, the Assistant Commissioner, was despatched to Charing Cross.

'It sounds,' said Jack, 'a horribly messy sort of murder.'

'I understand it was,' agreed Bill. 'It doesn't sound as if there's much of what you might call the doings inside the compartment, but the bloke is plastered fairly liberally across the coachwork and window.'

'That,' said Jack, drawing his breath in sharply, 'is revolting. It makes you realise the thinking behind those notices you get on the train. *Passengers Must Not Lean Out Of The Window.* Granted that our victim is spread across a fair bit of Sussex, I don't suppose the Railway Police have identified him, have they?'

'No, they haven't. They're leaving that to us, God bless' em.'

'Whose responsibility is it to investigate the murder?' asked Jack curiously.

Bill clicked his tongue. 'That's a nice question. Strictly speaking, the Railway Police have the authority, but they're more than happy to hand it over to us at the Yard. Their chief concern is to ensure the railway runs smoothly. They can deal with most incidents, but a murder investigation is a bit more than they want to bite off.'

'So you're in charge?'

'When the train arrives, I will be. Ideally, I'd like to have had the coach uncoupled and all the passengers detained at Turnhill Percy, but it wasn't practical, I'm afraid. Turnhill Percy is a one-horse place with a single platform and no facilities to speak of, so they kept the compartment coupled to the train. The police sealed off the compartment, stuck a canvas sheet over the outside, took a note of the names and addresses of everyone who was on the train and that's about it.'

'Couldn't the murderer have left the train before the police did their headcount?' asked Jack. 'I think I might be tempted to make a jump for it if I found myself with a corpse on my hands.'

'He *might* have done,' agreed Bill. 'An examination of the tickets will tell us if there's any tickets issued that can't be accounted for. The Railway Police don't have a great many options. We can't detain people indefinitely while we ponder over the niceties of who did what. I imagine there'll be enough complaints for the railway company to deal with as it is. There's a limit to how long a train can block the rails.'

'Do you know when it happened?' asked Jack.

'Just after West Hassock, apparently. The passengers – including Isabelle – felt a terrific jerk just before the train ran under the West Hassock road bridge. The Railway Police checked the permanent way back from where the communication cord was pulled and found fairly unmistakable evidence on the wall of the bridge. That means we've got a definite time for the murder, which is something, I suppose.'

'A definite time for when the bloke got his head knocked off, anyway,' said Jack thoughtfully. 'Not that there's any reason to think there's much difference. The murderer wouldn't want to hang around with his victim longer than he could help.'

'Do you know when the train's due?' asked Arthur.

'It should be here soon,' said Bill Rackham with a glance at the clock. 'The railway people said it shouldn't be long.'

As if on cue, there was a deafening squawk from the public address system above their heads as the arrival of the delayed Two Fifteen from Hastings was announced, followed by a series of puffing wheezes as the train grunted its way into the station. There was a final burst of steam, a long sigh from the air brakes, and then, with a slamming of doors, the passengers alighted.

Two of Rackham's constables walked down the length of the train and took up guard beside a compartment draped with a green canvas sheet. After listening to Bill's account of the murder, Jack was heartily glad it was covered.

A uniformed police inspector stepped down from the train and, extending his hand, helped Isabelle onto the platform. A tall man in a shabby trench coat alighted next, followed by two Railway Police constables.

'Isabelle!' called Arthur, striding towards her.

Isabelle's shoulders sagged in relief.

'I'm so glad to see you,' she said, kissing him on the cheek. 'Poor Arthur, you must've been worried silly when you got my telegram.'

She turned to the inspector beside her. 'Inspector Whitten, this is my husband, Captain Stanton, my cousin, Major Haldean, and this is Inspector Rackham of Scotland Yard. And this,' she added, turning to the man in the trench coat, 'is Mr Leonard Duggleby.'

Jack rather liked the look of Duggleby. He had a lean, scholarly face, dark hair flecked with grey at the temples, mild blue eyes and a hesitant, slightly shy, manner.

'Pleased to meet you,' said Duggleby. 'I could wish the circumstances were different, though. I didn't,' he added with an ironic lift of his eyebrows, 'intend to get caught up with the police.'

'I hope we won't have to detain you for very long, Mr Duggleby,' said Bill in a reassuring sort of way. 'We appreciate your help.' He raised his voice to carry over the clamour of the disgruntled group of passengers who had formed a knot round the harassed official at the gate. 'Have you any urgent business you need to attend to?'

'Unfortunately, no. I only wish I had.'

'I wish those people were as cooperative,' muttered Rackham. He jerked his head in the direction of his sergeant. 'Sort that lot out, will you?'

'Very good, sir,' said the sergeant. He strode forward accompanied by the two constables. 'Move along there, ladies and gentlemen,' he intoned in an official bellow. 'Move along there, please!'

'It's an absolute *disgrace*!' thundered a lady in a feathered hat and a black-beaded dress to the accompaniment of rumbled support from her fellow travellers. 'Not only has our journey been disrupted, we have been compelled – yes, *compelled* – to give our names to the police!'

'Shockin', I call it,' agreed a bowler-hatted tradesman, hooking his thumbs into his expansive braces.

'Absolutely,' fumed a man who looked like a bank manager, emphasising his point by striking his furled umbrella on the floor. 'Outrageous!'

Mme. Clouet favoured everyone with an outburst in French, bewailing her late arrival. Isabelle broke away from Inspector Whitten to retrieve a straying Michel and presented him back to his mother. 'That poor woman,' she said, with a grin to Arthur. 'She'll never want to get on a train again.'

'Come on, ladies and gentlemen,' intoned the constable in a patient way. 'The sooner you leave, the sooner you'll be home.'

A bright-looking man in wire-rimmed spectacles stopped by the other side of the gate. 'I say, what's happened?'

'Hades,' groaned Bill. 'That's Burgess of the *Monitor*. That's all we need.'

Burgess had caught sight of Jack beyond the barrier. 'Haldean! What's the story?'

'It's too long to explain,' called Jack. 'I'll catch up with you later.'

'There's been an incident on the train,' said Bill soothingly. 'Nothing to worry about.'

The feather-hatted lady looked at him in acute disgust. 'Since when has *murder* been nothing to worry about, young man?'

'*Murder?*' echoed Burgess in delight.

'Get these people off the station,' said Bill in tight restraint to the sergeant. '*Now.*' He turned to a man in railway uniform who edged his way through the throng.

'Inspector Rackham? We're going to shunt the compartment with the body in it over to the sidings.'

'Thanks,' said Bill and plunged into a discussion of details.

Beyond the barrier, Burgess, notebook in hand, had buttonholed a group of passengers.

'I ought to be doing that,' said Duggleby to Jack, looking wistfully at the busy Burgess. 'Interviewing the passengers, I mean. I'm a journalist,' he added, in response to Jack's enquiring look.

'Freelance?' asked Jack.

'Very free, unfortunately.' His rather melancholy face lightened. 'You're Jack Haldean, the author, aren't you? Mrs Stanton told me about you and I could see you knew that reporter. I suppose I'd better try and write something but I can't tell you how beastly it was. It'd be different if I wasn't involved.'

'You might as well give it a go,' said Jack. 'A first-hand account of discovering a murder must be worth something.' He paused. 'You did discover the body, didn't you?'

'Yes, I did,' said Duggleby gloomily. 'I suppose that means I'm suspect number one, but all I actually did was walk into a railway compartment.'

Bill, accompanied by Inspector Whitten, walked back along the platform to them. 'I suppose I should be grateful to Burgess,' Bill said with a laugh. 'All the passengers are pouring out their woes to him, which lets me off the hook for the time being, at least. Mr Duggleby, if I can take your statement, one of my constables will accompany you back home.'

'I can make my own way home,' began Duggleby, then stopped. 'You're checking up on me, aren't you?' Bill didn't reply. 'Do you think I murdered him?' he asked wearily. His mouth quivered. 'If you knew me, you'd realise I simply *couldn't* do it. Even if I wanted to, I'd be bound to make a hash of it. I can plan things but something always goes wrong. Like journalism,' he added, with a wistful look at the crowds surrounding Burgess.

That, thought Jack, showed an uncomfortable degree of self-knowledge. Duggleby struck him as a man who would be a fish out of water in the hurly-burly of Fleet Street.

'You'll appreciate there's a routine to follow in a case of this sort, sir,' said Bill smoothly. 'The railway authorities have placed a room at our disposal, so if I could trouble you to come along, we'll get it over and done with as quickly as possible.'

'Bill,' broke in Isabelle. 'Have you got the jewels? The jewels that were on the train?'

'Yes, I have,' said Rackham. 'Inspector Whitten's just given them to me.' He put a hand in his jacket pocket and drew them out. 'That's an interesting little collection to find kicking about on the floor of a railway carriage.'

'Good God!' Jack took the sapphires from Bill's outstretched hand and looked at them wonderingly.

'Nice, aren't they?' said Bill. 'Especially if they're real.'

'They're real enough,' broke in Duggleby. 'I used to work for a jeweller. They're absolute beauties.'

'Where on earth did they come from?' asked Arthur, wonderingly.

'That's just it,' said Isabelle excitedly. 'I've got an idea. Jack, you know Celia Leigh, don't you?'

'Celia? Of course I do.'

Isabelle hesitated. Jack had been rather smitten with Celia Leigh at one time and she felt she might be on dodgy ground.

He seemed to know what she was thinking, because he suddenly grinned. 'There's no need to look like a stuffed frog. I'm not going to break down and start sobbing at the mention of her name.' He turned to Bill. 'Old girlfriend,' he said in explanation. 'She's engaged to Ted Marchant, isn't she, Belle?'

'More or less,' said Isabelle, with some relief that Celia Leigh wasn't a hands-off topic, 'but that's not what I wanted to tell you. The thing is, Celia's related to Mrs Paxton. You know? The old lady who was murdered in Topfordham.'

Bill looked up alertly. 'Mrs Paxton? Hang on, that's the Napier case, isn't it? What are you getting at, Isabelle?'

'The man who was killed got on the train at Market Albury,' said Isabelle. 'That's not far from Celia Leigh's house in Madlow Regis. In fact, the train he arrived on in Market Albury must've come through Madlow Regis. I wondered, as there were sapphires involved in the Topfordham case, if these sapphires were the same ones?'

'They *might* be, I suppose,' said Bill doubtfully, weighing the sapphires in his hand. 'I must say the connection doesn't seem immediately obvious.'

'What if the man I saw was a thief?' asked Isabelle. 'These could be the sapphires that belonged to Mrs Paxton. He could've stolen them from the Leighs.'

'Did the Leighs inherit the sapphires?' asked Arthur.

'As a matter of fact, I don't know,' admitted Isabelle, her face falling. 'However, they'll know who did, won't they?'

'It's worth a telegram, Bill,' said Jack. 'There can't be that many strings of priceless jewels kicking about.'

'All right,' agreed Bill, slipping the jewels back into his pocket. 'I'd better get them authenticated first, though.' He glanced at Duggleby. 'No slight on your opinion, sir, but I want to make sure they're genuine before raising the hue and cry.'

'They're genuine, all right.'

'As you say. Thanks for the tip, Isabelle. If you're right, that's one part of the puzzle solved straight away.'

Jack clicked his tongue. 'Part of the puzzle, yes. But granted the man was a thief, why on earth didn't the murderer take the jewels?'

'Search me,' said Bill. He turned to Duggleby. 'Mr Duggleby, you spotted the sapphires. Were they out in the open?'

Duggleby breathed deeply and steadied himself. 'I'd better explain. I went into the compartment. I saw . . . saw *him* right away.' He put a hand to his mouth. 'I'm not proud of this, but I froze. I backed away and leaned against the door. Then – I told you, I'm not proud of this – my legs went and I slid down the door so I was more or less sitting on the floor. I don't know how long I was there. I had my eyes shut and had to nerve myself to open them. When I did, I simply couldn't bear to look at him again, but I saw something glinting under the seat. I pulled out the glinting thing and it was the necklace. For some reason, that made it worse. It was so bizarre, finding something like that on top of everything else. And then . . . And then . . .'

He stopped and swallowed. 'I knew the jewels were worth a fortune,' he said with a break in his voice, 'then it suddenly struck me that I was in a compartment with a dead man. Even if I picked up the stones and surrendered them later, people might think I'd killed him. I flung them away and scrambled out of there as fast as I could.' He turned to Isabelle. 'That's when you came along. I was grateful to you.' Instinctively Isabelle reached out a hand to his trembling arm. 'Thanks,' he said eventually.

'So the killer might not have realised our man had the jewels on him,' said Jack, after an awkward pause. 'They weren't in a case, were they?'

'No. I told you. I saw them glinting.'

'That's a clear enough story,' said Bill. He put the sapphires back in his pocket, then summoned one of the constables with a wave of his hand. 'Mr Duggleby, if I can ask you to go with the constable, I'll be with you as soon as possible.'

After Duggleby had been escorted away, he turned to his friend. 'Jack, the railway people are going to move the coach into a siding. Shall we meet there in about half an hour?'

'That's fine with me,' said Jack. 'Isabelle, why don't you let me buy you tea and you can give me a blow-by-blow account of what happened?'

'Tea!' she repeated with a sort of blissful intensity. 'Lead me to it.'

It took Isabelle three cups of tea and a macaroon before she considered herself suitably fortified for the journey home. Once she and Arthur had departed, Jack hunted out what a helpful railway official referred to as The Fatal Compartment.

The coach had been shunted to the far reaches of the station. The siding was a neglected little backwater of sooty pillars bounded by a grimy wall housing railway offices.

The coach itself looked lonely without its companion coaches and engine. Two policemen stood on guard outside the open door and three more policemen stood outside the railway offices.

The green canvas cover had been removed from the coach, revealing a compartment painted in the Southern Railway colours of olive green and black with a yellow number 3, indicating Third Class, emblazoned on the door. The only difference between this and any other compartment were the dark, sinister stains that fingered out from the window and across the coachwork. It looked as if someone had thrown a pot of dark lumpy paint at the door.

The policeman outside the offices touched his helmet as Jack approached. 'Are you looking for Inspector Rackham, sir? He'll be along in a few minutes.'

Jack found a space amongst the assorted trunks and bags on a wooden, iron-wheeled trolley and sat down to wait for Bill. At the far end of the platform the smoke-smudged sunlight hazed across the open end of the great blackened arched glass of the roof.

The hubbub of the crowds on the concourse and the whoosh and clank of the trains softened into rhythmic industrial music. It was, he thought, as he looked at the shining rails stretching out into London through the flickering veil of dust, like being inside a piece of modern art, a picture with riveted girders and astonishing angles.

He stood up as Bill came along the platform.

'Hello, Jack. Sorry I wasn't here, but I've just got Duggleby off my hands.' He nodded at the office. 'Shall we go in? I had the body put in here until it can be moved to Charing Cross Hospital. The divisional surgeon can take a look at him there, but we might as well see what we can discover in the meantime.'

'Right you are,' said Jack, following Bill into the office.

It was a high-ceilinged, sooty-smelling room with a pair of wooden filing cabinets, four chairs and a table. Two grimy windows looked out onto Craven Street and two more looked out onto the platform. Bill lit the gas lamp and the mantle hissed and glowed in a fitful kind of way. It seemed to make the daylight gloomier. The paintwork, of olive green and discoloured cream, did nothing to brighten the surroundings.

If I had to work in here, thought Jack, I'd turn my toes up and fade away from sheer depression. However, even if the office had been glowing with colour and radiant with light, it would be hard to feel cheerful, looking at the human shape beneath the blue cloth on the table.

Bill turned to the two policemen at the door. 'Let me know when the mortuary men arrive, but don't let anyone go into that compartment until I've given them the say-so. Not that,' he added to Jack as he closed the door, 'it'll make very much difference. Inspector Whitten decided early on he was going to hand the case over to us, but not before the Railway Police traipsed all over the compartment. A Doctor Lomax was called to Turnhill Percy to pronounce that our man was officially dead and he had a good poke around, too. In fact,' he added ruefully, 'everyone seemed to be called in at Turnhill Percy.'

'Which is understandable but a real bind, all the same,' said Jack sympathetically. There was a small brown leather suitcase by the foot of the table. 'Does that belong to our man?'

'I hope so. The case was on the luggage rack above our chap's head. Inspector Whitten and his men have been through it like a dose of salts. They didn't bother with fingerprints or any niceties of that sort, just rummaged through the contents, shoved everything back in, and expected a pat on the back. By the way, Mr Duggleby was right about the sapphires being the real McCoy. I've had them authenticated. A bloke from Sheringhams examined them. They're worth a fortune.'

'A fortune being?' asked Jack.

'Get ready for this,' said Bill with a grin. 'Would you believe about thirty-five thousand pounds?'

'Bloody hell!' Jack gaped at him. 'Thirty-five *thousand*?'

'Not bad, eh?'

Jack gave a long, slow whistle. 'Blimey, Bill, that's incredible! Well, that answers one question. Whatever the motive for the murder was, it wasn't robbery.'

'Absolutely. I suppose, technically speaking, as Duggleby was the first person to discover the body, he should be the prime suspect, but I can't see it somehow. He struck me as a pathetic sort of beggar.'

'M'yes. I can't see he'd commit a murder and leave a string of sapphires lying on the floor. The time's wrong, too. From what Isabelle said, it was a good ten minutes from feeling the train jolt when the body hit the bridge, to finding Duggleby dithering outside the compartment.' He looked at the blue-covered body on the table. 'If Duggleby had stuck a knife in this poor beggar's ribs and bundled him out of the window, he'd hardly hang around outside the door to tell the first person who walked past all about it.'

Bill nodded. 'I think you're right. I took his statement, of course. He's thirty-eight years old and lives in a cheap boarding house in Murchinson's Rents, off Shoe Lane near Fleet Street. He served in the Royal West Surreys in the war and was invalided out with a dicky chest. He's a journalist and gave the name of a couple of magazines who've published his articles.'

Bill laughed. 'He certainly doesn't have a newspaperman's nose for a story. The difference between him and Burgess of the *Monitor* was laughable.' He shook his head with an indulgent smile. 'He'll get something out of it, I suppose.'

'Burgess certainly will.'

'Burgess,' said Bill, 'is in seventh heaven. Not only has he got a murder to keep him happy, he's got a string of sapphires to write about.'

'He doesn't know they could be the Topfordham sapphires, does he?'

'No he doesn't,' said Bill emphatically. 'And neither, I may say, do we. I've told our Mr Duggleby to keep stumm about it, too. This is sensational enough without throwing Mrs Paxton's murder into the mix. Ideally, I wouldn't have mentioned the sapphires to Burgess at all but Tetlow, the ticket inspector, was full of it, so I had to come clean. I've sent a telegram to the Leighs and with any luck we should receive an answer to that soon. Anyway, do you want to look at the suitcase first or the body?'

'Let's take the case first, shall we? If I must pore over decapitated corpses, I like to work up to it.'

'Right you are.' Bill laid the suitcase flat on the dusty wooden floor and clicked open the catch.

Jack ran his hand over the leather case. 'It's good quality. Marked with the initials A.P., I see. Rather old now, perhaps, but it must have cost a fair bit when it was new.'

On top of the clothes in the case were two cheap editions of *The Four Just Men* and *The Crimson Circle* by Edgar Wallace.

Jack took the books out and flicked through them. 'Our man's written his name on the flyleaf which is obliging of him. Andrew Parsons.' He cocked his head to one side. 'Granted that the victim might be a thief, I don't suppose the name Andrew Parsons means anything to you, does it?'

'Not a thing,' said Bill, 'I'll get the Records Department to see if we've ever run across him before.'

'Hello,' said Jack. 'What's this?'

Tucked inside the book were two pieces of white, plain card about the size and shape of a visiting card. One of the cards had a little drawing in pencil, a cross with what looked like a halo over the top of it. Jack looked at it with a frown.

'What on earth's that for?' asked Bill. 'A bookmark, perhaps?'

'Perhaps.' Jack put down the books and took a newish light overcoat from the case and examined it carefully. It was a perfectly ordinary cheap overcoat of the sort made by Cross and Co. and, Jack ruefully thought, sold by the hundred in every city in Britain. The pockets contained the screwed-up wrapper from a bar of Nestlé chocolate and a well-washed fine linen handkerchief embroidered with an elaborate A.P.

Jack put the coat to one side. 'He's written his initials on the inside of the collar with indelible pen, but that's about it for the coat, I think.' He quickly rummaged through the rest of the case. It contained a pair of pyjamas, a cheap shirt, a pair of socks, a set of underwear, a safety razor, a packet of blades and a tooth-brush. 'No laundry marks,' said Jack, 'but there's something wrapped in the pyjamas.'

He drew out a man's hairbrush and a hand mirror. 'I say, these are rather nice.' The brush and the mirror were backed in a hard, heavy black wood. 'It's ebony, I think.' On the back of both the brush and the mirror, let into the wood so it was smooth with the surface, were the initials A.P. in stylised loops of silver wire.

'That's a pre-war set, I'd say,' said Jack, weighing the mirror in his hand. 'My father had something very similar. They're the sort of quality I'd expect to go with the suitcase. The clothes are cheap enough but the toiletry set and the case fit, if you know what I mean. They're old and expensive.' He picked up the handkerchief once more. 'So's this.'

He rocked back on his heels, frowning. 'There's definitely two sorts of belongings here. His suit, shoes and coat are new and cheap but these things aren't.'

'Someone who's down on his luck?' suggested Bill.

Jack nodded. 'It'd be a familiar story, that's for sure.' He repacked the suitcase and glanced up at the table. 'Come on. Let's have a dekko at the body.'

'Right-oh,' said Bill. He took hold of the blue sheet. 'Brace yourself. I've seen him once already. This is nasty.'

It was.

Jack recognised the blue suit and the sturdy shoes from Isabelle's description, but the man himself was a battered wreck. His shirt and waistcoat were torn with the impact and dark with blood but his jacket was lying draped across him, untouched.

'He'd taken off his jacket and put it on the seat beside him.' said Bill.

Jack swallowed hard. 'Poor beggar,' he said eventually. 'Can we cover up his head? Or, at least, where his head was. I saw quite enough poor devils like that in the war not to want to look at any more.'

'Me too,' said Bill and adjusted the sheet.

'That's better,' said Jack with a sigh of relief. 'I can think straight now. Look at his wristwatch, Bill. It's suffered a bit, but I'd say it's old and very good quality.' Jack stepped back and looked at the body appraisingly. 'D'you think he'd been in the army? That way of wearing his watch with the glass on the inside of his wrist is a real soldier's trick.'

'You're probably right. Mind you, roughly half the men in Britain have been in the army, so it hardly narrows things down.' Pulling a face, Bill undid the strap and, holding the watch in his hand, grunted in approval. 'It's real gold, I'd say.' He flipped open the back. 'There's something marked inside.' He turned it to the light. It was a cross in a circle. 'That's been scratched in with a compass point, I bet.'

'It's the same symbol as on the card in the book,' said Jack. He clicked his tongue thoughtfully. 'This mix of belongings is interesting, Bill. Let's have a look at the knife.'

He bent closer and examined the hilt. 'Straight between the fourth and fifth ribs, by the look of it. That's a direct blow to the heart. There wouldn't be much blood from the knife-blow.'

'You're right,' said Bill. 'It might be luck or he could've been stabbed by someone who knew what he was doing.' He drew his breath in sharply. 'By George, that knife's a trench dagger! I've got one like it kicking around in a drawer at home somewhere.'

'A French dagger, going off the shape,' added Jack.

'You're right. I'll leave it to the surgeon to get it out, but I'll be surprised if we're wrong.'

He turned back the flap of the dead man's jacket and slipped his hand into the inner pocket. 'Here's his wallet. I say, look at this. He *did* come from Madlow Regis. He's got a single ticket from Madlow Regis to London.' He ran his thumb over the edge of the banknotes in the wallet. 'He's got three pound notes and one ten bob, plus thirty francs in notes.'

'French money? Put them together with the French dagger and there seems to be a definite Continental whiff to this case.'

'And what's this?' Bill pulled out a piece of paper, evidently a torn-out picture from a magazine. 'I say, Jack! It's a photo of the sapphires!'

Jack took the piece of paper. The sapphires so dominated the picture, it took a moment or two to see past them to the woman who was actually wearing the necklace. And yet, thought Jack, she had a very definite personality, with a firm chin, commanding, clear eyes and an imperious expression. Underneath the picture was written *Mrs Francis Leigh, Breagan Grange, Madlow Regis, Sussex.*

'That's them!' said Bill. He took the sapphires from his pocket and compared them with the picture. 'There's no two ways about it.'

'So the sapphires do belong to the Leighs. My word, that's one up for Isabelle, all right. I've met Mrs Leigh. She was at Isabelle's wedding. She struck me as a bit of a tough egg.'

Jack took the paper from Bill and rubbed it absently between his fingers. 'I wonder which magazine it is? Not top-quality paper, so not one of the monthlies such as *Vogue* or *Eve* or *Modern Woman* or anything like that. I'd say it was one of the weeklies, price tuppence. *Poppy's Paper* or *Woman's Companion*, perhaps, but there's dozens of them to choose from.'

'Is that important? The main thing is that we know our man here knew about the sapphires.'

'Absolutely. I just thought that his choice of magazine could tell us something about who he was and where he came from.'

'Fair enough,' said Bill abstractedly. 'There's something in his other jacket pocket, too. It feels like a squashy book . . .' He gingerly unbuttoned the flap of the pocket and drew out a stack of white bank notes secured by a rubber band.

Jack gazed at the notes in utter astonishment. 'Holy Moses, Bill! How much is there?'

Bill counted up the notes in a dazed sort of way. 'Fifty quid.' He ruffled his thumb over the edge of the notes. 'Fifty quid in fivers, just stuck in his pocket.'

'He must have pinched it,' said Jack. 'I bet Belle's absolutely right about him being a thief. Imagine wandering around with fifty quid in fivers and a string of sapphires! What else was he carrying? At this rate, we'll find the Crown jewels tucked into his socks.'

Bill delved into the pocket again and froze. 'Crown jewels, eh?' He pulled out two sapphire earrings. 'You're not so far off.'

'Strewth,' breathed Jack, seeing the blue glint on Bill's outstretched hand.

Bill swallowed. 'It's a good job we're honest men,' he said in a regretful sort of way. He looked at the sapphires for a few moments then, with a sigh, opened his briefcase and put them away. 'Let's see what else he's got on him.'

The results of the rest of their investigation were nothing like as spectacular. They amounted to seven shillings and fourpence, an open packet of Woodbines, a box of Swan matches, a much-used pipe, a cheap leather tobacco pouch with strong Ship's tobacco, a smoker's penknife, a used London bus ticket for the day before yesterday, a stub of pencil and five francs, four centimes in coins.

Bill jingled the francs in his hand. 'As you said, there's a very definite Continental whiff to this,' he said thoughtfully.

'He didn't use French matches,' commented Jack, looking at the box of Swan. 'Mind you, I don't blame him. They're foul. He hasn't any keys on him.' He stepped away from the body. 'Shall we have a look inside the train? I think we've found out more or less all we can here for the time being.'

They walked out of the office and across the platform to the compartment. Carefully avoiding touching the coachwork, they mounted the steps into the compartment.

Isabelle had told Jack there was little trace of the murder inside the compartment, and she was right.

The blue-upholstered seats faced each other between pale yellow wooden-clad walls under the white roof. A *Smoking* sign was etched into the glass of the window. Beneath the mesh of the luggage rack, the walls were decorated with neat frames containing brightly coloured advertisements for seaside holidays at Eastbourne and Brighton, an advert for Johnnie Walker Red Label whisky and a map of England from London to the coast with the railway lines prominently marked.

Jack looked at the seaside advertisements with an unexpected lump in his throat. The mind that found pleasure in the images of bright sunshine and children playing on an idealised beach seemed so very far away from the sort of mind that rammed a knife between a man's ribs and bundled him out of the window.

'It's weird, isn't it?' he said. 'You wouldn't know anything had happened.'

He knelt down and peered beneath the seat.

'Looking for something in particular?' asked Bill.

'Just looking,' replied Jack in a muffled voice. 'A string of emeralds to go with the sapphires, perhaps? Hello! There *is* something here!' He popped his head back out like an inquisitive tortoise. 'Pass me my stick, will you?'

With his stick in hand, Jack looked at the floor and grimaced. 'Ah well, my suit's seen better days,' he said with an air of resigned martyrdom. He lay flat on his stomach and reached under the seat. 'Got it!'

Propelled by the stick, a dull metal something shot out from under the seat and onto the floor of the compartment.

'It's the sheath of the knife!' said Bill.

'There's something else, too,' came the voice from under the seat. 'Here it is.' He handed out a highly polished flat wooden jewel-case. It was lined with white velvet and clearly showed the indentations where the necklace had been. 'I haven't finished yet,' called Jack.

He batted first one, then the other, of a pair of fawn-coloured fine leather gloves into the compartment, then wriggled out from under the seat and levered himself to his knees.

'Well done,' said Bill.

Jack brushed himself down. 'I'll send the cleaner's bill to Scotland Yard.' His eyes were bright with excitement. 'There's bloodstains on one of the gloves, Bill. Look, you can see where the end of the index finger has snagged slightly.'

Bill picked up the gloves. 'By jingo, they're French,' he said, looking at the label. 'Look. *Marcoux et Cie,* Paris.'

'More French stuff,' said Jack. 'That's quite a haul. 'So we've got a pair of French gloves paired with a French dagger. *Ergo* we're looking for a Frenchman?'

'Perhaps,' said Bill. 'But anyone can buy a pair of gloves in Paris and there's thousands of trench knives, French and otherwise, kicking about. It's suggestive though, isn't it? I wonder if Parsons had any dealings in France? That's something we can find out.'

'They're nice gloves, aren't they? Kid, I'd say. A murderer in kid gloves.' He raised his eyebrows expressively. 'That'd make a snappy title for a magazine story. Which one's bloodstained? The right? So we're looking for a right-handed murderer with a taste in good gloves.'

Rackham rubbed a piece of the material between his fingers. 'They're very flexible. Perfect for this sort of work.'

'Ghoul,' commented Jack with a smile.

Rackham opened his briefcase, wrapped up the gloves, the jewel-case and the knife-sheath and put them away. 'I'll have them fingerprinted back at the Yard.'

He stopped and looked out of the open door of the compartment as footsteps sounded along the platform. A police constable hurried up to them, telegram in hand.

'This has just arrived, sir,' he said to Bill.

Rackham took the envelope. 'Thank you, Marston.' He slit the envelope and read the contents with a broad grin.

'This is from Mr Francis Leigh in reply to the telegram I sent him. Thanks to Isabelle, Mr Leigh now thinks Scotland Yard is composed of miracle workers. Listen to this. *Just discovered robbery. Jewels and money missing from safe.* Well, I can get in touch with Mr Leigh and tell him his property's safe. Is there anything else you want to look at, Jack?'

'Not really. I think I'll shoot off. I know you're going to be busy.'

'All right. I'll look in on the Stantons this evening, though. You'll be there, won't you?'

'Absolutely I will,' said Jack, climbing down from the train. 'See you there.'

FIVE

Later that evening Jack arrived at Isabelle and Arthur's flat in Lydstep Mews.

'We've got a visitor, Jack,' said Isabelle, as she hung his coat and hat in the hall wardrobe. 'It's all right, Lizzie,' she called to the maid who had appeared at the end of the hall. 'I'll

see to Major Haldean. Jack, I'd better warn you. Celia Leigh's
here.'

Jack grinned at his cousin's expression. 'Is she?' He laughed.
'Stop looking as if you're standing by the sickbed of a dying
pal, Belle. It all fizzled out with Celia ages ago. She thinks I'm
essentially frivolous so that was that, really. Mind you, we weren't
on Tristan and Isolde terms, just supper and a spot of dancing.
I never stood under her window, serenading her with a mandolin.'

Isabelle giggled. 'I can't think she'd have appreciated it if you
had done. I don't know why,' she added, looking puzzled, 'she
and Ted haven't announced their engagement yet. I hope they
haven't had a row.'

'So do I,' Jack agreed. 'Why's she here?'

'To see me, of course. I'm hoping,' she said with repressed
excitement, 'that she'll tell us all about the sapphires. There's
something odd about the sapphires,' said Isabelle, lowering her
voice as they approached the sitting room door. 'Celia's being
very cagey about them.'

Celia Leigh, a tall, good-looking girl with fair hair and an
earnest expression was sitting on the green sofa under the window.

'Jack, darling! Isabelle said you'd be calling. It's so nice to
see you again.'

'And you,' he said, taking her hand with a warm smile. 'Tell
me, are congratulations in order? For you and Ted Marchant, I
mean?'

Celia's mouth contracted into a straight line. 'No, they aren't.
If Ted doesn't come to his senses, I'm not sure congratulations
ever *will* be in order. He's got this idiotic idea of going off to
Singapore, of all places.'

'Just for fun or because he promised his mother?'

Celia looked at him suspiciously. 'His mother's been dead for
years. Why on earth should he have promised her he'd go to
Singapore?' Her suspicion increased. 'You're joking, aren't you?'

'Just a little badinage, don't you know?'

Celia sighed. 'I see you haven't improved, Jack. Ted's been
offered a job with a mining company. He says we can't afford
to live in England.'

'Bad luck,' said Jack with genuine sympathy. 'What are you
going to do?'

'I don't know,' said Celia. 'He's not like you, Jack. He wants to be settled. He likes security. I want him to buy some land and have a farm. He grew up on a farm. I *know* that's what he really wants to do.'

'He couldn't do anything better,' agreed Arthur enthusiastically.

Jack grinned to himself. A month ago, Arthur, tremulous with excitement, announced that his dearest wish had come true and he had at last persuaded his Aunt Catherine to let him manage her estate at Croxton Ferriers.

It wasn't, in Jack's opinion, a job for the faint hearted. The estate had been neglected for years and it would take an enormous amount of work to get the place on its feet again.

Arthur, who dreamt of living in the country, cheerfully embraced the idea of hard work. What made it better, in his opinion, was that the job came with a house he described as a little Jacobean gem. Isabelle had taken one look at the gem and flatly refused to go anywhere near it until it was in a rather better state of repair.

'Can't Marchant find anywhere?' asked Arthur.

'It's not so much can't as won't. Money, you know. Ted thinks he'd need at least two thousand pounds or so to get anywhere suitable and that's beyond him, unfortunately. I think we could manage with somewhere a lot smaller, but Ted doesn't agree. He says in Singapore I can have the sort of life I deserve, but that's nonsense. Ted will insist I want all sorts of things that I simply don't need. As a matter of fact, there's very little I do need. It would be inspiring, don't you think, to live close to the earth in a really *simple* way. It would be so much easier to be in touch with the essential verities, to concentrate on what's truly important, without all the needless trappings of modern life.'

'Electric light and running water are always handy,' murmured Jack.

'You sound just like Ted,' said Celia, shocked. 'I don't propose to live in a slum. It'll be perfectly simple to install a generator for electricity and I have no intention of living without modern plumbing. Absolutely not. Ted's just being stubborn. I *loathe* the idea of living in Singapore.'

Jack, Isabelle and Arthur swapped glances. 'What about the

sapphires?' asked Jack. Despite having just been reminded why he and Celia could never have been counted as twin souls, he had a lot of sympathy for her. Ted Marchant was a sound enough bloke but a bit of a he-man. He could well imagine him thinking he knew better than the little woman. What's more, he could well imagine him saying it. 'Couldn't the sapphires be – er – cashed in?'

'I wish,' said Celia ruefully. 'I know they've been in the family for generations, but I could put the money to much better use. There's so much that needs doing on the estate that I think Dad could be persuaded, but there's no chance of that happening.'

'Why ever not?' asked Arthur, refilling her cocktail.

'The sapphires don't belong to us, that's why not,' she said, sitting down once more. 'They belong to Evie, and don't we all know it! She absolutely adores them. She even had a photograph taken of them for the press.'

'I've seen it,' said Jack. He didn't think Celia would appreciate knowing where he'd seen it.

'Have you? Well, you can imagine that we simply couldn't credit Isabelle finding them on the train. Evie didn't know they'd gone until the telegram from the police arrived and then all hell broke loose. She nearly had a fit when she thought how close she'd been to losing them.' She smiled cynically. 'It was the most emotion I've ever seen her show. Anyway, when I heard it was Isabelle who'd found them, I simply had to come and get the story from the horse's mouth.'

Isabelle laughed. 'You could find a more flattering way of putting it. As a matter of fact, it wasn't me who found them, it was a Mr Duggleby. You'll have to tell Arthur who Evie is, though, Celia. I can see he hasn't a clue.'

'Sorry, Arthur,' said Celia, sipping her cocktail. 'Evie's my stepmother, although that sounds too like Cinderella for words. She and Dad got married last year.'

'She came to our wedding, Arthur,' said Isabelle. 'She had the most mouth-watering green linen dress with a long cream-and-gold stole. I think,' she continued knowledgeably, 'it was by Drécoll.'

'Crikey,' put in Arthur. 'I could hardly tell you who was there, let alone what they were wearing. I only,' he added with a grin, 'had eyes for you.'

Isabelle smiled. 'That's very sweet of you, but I don't believe a word of it. Men never look at clothes properly. Was it a Drécoll?' she demanded of Celia.

'It probably was,' said Celia. 'Evie always *looks* wonderful,' she said significantly. 'A real lily of the field, if you know what I mean.'

'Not in touch with the essential verities?' suggested Jack, wickedly. 'Addicted to electric light and running water and needless trappings, perhaps?'

'You may laugh, Jack,' said Celia, 'but Evie is a perfect example of, to my mind, all that is truly wrong with our modern life. All she really seems to care about is what she wears and being seen with the right people in the right places, you know? Dad says it's only natural because she used to be very hard-up, apparently, and it's only to be expected she should want to enjoy life now she can.'

'That's very generous of him,' commented Isabelle.

'Oh, Dad's completely unreasonable about Evie. Nothing but the best, whether it's clothes, holidays, parties – or sapphires. Even the sapphires weren't good enough as they were. Evie said they looked old fashioned, so Dad's having them re-set.'

'How did she come to own them?' asked Jack. He looked at Celia and chose his words carefully. 'Look. I don't want to trample on your finer feelings, but the sapphires are the ones Mrs Paxton owned, aren't they? I'm sorry if it's a delicate subject. Isabelle told me she was a relative of yours.'

'Mrs Paxton was my great-aunt but she quarrelled with Dad ages ago. I never actually met her. Yes, the sapphires belonged to her, poor woman.'

'Gosh,' muttered Arthur. 'When the papers rumble the connection with Terence Napier they'll love it.'

Celia shuddered. 'That's all we need. Dad's been up in arms about Uncle Terry and this'll just about put the tin lid on it. Dad believes he's totally innocent, but he can't be, can he? He whizzed Aunt Constance off to Paris and obviously did everything he could to get into her good books. The only reason he'd do that is because she was rich. Anyone else can see the truth of the matter a mile off, but not Dad. Dad isn't awfully good with people.'

'Your father?' said Isabelle, shocked. 'I like your father. He's always been very sweet to me.'

'Oh, he's a dear,' agreed Celia, 'but he's not very good at seeing what someone's actually like, you know? He always thinks the best of everyone. If he doesn't like something about them, he'll ignore it and carry on pretending everything in the garden's lovely. I'll say this for Evie, as soon as Dad let her know what happened to Aunt Constance, she cut short her holiday and came home and she's actually been very good about sparing his feelings. I mean, I know she thinks that Terence Napier simply has to be guilty, because there's nothing else she *can* think, but she hasn't said as much to Dad.'

'What's Terence Napier like?' asked Jack. 'As a person, I mean.'

'I don't know,' said Celia, shaking her head. 'I can hardly remember him. His parents died when he was very young and he lived with us, but I couldn't tell you what he's like now. He studied art, and was up in London at the Slade most of the year. He lived in Paris for a time and then there was the war, so I honestly can't remember him. It's different for Dad. Uncle Terry was like a younger brother to him.'

'Haven't you seen him since the war?' asked Arthur.

Celia shook her head. 'No, I haven't. As soon as the war was over, he headed for the South Seas. I've always pictured him like someone out of Somerset Maugham, living under a palm tree and cracking open coconuts and so on. Dad never really kept in touch – you know what men are like – but even now he believes Uncle Terry is the same boy he grew up with. I think the truth of the matter is that Uncle Terry had a nervous breakdown after the war and that changes people, doesn't it? I mean, going off to the South Seas is all very romantic, but it's a bit out of the ordinary, isn't it?'

'So what actually happened?' asked Arthur, putting more ice in the cocktail shaker. 'I read about it in the newspapers but I can't remember the details.'

Celia frowned. 'I'd better explain how Aunt Constance came to have the sapphires. They were part of the Breagan Stump

Bounty. It was discovered in seventeen something or other. You've heard of it, haven't you?'

Jack nodded. 'Yes, of course. It's in the British Museum, isn't it?'

'Parts of it are, yes. I can't say I've ever taken much interest, but the coins and some Roman jewellery went to the Museum years ago. However, the sapphires were always kept in the family. They were uncut when they were found but they were made into a necklace. They've always gone to the eldest girl in the family when she got married. When Aunt Constance married they went to her and,' she said, taking a cigarette from the box and putting it in a holder, 'they should have come to me. Or should have done when I got married, at any rate.'

'Bad luck,' said Jack, leaning forward to light her cigarette. 'Was it a formal arrangement?'

'No, not at all. It was just the way things always happened. That's the problem, of course. Still,' she added with an ironic smile, 'at least they're still in the family. It's just as well my grandfather never got near them. If he'd got hold of the sapphires, they would have vanished long since.'

Her smile faded. 'Aunt Constance was in possession and, legally speaking, she could dispose of them however she liked. She was left very badly off when her husband died and thought about selling the sapphires. Dad was keen they shouldn't be sold, so got together enough money to buy Aunt Constance an annuity. In return, she made a will leaving the sapphires to him, to ensure they'd stay in the family. What Dad was really afraid of was that she'd give them to her son, Sandy. Aunt Constance absolutely doted on Sandy. She thought he was the complete cat's whiskers, but he was even worse than my grandfather. My grandfather was an inveterate gambler but Sandy Paxton was a crook, pure and simple.'

'A real crook?' asked Jack.

'Oh yes,' said Celia, nodding vigorously. 'We've never spoken about him at home much, because Dad gets all hot under the collar if his name's mentioned, but I've managed to piece the story together. Aunt Mary – she's not an aunt really, but a neighbour I've known for years – has told me quite a lot about him. From what I can make out, there were a series of robberies

– furs, jewels, money and so on – from country houses he'd been invited to and people began to talk.'

'He sounds an absolute charmer,' said Isabelle.

'He was,' said Celia. 'Seriously, I mean. He lived off his charm. He was an actor for a time, after he got kicked out of Oxford. His speciality was making up to rich women. From what I can make out, he'd get silly women to fall in love with him, write compromising letters – I can never get over how many letters women used to write! – and then buy him off.'

Isabelle's eyebrows shot up. 'Blackmail?'

Celia shrugged. 'What else can you call it? Dad lost patience with Aunt Constance over him in the end. When the war came, Dad reckoned it was Sandy's chance to put the past behind him and make good. Reading between the lines, I think Dad more or less bribed Aunt Constance to get him to join up and, when Sandy was officially posted as missing, Aunt Constance blamed Dad and cut off relations completely. She never spoke to him again. And that,' she added, leaning forward, 'is where Evie comes in.'

'Go on,' said Jack, lighting a cigarette.

'Evie was a war widow. During the war she met Aunt Constance through some charity or other for the bereaved and they became very close.'

She contemplated the end of her cigarette for a few moments. 'That's that, really. As I said, the sapphires legally belonged to Aunt Constance and, although I think it was very mean spirited of her to go back on the arrangement she had with Dad, there's nothing he can do.'

'Possession being, as they say, nine points of the law,' put in Arthur.

'Exactly.' She blew out a long mouthful of smoke. 'The ironic thing is, they did come back into the family, despite Aunt Constance. Well, they came to Evie, at least.'

'From what you've said, that's not quite the same thing though, is it?' commented Isabelle.

Celia shrugged, then brightened. 'You never know. At least we've got them. Dad suggested that Evie has the sapphires re-set and he told me to hope for the best. He hopes she'll agree to sell a couple of the stones. If I had some money, I might be able to make Ted see sense and drop this silly idea about managing a tin mine in Singapore.'

She stubbed out her cigarette and looked up as a ring on the doorbell sounded, followed by footsteps in the hall as Lizzie, the maid, went to answer it.

'That'll be Bill Rackham, I expect,' said Jack.

'Rackham?' asked Celia. 'Inspector Rackham? He's the man who spoke to Dad.'

'Yes, he's a friend of mine,' said Jack.

'A policeman?' queried Celia, with raised eyebrows. 'Oh, I was forgetting. You do detective things, don't you? I'd forgotten. You're always so flippant, I'd forgotten just how capable you are.' She shot him an admiring look. 'That's a very admirable trait.'

Jack instinctively drew back. There was something in that look which no engaged or semi-engaged girl should direct at an unattached man, particularly one for whom she'd once had tender feelings.

'I must tell Dad about you,' continued Celia. 'He's hired a private detective to look into this idiotic idea he's got about Terence Napier, but if he's going to hire anyone, he might as well hire you.'

'I'm not a taxi,' said Jack with a grin.

Celia looked at him blankly. 'Of course you're not. I said you were a detective, not a cab driver. It's not the same thing at all. I suppose,' she said, as if she were talking about an alien species, 'you have to know heaps of policemen.'

'Bill Rackham's a friend of ours, too,' said Isabelle, catching the hint of snobbery in Celia's voice and determined to squash it. 'I like him very much.'

The door opened and Lizzie showed Bill into the room.

'Miss Leigh?' he asked, as they were introduced. 'I'm meeting your father tomorrow. He's coming to the Yard to reclaim his sapphires.'

'He was very complimentary about you, Mr Rackham,' said Celia. 'He thought it was marvellously quick work.'

'That wasn't me,' said Bill with a smile, pushing a lock of ginger hair out of his eyes. 'We were set on the right track by Mrs Stanton. No, not a cocktail, Stanton, thanks,' he said in

answer to Arthur's question. 'I'd rather have a whisky and soda.'
He took the glass with satisfaction. 'Thanks. I've earned this.'

He looked at Celia enquiringly. 'Have you explained how the
sapphires and money came to be stolen this morning?'

'No, I haven't, actually,' said Celia, turning to Jack, Arthur
and Isabelle. 'A man came to the house this morning, supposedly
looking for work. Dad found him hanging around the garden and
didn't like the look of him, so turfed him off the premises. There's
an old right of way that runs through the grounds, so it's perfectly
easy to get in, but passers-by aren't meant to come up to the
house, of course. He must've got into the study – the French
windows open onto the garden – and looted the safe. Dad said
there was some money missing, too.'

'We found fifty pounds in his jacket pocket,' put in Bill.

'There was fifty pounds missing from the safe,' said Celia.
'That must be it.'

'I'd say so,' said Bill. 'The man murdered on the train was
one Andrew Parsons. From what your father told me, the safe
seems a very old-fashioned affair and Andrew Parsons was an
expert safe-cracker.'

'So I was right,' said Isabelle triumphantly. 'He was a thief.'

'Absolutely he was,' said Bill. 'The Records Department turned
him up.'

Arthur sipped his cocktail with a frown. 'I still don't get it.
Why murder someone and leave the sapphires?'

'We think the murderer didn't realise Parsons had the sapphires,'
said Jack. 'Leonard Duggleby said they were pushed under the
seat. Tell us what you've unearthed about Parsons, Bill.'

Bill took a cigarette from the box on the table. 'There's no
fingerprints or photographs on file, worse luck, as we never laid
hands on him, but we had a record of him, all the same. You
remember we found two cards in his things, Jack? Well, Parsons
left a card in the Leighs' safe. He'd drawn a motif on it, a little
cross with a circle over it like a halo. That motif was well known
to the Yard a few years ago. Parsons, would you believe, is none
other than the Vicar.'

'The Vicar?' repeated Celia, puzzled. 'A clergyman, you
mean?'

Jack laughed. 'From the sound of it I don't think he's a minister of the established church.' He looked at Bill. 'It's a play on the name *Parsons*, isn't it?' Bill nodded. 'Come on. Who the dickens is the Vicar?'

'The Vicar,' said Bill, 'had a pretty fierce reputation as a crook before the war.' He hunched forward. 'There's always been a question mark over him. He was supposed to have been killed in 1915. He was cornered in a warehouse in Lambeth. The place caught fire and a charred body was recovered but, as you'd expect, there's always been rumours it wasn't his body and that he got away scot-free.'

'Hang on,' said Jack, getting up and refilling his glass. 'This is beginning to ring a bell. I wrote a series about past crimes for *On The Town* a couple of years ago. If he's the man I'm thinking of, he pulled off a good few robberies in France. Is he the chap who stole a small fortune in diamonds from the Calais Mail Train in 1911 or thereabouts?'

Bill nodded. 'That's the one. The diamonds belonged to a Wenzel Osterhagen, the American butter king. I read up on the case this afternoon and I don't think the diamonds were ever on the train. Mrs Osterhagen's maid could have easily stolen the diamonds beforehand and passed them on to the Vicar. She resigned shortly after the robbery and set up a fashionable milliners in New York, having apparently come into a considerable amount of money. The really rotten thing about the whole business, though, is that the train guard was murdered. If the maid did steal the diamonds, the guard's murder was nothing more than a blind.'

Isabelle gave a little cry. 'That's horrible!'

'It didn't end there,' said Bill. 'A string of thefts, a raft of assaults and at least three murders were attributed to him.'

'Good God!' said Arthur. 'I'd have thought that would have started a real hue and cry.'

'You'd think so, Stanton, but all the victims were petty crooks and known informers and not the types to attract much sympathy. They'd promised to squeal on the Vicar but he got to them before we did, poor devils. We know it was the Vicar because he always signed his crimes with that cross and halo. Sometimes it would be chalked on a wall, sometimes it was drawn on a card or a piece of paper, but he always signed it.'

'But why?' asked Isabelle and Celia together. 'That's really creepy,' added Isabelle with a shudder. 'Why advertise yourself like that?'

'Mainly because it is creepy, I imagine,' said Bill. 'He had a fair old reign of terror in the underworld before the war. He was a real hard case.'

'I wonder if he's been holed up in France?' said Jack. 'There was a definite French theme to the things we found on him. Was the knife a French trench dagger?'

'It was. I had a good look at it after the doctor got it out. Unfortunately, as far as we're concerned, it's a type which was produced by the thousand. It had a plain wooden hilt, as we saw, Jack, a steel cross guard and a blade about seven inches long. It's a very efficient weapon.'

'Vengeance,' said Jack. 'If I know the type, it had *Le Vengeur 1870* inscribed on the blade.'

'It did.'

'I'm going to have nightmares at this rate,' complained Isabelle. 'It was bad enough finding the man in the first place without you going on about daggers. Why on earth did it have *Vengeance* written on it?'

'Because of the Franco-Prussian war,' said Jack absently. 'The French had some scores to settle. It seems as if someone else did too. We were looking for a motive, weren't we, Bill? I wonder if it's revenge? Someone who wanted to be revenged on the Vicar, perhaps?'

'You might be right,' said Bill. 'It's worth bearing in mind, certainly.'

'Who could that be?' asked Isabelle.

'An old associate of the Vicar's, perhaps?' suggested Jack. 'Actually, Bill, I wonder if that is the reason? The Vicar was supposed to have died in 1915. What if someone, someone with a grudge, spotted him, still alive and kicking, and decided to finish off the good work that should have been completed years ago?'

'You don't know that,' said Arthur. 'You don't know anything, really. You're just guessing.'

'True,' admitted Jack.

'I'll tell you what I think is odd, though,' continued Arthur.

'If the Vicar was supposed to have died in 1915, why would he come back to England? And, if he did come back, wouldn't he try and conceal his identity?'

'I think Arthur's got a point,' said Isabelle. 'Are you absolutely sure it was the Vicar?'

'Who else could it be?' asked Bill. 'Why should anyone try and make out it's the Vicar when it isn't? It's not like saying someone's Jack the Ripper, say. The Vicar had an unenviable reputation in the underworld, but he was virtually unknown to the public. Andrew Parsons is a very obscure figure. It wasn't his name that gave him away, but the cross and halo on the card.'

'Andrew Parsons,' said Isabelle thoughtfully. 'Andrew Parsons . . . Did he have his initials on any of his things?'

'As a matter of fact he did,' said Bill, puzzled. 'His case and toiletry set and so on.'

'His initials,' repeated Isabelle, slowly. 'A.P.' She looked up sharply, her eyes bright. 'Jack! A.P.! *France!*'

'What about it?' he asked.

'Don't you see?' she said excitedly. 'Celia, what was the name of Mrs Paxton's son?'

'Sandy,' said Celia. 'I told you so earlier.'

'But he was actually called Alexander, wasn't he? Alexander Paxton. A.P. The same initials as the Vicar. What if Paxton *is* the Vicar?'

'Hang on a minute,' said Bill, blinking. 'The Vicar's called Andrew Parsons not Alexander Paxton.'

'That could be just a blind.'

Jack clicked his tongue. 'The pun on the name *Parsons* doesn't work if the Vicar's actually called Paxton, does it?'

'Excuse me,' said Celia repressively. 'This is a relative of mine you're discussing.'

Isabelle wriggled impatiently. 'Come on, Celia. It was you who told us Sandy Paxton was a crook. After all, he disappeared, just as the Vicar did.'

'He was posted as missing,' said Celia blankly. 'That means he's dead.'

'I know what it usually means,' said Isabelle impatiently, 'but what if he's alive? According to the papers, Terence Napier said Sandy Paxton had deserted and was still alive. Mrs Paxton must've believed he was alive, otherwise she wouldn't have gone to France with Terence Napier.'

'Well, if you're going to believe the word of a man like that . . .'

'He could be telling the truth.'

'Come off it, Isabelle,' said Jack witheringly. 'Sandy Paxton might or might not be alive but the Vicar was killed – or supposedly killed – in 1915. Sandy Paxton was certainly alive until he was posted missing on the Somme which, as you'll recall, was in 1916.'

'We don't know that,' said Isabelle stubbornly. 'He could've been leading a double life. We don't know either of them were killed when they said they were.'

'True,' agreed Jack.

'And,' she said, pressing home her advantage, 'Celia told us he'd been an actor. It'd be easy for him to pretend to be someone else. In fact, that could be it, couldn't it? Sandy Paxton might not have been the real Vicar but he could've been pretending to *be* the Vicar.'

Jack rolled his eyes to heaven, but Arthur looked impressed.

'That's an idea, Isabelle,' said Arthur. 'How old would Paxton be, Celia? If he was alive, I mean?'

'He'd be about forty, I suppose.'

Bill clicked his tongue. 'The age is about right, as far as that goes, but if Sandy Paxton stole the sapphires, Miss Leigh's father would have recognised him when he turned up at the house yesterday, wouldn't he?'

'Of course not,' said Celia. 'He's dead. I keep on telling you he's dead.'

'Just pretend, Celia,' said Isabelle. 'Just for the moment, yes? If he was alive, would your father have recognised him?'

Celia frowned in disapproval but tried hard. 'Actually, I don't think he would,' she said slowly. 'Dad disapproved of Sandy intensely and had as little to do with him as possible.'

'You see?' said Isabelle. 'It could have been Sandy Paxton. If your father was convinced he'd died years ago, he wouldn't expect to see him, would he?' She looked at Bill and suddenly grinned. 'I can see you're not convinced.'

'I can't say I am,' said Bill. 'I can't see why Paxton, or anyone else for that matter, would pretend to be an obscure crook from years ago. Even if the man on the train was Paxton, it doesn't tell us who killed him.'

'I suggested a confederate before, Bill,' said Jack. 'Did the Vicar have any associates?'

'He had people who worked for him, certainly. As far as we know, they're all dead.'

'What if one isn't dead? What if the murderer is a disgruntled ex-confederate?'

Isabelle sat up straight. 'Could *he* be Sandy Paxton? The confederate, I mean?'

'Dash it, Belle, they can't all be Sandy Paxton,' said Jack with a laugh. 'Although, to be fair, I think there's more chance of Paxton being one of the Vicar's hangers-on than the Vicar himself.'

'Why's that, Jack?' asked Bill.

'Well, let's say Paxton is alive.'

'Ridiculous,' muttered Celia.

'Let me play around with the idea,' said Jack with a smile. 'We know there was a lot in the papers about the sapphires after Mrs Paxton was killed. Anyone – any prospective thief – could have read about the sapphires and decided to have a crack at them, but there's no doubt that if Sandy Paxton saw them, he'd be fascinated.'

He broke off and looked at Isabelle. 'For your benefit, old prune, and just to show I've been paying attention, I'm going to use Sandy Paxton's name as a stand-in for the Vicar's partner. Celia, bear with me. Let's say the partner – who could be Paxton – gets in touch with his old pal, the Vicar, and they travel down to Breagan Grange to give the place a once over. Parsons, the Vicar, might have hoped to get into the grounds but he can't have expected to find the house open for him to stroll into. It sounded like an impulsive robbery and maybe it was.'

Bill nodded. 'You mean the Vicar saw his chance and took it?'

'Double quick, I imagine. Now, Sandy Paxton isn't expecting Parsons to have the stones, so Parsons keeps stumm about the fact he's got them. Then, on the train, the Vicar is actually looking at the necklace when Sandy Paxton comes in to the compartment. Parsons shoves the sapphires under the seat to hide them. There must be some reason why they were under the seat. Paxton doesn't know that the Vicar has the jewels but catches on that he isn't being straight with him and they quarrel.'

'As a matter of fact, Parsons could have started the quarrel on purpose,' said Bill. 'If he had the stones and didn't want to let on, he'd want a reason to fall out with the man so he wouldn't have to share the proceeds.'

'You might be right. However it started, though, Parsons comes off worse, and Paxton, or,' he added, with an eye on the rebellious Celia '– whoever the murderer actually is – skips as fast as possible, not knowing he's leaving a fortune in jewels under the seat.'

'Isabelle saw Parsons get on the train at Market Albury, didn't you?' said Arthur. 'Was there anyone with him?'

'I didn't see anyone,' said Isabelle, 'but that doesn't mean he wasn't there. The other man could have made a point of not speaking to him on the platform or he could have been on the train already or got on after Market Albury.'

'This is all complete nonsense,' said Celia in bewilderment. 'You can't possibly know any of this is true. You weren't there.'

'We've got to account for a murdered man, Miss Leigh,' said Bill. 'That does involve a certain amount of speculation.' He grinned at Isabelle. 'However unlikely some of it may sound.'

Celia sighed. 'If this man stole my stepmother's necklace, then he only has himself to blame for the consequences, no matter what his name is.' She rose to her feet. 'I really must be getting off. Isabelle, do you fancy coming shopping with me tomorrow? I'd like a new hat and I could really do with a new bag.'

'Absolutely,' said Isabelle happily. 'Hats *and* bags.'

'Steady on,' put in Arthur with a laugh. 'Don't get carried away.'

'I'd love to come,' said Isabelle, ignoring him. 'Shall we have lunch together?'

'I'm meeting Ted for lunch.' Celia sighed. 'I hope I'll be able to talk some sense into him. Shall we say the entrance to Marshall and Snelgroves at two? That's settled, then.'

'I'll get off as well,' said Bill, standing up. 'By the way, Isabelle, did you talk to Burgess from *The Monitor*?'

'Yes, I did. Why? There wasn't any reason I shouldn't have done, was there?'

'None whatsoever. It's just that if the press haven't been in touch already, they will once Burgess' story breaks.' He grinned. 'If I were you, I'd be tempted to leave the phone off the hook.'

SIX

At half past nine the next morning, the door to Isabelle's and Arthur's flat was opened by Lizzie, the maid, who, contrary to her usual custom, opened the door a crack and peered out cautiously, obviously prepared to slam it back in place. She sighed and visibly relaxed when she saw Jack.

'Thank goodness it's only you, sir,' she said, opening the door wide.

'Only me?' asked Jack, coming into the hall. He shed his panama into Lizzie's waiting hands, his eyes crinkling in a smile. 'I'm devastated, Lizzie.'

Lizzie's hand flew to her mouth. 'I'm so sorry, sir, I didn't mean it like that. Of course I didn't, only I've done nothing this morning but run back and forth to the door and the telephone with blessed reporters all a-clamouring for the mistress to talk to them. There's been more than a few,' she added with a certain amount of pride, 'who want to talk to me, would you believe! I reckon my name's going to be in the paper too! Cheek, I calls it. Not that,' she said virtuously, 'you'll catch me saying nothing I shouldn't but they sort of worm things out you, don't they? Cook told me to mind my tongue but I said to her, I hopes I know better than to stand and gossip to the likes of them with nothing better to do than to waste honest folks' time. You wouldn't *believe* what it's been like.'

She paused for breath and Jack, who could see she was thoroughly enjoying herself, was able to get a word in edgeways. 'I certainly would believe it. I had to dodge round the press myself to get into the flats.'

'You know what I'm talking about, then,' said Lizzie fervently. 'Half past six the phone started ringing. Would you credit it? I feel like I've done a full day's work already with that wretched telephone and the breakfast isn't cleared off the table yet.'

'Is that you, Jack?' called Isabelle, appearing in the hall, a piece of toast and marmalade in her hand. 'We're under a state of siege. Come on in and have some breakfast. Lizzie, bring through another pot of tea, will you? Poor Lizzie,' she said as she led the way into the dining room. 'Although she's actually,' she added in an undertone, 'having the time of her life.'

'Morning, Jack,' said Arthur from the breakfast table. He had the *Daily Monitor* propped up on the coffee pot. 'By jingo, can you believe the fuss? We've had to put Lizzie on guard duty.'

'She seems as if she's coping,' said Jack, reaching for the coffee pot.

'She doesn't think you're displaying the appropriate hysterics, Isabelle,' said Arthur with a grin. 'She said that you were being very brave, but I could tell she doesn't approve. Both she and Cook think you should have taken to your bed.'

Isabelle gave a gurgle of laughter. 'What, and be brought round with smelling salts and burnt feathers, you mean? Fat chance. You have seen the paper, haven't you, Jack?' she asked, spreading it out on the table. 'Look, there's a picture of me. It's not very flattering,' she added critically between mouthfuls of toast. 'I look like a startled rabbit.'

'Don't crunch down my ear like that,' begged Jack, moving her hand. 'I must say I've seen you looking brighter,' he added diplomatically. 'Oh, blimey, is that me?'

'Absolutely it is,' said Isabelle. 'There's quite a lot about you, Jack.'

'Strewth! Is there?'

Isabelle turned the pages of the *Monitor.* 'Here we are. *Mrs Isabelle Stanton is, of course, the cousin of detective-story writer Jack Haldean, whose talents as a sleuth have been called upon more than once by Scotland Yard. Readers may recall the events surrounding the launch of the flying boat Pegasus . . .* and so on and so on. And look, there's a piece by Leonard Duggleby, too. *Special report by Leonard Duggleby see page six.*'

'I'm glad he had enough about him to get into print,' said Jack. 'He was having collywobbles about the whole thing when I spoke to him yesterday.'

'Poor Mr Duggleby,' said Isabelle, her voice obscured by toast. 'This could be his big break. I hope it is, anyhow.'

'They haven't caught on to who the victim is,' said Arthur. 'When they do, I imagine all the old stories about the Vicar will be rehashed.'

'Of course they will. Burgess and his newspaper pals will think they're in heaven with a story like that. They haven't made the connection with Terence Napier, have they?'

'There's nothing in the *Monitor.*'

'It can only be a matter of time before they do.'

'Then it'll be the Leighs' turn to be hounded, I suppose,' said Isabelle as the telephone rang in the hall.

'Not again!' grumbled Arthur. 'We must have spoken to everyone in Fleet Street already. I can't believe it's more reporters.'

It wasn't.

'Isabelle!' said the breathlessly excited voice down the phone. It was Ethel Tibberton, an old and gushing school friend. 'That *is* you in the paper, isn't it? How madly *thrilling,* darling! You must tell me all about it.'

A couple of hours later and over a dozen old friends later, Isabelle was beginning to wish that the telephone had never been invented. The only call she really appreciated was one from Celia Leigh.

'Isabelle, I've just been speaking to Dad on the phone. Both he and Evie are absolutely soggy with relief that the sapphires are safe and want to thank you personally. Dad said he's going to drop you a line and I wouldn't be surprised if they called. They're anxious to get in touch with this man, Duggleby, too. Dad wants to know if he should offer Mr Duggleby a reward but, naturally, doesn't want to offend him.'

Isabelle thought it over. 'That's a bit delicate, Celia. It's obvious Mr Duggleby could do with the money, but I can't help feeling it'd be a bit like offering a reward to Arthur or Jack.'

'That's awkward. What do you suggest?'

'Tell your father to offer a reward as a thank-you,' said Isabelle, after some thought, adding, beneath her breath, 'tactfully.'

'Thanks, darling. I'll let him know. See you at two o'clock.'

Isabelle hung up the phone and it promptly rang once more.

After dealing with yet another old friend who expected her to be in rhapsodies about sapphires, murders and mysterious corpses, she marched into the sitting room.

Arthur looked at her in surprise. 'You look upset about something.'

'That's putting it mildly.' She flung herself into an armchair. 'I can't *believe* how many times I've had to go over the story. Maybe I'm being unfair, but there's something positively ghoulish about it all.'

'Why don't we,' said Jack, folding up the newspaper, 'do the manly thing and cut and run? You could station Lizzie beside the phone to field any calls and we could sneak out the back and have an early lunch at the Criterion, say?'

She beamed at him. 'Sometimes, Jack, you have some really good ideas. Let's do it.'

'What a relief to escape,' said Isabelle as they settled themselves at their table under the gold-roofed splendour of the Criterion. 'What do you fancy for lunch, Arthur?'

'That depends,' said Arthur, picking up the menu. 'Do you want the four-bob lunch or shall we push the boat out and spare no expense?'

'Six shillings and sixpence *and* a tip,' muttered Jack with a grin. 'Steady on, old thing.'

Isabelle pondered the bill of fare. 'Let's go for the four-bob option, shall we? I'd better not have a huge lunch as I'll have tea with Celia later on.'

'We might as well make the most of it,' said Arthur. 'It's not long before we move to Croxton Ferriers.' He sighed happily. 'I can't wait to get to work. The land's been neglected but it's got such *promise*, Jack.'

'It's not the land so much as the house at Croxton Ferriers which bothers me,' said Isabelle dubiously. 'Are you sure we've got running water, Arthur? Apart from down the walls, I mean?'

'It's fine,' said Arthur. 'It's even got a roof now.'

'And floors? That are safe to walk on, I mean?'

'It will have. Rock solid. Don't worry.'

'If you say so,' agreed Isabelle in a benefit-of-the-doubt sort of voice.

The waiter arrived and for a little while the conversation centred round food. Over his anchovy eggs Arthur returned to his favourite theme of plans for the future, when he broke off, looking at his wife quizzically. 'I don't think you've heard a word I've said, Isabelle. Are you all right?'

'Yes . . .' She seemed very doubtful.

'Well, either you are or you aren't,' said Jack. 'Are you thinking about yesterday?'

'No. At least, I don't think I am.'

'What on earth is it?' asked Jack with a laugh. 'You must know what you're thinking about. Get it off your chest, old bean.'

Isabelle wriggled her shoulder blades. 'I'm feeling very uneasy, for some reason.' She paused and wriggled again. 'It's as if I'm being watched.'

Jack put his hand to his face so his eyes were shielded by his palm and took careful stock of the restaurant.

At the next table there was a giggling woman in a red straw hat with elaborate feathers, sitting across from a flannel-suited man with a Brigade of Guards tie. Her attention was divided between the Guardee and the Pekingese on her knee, to whom she was feeding titbits from her plate. They weren't watching anyone but themselves.

At the next table on, a vacuous, gleaming fair-haired youth in a yellow waistcoat and a monocle was trying to light his companion's cigarette in its nine-inch holder without setting fire to her trailing silk scarf, while, next to them, four earnest bald-headed men in morning suits, who looked like bank officials, were solidly munching their way through roast beef.

Beyond them, an older couple, who, to Jack's eyes, had County written all over them, were dealing with whitebait, while at the adjacent table a white-moustached, military-looking man was beaming in an avuncular fashion at a prettily-dressed girl of about thirteen and her Eton-suited brother as they tucked into ice-cream.

A stout lady in black was ruining the teeth of her Pomeranian by feeding it sugar cubes while her husband placidly sipped his coffee. Beyond them, three very smart ladies picked at fruit salad. The other tables in the restaurant were too far away to count, but no one seemed to be paying them any particular attention.

'There isn't anyone watching us now,' said Jack quietly. 'A couple have just gone out, though. The man was wearing a topper and the woman had a maroon hat and coat, but that's all I can tell you about them.'

'It's gone, in any case,' said Isabelle in relief. 'The feeling, I mean. It was really odd. It was as if I had a ghostly finger poking into my back.'

'Why should anyone be keeping an eye on you?' asked Arthur. 'Unless it's more reporters, I suppose.'

'They'd hardly come in here,' said Jack. 'And they certainly wouldn't just stand and stare.'

Isabelle shook herself briskly. 'I don't suppose it's anything but imagination.' She straightened her shoulders, obviously drawing a mental line under the conversation. 'Let's talk about Croxton Ferriers. I'm going to be madly domestic, Jack, and Arthur's positively rural. You're off to look at milk separators this afternoon, aren't you, darling?'

'I've got hopes of building up the dairy herd,' said Arthur. 'I want to look at fresh stock, obviously, but with some new machinery, including a really up-to-date milk separator, we can really start to make things happen . . .' The conversation drifted off into strictly agricultural paths.

After lunch, Isabelle made her way to Oxford Street and Marshall and Snelgroves. Arthur, with undisguised enthusiasm, took Jack off to Clough and Holland's, the agricultural machinery suppliers on Dover Street, talking happily about milk yields.

Isabelle was on New Bond Street when she first became aware of a vague uneasiness, a little niggling sensation between her shoulder blades. It was the same sort of feeling she'd experienced in the Criterion.

She stopped to look at the display of hats in Walpoles and was momentarily distracted by a peacock-blue brimless silk cloche hat with an embroidered ribbon and matching silk scarf, a mere five and a half guineas. Five and a half guineas! She clicked her tongue. That was well over a week's household expenses, but it was lovely. She wondered what Arthur would say . . .

The little niggling sensation increased and she suddenly wished, very strongly, that Arthur was there. It was as if she was being watched. She stepped back a pace from the plate-glass window, ostensibly still looking at the hats, but actually trying to see the reflections in the curved glass.

In all the strolling crowds, no one seemed to be paying her any special attention and she unconsciously relaxed. Maybe, she thought impatiently, it was nothing more than nerves. She turned and walked briskly away from the milliners.

Arthur had warned her she could suffer a reaction to the events of yesterday. Maybe this was it. Yesterday had been dreadfully long and wearisome, and, what with reassuring little Agathe's mother, calming down Mr Duggleby, patiently answering interminable questions and putting on a brave face for Arthur, her own emotions seemed to be steamrollered into non-existence. And yet, in the privacy of her own thoughts, she acknowledged it had been a horrible shock. (*There was that sensation between her shoulder blades once more!*)

She tried to firmly put the memory from her mind as she paused on the kerb at the corner of Maddox Street to wait for a break in the traffic.

The sensation, the near physical sensation of fingers on her spine grew and she suddenly went from vague fear to near terror. It *wasn't* just nerves!

The crowd on the tight-packed pavement moved with a restless lurch, she turned her head, caught the sight of a looming shape, then there was a sharp shove in her back. She staggered forward, losing her footing on the kerb. Arms flailing, she fell forward. A car, its radiator grill suddenly huge, was above her head. She tried to twist out of the way, heard screams, shouts, a squeal of brakes, a moment of intense pain, and then there was nothing at all.

SEVEN

Leonard Duggleby came up the steps of Piccadilly Circus underground station, pulling his hat over his eyes to shield them from the sun as he emerged from the depths. For a moment the light, reflecting from the innumerable windows of the tall, smoke-streaked, cream-coloured buildings, dazzled him.

Blinking in the glare, he walked towards the seemingly unstop-
pable stream of black taxis, yellow and red buses and patient
plodding horses, all funnelled round the tall green fountain
surmounted by Eros on his bronze plinth in the middle of the
square.

'Paper!' shouted a newsvendor in a hoarse Cockney rasp as
Duggleby threaded his way through the crowd. 'Get cher paper
here! Murder on the train latest!'

Duggleby hesitated on the kerb, stopped, turned back, felt in
his pocket for a penny, and bought a copy of the *Evening Standard.*
There wasn't, he thought as he glanced at the headlines, much
he could learn from the newspaper, but it was worth having a
look, all the same. Newspaper in hand, he plunged back into the
crowd towards the kerb.

There was a chorus of shouts, a blast of horns and the crashing
of glass. The policeman on point duty gave a startled shout, then,
seizing his whistle, gave a shill blast as he ran across the road.
A horse pulling a furniture wagon reared in its traces, a taxi
clipped the side of a car, crumpling its wheel, and a bus, the
passengers on the open upper deck crying out in alarm, slewed
across the road.

Leonard Duggleby felt the back of his jacket gripped and
pulled. Gasping for breath as his collar bit into his throat, he
sprawled in a heap on the pavement, the Cockney newsvendor
towering above him.

'What the blinkin' hell were you *doin'*?' demanded the news
vendor. 'You could have been killed, leapin' orf the kerb like
that!' A sea of concerned faces gazed down at him. 'Jumped out
like a bleedin' salmon, you did.'

Duggleby pulled his collar loose and scrambled to his knees.
'I was pushed,' he said faintly. A fit of coughing overcame him.

'What's going on?' The policeman who'd been on point duty
carved his stately way through the alarmed, if eager,
spectators.

'He woz pushed!' said the newsvendor. 'Someone pushed this
geezer into the traffic!'

'Pushed?' repeated the policeman incredulously. 'Who pushed
you?'

Duggleby shook his head in bewilderment. 'I don't know.'

The policeman reached down his arm and Duggleby got to his feet.

A second policeman joined them. 'What's happened?' he demanded.

Various members of the crowd eagerly attempted to tell him.

'Hold on, hold on,' said the constable, shaking his head in disbelief. 'Quiet down, everyone! First things first. Let's get this traffic moving, for a start.' He looked to where the car and the taxi had drawn up beside the kerb, raising his voice as the driver and the motorist climbed out onto the pavement. 'Anyone hurt? No? That's the main thing.' He ushered the crowd in front of him. 'Move along there, ladies and gentlemen, move along! Now then,' he said, turning back to Duggleby, 'are you all right?'

'I think so,' said Duggleby shakily, with an unsuccessful attempt at a smile. 'That was scary. No bones broken, thank God. In fact,' he added, straightening out his clothes, 'I seem to be very lucky. No damage done.'

'You go and have a sit-down in the pub, sir,' said the policeman, pointing to The Crooked Staff. 'We'll come and have a word with you in a few minutes. And I'll need to speak to you, sir,' he added to the irate motorist who, with the taxi-driver close behind, had elbowed his way through to the circle surrounding Duggleby.

'And I want to speak to the clown who jumped out in front of me,' snapped the motorist, a large man with a red face and an aggressive moustache. 'What the devil happened? My wheel's a complete wreck and my lights are broken. I'll be very surprised if I'll be able to drive that car again in a hurry.' He glared at Duggleby. 'Dammit, I nearly killed you! What the devil came over you, sir!'

'I was pushed,' repeated Duggleby wearily.

''E woz pushed,' echoed the newsvendor.

'Pushed?' The motorist snorted in disbelief. 'Nonsense.'

''E woz pushed,' repeated the newsvendor, doggedly. ''E woz pushed.'

'Pushed,' muttered the crowd.

The motorist stopped dead in his tracks and stared at Duggleby. 'But dash it, man, was it an accident?' Duggleby shook his head. 'But who pushed you? Someone who was with you?'

Duggleby shook his head once more. 'No one was with me.'

'But you *can't* have been pushed,' said the motorist. 'Why, that'd mean someone deliberately tried to kill you!'

Duggleby buried his face in his hands. 'I rather think they did.'

It was getting on for half past four when Arthur and Jack arrived back at the flat.

The door to the kitchen at the end of the corridor opened as they came in. Lizzie poked her head out. 'Oh, it's you, sir. And you, Major Haldean.' She sounded disappointed.

Arthur paused in the act of hanging up his hat on the hall-stand and looked at her questioningly. 'Why shouldn't it be us?'

Jack smothered a grin at this less than rapturous welcome. 'That's more or less what you said when I arrived this morning, Lizzie. Are you expecting someone?'

'I wasn't expecting anyone, sir,' said Lizzie, flushing as she came into the hall. 'And I didn't mean it shouldn't be you, of course I didn't. It's just that you know the mistress asked me to answer the telephone for her? Well, Miss Leigh telephoned at gone three o'clock and said the mistress should have met her at two and where was she? I was hoping you was the mistress, if you take my meaning, because me and Cook think she's ever so brave with what happened on the train, and we were worried.'

Her face contorted into a frown of concern. 'Cook doesn't hold with trains. She thinks as how it wouldn't be a wonder if the mistress was took funny, because her aunty – mind you, she is sensitive – was struck all of a heap for days when she had a nasty experience on a train.'

'Whatever happened to Mrs Travis' aunt?' asked Jack inquisitively.

Lizzie pursed her lips primly. 'Nothing I can discuss with a gentleman. But Cook and me wondered if the mistress had started to dwell on what happened yesterday and had come over all peculiar somewhere.'

'It doesn't sound very likely,' said Arthur good humouredly. 'I appreciate your concern but can't see Mrs Stanton coming over – er – all peculiar.'

'What's happened to her then, sir?'

Arthur frowned. 'As a matter of fact, I don't know. Miss Leigh rang at just gone three, you say? I wonder where Isabelle's got to?'

His face cleared as the telephone jangled beside him. 'That's probably her now.' He picked up the phone. 'Mayfair two-five-seven.'

Jack saw Arthur's face alter as a tinny voice sounded clearly over the telephone.

'Excuse me,' said the voice hesitantly, 'but is that Captain Stanton, by any chance?'

'Yes, this is Captain Stanton.'

There was a sigh of relief. 'We met yesterday, Captain. This is Leonard Duggleby.' He sounded ridiculously apologetic. 'I hope you remember me.'

'Mr Duggleby?' said Arthur, unconsciously trying to put the man at his ease. 'Of course. What can I do for you?'

'Well, something rather disagreeable has just happened and I . . . I do hope you forgive the intrusion, but . . . but . . .' He swallowed and got out the words in a rush. 'Is Mrs Stanton all right?'

Jack saw Arthur's hand tighten on the receiver. 'As far as I know.' He exchanged a worried look with Jack. 'Why do you ask?'

'It's . . .' The man's hesitation was maddening. 'Look, I don't want to sound overly dramatic but . . . but . . .'

'*What?*' demanded Arthur.

'I think someone's tried to kill me,' said Duggleby lamely.

Arthur was incredulous. '*Kill you?*'

'It sounds crazy, I know, but I couldn't have been mistaken, I really couldn't, and there isn't any reason why anyone should do such a thing unless it's connected with yesterday somehow. When I picked myself up, and sorted myself out, I thought about Mrs Stanton. I hope you don't mind me ringing, but she gave her address and telephone number to the police yesterday and I thought I'd remembered it correctly. I simply had to call and find out if she was all right.'

Jack saw the expression on Arthur's face. He stepped forward and took the telephone from his friend's unprotesting hand. 'Duggleby? This is Jack Haldean. You say someone tried to kill you?'

'I can't think of any other explanation. I was crossing Piccadilly Circus when there was a sharp shove in my back and I went sprawling into the traffic, right in front of a car. Fortunately, the driver had his wits about him, or I wouldn't be here now. I'm ringing from a public telephone in Piccadilly near The Crooked Staff. The policeman on duty told me to wait here until he could speak to me. I don't want to make a fuss, but I'm worried.'

'I'm not surprised. I'm glad to hear you've come to no harm, Mr Duggleby. Stay where you are until the police have spoken to you.'

'Yes, of course I will.' He hesitated once more. 'Is Mrs Stanton all right?'

Jack glanced at Arthur. 'As far as we know. We haven't seen her for a while.'

'Come on, Jack,' muttered Arthur in a dried-up voice. 'We have to find Isabelle.'

Jack nodded and spoke to Leonard Duggleby once more. 'I need to see you. I'll be in touch soon.' He hung up the receiver.

Arthur was at the door. 'Come *on*, Jack! We have to find Isabelle!'

'Wait a moment.' Jack picked up the telephone. 'Let me speak to Bill Rackham first. If anything has happened, he should know.'

Alive with impatience, Arthur waited for Jack's call to be put through. It seemed to take an endless amount of time for the connection to be made. As Bill's voice sounded over the telephone, Arthur gripped the hall table, his knuckles showing white.

'Bill? It's Jack. I'm with Arthur at the flat . . .'

Arthur strained to hear but the words – Jack's words – were coming from a dark place very far away. The brightly painted hall suddenly seemed full of shadows. He sensed rather than saw Lizzie beside him and knew she was holding her breath.

Jack put down the phone slowly. He swallowed before he spoke. 'There was a woman knocked down on New Bond Street. She was taken to the Royal Free.' He put his hand on Arthur's arm. 'She's going to be all right.'

Arthur closed his eyes and swayed in relief. 'Thank God,' he muttered. 'Thank God.'

Released from tension, Lizzie suddenly burst into tears. 'I'm sorry,' she sobbed, dabbing her eyes. 'I'm so sorry, but I was that *worried.*'

'Go and make a cup of tea,' suggested Jack. 'I think you need one. Captain Stanton and I are going to the hospital. Come on, Arthur. Let's go.'

Accompanied by Dr Hawley, Arthur and Jack entered Isabelle's room. She was asleep, her chestnut hair spread over the white pillow and one arm over the bedspread. Her face was bruised and there was a bandage round her head but she was alive. Arthur walked very quietly to her side and gazed at her speechlessly.

Dr Hawley, a brisk, no-nonsense man, stayed at the back of the room. He raised his eyebrows at Jack in enquiry. 'I take it you identify the patient?

Jack drew his breath in. 'Yes,' he managed to say. His voice was hushed. 'That's Mrs Stanton.'

Isabelle's eyes flickered open. 'Arthur?' Her voice was the thinnest of whispers.

'I'm here,' Arthur said unsteadily.

Isabelle smiled and reached out her hand to him.

Dr Hawley tapped Jack on the arm. 'We'll wait outside, major.'

In the corridor, Dr Hawley looked satisfied. 'I was very pleased to see the patient recognised her husband. I didn't think there was any lasting damage, but head injuries can be very tricky things.'

'She will be all right, won't she, doctor?' asked Jack anxiously.

Dr Hawley assumed the hearty common sense he used to reassure relatives. 'She'll be very stiff and sore for a while, but there's no bones broken, thank goodness. As long as she has complete rest tonight, she should be discharged tomorrow. I realise the patient's husband is understandably anxious, but it would be best if his visit was as short as possible. I can't allow any other visitors.'

The fact that the doctor referred to Isabelle as 'the patient' suddenly irritated Jack. It wasn't unkind but it was anonymous. Isabelle was a person who *mattered,* a person with a name and people who cared about her. 'I'll make sure I tell Mrs Stanton's parents, Sir Philip and Lady Rivers, as much.'

At the mention of the gentry, the doctor's manner subtly altered.

He shifted back a step and put his head to one side quizzically. 'Sir Philip and Lady Rivers, eh? Yes, yes, of course.' He coughed. 'Naturally, I would make an exception in their case.'

Good old snobbery, thought Jack. It never fails.

'I'm sure Mrs Stanton will be relieved to see her mother. Incidentally,' said the doctor, regarding Jack as an individual for the first time, 'I'm very glad you and Captain Stanton turned up. We had no way of knowing who Mrs Stanton was. Her handbag was picked up at the scene of the accident but there was nothing in it to identify her. She regained consciousness shortly after the accident but was quite unfit to answer any questions. Since being admitted, she's been asleep. How did you know she was here?'

'We telephoned Scotland Yard.'

'Scotland Yard?' Dr Hawley's eyebrows shot up. 'Good heavens, whatever for? That seems a somewhat extreme reaction. After all, Mrs Stanton can't have been missing for very long.' He looked at Jack doubtfully. 'Does Captain Stanton usually panic in this manner if his wife is absent for a few hours?' His eyebrows reached further heights. 'Is he subject to nerves?'

The doctor clearly thought, however correct his actions had proved to be, Arthur was madly over-possessive if not next door to a basket case.

'It's not nerves, doctor, it's circumstances. Did you see the papers this morning? About the murder on the train?' Jack gave the doctor a brief account of what had happened, ending with the telephone call from Leonard Duggleby.

Dr Hawley was thunderstruck. 'God bless my soul! Do you mean to tell me you suspect Mrs Stanton's accident to have been caused *deliberately*?' He broke off as Arthur came out of the room. 'Captain Stanton, Major Haldean tells me that you believe your wife was the victim of a calculated attack. I can hardly believe it, sir. Surely you're placing too much emphasis on what has to be a simple accident.'

'Hardly,' said Arthur. His face was very grim. 'Isabelle told me she was pushed.'

'But . . .' Words failed the doctor. He stared at the two men. 'What on earth are you going to do? If there is any truth in this fantastic story, that is.'

'I think we'd better ring Scotland Yard,' said Jack. 'It might be as well if Mrs Stanton has a police guard.'

The doctor stared at him, once more struggling for words. From his expression, Jack guessed Dr Hawley had a shrewd suspicion he was either dealing with a couple of complete romancers or a pair of practical jokers.

Doctor Hawley suddenly brightened. 'Scotland Yard? Yes, of course, that probably would be the best idea. Ring Scotland Yard by all means, gentlemen. You can use the telephone in my office. I'll see you have the correct number.'

Jack smiled. The doctor thought he had called their bluff. 'Thank you very much. It's very helpful of you.'

And that, thought Jack with some satisfaction, as they set off for Dr Hawley's office, had well and truly had taken the wind out of his sails.

The following afternoon Isabelle, a bandage round her head, sat beside her mother on the big sofa by the window of the flat, looking out onto the afternoon sunshine of Lydstep Mews. Sir Philip and Lady Rivers had come up to London to take Isabelle back to Hesperus with them. That, as far as Arthur was concerned, solved a real problem. He had to go to Croxton Ferriers but he hated the idea of leaving Isabelle alone.

Aunt Alice, thought Jack, looking at Isabelle's mother affectionately, really was the goods. She didn't, thank goodness, panic. Her good sense and calm had reassured Arthur and the fact she and Uncle Philip were staying in the flat had given Lizzie and Mrs Travis, the cook, something to think about apart from the worry, as Mrs Travis volubly expressed it, of not being able to step over the doorstep without being murdered.

Uncle Philip, standing with one arm resting on the mantelpiece, was chatting to Bill Rackham. They were waiting for Leonard Duggleby.

It was Jack's idea that Duggleby should call. The attempt on Isabelle and the attempt on Duggleby were so clearly connected, it made sense to both Jack and Bill that the two should compare notes.

The doorbell sounded and, moments later, Lizzie showed Leonard Duggleby into the room. He looked understandably ill at ease but his anxiety was swallowed up by concern as he saw Isabelle.

His long face lengthened as he sat down, his attention fixed on Isabelle. 'I say, Mrs Stanton, you look as if you've taken a dickens of a knock.'

'I did, rather,' said Isabelle. 'I'm still awfully stiff and creaky. I can't really say much about what happened, but I understand from the people who saw it that I was lucky to escape in one piece. I gather you were lucky, too.'

'I suppose I was.' He smiled shyly. 'I don't know if you feel the same, but it's so hard to believe that someone seriously tried to . . . er . . . kill us.' He completed the sentence with an apologetic lift of his eyebrows. 'I'm sorry to put it like that. It seems so ridiculously melodramatic.'

'It was real enough,' said Isabelle with a shudder.

'You'd had the jumps earlier, didn't you?' said Jack. 'When we had lunch at the Criterion, I mean. You were certain someone was watching you.'

'You never mentioned that, dear,' said her mother.

Isabelle nodded, then winced, touching her bandage. 'I think that's why I managed to get out of the way. I think I'd been on my guard all afternoon. It was the creepiest feeling, you know?'

'Did you spot who was watching you?' asked Bill.

'Jack saw a man in a top hat and a woman in a maroon outfit leave the restaurant. It could have been them.'

Duggleby gave a little start. 'A man in a topper?'

'I only got a glimpse of their backs, worse luck,' said Jack.

Sir Philip blew out his cheeks in discontent. 'It's precious little to go on, by gad.'

Duggleby looked at Jack thoughtfully. 'And this was at the Criterion, you say? That's in Piccadilly, where I came to grief,' he added. 'It's quite a coincidence, isn't it? Only I don't suppose it's a coincidence at all. I saw a man in a topper that morning, when I was in Fleet Street. He was standing by the Cheshire Cheese. I had an uncomfortable feeling about him. It's exactly as Mrs Stanton says. It felt as if I was being watched.'

'Would you know him again?' asked Bill.

Duggleby hesitated. 'I'm not sure. I had this rummy feeling that someone was keeping tabs on me. I looked round and this chap, the one outside the Cheshire Cheese, turned and walked quickly away. I *might* know him again, but it was only a passing glance, you understand. What's the idea? That this man in a topper followed Mrs Stanton when she left the restaurant?'

'It seems likely enough,' said Bill. 'He saw his chance and took it. The same applies to you, Mr Duggleby. He'd marked you out that morning and took care to know where you were. Mrs Stanton's been tucked up safely in hospital since the accident, but have you had any other incidents since your experience in Piccadilly?'

'No,' said Duggleby thoughtfully. 'That is . . .' He shook his head. 'I've felt as if someone's watching me from time to time, but it's all so very nebulous.' He half-laughed. 'Believe you me, I've taken care crossing the road, though.'

'This is crazy!' protested Isabelle. 'I can't go on like this, constantly looking over my shoulder to see if a man in a top hat's there. Neither of us can.' She suddenly broke off and swallowed. 'It's *frightening.*'

Arthur crossed the room and, sitting down beside her, put his hand on her shoulder. 'You're not going to face anything like that again.' He glanced up at Jack. 'Haven't you got any ideas? Who is this man? Why did this happen?'

Jack glanced at Bill. 'The why's obvious enough, I'd say. It has to be connected with Parson's murder. You know something, Belle – or, at least, the murderer thinks you do – and he doesn't want either you or Duggleby to work out what it is.'

'Somehow or other you're a danger to him,' agreed Bill.

'But I don't know anything!' protested Duggleby.

Jack shook his head. 'That's not quite true, is it? Don't forget, you've seen the bloke in the topper. I've seen him too, even though it was only a glimpse. Bill, we were looking for Parson's partner, weren't we?'

'Parson's partner,' repeated Bill. 'The man in the top hat could be him. If he was Parson's partner, it sounds as if he might be a high-class fence.'

'Yes,' agreed Jack slowly. 'That's one possibility.' He broke off as the doorbell rang.

'We weren't expecting anyone,' said Arthur with a groan. 'I'll tell Lizzie to get rid of them.'

There was the hum of voices in the hall and a few moments later, Lizzie came into the room. 'It's a Mr and Mrs Leigh,' she said. She looked at Isabelle. 'I said you'd just come out of hospital, ma'am, and they said they were that sorry to hear it, and that they wouldn't disturb you if you weren't up to seeing them, but they'd really like to thank you for what you've done.'

Isabelle looked at her mother. 'You and Dad know the Leighs, don't you?'

'Yes, dear, we do. I really think we'd better see them, even if it's only for a few minutes.'

'All right,' said Arthur. 'Show them in, Lizzie.'

Duggleby looked up with interest. 'Mr and Mrs Leigh? The people who own the jewels, you mean?' Isabelle nodded. 'I was going to drop them a line. My landlady told me they'd called, but I wasn't in. I couldn't think what on earth they wanted to see me about.'

'Probably to give you their grateful thanks, my dear feller,' said Sir Philip, looking at Duggleby approvingly. 'After all, it's thanks to you that their precious sapphires didn't go west.' He stood up and straightened his waistcoat as the door opened.

EIGHT

'**M**rs and Mrs Leigh,' said Lizzie, ushering them in.

It was always an event when Evie Leigh entered a room. The picture in the magazine, thought Jack, had captured her features perfectly, but it couldn't convey her sense of unspoken authority. She wafted in on a cloud of expensive scent, every inch the embodiment of *chic*, from her fine leather shoes with slim heels to her wide-brimmed hat with a turquoise feather.

Evie Leigh looked quickly around the room and fastened on Isabelle. 'Mrs Stanton!' She came towards the sofa and sat down, her Egyptian blue silk shawl billowing around her.

That hat, thought Isabelle, remembering the cloche hat in the Walpole's shop window in New Bond Street, probably cost at least a fortnight's household expenses and maybe more. She spared a glance for Frank Leigh, standing behind his wife, looking solid, square and very ordinary.

'What a perfectly *dreadful* thing to have happened!' said Evie earnestly. 'Frank and I absolutely had to see you. I *had* to thank you personally for restoring my sapphires. I could hardly credit it when your little parlourmaid told us that you'd only just come home from hospital. These frightful motorists who think they own the road are just too bad, aren't they? We won't stay long, of course, but we really were *desperate* to give you our thanks.'

'It really is very good of you to take the trouble,' said Isabelle. 'You know my mother, of course, and my father . . .'

'Of course,' murmured Evie. '*Dear* Lady Rivers, you must have been positively eaten up with anxiety. And Sir Philip, too.'

'And this,' said Isabelle, continuing with the introductions, 'is Inspector Rackham of Scotland Yard.'

'Oh dear! I do hope we're not interrupting anything official.' She smiled engagingly at Bill Rackham.

Bill, Jack noticed with some amusement, couldn't but help smiling back in a dazzled sort of way. It wasn't that Evie Leigh was remarkably good looking exactly – she must be nudging forty for a start – but she was certainly striking, exquisitely made up and very definitely Someone. 'You're the policeman who gave my husband the sapphires, aren't you? How utterly unexpected to find you here.'

'And this,' continued Isabelle, 'is my cousin, Major Haldean.'

'Major Haldean?' said Frank Leigh, his eyes narrowing in a frown. 'We've met before, of course.' He was obviously turning something over in his mind. 'Major, Celia tells me that you've got a knack for solving problems. She was insistent I ask you for help.'

'Frank, you're not going to buttonhole the major about Terence Napier, are you?' interrupted Evie. 'Leave the poor man alone. I'm sure he's got better things to do than listen to our affairs.' She smiled apologetically at Jack. 'I'm sorry, major. You must be constantly asked for advice and it must be *such* a bore.'

'It doesn't actually happen very often, Mrs Leigh,' said Jack.

Frank Leigh took this admittedly thin encouragement as a signal to go ahead. 'Are you free this evening? Perhaps you could join me for a drink at my club?'

'I'd be delighted, sir.' Jack couldn't see he had much chance of finding Terence Napier where the entire police force had failed, but it would be interesting to get Frank Leigh's account of what happened at Topfordham, all the same.

Mr Leigh's rather anxious face relaxed into a warm smile. 'Excellent. Shall we say six o'clock at the Senior Conservative? That's settled, then.'

Evie gave a world-weary sigh and, as if dismissing the matter, looked at Leonard Duggleby, her eyebrows drawing together as she registered the shabbiness of his appearance. 'And you are?'

'This is the man you really want to thank,' said Arthur, putting a hand on Duggleby's shoulder and bringing him forward. 'This is Leonard Duggleby.'

Evie's frown vanished. She stood up and held out her hand, her face glowing with delight. 'Mr Duggleby! How *wonderful* to meet you at last!'

Duggleby shook her outstretched hand in a sheepish sort of way.

'Frank!' she said, turning her head. 'This is Mr Duggleby! Mr Duggleby, we called to see you.' Duggleby started to reply but was cut short by Evie Leigh. 'We're absolutely *prostrate* with gratitude, Mr Duggleby. So many men in your position would have simply pocketed my sapphires and said nothing about it.' She gazed at him in a sort of rapture.

Duggleby gave an awkward cough and tried to speak.

Evie Leigh silenced him with a wave of her hand. 'Your honesty is positively *shining*. It is truly inspiring to find such goodness in the world. I felt utterly elated. Didn't I, Frank?'

Frank Leigh stepped forward and shook Duggleby's hand. 'We're very grateful indeed.'

'I can hardly be expected to be thanked for honesty,' muttered Duggleby awkwardly.

'Nevertheless, I think we were very fortunate that you found the jewels,' said Frank Leigh with feeling. He looked at Duggleby appraisingly, taking in his worn suit and his down at heel shoes. 'Perhaps I could have a word with you later. I really would like to mark your actions in some way.'

'Please, Mr Leigh, there really isn't any need,' said Duggleby, wriggling with embarrassment. 'All I did was walk into a railway compartment. There really isn't any more to it than that.'

'There's a great deal more to it,' said Frank Leigh warmly.

'I think it's wonderful to come across you like this,' said Evie. 'I had no idea you were friends of Captain and Mrs Stanton.'

Duggleby looked at Isabelle in a rather startled way. 'Friends? I wouldn't say that.' He stopped abruptly, his discomfiture increasing by the second. He looked at Isabelle and Arthur apologetically. 'I'm sorry. That sounded very ungracious.'

'What Duggleby means,' explained Arthur, 'is that we hadn't met until he and Isabelle found Parson's body on the train.'

'And we seem to be paying the price,' said Duggleby ruefully. 'Poor Mrs Stanton was knocked over on Oxford Street and some idiot nearly did for me by pushing me under a car in Piccadilly Circus.'

Frank Leigh took a step back. 'What? You had an accident as well?' Duggleby nodded and Frank Leigh turned to Bill. 'That has to be more than a coincidence, surely?'

Bill cleared his throat in an official-sounding cough. 'So I'm inclined to believe, Mr Leigh. We know there's a dangerous man at large, and I'm afraid it looks as if he's set his sights on both Mrs Stanton and Mr Duggleby.'

'But this is absolutely dreadful,' said Evie Leigh. 'What's to stop it happening again?'

Lady Rivers made a little sound in her throat and reached out for Isabelle's hand. 'Jack, Mrs Leigh's right. How do we stop it happening again?'

'I can't make out why it happened in the first place,' muttered Sir Philip. 'It's got me stumped.'

'They must think we know something,' said Isabelle. 'They must think that both Mr Duggleby and I know something about how Parsons was killed.'

'We have to get to the bottom of it,' said Arthur. 'If we can work out what it is that Isabelle and Duggleby are meant to know, then we can make sure that the devil behind it knows his secret isn't a secret any longer.'

'Tell the newspapers about it you mean?' asked Bill. Arthur nodded. 'That's not such a bad idea, Stanton,' he said thoughtfully. 'Once the cat's out of the bag, then both Mrs Stanton and Mr Duggleby can breathe freely once more.'

'If we can discover what the cat is,' murmured Jack.

'But I don't know *anything!*' said Duggleby. 'All I did was walk into a railway compartment.' He lit a cigarette with trembling fingers. 'That's all.'

Jack reached across and briefly put a hand on his shoulder. 'Easy does it.'

Duggleby let out a long mouthful of smoke and slumped back in his chair. 'Sorry,' he muttered.

Isabelle swallowed and braced herself. 'Can we assume that whoever killed Parsons tried to kill me and Mr Duggleby?' Jack nodded. 'In that case, the murderer must think we spotted him.'

Duggleby was about to protest, but Jack waved him quiet. 'Did you spot anyone on the train, Belle? Anyone you noticed particularly, I mean?'

Isabelle frowned in remembrance. 'No,' she said reluctantly. 'I can't say I did. Everyone was so ordinary. The only man who stood out on the platform at Market Albury was Parsons himself. He had a sort of devil-may-care, dangerous air about him. He was very pleased with himself, I could tell.'

'How did that come across?' asked Jack.

'It just did. He looked at me, in a meaningful sort of way, you know?' She couldn't help smiling slightly. 'He was definitely interested.'

'Was he, by Jove?' said Arthur.

'It made me feel a bit uncomfortable, actually.' She turned to Evie Leigh. 'Mrs Leigh, you met him when he came to your house, didn't you? How did he strike you? A bit raffish, perhaps?'

'I can't really say he was,' drawled Evie Leigh. 'I thought he was more obsequious, than anything. I didn't care for him at all. Frank, did he strike you as raffish?'

'I don't know about raffish, exactly, but I didn't like his attitude, that's for sure. I wasted no time in getting rid of him. I only wish I'd made him turn out his pockets first,' he added ruefully.

'It's a great pity you didn't avoid him altogether, Isabelle,' said her father.

'I didn't speak to him at all, Dad, until I absolutely had to.'

'And why the dickens did you have to, eh?'

'Because of the French family on the platform,' said Isabelle, a trifle wearily. 'You remember, I told you about them? There was a Frenchwoman, Mme. Clouet, who was waiting for the train with her three children. I got roped into help.'

'That's right,' said Jack. 'You said you been enrolled as nursemaid. It was little Agathe who found the sapphires in the compartment, wasn't it?'

'Yes. Little Agathe was fairly well behaved but the two boys were a real handful. One of them – Michel, I think it was – was playing hide and seek on the station platform with his brother and ran slap into Parsons. Little Michel fell over and hurt himself and, although Parsons made the best of it, he was clearly far angrier with the little boy than he deserved. Mme. Clouet tried to apologise, but her English was very limited, so I weighed in with my best French and tried to pour a bit of oil on the troubled waters, so to speak. Parsons subsided, but he clearly quite liked me and more or less suggested we travel up to London together.'

'I wish I'd been there,' muttered Arthur. 'I'd have given him something to think about.'

'Don't be such a caveman, darling,' said Isabelle, but she looked pleased, all the same. 'I could cope. Partly in order to get away from him and partly because Mme. Clouet was so hopeless at managing the children, I travelled with her, and it was when I was taking little Agathe for a wash and brush-up that I came across you, Mr Duggleby. That's it, really,' she added with a shrug. 'I didn't see him speak to anyone else and no one, as far as I know, was keeping tabs on him. I don't know what I'm supposed to have seen or done that could be dangerous to anyone.'

'There must be *something*, though,' said Jack. 'There was a fairly strong French theme to the things we found in the compartment. I don't suppose this Mme. Clouet could have set up the encounter with Parsons, could she, Belle?'

'I can't see it, Jack,' said Isabelle doubtfully. 'I'm sure she was exactly what she seemed. A nice, cultivated Frenchwoman, who was hapless at managing her children. Besides that, I travelled in the same compartment with her and she never stirred.'

'That's fairly conclusive,' said Jack. 'What did you think of Parsons, Belle? Apart from the fact he had a roving eye, that is.'

'I think he'd been in the army,' said Isabelle, after a moment's reflection. 'Not an officer, I'd say, but I definitely thought he'd been in the army.'

Jack and Bill swapped glances with each other. 'So did we,' said Jack. 'What gave you that impression?'

Isabelle looked puzzled. 'I don't really know . . . Wait a moment! After little Michel ran into him, Mme. Clouet was all over him, apologising, and he was obviously trying to get rid of her by saying it didn't matter and so on. He said it was all *san fairy ann* which is a real army expression. I had to tell her he meant *ça ne fait rien*. She didn't have a clue what he was on about.'

'I don't blame the poor woman,' said Jack with a grin. 'Army French bears no relation to the real thing.'

'San fairy ann is a common enough phrase,' said Bill. 'Anything else, Mrs Stanton?'

'No, I don't think so, but she was apologising away for all she was worth and I couldn't help but take a hand.' Jack gave a stifled exclamation and she broke off. 'What is it? You look as if you're sucking lemons.'

'Hold on,' Jack said excitedly. 'Bill, did the Vicar speak French?'

'Yes,' said Bill. 'Fluently, by all accounts. After the Calais coach robbery it was assumed he was French. It was only because an informer squealed that we knew he was English.'

'But the man Belle saw *didn't* speak French,' said Jack triumphantly.

'Good God,' said Bill under his breath. 'I wonder if that's it? Parsons could speak French and the murdered man couldn't.'

'And therefore the murdered man wasn't Parsons,' finished Jack. 'Bill, that's it!'

Isabelle gazed at him. 'I knew it!' she said triumphantly. 'Didn't I say as much? All those things you found in the compartment were fakes.' She would have said more but broke off with a glance at Frank and Evie Leigh.

'The things in the compartment can't all have been fakes,' said Bill. 'Anyone can write a name in a book, I suppose, but the watch, the brush and mirror, the suitcase itself, all convinced me. They looked authentic. Besides that, what about the cards with the cross and halo on them?' He nodded at Frank Leigh. 'Mr Leigh found a card in his safe. That's Parson's trademark.'

Jack linked his hands round his knee and leaned back in his chair. 'You're right. Maybe the things we found really did belong to Parsons. But if Parson's things were there, it's likely that Parsons himself was there.' He broke off, his head on one side, waiting for his friend to finish the sentence.

'With his confederate,' said Bill slowly. 'Damn me! We were looking for Parson's confederate. We thought the confederate had killed Parsons but he didn't. It was the other way round. Parsons killed *him*. The Vicar isn't the victim but the murderer.' He nodded his head slowly. 'I bet that's it.'

'Exactly,' said Jack softly. 'That's the secret.' He looked at Isabelle. '*That's* what you and Duggleby knew, Belle! The man who was murdered didn't speak French and so therefore he can't be Parsons. Parsons – the real Parsons – must have been at Market Albury and seen your little incident at the station.' He turned to Duggleby. 'Did you see what happened on the platform?'

'No. No, I didn't. You can't be right, surely? It seems so little to go on. There has to be another explanation. Maybe Parsons was only pretending not to understand this Frenchwoman.'

'I don't see why,' said Isabelle. 'As I said, it wasn't important.'

'Well, I didn't see Parsons on the platform,' said Duggleby stubbornly. 'I didn't see *anything*.' He looked up, his face strained. 'Doesn't that prove you're on the wrong tack?'

'You knew what happened, though,' said Isabelle. 'I told you about it.'

'You're the chief witness, Mr Duggleby,' said Bill. 'You and Mrs Stanton were together on the train. You spoke to me at Charing Cross and to Inspector Whitten at Turnhill Percy. If Parsons was keeping an eye on what was happening – and I bet he was – he must have known you'd talked to Mrs Stanton. He probably didn't see the danger immediately. As you said, the incident on the platform wasn't important, but once he realised the implications, he'd have you lined up as a possible threat.'

Isabelle had gone pale. 'So Parsons – the Vicar – is the man who tried to kill me?'

'What do you actually know about this man, inspector?' asked Evie Leigh.

'Very little, I'm afraid.'

'A vicar?' questioned Sir Philip, shocked. 'You mean to tell me a man in holy orders is a *murderer*?'

'It's a bad joke, Dad,' explained Isabelle. 'Parsons, you know?'

'But you must be able to apprehend him, surely! A man like that can't be that hard to find.'

'Unfortunately, Uncle Phil,' said Jack, 'as far as us honest folk are concerned, the average crook doesn't have a striped jersey, a black mask and a bag marked *Swag*. Things would be a lot simpler if they did.'

Sir Philip drew a discontented breath. 'It seems quite incredible to me that a thief and murderer should be allowed to roam unchecked.'

Duggleby buried his head in his hands. 'What I am going to do?' He sounded close to panic. 'I don't mind telling you, I'm scared. I'll have to get away from London. It's so unfair! All I did was board a train. That's all.'

'You saved my sapphires,' said Evie Leigh, softly. She turned to her husband. 'Frank, can't we do something?' She lowered her voice. 'I wanted someone to come to Breagan Grange. I want them to investigate the temple. Why can't we ask poor Mr Duggleby? He'll be safe with us at the Grange.'

'It's an idea,' said Frank. He frowned, considering the idea. 'Why not?'

He cleared his throat. 'Mr Duggleby, we were looking for someone to make a proper study of an old temple and caves in the grounds of our place in Sussex. Would you fancy the job?'

Duggleby looked up eagerly, then his face fell. 'What sort of study? I'm not an architect.'

'You're a journalist, I understand. Surely you know how to go about looking things up, eh? It's not so much the architecture, it's the history of the place. There's some very odd stories around the temple and I'd like to know if there's any basis in fact. There might be local legends and so on you can uncover. Would you fancy the job?'

'Yes,' said Duggleby slowly. 'Thank you, sir. Yes, I'd like it very much.'

'We'd pay you of course.' Frank Leigh held his hand up. 'Now don't argue, my dear chap. The labourer is worthy of his hire. I'll be very obliged if you take the job on.' He glanced sympathetically at Duggleby's clothes. 'Perhaps it would be as well if I gave you something in advance to cover any necessities you need to buy. We were returning to Breagan Grange this evening. Why don't you run down with us in the car?'

'That's an excellent idea,' said Evie Leigh approvingly. 'What do you propose to do, Mrs Stanton? Are you staying in London?'

'Isabelle's coming to us at Hesperus,' said Lady Rivers. 'That's been already decided.'

'I think that's very wise,' said Evie Leigh approvingly.

'Will there be any danger?' asked Arthur. 'If you contact the newspapers, Rackham, and let them know what we've worked out, I mean? Once the Vicar knows we know, we can all rest easy again.'

'I hope so,' said Bill. He glanced at the clock. 'I need to get back to the Yard. If I get my skates on, it'll be in the evening editions. I'm much obliged to you all for your help.' He inclined his head towards Jack.

'I'll see you out,' said Jack, taking the hint and standing up.

They went into the hall together and closed the door behind them.

'I just hope this idea about telling the press works and keeps Mrs Stanton and Duggleby safe,' said Bill as they walked down the hall. He jerked his thumb over his shoulder. 'Duggleby's a bit jumpy, isn't he? I think it's good of the Leighs to offer him house room. He looks as if a few square meals wouldn't do him any harm. I don't suppose you've got any bright ideas about where we could lay our hands on Parsons, have you?' he added hopefully.

'We think he was in the Criterion, remember? With the woman in the maroon hat.'

'That's not much use in identifying him, is it?'

'No, I suppose not,' agreed Jack. 'Identification . . . Bill, why did Parsons change places with his victim?'

'To confuse us, I suppose,' said Bill with a shrug. 'Being dead's a dickens of a good cover.'

'Yes, but as far as Scotland Yard were concerned, the Vicar was dead already. You hadn't heard of him for years. What I'm getting at is this. The man on the train is somebody, somebody whose identity the murderer doesn't want us to know. He has to be associated with Parsons because of the things we found on the train.'

'You mean the identity of the victim will lead us to Parsons?'

'More or less, yes.'

'It's a thought,' said Bill. 'I could see Isabelle dying to tell us it was Sandy Paxton.'

'Mmm, yes. I thought it was very tactful of her not to air that idea in front of the Leighs. The trouble is, even if it was Paxton, how would that lead us to the Vicar?

'It wouldn't, as far as I can see.' Bill laughed. 'Perhaps it's Terence Napier having another pop at the sapphires.' He held his hand up as he saw Jack's expression. 'It's a joke!'

'I know,' said Jack easily. 'Joking aside, it can't be Napier because Mr Leigh would've recognised him when he came to the house. The man who stole the sapphires is certainly the man Belle saw at Market Albury and the man who was murdered on the train. He's somebody. Who?'

'Think about it,' said Bill seriously. 'Your guesses have a way of coming good. Incidentally, talking of Napier, what on earth are you going to say to Mr Leigh about him when you meet up?'

'I'm just going to listen, I think,' said Jack with a shrug. 'It'd be rum if there was a connection between the murder in Topfordham and the murder on the train, though.'

'What sort of connection?'

Jack held his hands wide. 'I don't know. There's the sapphires, of course.' He stuck his hands in his pockets and scuffed his foot idly. 'I suppose there's no doubt that Terence Napier is guilty, is there?'

'Not really. Mr Leigh thinks otherwise, of course. He's perfectly entitled to his view, but he's hardly unbiased.' He saw his friend's expression and laughed. 'Blimey, Jack, are you short of something to do? I would've thought the murder on the train was enough to be going on with without getting involved in the Terence Napier affair.'

'You wouldn't have any objections if I did though, would you?'

Bill shrugged. 'Be my guest. It wasn't a Scotland Yard matter in any case. The local force handled it. It was your old pal,

Major-General Flint who took the lead. I've heard Superintendent Ashley talk about him.'

'General Flint?' said Jack with a grimace. 'He doesn't like me.' He thought for a moment, then gave a wicked grin. 'D'you know, I might take up the Napier case just to annoy him. I bet Ashley would give me a hand. Flint's not one of his favourite people either.'

'I'm sure Ashley would, but you can't go poking your nose into a murder just to irritate the chief constable.'

'Can't I though?' said Jack. 'It depends. D'you know, I'm quite looking forward to my talk with Mr Leigh.'

NINE

Superintendent Edward Ashley, a broad-shouldered, good-natured-looking man in his forties, waved cheerily as the blue and silver Spyker drew up to the grass verge beside his neat, semi-detached house in the outskirts of Lewes.

'Haldean! Good to see you again,' he said, scrambling into the car. 'Thanks for coming to pick me up.'

'It's the least I could do,' said Jack, putting the car into gear and pulling away from the kerb. 'It's good of you to come with me. I can't help but feel the inhabitants of Topfordham might be a bit more forthcoming if you lend your official weight to my nosing around.'

'As far as that goes, I'm actually unofficial at the moment,' said Ashley. 'It's my day off. That's why I suggested you come down today. The Chief's a bit precious about the Napier case. He won't be jumping for joy if he knows you're looking into it.'

'I say, Ashley, I'm not going to get you into trouble, am I?' asked Jack anxiously.

'Nothing I can't handle,' said Ashley easily. 'What I do on my day off is my own affair and if I choose to spend it in Topfordham with an old friend, that's up to me.' He smiled slowly. 'And, naturally, if I happen to come across anything that's pertinent to a police investigation while I happen to be just passing the time of day, so to speak, I would be failing in my duties if I didn't act upon it. Not that,' he added, 'I can see what it is you're actually hoping to find. As far as the Chief's concerned, the Napier case is all done and dusted and, I must say, that for once I agree with him.'

'M'yes,' said Jack, slipping the car into third. 'Apart, that is, from the small matter of finding Napier himself.'

'That is a bit of a flaw,' admitted Ashley. 'Have you any thoughts as to where he might be?'

'I haven't a clue,' said Jack. 'As I said on the phone, I had an interesting conversation with Mr Leigh. He can't deny the evidence but he's convinced there's been some ghastly mistake. He's so convinced of Napier's innocence that he's hired his own private enquiry agent, a chap called Wood, and despatched him to Topfordham. I don't know how far he got or if he found anything worthwhile.'

'A private enquiry agent?' asked Ashley dubiously. 'I doubt he'll turn anything up.'

'That's a depressing view, Ashley.'

Ashley snorted cynically. 'Come on, Haldean, you know what private agents are like. They're all right for gathering divorce evidence and guarding the presents at society weddings but damn all else. Where's he from?'

'An outfit called the Rapid Results Agency in Victoria. I've never heard of them.'

'Me neither,' said Ashley with a shrug. 'These places spring up like mushrooms, though. What's Mr Leigh hoping you'll do?'

'Be brilliant,' said Jack with a grin. 'Tootle down to Topfordham, find that whoever bumped off Mrs Paxton, it wasn't Terence Napier and produce the real villain like a rabbit from a top hat. I must say,' he added, his grin fading, 'that seems a little unlikely. I've got an unreasoning aversion to any solution General Flint's come up with, but he does seem to have been very bright about the whole business. I'm surprised he didn't announce Mrs Paxton's death was suicide and leave it at that.'

'General Flint had help,' said Ashley. 'It was the local doctor, a chap called Mountford, who balked at the idea of Mrs Paxton doing herself in. He knew her as well as anyone in Topfordham and just couldn't believe it.'

'Ah-hah! I thought it was unusually inspired.'

'As you say, ah-hah! There's no doubt about it, the doctor deserves a lot of credit.'

They were well into the countryside by now. Ashley relaxed back into his seat, watching the dancing yellow of the cornfields hemmed in by green hedges under a cornflower-blue sky roll by.

'Haldean,' said Ashley thoughtfully. 'You don't think there's any connection between the Napier case and the murder on the train, do you? Apart from the sapphires, of course.'

Jack sucked his cheeks in. 'Not really. There could be, of course. Anything's possible, but if there is a connection, it doesn't jump out, does it? Isabelle thinks there is. She's convinced that the man who was murdered on the train is Mrs Paxton's rather unsatisfactory son, Sandy Paxton.'

'*Sandy Paxton?*' repeated Ashley incredulously. 'Why on earth does she think that?'

'Because he was supposed to have deserted in France – I don't know if he's dead or really did desert – and there were French things in the railway compartment. That's link one. We were meant to think that the victim was Andrew Parsons, also known as the Vicar, but we know that's not the case. However, we found a suitcase and hairbrush initialled with the letters *A.P.,* which could easily, as Belle says, stand for Alexander – or Sandy – Paxton. That's link two. Sandy Paxton was, not to beat about the bush, a crook, and the bloke who got bumped off was a crook. That's link three. As the bloke in the train could have been just about anyone, who's to say she's wrong? No one can disprove it.'

'I can't disprove there are fairies at the bottom of my garden but that doesn't mean they're there.'

'Very cutting,' said Jack with a laugh. 'It's a possibility, but that's all.'

'How is Mrs Stanton?' asked Ashley. 'I tell you, when I read what had happened to her, my blood ran cold. I think you did the right thing, bringing the newspapers into it. There haven't been any more accidents, have there?'

'No, thank God. As far as that goes, the plan seems to have worked. Arthur's busy with their new place in Croxton Ferriers, so Isabelle's staying at Hesperus for a few days until she recovers

completely. There haven't, I'm glad to say, been any more alarms.
Mr Leigh's invited me to stay at Breagan Grange after I've been
to Topfordham and Isabelle's invited too. Mr Leigh's daughter,
Celia, is an old friend of hers. I'm staying at Hesperus tonight
and Belle and I are driving over tomorrow. Poor old Belle is a
bit stiff and sore, but she's fine.'

'Thank goodness for that,' said Ashley fervently. 'What's our
first port of call in Topfordham, by the way?'

'I dropped a line to Dr Mountford after I'd spoken to Mr Leigh
to say I'd appreciate a word with him. I knew he'd been called
in but I didn't realise he'd actually spotted the crime.'

'He's the man we need to speak to,' said Ashley. 'Dr
Mountford's it is.'

Doctor Mountford's house in Fiddler Lane was built of large
Jacobean blocks of honey-coloured stone festooned with ivy.
It seemed to have grown up from the small lawn and the cheerfully higgledy-piggledy mass of old-fashioned cottage garden
flowers that crammed the borders of the path and surrounded
the walls.

The door was opened, not by a servant, but by a solid-looking
woman with an inquisitive, kindly face.

'Mrs Mountford?' asked Jack, raising his hat. 'I'm Jack
Haldean and this is Superintendent Ashley. I dropped your
husband a line to ask if he could spare us a few minutes.'

'I know,' she said happily. 'Please come in.' She ushered them
into the hall, regarding them with keen anticipation. 'James –
that's my husband, Dr Mountford – and I were *itching* with
curiosity when we got your letter.' She lowered her voice to a
conspiratorial whisper. 'I've heard of you, Major Haldean. A very
good friend of mine lives in Breedenbrook, where the man was
murdered in the fortune-teller's tent at the village fête. She told
me all about how you sorted it out, and it was in the papers, of
course.'

'You're famous, Haldean,' muttered Ashley with a grin, rather
to Jack's discomfiture.

'Our village fête isn't for another fortnight,' added Mrs
Mountford in a slightly worried way. 'There isn't going to be a
murder there, I hope.'

'Not as far as I know,' said Jack with a laugh, as she took their hats and coats and hung them on the stand.

'Then it must be about Mrs Paxton,' said Mrs Mountford with an air of triumph. 'It is, isn't it?' Jack nodded. 'I *told* James it would be. James will be delighted to see you but he's in his morning surgery at the moment. He always breaks off for elevenses, though, if you don't mind making do with me until then. We'll have morning coffee when James joins us, if that's all right. It makes things so much easier in the kitchen if we can keep to the ordinary routine.'

'That's fine,' said Jack cheerfully. He had taken an instant liking to the kindly looking, motherly Mrs Mountford.

She led them down the hall and showed them into a sun-lit sitting room with chintz curtains and faded armchairs.

'Please sit down,' she said, perching herself on the edge of a chair. Her bright eyes and expectant poise reminded Jack irresistibly of a bird hopeful of breadcrumbs.

'You were quite right, Mrs Mountford,' said Jack, 'that I want to know more about how Mrs Paxton met her death. Her nephew, Mr Francis Leigh, has asked me to look into the business.'

Mrs Mountford gave a distracted sigh. 'It's very sad for him, isn't it? Mr Leigh, I mean. It was even sadder for poor Mrs Paxton, of course, but Mr Leigh is convinced his cousin – Terence Napier is Mr Leigh's cousin, isn't he? – is innocent, but James is *certain* Mr Leigh is barking up the wrong tree.'

That, in Mrs Mountford's view, was clearly the last word on the matter.

'I think it's very nice of Mr Leigh to be so loyal to his cousin,' she continued, 'but, as James says, you can't alter facts. Mr Leigh's employed a private eye, hasn't he?' She pronounced this term very dubiously. 'James spent quite a long time with him. He's a Mr Wood, a Mr Aloysius Wood.'

Mrs Mountford screwed up her face doubtfully. 'He *said* he was a detective but I always thought detectives – real detectives, I mean, not policemen or Sherlock Holmes and *of course* not you, major – were greasy little men in shabby overcoats, but this one was a real gentleman. I know that since the war, people do all sorts of things they wouldn't have dreamt of doing before, but I was surprised to find he was a detective. He doesn't think

Terence Napier is guilty but, as I said to James, if Mr Leigh's employing him, he more or less has to think that, doesn't he? Because if Terence Napier isn't guilty, who is?'

She paused for breath and Jack leapt into the miniscule conversational gap.

'Have you any ideas, Mrs Mountford?'

She drew back. 'I hardly like to say. Mr Wood thought the servants might know more than they're saying and, of course, it's hard not to think of the servants when something like this happens, however unfair it might be. I've never known such an uproar in all my born days. The entire village was set by its ears. Nothing else but Mrs Paxton was talked about morning, noon and night. It was enough of a sensation when her nephew turned up and whisked her off to Paris, but this is beyond *anything*. I'm just thankful that if she had to be killed so dreadfully, it was her nephew who did it and not someone we'd known in the village. An outsider makes it easier to understand, you know? I know everyone has to come from somewhere, but I'd hate to think we'd nurtured a murderer in our midst. James didn't like Terence Napier *at all* and nor did anyone else who came across him.'

'He was an artist, I understand,' said Jack, who'd had a glowing, if partisan, account of Terence Napier from Francis Leigh.

Mrs Mountford sniffed. 'That's what he *said*. Or, at least,' she amended with scrupulous honesty, 'that's what Mrs Paxton said. She was terribly proud of him, although I couldn't see he was anything to write home about. Florence, Mrs Paxton's maid, described him to our cook, Mrs Abbot, as a great thin streak of nothing, who looked down his nose at you in a sneering sort of way as if you weren't fit to breathe the same air as him. I must say, that's what James thought too, although we never guessed what he had planned, of course. James,' she said indulgently, 'wouldn't say a word about why she went to Paris with her nephew, as Mrs Paxton had told him in confidence. Bless him, it was all round the village!'

'How exactly did the news get out?' asked Jack curiously. It wasn't, he thought, necessary to pump Mrs Mountford. She wasn't a pump so much as a tap.

'Mrs Paxton's maid, I expect,' said Mrs Mountford. 'Mrs Henderson, I think it was, broke the news and her Mavis was very friendly with Mrs Paxton's Florence. You know how hard it is to stop talk from getting round and Florence was a great one for keeping up to the mark.' She leaned forward confidentially. 'I can't see someone like Florence Pargetter letting an opportunity like that pass her by. She was shrewd as well, and never minded putting two and two together.'

'That often makes five,' said Ashley with a smile.

'As a matter of fact, where Florence was concerned, it usually made four,' said Mrs Mountford. 'It was positively uncanny, sometimes, the way she hit the nail on the head and she was never backwards in coming forwards, as they say, with what she thought.'

Florence, thought Jack, sounded like somebody worth talking to. 'Where is she now?' he asked. 'Florence, I mean. Is she still at Mrs Paxton's old house?'

'Why, no,' said Mrs Mountford, her eyes circling. 'She's gone. The house has been shut up and instructions given to the house agent. If I was Mrs Leigh – she owns the house now, of course – I'd have wanted the servants to stay on, to keep it aired and fresh, but Mrs Welbeck, the housekeeper, she went back to Leeds, so I believe, almost immediately. Mrs Leigh wanted her to stay on, but she only offered to pay board wages, so she upped and left. She wasn't even here for the inquest. The coroner was very annoyed about it and said the police should have made it clear to her she was expected to attend, but there was nothing much they could do. Florence gave evidence, of course, as did James.'

'How was it known that Mrs Welbeck had gone to Leeds?' asked Jack. 'Florence, perhaps?'

Mrs Mountford nodded. 'That's right, but she didn't leave an address, so that wasn't much help. I think,' she said doubtfully, 'that she might have had a little nest-egg tucked away, so she might not have needed another position, not right away at least.'

'Why d'you think that, Mrs Mountford?' asked Ashley. 'That she had some money, I mean?'

Mrs Mountford hesitated and looked at the door. 'It's just as well James isn't here. He hates me repeating gossip. I know I shouldn't really, but Florence said as much to Mrs Henderson's Mavis who told Mrs Beeding's Doreen who mentioned it to our cook. Actually,' she added parenthetically, 'I wouldn't be surprised if that's why Mrs Welbeck left as quickly as she did.'

Jack looked a question.

'*John Bright,*' said Mrs Mountford as if that explained everything.

'Who?' began Ashley, but Mrs Mountford cut him off.

'John Bright was Mrs Paxton's outdoor man. Bright's lived man and boy in the village, apart from when he was conscripted during the war, but I never cared for him. He had far too much of an eye for both girls and money. His father was just the same, a real old reprobate and didn't his wife let him know about it! The rows they had were an absolute *scandal.* Saturday nights, regular as clockwork – the pair of them drunk as lords, of course – and all on the public street as well, so everyone knew their business. They're long gone, of course. Bright's been at The Larches ever since the war and he had enough sense to make sure that he always kept on the right side of Mrs Paxton, but it was absolutely *disgraceful* how he behaved and I can't blame Mrs Welbeck for taking umbrage.'

'What did he actually do?' asked Jack. 'To put Mrs Welbeck's back up, I mean?'

As Mrs Mountford stopped, flushing, he wondered warily if the answer would strain her sense of propriety to breaking point, but Mrs Mountford gathered up her forces and continued.

'Well, not to put too fine a point on it, Florence caught him kissing Mrs Welbeck.'

That wasn't too bad.

'And . . . er . . . his attentions were unwelcome?' asked Jack delicately.

'I should think they were! And really, there's no reason why she should be expected to tolerate that sort of thing,' said Mrs Mountford with stern reproof. 'Florence said Mrs Welbeck stormed in from the outside, with her cap disarranged and all her teeth off to one side and she was *furious* with Bright, banging pots and pans about and generally in a real temper. Well, I don't want to be unkind, but she wasn't the sort who'd attract the John Brights of this world or any man, really. Florence thought it was screamingly funny, and I suppose you can see why, but it isn't, really. Florence said – and it sounds like sheer cattiness but you *can* see her point of view – that the only reason anyone, including Bright, would want to kiss Mrs Welbeck is money. That's why she thought she had a bit tucked away. Florence,' she added, somewhat unnecessarily, 'and Mrs Welbeck never really got on.'

'That sounds like an understatement,' said Jack.

'Mrs Welbeck was much older than Florence, of course,' said Mrs Mountford, pursing her lips, 'and mind you, I don't think anyone *did* get on with Mrs Welbeck much. She hadn't been here long – only a matter of a few weeks at the most – and she was a bit stand-offish.'

'Where's Florence now?' asked Jack once more.

'I told you, she's gone,' said Mrs Mountford. 'Nobody knows where, either, which is very mysterious. Florence wasn't at all like Mrs Welbeck. She did have friends but none of them have heard a word from her.'

'When was this, Mrs Mountford?' asked Ashley.

Mrs Mountford screwed up her face in remembrance. 'It must be three weeks ago now. She did give evidence at the inquest and thought herself very grand in consequence. She didn't want to stay on at Mrs Paxton's after Mrs Paxton died, because, as I say, it was only board wages and Florence could do a great deal better for herself. She had talked about going up to London and leaving service altogether – becoming a waitress or some such – but you'd have thought if she had done, she'd have let one of her cronies know. I don't know if she had a new position in mind, but she was excited about something, that's for sure.'

'Is John Bright still at Mrs Paxton's old house?' asked Jack.

'No,' said Mrs Mountford. 'No, he isn't, and no one knows where he's gone either. He hasn't been seen for the last week or so but where he's got to, I really couldn't say.'

'He's missing?' asked Jack slowly.

'I wouldn't call it *missing*, exactly,' said Mrs Mountford, 'but it's about a week since anyone's seen him. His wages had been cut, of course, so he might have gone to find another job. I doubt if anyone in the village would employ him.'

Jack's mind was racing. About a week? And, less than a week ago, an unidentified body of a man was found on a train . . .

'Has he gone off before?' asked Ashley.

'I don't *think* so,' said Mrs Mountford. 'No, never. He was always careful to keep on the right side of Mrs Paxton. She wasn't the sort of person people felt easy about confiding in, so I imagine she never got to hear what the general opinion of Bright was. Not that,' she said judiciously, 'I suppose it would have mattered to her much.'

Mrs Mountford's voice faded into the background. Was there any way of establishing if it was Bright? Jack thought of the mangled remains at Charing Cross and shuddered. He couldn't ask anyone to look at that body. Beside that, there was no point. As well as being absolutely hideous the remains were completely unrecognisable.

'That's why Mrs Welbeck seemed to suit her so well,' continued Mrs Mountford, blissfully unaware of his inattention. 'In a small village like this, it's accounted as rather unfriendly if someone wants to keep themselves to themselves, although it's a virtue in a way, I suppose. Mrs Paxton thought it was a virtue, according to James.'

No, he couldn't ask anyone to look at the body in the train. Not only did he shrink from the idea, Bill and the police would never confront a member of the public with *that* unless there was a more than racing certainty they could identify him.

'If Mrs Paxton talked to anyone, it was James. She was never what you would call a chatty woman, but she trusted James. She told James that although Mrs Welbeck wasn't anything much to look at – bad skin and rabbit teeth, poor woman – that was a good thing, as she wouldn't be likely to be off dallying with followers, unlike Florence, who, I must say, always did attract attention.'

Hang on! Evie and Frank Leigh had seen the man at the house. If there was a photograph of Bright, that would do the trick.

'Mrs Mountford,' he said, cutting across her flow of words, 'I don't suppose you know where I could get a photograph of Bright, do you?'

'A photograph of Bright?' she said, brought up short in astonishment. 'Whatever . . .? No, I can't think who'd have a photograph of him. There'd be one of Florence, I imagine, as she always went on the Servants' Church Outing, organised by Mrs Billington, the vicar's wife – they usually have their photo taken on the charabanc or by the sea – but that's ladies only, so Bright wouldn't be in that. No, I can't help you there, major, I'm afraid.'

She put her head on one side, listening as the grandfather clock in the hallway geared up with a series of clunks and whirrs before it wheezily donged out the time.

'Eleven o'clock,' said Mrs Mountford. 'I'll just go and see James knows we're going to have coffee in here instead of the surgery. If you can just excuse me for a few moments . . .'

She bustled out of the room, leaving Ashley looking quizzically at Jack.

'Why d'you want a picture of Bright?'

Jack hesitated. The idea which had seemed so compelling when it had occurred to him minutes before now seemed, as he had to say it out loud, full of flaws.

'It occurred to me that, as Bright disappeared about a week ago, he could be the man on the train,' he said reluctantly. He saw Ashley's startled expression and held his hands up dismissively. 'It's just an idea. I know there's a lot of problems with it.'

Ashley sat back, his brow furrowed. 'I should think there are.' His frown deepened. 'You and Rackham worked out that the man on the train was an associate of Parsons. That can't be Bright. He's a village lad born and bred. He doesn't sound like much to shout about, I grant you, but he could never have been the associate of a real crook like Parsons. Besides that, he lived here until he was conscripted, and conscription didn't come in until 1916. Parsons was dead by then, or was thought to be, at any rate.'

'I know, I know,' said Jack.

'Add to that, whoever the man was, he was an expert safe cracker, otherwise he couldn't have got hold of the sapphires in the first place. I can't see any jobbing gardener having that sort of knowledge. Not and continue to be a gardener, I mean, and Bright had worked for Mrs Paxton since the war, according to Mrs Mountford.'

'I know,' said Jack. 'I thought of that almost as soon as I asked about the photo. My idea was to show it to Mr and Mrs Leigh and see if they recognised him as the man who stole the sapphires. It was just the coincidence of dates that got to me.'

Ashley shook his head doubtfully. 'If his wages had been cut,

Bright would want to move on. A handyman and gardener can find work almost anywhere and, from the sound of it, he'd made himself none too popular roundabout.'

'You're absolutely right,' said Jack as Mrs Mountford came along the hallway, her voice clearly audible.

'Here's James,' she announced, sweeping into the room ahead of her husband in the manner of a tug-boat towing in an ocean liner.

'I hope we're not disturbing you, doctor,' said Jack.

'Not at all. It's a pleasure to meet you.' Dr Mountford hitched his trousers up at the knee and sat down in one of the shabby armchairs, his eyes crinkling indulgently as he looked at his wife. 'Mildred's been on pins ever since we received your letter. Milly, shall we have coffee?'

'Yes, dear,' said Mrs Mountford ringing the bell. 'That's all arranged.'

An elderly parlourmaid brought in the coffee promptly and Mrs Mountford, who was obviously bursting with pride, managed to contain herself until she had poured it out. When the parlourmaid had gone, Mrs Mountford wriggled forward in her chair. 'Of course, no one knew it was a murder until James spotted it. James was commended by the coroner.'

'That was very acute of you, sir,' said Ashley warmly.

Dr Mountford's weather-beaten face became slightly more coloured. 'I knew Mrs Paxton,' he said simply. 'She was the sort who clung to life.'

He stirred his coffee thoughtfully. 'There's another thing, too. When I met Terence Napier, I thought he was a thorough-going rotter. Long haired with an affected way of speaking, and, for all Mrs Paxton's obvious affection for him, I didn't think he had any affection for her. To say I was expecting a murder is to put it far too strongly, but I was expecting some sort of trouble. I told that chap, Wood, Mr Leigh's private detective, as much.'

'Did you know Mrs Paxton had a son?' asked Jack. 'Before Terence Napier came on the scene, I mean?'

The doctor nodded.

'You never said anything to me!' interrupted Mrs Mountford indignantly.

Dr Mountford smiled sheepishly and contented himself with

a murmur of '*Ethics, dear,*' before continuing. 'Yes, I knew she had a son. She kept his photograph in the parlour. The question is, granted Mrs Paxton told me they were going to Paris to find him, was he in on the scheme with Terence Napier?'

'It's an intriguing thought,' said Ashley cautiously. 'However, what I will say, that whether Napier was working alone or in cahoots with Sandy Paxton, he'd have been lucky to have got away with it, even if you hadn't realised it was murder and not suicide.' He put his head on one side and looked at the doctor. 'It was you who spotted the will was false, wasn't it, sir?'

'I suppose it was,' said Dr Mountford, rubbing the side of his nose in an embarrassed sort of way, 'but anyone who knew anything about Topfordham would've seen it. That was sheer bad luck for Napier. I suppose he just copied the signatures from the previous will and left it at that. If he'd known more about the village he wouldn't have made the mistake of having two witnesses who were dead.'

Mrs Mountford wriggled in her chair. 'I don't understand, James. Surely if Sandy Paxton was behind the plan – although it seems a very wicked plan indeed – it would've been easier for him to come home and charm his mother into altering her will.'

'You're forgetting who Sandy Paxton is, Milly,' said Dr Mountford. 'He's a deserter. That, by itself, wouldn't matter in this day and age and that's what I told Mrs Paxton. However, not to put too fine a point on it, he is or was a crook and that *does* matter. With that black mark against his name, he wouldn't be offered amnesty. He'd have every chance of going to prison for desertion and there's probably other offences outstanding as well.' Dr Mountford sucked his cheeks in. 'I'd say it would be very awkward for our Mr Paxton to claim anything his mother left him in her will.'

'That's very true, doctor,' said Ashley, 'but I still think Napier would've been lucky to have got away with it.'

'It might've been more convincing, if Terence Napier had been given more time, Ashley,' said Jack. 'Say Mrs Paxton and Napier hadn't quarrelled. Napier could have become a regular visitor and no one would have thought anything of it.'

'But surely Mrs Paxton would realise she'd been swindled as soon as she saw her will?' asked Mrs Mountford.

'If she'd seen the will, she'd certainly know it was a forgery,' agreed Jack, 'but I very much doubt Napier would leave it in the desk. If he'd had enough time, he could have put the will into her papers after she died without anyone being any the wiser. It sounds as if the quarrel caught him on the hop, so he had to act quickly and hope for the best.'

'It's all very sad,' said Mrs Mountford with a sigh. 'You think so too, don't you, James?'

The doctor nodded gravely and, taking his pipe from his pocket, absently filled it with tobacco from the jar. 'Very sad, indeed. After Mrs Paxton spoke to me about going to Paris with Napier, I was worried. She was certain of success. I knew she'd be heartbroken if she didn't find him and, from what she'd told me of young Paxton, thought there was every chance she'd end up being heartbroken if she did.'

His face lengthened. 'It's hard to explain the Sandy Paxtons of this world. He seemed to have every advantage and yet he went wrong. From what I could make out, his mother made excuses for him and covered things up, and was rewarded with crocodile tears and promises of reform. It's the psychology of the thing I find interesting.'

Ashley blinked and Dr Mountford smiled fleetingly. 'Even in a one-horse place like this, we've heard of psychology. You know he became an actor after he was sent down from Oxford? Mrs Paxton didn't approve, but still continued to support him. What she did resent – resented bitterly – was him marrying an actress.'

'I didn't know he was married,' said Jack in surprise. 'Neither Frank Leigh nor his daughter, Celia, mentioned it.'

'He had the sense to keep it quiet,' said Dr Mountford. 'When his mother *did* find out, she was furious. She read him the riot act and cut off her support. She'd been supplanted, you see, and Mrs Paxton wasn't a woman to forgive or forget very easily.'

Mrs Mountford shook her head sadly. 'I can't imagine treating any of our boys like that.'

'I'm glad to say you're a very different person, Milly,' said the doctor. He sighed. 'To be fair to Mrs Paxton, none of our boys gave us anything like the problems Sandy gave his mother. She did try.'

'You said that she tried to get him into the Church,' said Mrs

Mountford, with an ironic twist to her voice. 'Goodness knows why. From what James has told me it's hard to think of a less likely profession for him to adopt.'

'She didn't try and get him into the Church, Milly,' said the doctor. 'She said she hoped he *might* enter the Church, which is a very different state of affairs. One of his friends was a minister, or so he told his mother, at any rate, and he wanted to follow in his footsteps. It seems pretty unlikely to me.'

Jack, cup of coffee in hand, froze. 'A *minister*?' he repeated slowly.

'That's what she said. She believed him. I don't know if I would.'

'I might,' said Jack. 'Did she say *minister*, doctor, or *vicar*?'

Beside him, Ashley let out a sudden breath. 'By George!' he muttered. 'The Vicar!'

The doctor and Mrs Mountford looked at them curiously. 'She said *vicar*, I think,' said the doctor. 'The two terms are more or less interchangeable, aren't they?'

'Yes,' said Jack, trying to keep the excitement out of his voice. 'Yes, I believe they are.'

In the small and inquisitive village of Topfordham, it was hard to find somewhere where they were free from observation, but the Malt and Shovel was a haven of calm.

Two middle-aged clerks were taking an early lunch, three travelling salesmen, identified by their cases of samples, were playing five-o-one on the dart board and six elderly, bewhiskered men, pipes lit and half-pints close to hand, were bent over a game of dominoes. A ginger cat was spread somnolently in the warmth of the diamond-barred sunshine flooding through the leaded window onto the oak window sill.

By common consent, neither Jack nor Ashley said anything about the case until they were sitting at a table by the window with a pint of bitter, a cheese sandwich and a pork pie apiece.

Ashley took a swig of beer and wiped his mouth. 'What d'you reckon?' he asked.

'It's interesting, isn't it?' said Jack. 'Where on earth have all the servants got to?'

Ashley looked at him, beer in hand. 'I can't see there's any great mystery about that, Haldean. I'd have expected you to be leaping up and down about the Vicar, not fretting about the servants.'

'Never mind about the Vicar for a minute. I'll leap as high as you like later. What about the servants? Don't you think it's odd that they've all vanished?'

Ashley shrugged expressively. 'Not really. Mrs Paxton was dead, the house was shut up and, although Mrs Leigh was probably only too happy for them to keep the place aired, she was only paying them a pittance to do it. You can't expect them to stay on in those circumstances.'

Jack put his hands wide. 'Perhaps, but wouldn't you expect them to mention where they were going? Maybe Mrs Welbeck did just take herself off but what about Florence? And what was she, to use Mrs Mountford's expression, cooking up with John Bright?'

'Who knows?' said Ashley without much interest, cutting his pork pie into segments. 'Where they were going to run off together, perhaps?'

'They left separately.'

'All right. So Mrs Welbeck goes off to Leeds, Florence decides to try her luck in London and John Bright can't get another job in the village so he ups and offs. It's only when you put all three of them together that it seems mysterious they've all gone.'

'I was wondering if there was a common reason,' said Jack. 'And if that common reason had something to do with Terence Napier.'

Ashley munched his way through a portion of pork pie before replying. 'It seems unlikely,' he said eventually. 'Napier slung his hook double quick, didn't he? I can't see him sneaking back into the village and picking them off, one by one, if that's what you're getting at.'

'That does seem unlikely, I agree,' said Jack. 'What I actually had in mind, you melodramatic old thing, was that they know where Napier is and he's bribed them to keep quiet. Actually,' he added, clicking his tongue, 'it would have to be no end of a bribe and they could stick around and be quiet without having to vanish into thin air. All right, let's say he's murdered them.'

'Come off it,' said Ashley. 'Bodies are blinking hard to dispose of. What would he do with them? He could hardly leave them lying about.'

'The dustmen would probably complain,' said Jack with a grin. 'I'll be honest, Ashley, I don't know what could have happened to them, but it just seemed so very odd.'

'What about Sandy Paxton?' questioned Ashley. 'That sounded a great deal more promising. I saw your eyes light up when the Mountfords talked about him going into the Church. I'm assuming, as you assumed, that what Paxton actually meant was that he'd taken up with Parsons, the Vicar. It sounds more probable than him actually considering holy orders.'

'I couldn't help *but* think it,' said Jack, taking a tentative bite of pie. 'Isabelle suggested that Paxton was the Vicar himself.'

'I don't think much of that idea.'

'That's more or less what I said. To be fair to her, as soon as the notion of the Vicar having an associate was floated, she suggested Paxton as a candidate, so that's one up to her. I like the idea of him telling his mother he was considering the Church. It would appeal to a certain sort of humour, you know? The sort of person who enjoys flaunting a secret. It's a sort of dare to themselves, I suppose.'

'That's right,' said Ashley with a nod. 'He could think it was really funny to talk about "the Vicar" when all the time he meant Parsons. I think I'd better let Inspector Rackham know what the Mountfords said.' He sucked his cheeks in thoughtfully. 'I wish we knew if Paxton did die on the Somme or really was a deserter. His mother was convinced he was alive, but he's officially dead.'

'Let's say he was alive,' said Jack, spearing a pickled onion. 'Apart from anything else, it's more fun that way. Adds a bit more mystery, don't you think?'

'That's all we need,' said Ashley grumpily.

'Maybe both Napier and Paxton were in it with the Vicar, as Dr Mountford suggested. They were cousins, after all. Come on, Ashley. You're not on duty now. Engage in a little speculation.'

Ashley laughed. 'All right, I'll play. Paxton and Napier could've been working together or Paxton could've moved in on his own account after Napier managed to mess it up *and* see off Mrs Paxton into the bargain. If the description of Napier wasn't so far adrift from the description of the murder victim, I'd have him down as a likely candidate to have another crack at the sapphires again, too.'

'You're right. The man who the Leighs saw – and Belle saw, too, for that matter – sounds nothing like Napier, which brings us back to Paxton.' Jack thought for a moment, then looked up, his eyes brightening. 'Wait a moment! Dr Mountford said Paxton's mother had a photo of him! If I can find it, I can show it to Isabelle and ask her if he's the man she saw at Market Albury.'

'You could ask the Leighs if he's the man who turned up at their house, as well.'

'Mrs Leigh has probably got Mrs Paxton's things,' said Jack. 'Who knows, it could be boxed up and at Breagan Grange. I'm going there tomorrow. If I can lay my hands on that photograph, that'll be a big step forward.'

'If he really was the man on the train, it'd be a massive step forward,' said Ashley.

Jack clicked his tongue. 'I wonder if it's really on the cards? Our train victim couldn't speak French. I'd assumed Paxton does.'

'Why?' asked Ashley. 'Because Napier told Mrs Paxton he'd seen him in France? We can't trust anything Napier said.'

'That's true,' agreed Jack adding chutney to his cheese sandwich. He ate without speaking for a few moments. 'I must say I'd hoped to get a bit further on today.'

Ashley put his beer down in surprise. 'I think you've come a dickens of a way.'

'M'yes. But even if our man on the train is Sandy Paxton, how does that lead us to the Vicar? I was convinced that once we'd identified him, we'd have the Vicar, and we haven't. And I really would like to know where the servants have got to.'

'You've got a bee in your bonnet about them,' said Ashley.

Jack cocked his head to one side. 'Are you in a hurry to get back this afternoon?'

'Not particularly. Why?'

'Because it strikes me,' said Jack, running his finger round the top of his pewter mug, 'that although Mrs Mountford seems to know everything that goes on in Topfordham, the only way to find out for certain if Mrs Welbeck, Florence Pargetter and

John Bright haven't told anyone where they're going, is to ask the people they're likely to have talked to.'

Ashley's eyebrows shot up. 'What? Interview all the servants in Topfordham, you mean?'

'Interview's a bit official. I was thinking of having a chat to Mrs Henderson's Mavis, as she seems to have been closest to Florence Pargetter, but you can call it an interview if you'd rather. Old-fashioned police work,' added Jack with a grin, taking a gulp of bitter. 'You should love it. Or do you have minions to do that sort of thing for you nowadays?'

'Minions be blowed,' grumbled Ashley. 'This is supposed to be my day off.'

TEN

'I don't know as who could tell you about Mrs Welbeck,' said Mavis blankly. 'Or John Bright, neither.'

Mavis Stainburn was a big, amiable, fair-haired girl with large, placid blue eyes, only too willing to follow Mrs Henderson's instructions and 'talk to these gentlemen'. She reached across the well-scrubbed kitchen table for the sugar bowl, stirred three spoonfuls into her tea and settled back happily.

Mavis had echoed more or less what they had learned from Mrs Mountford. Mrs Welbeck had departed in a huff back up north, John Bright had hung around until he, too, had taken himself off and as for Florence . . .

'I don't suppose,' said Ashley, 'that Miss Pargetter and John Bright could've gone off together, could they?'

Mavis blinked at him in slow disbelief. 'Flo go off with Bright?' She gave a rich laugh. 'She wouldn't give him the time of day. Mind you,' she added, 'it wasn't for want of asking. Quite struck on her, he was, for a time, but Flo wouldn't have any of it.'

'So there wasn't any special friendship between them?' asked Jack.

'No . . .'

He picked up the hesitancy in her voice and looked a question.

'There was something going on,' she admitted. 'I couldn't make it out. She didn't fancy him, nothing like that. She could do far better than him, but there was *something*. I saw them with their heads together a couple of times.'

'Could it be something to do with Terence Napier, perhaps?' suggested Jack.

Mavis digested the notion. 'Perhaps,' she said, then shook her head. 'No. That doesn't seem right, somehow.' Jack could see her struggling to put her thoughts into words. 'Florence was worked up about something. I don't know what. She should've told me,' she added, indignation clouding her good-natured face. 'She had no right, keeping things back. We were best friends but I've not heard nothing.'

It was slow work, but they learned quite a bit about Florence. How she could take off Mrs Paxton, with her snooty ways, so you would weep with laughing. And the vicar. Yes, and Mrs Welbeck, too, and anyone else you could care to mention in the village. She was a rare one for noticing, was Florence. 'My mum,' said Mavis, pouring herself another cup of tea, 'said that Flo was so sharp she'd cut herself one of these days, but she made me die, she did.'

'It's a real gift, to be able to mimic someone properly,' said Jack with a warm smile. 'You have to be a very keen observer. And, of course, a good mimic gets to know all sorts of things about the people they're impersonating.'

A slow smile spread across Mavis' face. 'I'd say so. Florence always knew what was going on.' Mavis laughed. 'She did all right out of it, too. She had some nice presents from folk who wanted to keep her sweet. Bits of jewellery, stockings and chocolates and so on. My mum,' she added with a sniff, 'didn't like it, but, as Flo said, if you don't want to be caught out, don't get up to anything you shouldn't in the first place.'

'What about Florence's mum? Did she approve?'

Mavis gave an incredulous snort. 'Mum? She didn't have no mum. She only had her gran and when she passed over, Flo went to the orphanage. They put her into Service. She reckoned she'd never have been in Service if she wasn't an orphan. We often spoke about what we'd do if we had the choice.' Mavis' expression became dreamy. 'I'd be a film star, and wear a fur coat and have jewels, just like they do in the magazines.' She looked at a pile of magazines on the kitchen sideboard and sighed.

'Which ones have you got?' asked Jack with interest, strolling over to the sideboard and flicking through the heap of magazines. 'I see. *Peg's Paper, Up To Date, Woman's Companion, Chit-Chat, Society Snippets, Joy, Love and Laughter Weekly* and *Film Life.*'

'Not one of yours, then, Haldean?' asked Ashley. He turned to Mavis. 'Major Haldean writes for *On The Town* magazine.'

Mavis' eyes bulged. 'Do you, sir?' she asked in awestruck tones. Unconsciously her hand reached up and she patted her hair into place. 'Flo would've loved meeting you. That's what she wanted to do. Be one of these people who find things out and write about it in magazines, I mean. Oh, I wish she was here.'

'I wish she was, too,' said Jack. 'I could've given her a couple of tips about how to get on, perhaps.'

Mavis nodded vigorously. 'She would've liked that. You might meet her, up in Lunnon. I reckon that's where she is. She had something in mind, I know. What's more, I'm sure it had something to do with a magazine. Mad about magazines, she was.'

'About magazines in general or any one in particular?' asked Jack, his hand resting on the pile.

Mavis ruminated for a few moments. 'She talked about *Joy, Love and Laughter.*' Slightly surprised, Jack held up the copy of the magazine. From Mavis' description of Florence, he'd had expected her to be more drawn to the acidic observations of *Chit-Chat* or *Society Snippets* rather than the fulsome sentimentality of *Joy, Love and Laughter.* 'Yes, that's the one. Mind you, we were all excited about it, because of the sapphires.'

Jack and Ashley exchanged glances. 'The sapphires?' questioned Jack.

'Yes, Mrs Paxton's sapphires. A big picture it was, with Mrs Whoever it is – the lady who's got them now, I mean – all dressed up, with them on. Flo wanted to take the magazine,' continued Mavis, 'but I wouldn't let her. I wanted to show it to mum. Flo fell out with me over it, but I said if she wanted it, she'd have to buy her own.'

As Mavis talked, Jack flicked through the magazine, remembering the feel of the picture he and Bill had taken from the dead man's wallet. The quality of the paper was right and so was the price. A tuppenny weekly, he'd said.

And there it was. The picture he had last seen in that gloomy room in Charing Cross, complete with a half-page article, describing the origin of the sapphires in reverent terms.

The writer rather spread themselves about the mysterious Breagan Stump Bounty, locked away in a golden box in the dark fastness of a cave for millennia, etcetera, etcetera. The fact that the sapphires had been locked away in the equally dark fastness of a bank for years and had only seen the light because an old lady was murdered wasn't mentioned. Murder, he thought, wouldn't induce the appropriate emotions in the readers of *Joy, Love and Laughter.*

'You say whatever Florence had in mind had something to do with this magazine?' he asked.

Mavis nodded. 'I think so. As I say, she was excited for some reason. I dunno why, but she was. Do you really write for a magazine, sir?' she added wistfully.

Jack smiled. 'Yes, I do. Would you like me to send you a copy of the next issue? I've got a story in it.'

'Oh, *yes,*' said Mavis in a sort of rapture. 'That would be lovely. My mum won't believe it when I tell her I've met you!'

'What would you call a sharp young woman who takes "nice presents" from people who want her to keep quiet?' asked Jack as he drove Ashley back to Lewes.

'I'd call her dangerously close to a blackmailer,' said Ashley. He looked at Jack speculatively. 'I know I laughed at the idea earlier, but I wonder if Florence Pargetter did know something about Terence Napier?'

Jack nodded. 'Maybe, but what seems to have really got her going was the picture of the sapphires in the magazine. The same magazine picture,' he added, 'that turned up in our victim's wallet.'

Ashley digested this slowly. 'Well, there's one thing about the victim in the train,' he said with a grin. 'Whoever it was, it wasn't Florence Pargetter.'

*   *   *

Jack spent that evening with Aunt Alice, Uncle Philip and Isabelle. The next morning, with Isabelle beside him in the car, he drove from Hesperus to Breagan Grange.

'You haven't been to Breagan Grange before, have you, Jack?' asked Isabelle as Jack negotiated the Spyker through Breagan Hollow and turned up the long drive to the Grange.

'No, I haven't,' said Jack, swerving to avoid a pot hole.

After the homely prosperity of Hesperus, he felt his spirits dulled by the sight of Breagan Grange. He had been told that Frank Leigh had found it a struggle to hold onto the Grange after his father had gambled away the family fortunes but he could have guessed at the struggle, if not the cause, from the unkempt air of the place.

The lawns on either side of the drive were ragged and the house itself, although beautifully proportioned, was badly in need of pointing and painting. Discoloured patches of grey grime and damp marred the white façade. Even the surrounding countryside appeared shabby and down at heel. The woods behind the house, climbing the slope of Breagan Stump, seemed dusty in the heat and the tops of the surrounding hills were scorched a dull dun colour.

'It looks as it could do with a bit of spit and polish, I must say,' he continued. 'If I'd just inherited a string of sapphires, I'd be tempted to cash them in and spend the money where it was needed.'

'So would I,' said Isabelle, 'but there's no chance of that, I'd say, judging from what Celia says.' She tutted in irritation. 'I do hate seeing a place run down like this.'

'I don't suppose Mr Leigh can do much about it,' said Jack.

'There's lots he could do,' said Isabelle robustly. 'He could put his foot down for a start and stop his wife squandering money.'

'Celia's been bending your ear, hasn't she?' said Jack with a sideways glance.

'I suppose she has,' said Isabelle with a giggle, 'but I do think she's got a point.'

'The real point is that Celia and her stepmother don't get on very well, isn't it?'

'What d'you expect? Celia didn't mind her father remarrying,' she added tolerantly, 'but if he had to jump off the dock again, she expected it to be with Mary Hawker. She's a neighbour,' she continued in answer to Jack's questioning look. 'Her husband's dead and she's obviously got a real soft spot for Mr Leigh. Celia likes Mrs Hawker. She's one of those efficient women, the sort who's always on committees and who ropes you into things. I bet she worked her socks off during the war. You're bound to meet her sooner or later.'

'She sounds a bit tweedy,' said Jack. 'It couldn't be that Celia's jealous of Evie's style, could it? After all, Celia's a bit tweedy herself.'

'D'you know, she is,' said Isabelle with rueful recognition. 'I've never thought of her like that, but you're right. By the way, Jack, try not to be too fascinating with Celia. She's fed up with Ted and I've got a feeling she's regretting having returned you to store. In fact,' she added, 'she's virtually said as much.'

'Oh, blimey, has she? I thought as much the other day, but I hoped it was a passing mood. I must try to be as repellent as possible.'

'Just be yourself,' suggested Isabelle. 'That should do it.'

'Thanks,' said Jack with a grin, turning the car into the broad sweep of gravel in front of the house. 'Forewarned is forearmed.'

When Jack came down to the hall after he had been shown to his room, he found Frank Leigh waiting for him, together with a plump, cheerful looking man of about thirty-odd with a round face, a thick thatch of butter-coloured hair and humorous blue eyes.

'Hello, Haldean,' said Leigh, with a brief smile. 'I heard you'd arrived.' He indicated the man beside him. 'This is Mr Aloysius Wood, who's been looking into things in Topfordham for me. Come into the study,' said Leigh, leading the way. 'We can talk in there without being disturbed.'

Jack was favourably impressed by Wood. Mrs Mountford, he remembered, had liked him too.

Frank Leigh looked at Jack expectantly. 'Did you discover anything in Topfordham?'

'Not exactly, sir, but I've got a few ideas.'

Frank Leigh and Aloysius Wood listened attentively as Jack ran through the events of the previous day.

'Wood went to Topfordham last week,' said Leigh when Jack had finished. 'You wondered about the servants, didn't you?'

'I didn't realise Bright had disappeared,' said Wood, looking worried. 'That's a clean sweep. I don't like the sound of that at all. I was concentrating on Mrs Welbeck and Florence Pargetter. As the general impression was that Mrs Welbeck had returned to the north of England, I've advertised for her in the *Leeds Mercury,* the *Manchester Guardian* and the *Liverpool Echo* as well as the national papers, but, so far, I've had no luck. Where Florence Pargetter has got to is anyone's guess.'

'Have any of the servants approached Mrs Leigh for a reference, sir?' Jack asked Frank Leigh. 'With Mrs Paxton dead, Mrs Leigh is the natural person for them to turn to.'

'No, no they haven't.' Frank Leigh moved uneasily in his chair. 'But look here, Haldean. Mrs Welbeck went more or less right away, Florence Pargetter left three weeks ago and Bright pushed off last week. Surely it's nothing more than coincidence.'

Jack looked at him curiously. He had the distinct impression that Mr Leigh was holding something back. There were strained lines round his mouth and his forehead was furrowed.

'Servants come and go all the time,' continued Frank Leigh, 'especially in the country. I'm more interested in Sandy Paxton.'

Jack rubbed his nose hesitantly. 'Yes . . . I'm not sure if I'm on the right lines or not, but there's a suggestion that Paxton was an associate of the Vicar's.'

'The Vicar?' exclaimed Leigh. 'The maniac who tried to murder Duggleby, you mean?'

'And my cousin, Isabelle, yes.'

Frank Leigh gaped at him. 'But that's incredible!'

'Is it?'

Frank Leigh started to speak, then fell silent. 'As a matter of fact, I suppose it *is* possible,' he admitted grudgingly.

'I also think,' said Jack, 'there's a possibility, not to put it stronger than that, that Paxton stole your sapphires.'

For a few seconds Frank Leigh looked completely thunderstruck, then he laughed dismissively. 'He can't be. The man who came here, you mean?' He put his hand to his mouth and sat for a while in silence. 'That can't have been Paxton. Dash it, he was *murdered.*' He shook his head, bewildered. 'Murdered on the train. You mean to tell me that you think that was my cousin, Sandy Paxton?'

'I think he could've been.'

Frank Leigh shook his head once more then sat back in his chair. He took a cigarette from the box on the study desk and lit it in an abstracted way, before pushing the box towards Jack. 'Sorry, major. Help yourself.'

Leigh smoked the cigarette down to the butt, stubbed it out slowly and took a deep breath. 'I have to say there's no reason why it shouldn't be true. Paxton was an actor.' He shrugged. 'I don't know if he was a good or bad actor, but he was certainly an actor. The man who turned up here could've been him.' He looked at Jack and shrugged. 'What on earth gave you the idea?'

'It was something Dr Mountford said. If Mrs Paxton confided in anyone in the village, she confided in him. She told him about the trouble she'd had with her son. She hoped Paxton would reform and even hoped he'd go into the Church.'

'A likely story,' said Frank Leigh with a snort of derision. 'That young devil? I don't think so.'

'No, neither did I. But when I questioned Dr Mountford, what Mrs Paxton had *actually* said was that Sandy Paxton had a close friend who was a vicar. He wanted to follow in his footsteps.'

Wood stared at him. 'My God,' he said quietly. 'I wonder if it's true.'

Frank Leigh sat in stunned silence. 'That,' he said eventually, 'is oddly convincing.' He shot an acute glance at Jack. 'It's all speculation, though, isn't it? I don't see how you can prove it.'

'Dr Mountford said Mrs Paxton had a photo of her son. I believe that all Mrs Paxton's things are here. I wondered if I could look for it.'

'Feel free,' said Frank Leigh. 'There's a fair few boxes to hunt through, though. Strictly speaking, they belong to Evie, but I can't see she'll have any objections.'

'I'll give you a hand,' said Wood. 'The boxes are in the old barn, aren't they, Mr Leigh?'

'Yes, that's right. They're in the hayloft. But you can't look now, Major Haldean,' he added, as the dinner gong sounded in the hall. 'It's time for lunch and Celia wants to take you and your cousin round the temple and cave this afternoon.' He smiled fleetingly. 'Duggleby's taken his role as an amateur archaeologist very much to heart. He's itching to show off his knowledge.'

After lunch, under Celia's direction, the party set off across the grounds to the wooded path that led up the slope of Breagan Stump to the temple. Frank and Evie Leigh were at the head of the group with Celia and Leonard Duggleby a few paces behind, while Jack and Isabelle brought up the rear.

'I don't want to be catty,' said Isabelle quietly to Jack, 'but don't you think Celia's getting a little bit too friendly with Mr Duggleby?'

There was no doubt that Celia had taken a real shine to Duggleby. Jack had noticed as much at lunch.

'At any rate, I think you can stop worrying,' said Isabelle, dropping back a few paces. 'Duggleby's an attractive man, you know.'

'Duggleby?' repeated Jack in hushed disbelief. Despite himself, he couldn't help feeling piqued. 'You must be joking. He's a weedy sort of beggar and years older than she is. He can't hold a candle to Ted Marchant.'

'Or you?' said Isabelle with a sly grin.

'Well, I . . .'

'I thought as much!'

'But what on earth does she see in him, Belle?' protested Jack.

'Duggleby's the sort of man who women want to look after. That's a very powerful urge, you know, especially with someone like Celia. It's why you always bring her up sharp. You're far too capable.'

'I suppose I should be grateful,' murmured Jack. 'Do girls really like incompetent men?'

'Not incompetent exactly, but she needs to be needed. She does the hero-worship bit, too. For instance, she never could give a toss about the temple and the cave, but now Duggleby's here, she's all for them. I hope she does manage to patch things up with Ted Marchant,' she added in a worried voice. 'If he'd only stop telling her what he thinks she wants and start listening to what she actually does want, things would be a lot better.'

She broke off abruptly as Celia, squeezing Duggleby's arm, broke off her rather giggly conversation and turned back to them.

'Isabelle, I hope you put walking shoes on. It can be ever so muddy along these paths, even in dry weather.'

'I'll be fine,' called Isabelle. 'Mr Leigh doesn't like it,' she added quietly. 'I saw him looking daggers at lunch and he made a point of dragging Ted's name into the conversation.'

'You're worrying too much,' said Jack uneasily. 'Celia's far too straight-laced to start flirting.'

'Celia's unhappy with Ted,' said Isabelle. 'That's dangerous.'

Frank Leigh reached the top of the path and turned to encourage the stragglers. 'Come on, Mrs Stanton. Nearly there! How did you find the climb?' he asked Isabelle. 'I did wonder if it might be a bit too much after your accident.'

'I'm fine, thanks. My head's still a bit sore but nothing to complain about.'

Jack walked out onto the grassy clearing. His first sight of the temple took his breath away. After the shade of the woods, the sunlight on the gleaming white limestone was dazzling. 'My word, sir, this was worth the walk!'

'It's not bad, eh?' said Frank Leigh with modest pride. 'Vanbrugh designed the house and we think the temple is his as well.'

The temple, thought Jack, certainly had the inspired stamp of a master. Against the shadows of the surrounding trees and the sparkling green of the wind-ruffled grass, the arched and colonnaded temple was as brilliant as the Mediterranean in midsummer. Beyond the trees, Jack could make out the elegant lines of the house and, beyond that, the sparkling turquoise of the lake. It seemed the essence of a dream of an urbane, classical world.

He swallowed. He didn't know why, but a sudden aversion to that wickedly innocent-looking temple on its inviting grassy mound flared up inside him.

'What d'you think of the temple?' asked Leonard Duggleby. 'Quite a sight, eh?'

'I've always felt a presence here,' said Celia, ignoring Isabelle's derisive snort. 'I told Len as much.' Isabelle and Jack swapped glances. So it was *Len* now, was it? 'Aunt Mary – Mrs Hawker – says there's something about the place which isn't quite canny.'

'I hardly think so,' said Evie.

Duggleby cleared his throat. 'I'm not so sure, Mrs Leigh,' he said hesitantly. 'I've sensed something here.'

'Stuff and nonsense,' said Frank Leigh robustly.

'Why have the trees been allowed to grow so thickly round the temple?' asked Jack curiously. 'As the house and the temple were built at the same time, I'd have thought that the temple was meant to be seen from the house and grounds.'

'Exactly,' said Celia. 'I think the trees were allowed to hide the temple.'

Frank Leigh sighed in exasperation. 'If you're determined to frighten yourself with fairy-tales, my girl, I can't help you. It's just superstition, eh, Duggleby?'

Caught between Celia Leigh and her father, Duggleby resorted to diplomacy. 'There are many superstitions connected with this area,' he agreed. 'Most of them can be satisfactorily explained. For instance, it's perfectly natural this area should be thickly wooded. We're in what was the ancient forest of Andred. The Anglo-Saxon Chronicles warned travellers to be wary of Andred. It covered a huge area and was so dense that even William the Conqueror's men couldn't penetrate its depths for the Domesday Book.'

Celia shuddered and Jack laughed. 'You'll have to try harder than that, Duggleby, if you want to make it less creepy. Incidentally, I'm amazed by your erudition,' he added lightly. 'Do you often curl up with the Anglo-Saxon Chronicles?'

'I've made some fascinating discoveries,' said Duggleby earnestly. 'My chief source has been a history of the area written in the 1830s by the local vicar, the Reverend Bertram Throckmorton, who was a noted antiquarian. There's a copy in the library in the house and it's been invaluable. It was the Reverend Throckmorton who excavated the Altar Cave.'

'The Altar Cave?' asked Jack.

'It's an absolute gem,' said Duggleby, ramming his glasses firmly onto his nose. 'The altar, I mean. Wait till you see it. The temple was built to make a fitting entrance to the cave. Throckmorton ascribes the altar to the native British god, Euthius. There's one other dedication to Euthius in Britain, but it's nothing like as fine as this.'

'The Breagan Bounty was found under the altar, wasn't it, Mr Duggleby?' asked Evie.

'That's right, Mrs Leigh,' said Duggleby earnestly. 'Throckmorton believes that the Breagan Bounty was hidden beneath the altar to put it under the protection of the god when this area was torn apart by the fall of Rome.'

'It was my ancestor, Jasper Leigh, who found it,' said Mr Leigh. 'He'd been on the Grand Tour, and built the temple as a memento of his travels.'

'There were human remains found, weren't there, Mr Duggleby?' said Celia raptly. 'Human sacrifices!'

Duggleby nodded earnestly. 'So the Reverend Throckmorton believed.'

Celia gave a contented little sigh. 'It's very sad, no doubt, but isn't it fascinating? I wonder if they had a priestess. A priestess,' she said dreamily, 'steeped in the wisdom of the ages. Men would have died of love for her. I wonder what she wore? Gold, perhaps, with purple robes and maybe a headdress, rich with exotic stones.'

Duggleby coughed awkwardly, taken off-guard by this flight of fancy.

'It seems unlikely,' said Frank Leigh looking dubiously at his daughter. 'I've never known you take much interest in the temple before, Celia.'

'It's different,' said Celia, 'when there's someone who can make it come alive for you. It's totally *thrilling*, isn't it Isabelle?'

'The bodies aren't still there, are they?' asked Isabelle guardedly.

'Of course not,' said Duggleby reassuringly. 'Mr Throckmorton had the bodies moved and interred in ground nearby the churchyard. He couldn't bury them in the churchyard, of course, because it was impossible to tell if they were Christians or not. The Altar Cave itself is most certainly not Christian.'

'Shall we go in?' asked Frank Leigh. 'You've got torches, have you, Duggleby?'

'There's two or three torches in the temple,' said Duggleby. 'I leave them there to be on the safe side. I like a spare in case the batteries run out.'

With an odd reluctance Jack entered the temple, Isabelle close beside him. It was a large, square, airy space, brilliantly white, with carved stone benches set around the walls, together with various Roman statues and an ornamental urn, the result, no doubt, of Jasper Leigh's Grand Tour.

Frank Leigh led the way to a brass-hinged cedar wood door. Reaching up, he took down a large key from the top of the architrave. 'We keep the cave locked up,' he said. 'We don't often get people poking around up here, but it has been known.'

The door opened onto a rocky passageway, filled with the echoing sound of running water. 'Have you got the torches, Duggleby?'

Duggleby opened a tin box beneath the marble bench near the door and handed out torches.

'Keep to the raised brick path,' warned Frank Leigh. 'There's a spring which runs through the cave and it's very muddy underfoot. You can see,' he added, directing the light from his torch, 'where the spring comes out of the cave wall.'

Evie Leigh looked at her shoes dubiously. 'I don't really want to get my feet wet, Frank. I'm sure Mrs Stanton doesn't either.'

'It'll be fine,' said Frank. 'There's a bridge over the actual stream, but watch out when we get into the cave. The stream runs though it and you've got to be careful of your footing. There's an old well that used to tap into it further along the course of the stream. The gardeners still use it occasionally. You think the well's Roman, don't you, Duggleby?'

'Judging by the bricks, it seems very likely, sir. The level of the water must have dropped considerably since Roman times.'

'The main course of the spring was diverted when the house was built so it drained into the new lake. It's a model of Georgian engineering.'

Duggleby was politely dismissive of the Georgians. 'I'm glad they didn't manage to divert the spring altogether. It would have ruined the effect of this carving,' he said, directing the beam of his torch onto the wall. A carved face was just about discernable in the torchlight. 'It's as if the water of the spring is the god's tears.'

'I can hardly see anything,' said Isabelle in a disappointed voice after a prolonged stare. 'It's all covered over with green slime.'

'It's been there for two thousand years or so, maybe even

longer. As I said, according to the Reverend Throckmorton, it's Euthius, a British god who was also worshipped by the Romans.'

'Why Euthius, I wonder?' said Jack. 'I mean, we're in Breagan Stump on the grounds of Breagan Grange in Breagan Hollow. Who or what is Breagan?'

'I don't know,' said Duggleby. 'I don't know where the name Breagan comes from, as a matter of fact. I must look it up.' Frank Leigh cleared his throat as if about to speak. 'Mr Leigh? Do you know?'

'Can't say I do,' said Frank Leigh in an unconvincing way.

There was a slightly awkward silence, then Duggleby continued. 'The spring is the original place of worship. Throckmorton considered the Altar Cave to be a later addition. We're at the heart of the old kingdom of the Celtic tribe of the Regnenses and both the Celts and their Roman masters saw springs and rivers as a barrier between the world of the living and the world of the dead.'

Celia gave a satisfied little gasp. 'How utterly *thrilling,*' she murmured once more.

She walked onto the bridge and shone her torchlight onto the dark ripples beneath. 'Just think. I'm standing between worlds. Here, on this side of the spring, is life but on the other side . . .' She gave a happy little shudder. 'It's as if the god is inviting us to enter the kingdom of the dead.'

The carving didn't, in Jack's opinion, look remotely inviting. He felt Isabelle's hand slip into his.

'I don't like it, Jack,' she said quietly. 'It's silly, I know, and Celia's being the biggest sort of idiot, but I don't like it.'

He gave her hand a reassuring squeeze. 'It'll be all right,' he said as the group set off again.

Beyond the bridge the rock of the wall had been carved into rough pictures.

'These carvings indicate this is a ritual processional route leading us to the Altar Cave,' said Duggleby. 'The carvings are mainly *dendrophori,* as you can see.'

'Den what?' asked Isabelle.

'Chaps carrying trees and branches,' said Jack, a remnant of Classical knowledge returning to him. 'It's Greek, but they seem to crop up all over the ancient world. I suppose the idea is that the woods are walking, that the woods have come to life. It's not all *dendrophori* though, Duggleby. There's some blokes carrying water-jars and some others carrying what I suppose are flaming torches.'

'Yes, there's some interesting local variations. The most interesting carvings of all are, as you'd expect, in the Altar Cave.' He raised his voice. 'Mind your head, Mrs Leigh! It's a narrow opening into the cave.'

The first thing Jack saw, as they crowded through into the Altar Cave was, oddly enough, a Victorian desk, two chairs, the frame of a wooden camp-bed, an old-fashioned oil lamp, an earthenware beer bottle and an ink-pot.

'What on earth are these things doing here?' he asked.

'The Reverend Throckmorton had them brought in,' said Duggleby. 'He says as much in his book. He liked to work in here. I've found lots of his bits and pieces.'

The roof of the cave, so low at the entrance that they had to crouch, opened to a space about twelve feet high or so. It was a substantial cave, measuring about twenty yards or so across at the widest extent and running back about the same distance. From all around them came the echoed, measured sound of dripping water and, from somewhere close by, the chatter of an unseen stream running through the cave.

'You'll see,' said Duggleby, shining his torch at the walls, 'that there's been the occasional landslip. Throckmorton dug it out and shored up the wall and roof all along this side with beams.'

'Is it safe?' asked Evie Leigh sharply.

'I hope so,' said Duggleby. 'I wouldn't like those roof beams to go, though.' He directed his torch light to the ground. 'Watch your step over the stream. Ideally there should be a handrail but it's only a plank bridge.' He grinned at Celia. 'The altar's on the other side. It's the barrier between life and death once more.'

Fortunately Celia, who was watching her footing on the slimy planks, wasn't moved to make another speech.

As they approached the altar, Jack felt his feet tread on very smooth ground. He looked down. He was standing on wooden boards. 'Why's the floor been boarded over?'

'That's where the graves were,' said Duggleby. 'Throckmorton found the remnants of wooden planks and the remains of sacrificial victims. The floorboards you're standing on are Victorian. Throckmorton had them placed there to mark the spot and so no one would fall into the graves.'

Isabelle gave a little gulp and reached for Jack's hand once more.

In front of the altar was a stone channel, ending in a dark-stained shallow stone basin and, beyond that, seven broad steps led up to the altar itself.

The stones of the altar were a blackened mass of carving; a staring face with huge eyes, a snarl of pointed teeth and stylised, waving hair.

'That gentleman,' said Duggleby 'is Euthius, or, at least, I think it is. There's no inscription on the altar but Mr Throckmorton found a couple of lead tablets addressed to Euthius by the spring. They were pretty vivid requests to wreak vengeance. *Euthius, consume mine enemy, Saturninus*, ran one. *Make his blood as water, his heart putrefied as rotting blood and his bowels a ribbon of flame.'*

'Poor old Saturninus,' said Jack. He looked at the staring face on the altar and clicked his tongue. 'I wouldn't like a character like that after me even if all he wanted was a cup of tea and a chat. Can I borrow your torch Duggleby?' He crouched down beside the altar and slowly worked his way round. 'What have we got? There's more chaps with trees – lots of trees – and on the other side there's a lot of curvy waves. Water?'

'I think so,' agreed Duggleby.

'With what look like dead fish with a spear through them in a heap at the bottom. Then there's what looks like someone about to sacrifice a lamb. D'you think it's a lamb? I don't think the artist was particularly great shakes, but it looks as if it could be a lamb to me. The knife's very clear and so's the blood.'

He looked back at the stone channel in front of the altar. 'I wouldn't be surprised if that's where the *coup de grâce* was administered. Then, on top of the altar, we've got – what? It looks as if it might be more water, but these waves are different from the other waves.'

'The Reverend Throckmorton thinks it's fire,' said Duggleby. 'Water, blood and fire seem to have been the chief symbols of the cult.'

'Water, blood and fire,' repeated Jack, rocking back on his heels. 'Are you sure it's a Celtic cult, Duggleby? I thought the Druids worshipped in stone circles and sacred groves, not in caves.'

'You're quite right. There's descriptions of human sacrifice by the Druids in Tacitus, Strabo and Caesar, but those are all in the open air. However, after Christianity became the state religion, the Emperor Theodosius in 391 A.D. outlawed pagan rituals and shrines. Throckmorton's opinion is that this is a very late Romano-British cult, driven literally underground.'

'The fish and the lamb are both Christian symbols,' said Jack thoughtfully. 'And on the altar both the fish and the lamb are shown coming to a sticky end.' He stood up and brushed off the knees of his trousers. 'It's very interesting, Duggleby, but I don't think I would have liked to meet Euthius' pals.'

He reached out and touched the altar stones. 'What's all this black stuff?' He rubbed his fingers together and sniffed them. 'It smells like soot.'

'It is. Mr Throckmorton states in his book that he was worried by the anti-Christian nature of the cult. He was troubled, he says, when he was alone in here, by sudden changes in temperature, from intense heat to deathly chills.' Duggleby gave an apologetic cough. 'He had a feeling of . . . er . . . evil.'

'I'm not surprised,' agreed Isabelle.

'Throckmorton decided to hold a service to clear the air,' said Duggleby earnestly. 'He was a thorough-going Classicist and cites Sidonius Apollinaris on the best way to convert a pagan altar to Christian use. Sidonius suggests that you sacrifice a white cockerel or some other ritual animal to the old god and tell them thanks very much, but the old dedication's off and from now on it's going to be a Christian altar. Throckmorton wanted to give it a go, but his bishop disapproved.'

'I imagine he would,' said Jack dryly.

'The bishop seemed to think that it was a Papist rite, which he had the strongest objections too. He gave a cautious thumbs-up to the idea of prayers, but insisted that any service should be conducted on the lines laid down by the Established Church.'

'So no animal sacrifices?' asked Jack with a grin. 'Even Catholics draw the line at those as a general rule.'

'So I believe. Anyway, Throckmorton tried saying prayers and whether it was an accident or not – I imagine everyone was fairly jittery – the candles got knocked over, the oil in the lamp caught on fire and, although no one was harmed, they all retreated in double-quick time. He says the altar seemed to be a mass of flames and the eyes of Euthius glowed white-hot. Fire again, you see? He was probably suffering from an overheated imagination. He was pretty rattled.'

'I don't blame the poor man,' said Isabelle. 'Can we go? I think I've had enough of ancient horrors.'

They made their way out of the cave. Jack stopped to look once more at the old camp-bed. 'Did Throckmorton sleep in here?'

'He doesn't say as much, but it looks like it, doesn't it?'

'Rather him than me,' said Isabelle firmly, leading him to the entrance. 'I wouldn't spend a night in here for all the tea in China.'

'It's a rum thing where the photograph of Paxton could have got to,' remarked Jack to Wood in the hayloft later that afternoon.

The loft was quite a pleasant place, with sunlight from gaps in the old tiled roof making the clouds of dust-motes dance in parallel shafts of light, but even so, Jack felt he had been stuck up here quite long enough. They had spent well over an hour hunting through the boxes from Mrs Paxton's house. He stood up and stretched his shoulders.

'I can't understand it,' said Wood, sitting back on his heels. 'The photograph's certainly not here.'

Jack took out his cigarette case and offered it to Wood. 'That,' he said, as he clicked his lighter, 'is a real shame. Odd, too. Dr Mountford said Mrs Paxton had a photo of her son in the parlour.'

'Do you really think Paxton was the bloke in the train?' asked Wood, blowing out a mouthful of smoke.

'I think it's possible.'

'I haven't thought about the murder on the train,' said Wood. He pulled on his cigarette broodingly. 'It's Mrs Paxton's death Mr Leigh wants me to explain. He's certain Napier is innocent. I wish I could find out where the servants have got to. It could be coincidence, I know, but I don't like the way all three of them have vanished.'

'Spell it out for me, Wood,' said Jack quietly. 'What's in your mind?'

Wood ran a distracted hand through his hair. 'Are they dead?'

'You're still not spelling it out.'

'All right, I will. Have they been murdered? I know it seems incredible, but what other explanation is there? Now you've worked out the Vicar's involved anything's possible.'

Jack held up his hand for silence. A sound came from below. 'There's someone there,' he said quietly.

They got up and walked to where the trapdoor to the loft opened out to the old stable below. The old boarded floor creaked beneath them.

A middle-aged, smartly dressed woman was standing at the bottom of the ladder. 'Mr Wood? Major Haldean?' she called.

'Mrs Hawker?' said Wood in surprise. He swung himself onto the ladder and climbed down, Jack following behind.

Mary Hawker held out her hand to Jack. 'We haven't met. I'm Mary Hawker. I believe you're looking into Mrs Paxton's death.'

'That, and other things,' he said with a smile, squinting in the early evening sun slanting through the barn door.

Isabelle had described Mary Hawker very well, he thought. A sensible, grey-haired woman with a briskly efficient air, who he could well imagine being the mainstay of various local committees. As Jack took her outstretched hand, however, he caught a fleeting glimpse of something else.

She looked from him to Wood and back to him, with a sudden, intent stare. She's frightened, he thought, with that sudden stab of insight which is hardly ever wrong, and then, as he saw the expression in her troubled brown eyes, added another layer to his first impression. For some reason she was frightened of *him*.

She gave a little insincere laugh. 'I've come to tell you it's time to get ready for dinner. It's still quite early but I thought you'd both want a bath after being up in the hayloft.' She turned and walked to the door. She cleared her throat and said, rather too firmly, 'I've only just arrived.'

It was such an unnecessary statement it made Jack pause. The sunlight illuminated her footprints in the dust. She was wearing shoes with a raised squared-off heel. He glanced back to where the ladder stood, leading up to the hayloft. By the foot of the ladder were quite a lot of footprints with a raised, squared-off heel. Mary Hawker had obviously been standing in the barn listening to them for some time.

Why?

ELEVEN

Leonard Duggleby perched himself on the stone balustrade of the terrace, looking out onto the sunlit gardens. Breagan Grange was a lovely house. It might have suffered from neglect but, compared to the squalor of Murchinson's Rents, it was an earthly paradise. He could be happy here . . .

He turned round at the sound of his name. Celia had come onto the terrace.

'I wondered where you had got to, Len.' She sized up the balustrade, then hitched herself onto it, beside him. 'I was so interested in hearing you tell us all about the cave this afternoon. I've always been a bit bored by all that ancient history, but you really made it come alive.' She paused. 'You're a very talented man.'

Duggleby looked sheepishly embarrassed at the compliment. 'It's a real pleasure to be able to find out about a place like this, without having to think of an angle, as they say in journalism. What I'd like to do is to find out as much about Euthius as I can. I'm hoping that the British Museum may help.'

'That's the real you, isn't it?' said Celia. 'An academic, I mean. You should be in a university, not Fleet Street.'

Duggleby laughed hollowly. 'That was never an option, I'm afraid. I'm just glad to be here, even if it's only for a short time. I'll never forget it, nor all your kindness to me.'

Celia paused. 'I don't want you to go away,' she said softly. 'Ted doesn't appreciate this place. You do.' She glanced away. 'Knowing you has made me wonder about Ted. I don't know if he's right for me.'

Duggleby's sheepishness increased. 'Celia,' he began awkwardly, then stopped. 'Look,' he said in a rush. 'I don't know quite how to put this, but I don't want to come between you and anyone else. You deserve all the good things in life, things I can't possibly give you.'

She looked at him earnestly and something in his expression made her catch her breath. 'Dear Len,' she said softly. 'There's always a way.'

In her room, Isabelle had dressed early for dinner. The dinner gong wouldn't sound till eight and she had acres of time on her hands. She walked idly to the window. The sun was on the terrace, but so was Leonard Duggleby, perched on the stone balustrade, chatting to Celia. That ruled out the terrace. She'd had quite enough of the god Euthius for one day.

The portrait gallery? That was a thought. She'd been whizzed through the gallery at great speed by Celia, who obviously thought her ancestors were the frozen limit of dullness, but Isabelle wouldn't mind filling in half an hour or so with a closer look at the pictures. Picking up her beaded bag, she walked along the corridor to the gallery.

The gallery itself was worth seeing, a long L-shaped, high-ceilinged room of beautiful classical proportions with arched windows looking onto the grounds. The low evening sun brought out the rich honey colours of the old oak of the floorboards and panelling. A door, midway along the room, had stairs leading, she knew, to the lower corridor and down to the main hall.

The faces in the portraits were fascinating. A seventeenth-century maiden, looking dopily at a dove, was a tubbier and dimmer version of Celia. A Cavalier, with a startling resemblance to Frank Leigh, regarded her with his painted eyes, doffing his feathered hat. An eighteenth-century divine, in high collar, full wig and sober clothing, Bible in hand, made her pause. He had a fleeting resemblance to . . . who?

She couldn't place it, but she'd seen that face before. His name was Ebenezer Leigh. There was a catalogue at the far end of the room that might tell her more about Ebenezer. She walked round the corner of the L to the catalogue when she heard the floor-boards creak. Someone had come into the gallery.

Isabelle looked round the corner. Frank Leigh was standing, pocket watch in hand, in the middle of the room. She was about to say hello, when she suddenly noticed the tension in his stance. Feeling like an intruder, she drew back.

The door midway along the gallery opened and Mary Hawker came in. Her shoulders sagged in relief as she saw Frank. She crossed to him quickly and put her hands on his arms.

'Oh, my dear, thank heavens you're here. Frank, I'm worried.'

My dear? thought Isabelle. That was very friendly.

She darted a look up and down the gallery. 'We're alone, aren't we? I'm sure Evie's door opened as I went past.'

'Relax,' Frank said soothingly. 'Evie's picking out what to wear for dinner. She won't be ready for ages. No one comes up here at this time of day.' He held her hands between his. 'Calm down, Mary. What on earth is it?'

At this point Isabelle's conscience won over her curiosity. She was about to tactfully cough and make enough noise for Frank Leigh and Mary Hawker to stand a decent distance apart before she came round the corner, when Mrs Hawker's next remark drew her up sharp.

'You must get rid of Major Haldean, Frank. He's dangerous. I overheard him talking to Wood. He's going to get to the truth. He's a clever man. Dangerously clever.'

'Dangerous?' Frank Leigh's voice was sharp with apprehension and then he gave a very unconvincing laugh. 'Nonsense. Why should the truth be dangerous?'

Mary Hawker gave an exasperated sigh. 'Frank! Don't pretend you don't understand. This is murder we're talking about. I don't blame you but this is *murder.*'

Isabelle held her breath.

Frank Leigh choked. 'I . . . I didn't know you knew.'

'Don't be an idiot, Frank. How on earth could I *not* know? Why on earth did you ask Major Haldean here?'

'Celia was all for it,' muttered Frank. 'What could I say? I couldn't refuse. That'd look far too fishy. It'll be all right, Mary. Haldean's not as clever as you think. After all, he thinks it was Sandy Paxton who was murdered on the train. I just can't believe it.'

Mary Hawker gave a snort of impatience. 'I don't care about

the man on the train. He's not important. I'm telling you, Frank, Major Haldean is dangerous. You have to get rid of him.' She paused and added, with an odd inflection in her voice, 'You have to get rid of Wood, too.'

It was a few moments before Frank Leigh replied and then he said very quietly, 'I can't.'

'You must!' Mrs Hawker spoke rapidly and Isabelle could tell she was close to tears. 'If Major Haldean finds out about him . . . I care about *you*. You're running your head into a noose. You have to act, Frank.' She gave a little, breathless gulp. 'I . . . I care. You don't know how much I care.' Her voice wavered and she broke into sobs.

Isabelle risked another swift glance round the corner. Frank Leigh, his arms round Mary Hawker, was holding her close. Isabelle drew back again, but as she did, a tiny movement from the door to the stairs caught her eye. She could see a flash of brilliant scarlet in the thin crack of the open door, then it swung closed very quietly and the catch clicked into place. Neither Frank Leigh or Mary Hawker heard the snick of the door.

'Chin up,' said Frank Leigh softly. 'Courage, my dear. We have to act naturally at dinner. Don't let anyone guess there's anything wrong.'

'I won't.' When she spoke again, her voice was steadier. 'Promise me you'll act, Frank.'

Frank Leigh took a deep breath. 'I'll do what I think is best. Trust me, Mary. Now, off you go.'

Isabelle heard her footsteps on the oak boards then, after a short time, Frank Leigh sighed heavily and left in his turn.

Isabelle waited for quite a while before she walked out into the gallery. She opened the door to the staircase where she'd seen that tell-tale flash of scarlet. Lingering in the doorway was the whiff of a distinctive, expensive scent.

Both the scent and the colour belonged to Evie Leigh. What had she made of the scene in the gallery?

'Mrs Hawker wants to get rid of you,' said Isabelle. She was in Jack's room. 'She was frightened, Jack. She's obviously head over heels about Mr Leigh. I think she'd do anything to protect him.'

Jack, his hands moving without any conscious thought, carried on dressing for dinner. 'And Evie Leigh was listening, you say? I wonder what she made of it?'

'It's not Evie Leigh I'm worried about, Jack, it's you. Mary Hawker wants Mr Leigh to get rid of you. She's dangerous.'

Jack automatically adjusted his braces and picked up his white tie. 'Are you sure, Belle?'

'After what I heard her say to Mr Leigh? He's a murderer, Jack. He admitted as much.'

'But dammit, Belle, who's he murdered?'

'I don't know! Mrs Paxton, maybe? After all, he thought he was going to inherit the sapphires.'

'He can't have murdered Mrs Paxton. Everyone, apart from Frank Leigh, believes that Napier bumped her off. If Frank Leigh had murdered Mrs Paxton, he'd hardly go round telling the world that Napier's innocent.'

'Couldn't it be a ploy to make us believe he's innocent?'

'But no one ever dreamt he was guilty!'

'What about Sandy Paxton, then? The man on the train, I mean? No, hang on, that won't work. Mr Leigh doesn't think it was Sandy Paxton,' she added in a disappointed voice. 'Actually,' she said, brightening, 'that doesn't matter, does it? He can still have killed him, no matter who he thought he was.'

'We'd worked out that the Vicar was the murderer, Belle. You can't honestly tell me you believe Frank Leigh's the Vicar. That's too goofy for words.'

'I don't really believe it, I suppose,' said Isabelle, wrinkling her nose. 'I was just trying to think of who it could be.'

Jack turned to the mirror and knotted his tie with an irritated frown, then his hands slowed. 'Wood thinks Mrs Paxton's servants have been murdered.'

'The servants? Why on earth should anyone kill them?'

'God knows. Because they knew too much, I suppose. If they do know anything, it has to be about Napier, but what is anyone's guess. And why pick them off one by one? It just doesn't stack up.'

'*Who* then?' said Isabelle in frustration. 'Mr Leigh admitted to murder, Jack. Mrs Hawker said he was running his head into a noose. He didn't contradict her. What is it about Wood that she's so afraid of you finding out? Could Wood have murdered someone, perhaps?'

'Blimey, Belle, they can't all be murderers.'

'Well, what then? Mr Leigh employed Wood to prove Terence Napier was innocent, so Wood's done a fair old bit of digging around. Could it be something Wood's found out or is going to find out?'

'From what you said, it sounded more as if I was going to find out something about Wood.'

'Yes . . .' Isabelle sat up straight in her chair. 'Jack! I've got it! Wood isn't Wood at all!' Her eyes shone with the light of discovery. *'He's Terence Napier.* Who would Napier turn to if he's been hunted by the police? Mr Leigh, of course . . .' Her voice trailed off. 'What are you grinning at me like that for?'

'I thought of that,' said Jack with a laugh. 'It's obvious. Wood can't be Napier. He went to Topfordham and had a long talk to the Mountfords. They'd have recognised him.'

'Yes, I suppose they would,' said Isabelle with a frustrated sigh. 'But if that's not it, Jack, what is it?'

'I'm dammed if I know,' said Jack, shrugging on his coat. 'Mrs Hawker seems very certain I'm on the edge of the truth. I only wish I was.'

Isabelle shuddered. 'Mrs Hawker's not to be trusted, Jack.' She laid her hand on his arm. 'She's a very determined woman and I'd say she's really stuck on Mr Leigh.'

'That sounds as if Evie Leigh had better watch out.'

'So she should. Don't underestimate Mrs Hawker, Jack. You're in danger.'

Jack straightened his waistcoat and drew his breath in. 'All right. I'll be on my guard.' He offered her his arm. 'Let's go down to dinner.'

It was something of a relief when dinner, a wearily drawn out meal of soup, fish, an entrée of beef, roast duck, strawberry jelly and a savoury of dressed prawns and fruit, was over. Mary Hawker was clearly on edge and Evie Leigh seemed ill at ease. She was, Isabelle noted, wearing a brilliant scarlet beaded shawl. She hadn't been mistaken about the scent, either.

Frank Leigh was clearly under a strain and Celia had evidently picked up the tension round the table. The only ones who seemed completely unaffected were Leonard Duggleby, who chatted about the cave throughout the meal, and Aloysius Wood, who, possessed of a very keen appetite, was heartily appreciative of the food.

When the ladies left, even Wood's breezy cheerfulness suffered a dent in the face of Frank Leigh's brooding silence. Jack drank his port as if it were a patent medicine instead of a pleasure and greeted the suggestion that they should join the ladies with rather more enthusiasm than was polite.

In the drawing room, Celia had turned on the wireless, Evie Leigh was flicking though a magazine and Isabelle was making very stiff conversation with Mary Hawker.

'I haven't got anything out of Mrs Hawker,' said Isabelle in a whisper as Jack, coffee in hand, sat down beside her. 'She's being very County. Dogs, gardens and Sales of Work. Celia's on edge and Mrs Leigh's bored witless. I don't blame her.'

The programme of dance music from the Savoy came to an end and Celia switched off the wireless. 'Let's *do* something,' she said to the company in general.

'All right,' said Frank Leigh after a pause. He looked round the room and made an obvious effort. 'We've got two bridge fours. What about bridge?'

'Good idea,' began Mary Hawker, but she was interrupted by a yawn from Evie.

'Not bridge, darling. I always get into trouble for overcalling and I find it fearfully hard to remember who's bid what.'

'The art is to distinguish between a hand with winning cards and a hand without losing cards,' said Mary Hawker, tartly. She was an excellent bridge player.

'But it takes so much *thought*,' complained Evie, 'and everyone always ticks me off for not paying enough attention. Shall we play a round game? Or Halma, perhaps? Frank?'

'Not for me, my dear,' said Frank with a dismissive laugh. 'Beastly game. I think I'll take a turn on the terrace.'

'Don't, Dad,' said Celia quickly. 'I've got an idea.' She cast a covert look at Duggleby and swallowed. 'I wondered about table-turning.'

Mary Hawker looked up alertly. 'Table-turning, Celia? Are you serious, dear?'

'Table turning?' repeated Frank Leigh blankly. 'What, you mean all holding hands and asking "Is anybody there?" Lot of damn nonsense. There's other ways of passing the time.'

Jack caught Isabelle's eye and had to look away quickly. It was a way of passing the time that involved Celia sitting in the dark and holding hands with Leonard Duggleby, something that Isabelle had obviously figured out right away.

Celia glanced at Leonard Duggleby and flushed. 'It isn't nonsense, Dad,' she protested, turning to Mary Hawker for support. 'You don't think it's nonsense, do you?'

'Certainly not, Celia, but it mustn't be approached in a frivolous manner.'

'I'm not being frivolous,' said Celia, clasping her hands together earnestly. 'We all felt something, a feeling, a presence, call it what you like, in the cave this morning. *Is* there anything there?'

'Dash it, Celia, of course there isn't,' snorted her father.

'But if there is – well, shouldn't we find out?' She paused, tracing an arabesque with her finger around the embroidery on her dress, then looked appealingly at Duggleby. 'You must want to know more about the cave. You said as much earlier on.'

'Well, I . . .' prevaricated Duggleby, then swallowed. 'Of course I do.'

Celia smiled encouragingly. 'Come on, everyone. You'll join in, won't you, Aunt Mary? You've been to lots of séances, I know.'

Frank Leigh stared at her and Mary Hawker coloured. 'I sometimes have sittings with Deirdre and Lucia Trelawney in the village. You know the Trelawneys, Frank. Very sincere, the pair of them. I've seen some funny things,' she said gruffly. 'Odd things, I mean, that I can't explain. Everyone must have done table-turning at some time,' she said defensively.

'Yes, on a winter's afternoon when there's nothing much else to do,' agreed Frank. 'I usually take myself off with a newspaper and leave the ladies to it. Evie, what about you?'

'I suppose Evie thinks it's too stupid for words,' broke in Mary Hawker.

Evie's eyes widened. 'I'd rather you didn't decide my opinions for me, Mary, darling.' She looked at Celia as if she'd just performed some difficult party trick, then gave an unexpected laugh. 'Why not?' She looked around the room. 'Mr Wood? Are you a believer in ghosts and spirits and things that go bump in the night?'

'Me?' said Wood with a smile. 'Not really. I've done table-turning but I've never seen anything that can't be put down to shoving.'

'That would be *quite wrong*,' said Celia severely. 'I hope no one is going to shove. I want to see what we can find out about the cave.' Her eyes sparkled. 'I feel as if I've been blind. All these years I've taken it for granted and yet here, here on our very doorstep, are wonderful things waiting to be discovered.' She shot Duggleby a succulent look. 'All I needed was someone to show me the way.'

'I . . . er . . . yes,' agreed Duggleby, then added, in a worried way, 'I must confess I've never actually sat in at a séance before. What do we actually do?'

'We sit round a table and everyone holds hands. It's got to be in the dark, of course.'

'That's right,' agreed Mary Hawker. 'The spirits cannot tolerate the harsh rays of artificial light. Then, when everyone's settled, we invite a spirit guide to join us.' She cleared her throat awkwardly. 'When I sit with the Trelawneys, my guide is Anatenzel, an Aztec princess. She was betrothed against her will to an Aztec prince but she was cast out by her people when she fell in love with a Spanish Conquistador. He only pretended to love her because he thought she had vast amounts of Aztec treasure. When he found she was penniless, he cast her off and she was murdered by the prince, who was maddened by love for her. Ever since she has tried to help poor souls who might find themselves on the wrong path.'

'Gosh,' muttered Jack. He looked at Mrs Hawker with new respect. With a lurid imagination like that, she could make a packet writing for the popular magazines. He didn't know if she was a dangerous woman, as Belle had maintained, but he marvelled at the yearning for romance concealed by that gruff exterior.

'We need a table, dear,' continued Mrs Hawker, looking at Celia. 'What about the card-table?' she asked, indicating the lightweight green-baize card table.

'Can't we sit by the window?' asked Duggleby, pointing to the very solid circular oak table positioned by the bay of the window looking out onto the terrace. 'That'll do, won't it? There's more room.'

'No one will be able to shove that table around,' muttered Isabelle to Jack. 'He is new to this, isn't he?

A discussion about the relative merits of the two tables ensued.

Frank Leigh gave the casting vote to the oak table on the grounds that if he was going to engage in complete tomfoolery, he was jolly well going to sit in comfort while he did it.

'Are you joining in?' Isabelle asked Jack.

Jack clicked his tongue. 'I'm not sure. As a good Catholic I'm not meant to dabble in Spiritualism.'

Isabelle's eyes sparkled. 'You don't think there's going to be any, do you?'

'I can't say I do. What if I take notes? Although that's going to be difficult in the dark.'

Celia was appealed to. Although disappointed Jack wasn't going to join in, she suggested he sat under the small reading lamp the other side of the room from the table, where the light wouldn't disturb them.

With Celia chivvying them on, everyone sat down. Celia, predictably, was next to Duggleby but with her father on the other side, which, thought Jack, might cramp her style. Mary Hawker sat beside Frank Leigh, and Isabelle, Evie Leigh and Aloysius Wood completed the circle.

Jack turned off the lights and groped his way back across the room to where the reading lamp shone over the back of the armchair.

'Everyone put their hands on the table,' said Celia. 'Make sure you're touching the fingertips of the person next to you.' There was a certain amount of giggling. 'Dad,' complained Celia, 'you've got to keep holding hands.'

'If I want to drink my whisky and soda, my girl, that's what I'll do, spirits or no spirits.'

There was a snort of subdued laughter from Wood. 'At least we're sure of some sort of spirit.'

'Please, Mr Wood!' chided Celia. 'Be serious.'

There was silence.

Time crept on. Jack lit a surreptitious cigarette. He sat back in his chair, blew out a mouthful of smoke, then very nearly swore.

From the table came a hollow plop, the sound of dripping water, the same sound he had heard in the cave that afternoon. It was followed by another drip and then another. Jack felt the hairs on the back of his neck rise.

'Is anyone there?' asked Celia in a wavering voice.

The only sound was the drip of water.

'Are you a spirit?'

A loud crack sounded. Celia gave a nervous yelp. 'Will you answer one rap for yes and two for no?'

One rap.

'Are you Anatenzel?' asked Mary Hawker shakily.

Two raps.

'Are you –' Celia Leigh broke off and swallowed – 'are you from the cave?'

One rap.

'This yes and no business is hopeless,' complained Wood. 'Can't you go into a trance or something, Mrs Hawker? It could speak through you then.'

'I can't summon up a trance for the asking,' said Mary Hawker in a worried voice. 'We could use the alphabet, I suppose. One rap for A, two for B and so on? Major Haldean, you can keep track for us, can't you?'

'Just as you like,' said Jack, jotting down the alphabet in his notebook and numbering the letters.

'Thank you, major. Spirit of the cave! Can you speak to us through the alphabet?'

Jack counted as a quick series of raps sounded. Twenty-five, then a pause, five and another pause, then nineteen. That spelt . . . 'Yes.'

It was handy, thought Jack, that the spirit should be so conversant with modern English. Another series of raps sounded.

'Did you get that, Jack?' asked Celia.

'"Peace",' said Jack, reading his notes. '"The barrier is broken".'

It was hard, in the dim light, with the stilled hush of breathing from the group at the table and that inexplicable drip of water, to remember that this was meant to be nothing more than a parlour game.

'Who are you?' asked Celia.

More raps sounded. '"Barita",' Jack read.

'That's a girl's name,' said Duggleby. 'A Romano-British girl's name.'

More raps sounded.

'"Euthius is trapped",' read Jack. '"Free him"!'

'How do we free him?' asked Celia. 'Can I free him?'

'"No",' Jack read. '"You are not the god's choice".'

Celia gave a little cry. 'Who, then?' she demanded.

'Hold on a minute,' said Isabelle. 'Do we want Euthius to be free?'

A long series of raps sounded. '"Darkness. Trapped",' said Jack, working out the message. '"Release him. Tree. Walking tree".'

'What on earth does that mean?' asked Mary Hawker.

'"The tree must walk to the cave",' Jack read. 'I'm not sure which tree,' he added.

'You'll have to be rather more precise with your instructions,' said Mary Hawker, addressing the spirit of Barita as briskly as if it were on a committee. She was very brisk indeed, with a nervous edge to her voice. 'What are you talking about?'

'"Follow the sign".'

'What sign? We haven't got a sign.'

They waited for an answer but there was silence, broken only by the dripping of the water. As the silence lengthened, that sound, too, became more and more spaced out, then stopped.

'I think,' said Evie with a little sigh, 'the spirit has gone. How extraordinary! Turn the lights on, Frank, darling.'

As the lights came on, she pushed her chair back and, interlinking her fingers, pushed her arms straight, stretching her shoulders, then stopped abruptly, staring at Aloysius Wood's hands.

Beside her, Wood had his hands clasped lightly together on the table. An ominous red stain rimmed his knuckles.

'What's that on your hands, Wood?' asked Frank.

Wood opened his hands slowly and stared in confusion at his palms. They were stained red.

Celia started to her feet, pushing her chair over with a choking noise. 'It's blood! Can't you see? It's blood! Oh my God, it's like the cave! First there was the water and now there's blood! The next thing will be a fire!'

'Calm down, Celia,' said her father. 'Wood must've cut himself somehow, that's all. Don't get so worked up about nothing.'

'Have you cut yourself, Wood?' asked Jack, as they all crowded round.

'No, no I haven't,' he said in a bewildered voice. He looked horribly shaken. 'I felt something sticky when you – the spirit I mean – was talking about signs, but I don't know how this stuff got on my hands.'

'But what's it a sign *of*?' demanded Celia.

'Guilt,' said Mary Hawker slowly. 'Blood's usually a sign of guilt.'

Wood scrubbed at his palms with a handkerchief. 'I'm not guilty of anything. This is *creepy*.' He looked wildly at the faces round him. 'Hasn't anyone else got anything on their hands? No? Why me? What have I done?'

Frank Leigh dropped a hand on his shoulder. 'Go and wash it off, Wood,' he began, when Mary Hawker gave a sharp cry.

'Wood! That's what the spirit was talking about! A walking tree. It's a sort of ghastly joke. Mr Wood, you're the walking tree!'

Wood froze, looking down at his hands. There was a long moment, and when he spoke, his voice was quiet. 'Yes, I am, aren't I?' He lifted his head and looked at her. 'The spirit wanted a walking tree to go to the cave.' He stood up like a man in a trance. 'I'd better go.'

'Now?' said Isabelle sharply. 'You can't! It's dark.'

Wood gave her a twisted smile. 'I think the powers, whatever they are, are probably more effective in the dark, don't you?'

'For God's sake, man,' protested Frank. 'You can't do it!'

Wood looked at him, then his smile broadened. 'Why not?'

'It's a preposterous idea,' spluttered Frank.

'Why? Do you believe in ghosts?' He held up his bloodstained palms. 'Do you believe in *this*?'

'I don't know what I believe,' said Frank Leigh in a harried way. 'It's all a lot of damn nonsense. It has to be.'

'Can the spirits harm me? Not if they don't exist. If they do exist, I'd better do what they say, don't you think?'

The argument went back and forth, but Wood was absolutely determined.

In the end, Wood, accompanied by Jack and Frank Leigh, carrying an oil lamp, torches and blankets made their way across the darkened gardens, through the temple and into the cave.

Jack put the oil lamp on the old Victorian desk. The thin beam of light only seemed to make the darkness greater. At the back of the cave, beyond the reach of the light, stood, he knew, the altar of Euthius. The cave echoed with the drip of water and, after the summer night, the cold was biting. A loathing for the evil figure carved on that darkened altar twisted his stomach.

This was just *wrong*. What had started as a silly evening pastime should remain just that. They couldn't possibly have heard a message from the dead. At that moment, even if Euthius himself had spoken from the altar, Jack would have refused to believe it. And yet . . .

There had been blood on Wood's hands. That had to be explained.

Another thing he couldn't explain was Wood's frame of mind. On the one hand he spoke as if the séance had been a genuine summons from another world, on the other he seemed to think it was all a trick. Even if it was a trick, that wasn't a very comforting thought.

Mary Hawker had told Frank Leigh to get rid of Wood. She could've easily suggested the idea of a séance to Celia. If she'd done it subtly enough, Celia would've been convinced it was her own idea.

It was Mary Hawker who had identified Wood as the man selected to spend the night in the cave and the upshot was that Wood *was* spending the night in the cave. Frank Leigh had protested, but as Wood's employer and host, he could have refused his permission outright.

Frank Leigh looked at the cheerless camp-bed and shuddered. He clapped his hand on Wood's shoulder. 'For heaven's sake, man, this is crazy,' he said gruffly. 'Come back to the house.'

'Not ruddy likely,' said Wood cheerfully. 'I've been challenged and I'm going to face it.' He patted his pocket. 'I'm armed, you know, and I've got a light, a good book – it's one of yours, Haldean, as a matter of fact – and a flask of whisky. If anything happens, I'm ready for it. Now off you go and leave me to Euthius.'

He accompanied them back down the passage to the cedarwood door. 'I'm going to lock myself in,' he said, putting the key in the lock. 'That should stop anyone fooling around. See you in the morning.'

Jack and Frank Leigh stood in the temple, the cloud-broken moonlight shifting across the marble floor and columns. As they heard the key turn in the lock on the other side of the door, Leigh heaved a deep sigh. 'I hope he's all right.'

They set off down the path, the light of the torch dancing before them. It was a little time before Frank Leigh spoke again.

'I don't like it, Haldean. I don't mind telling you, that séance rattled me. There's . . .' He hesitated. 'There's too much history in Breagan Stump. What happened in that cave was real. Even though it was nearly two thousand years ago, it's real and I don't like it.'

He motioned back towards the temple. 'You asked this afternoon where the name Breagan came from. I had a tutor when I was a boy. He called himself a philologist, very keen on the origin of words. He got me to look up *Breagan*. It isn't Roman or Celtic, it's Anglo-Saxon. They knew the place was somewhere to be avoided. Breagan comes from the word *gebrégan*. I've never forgotten that word.' He paused, uncomfortably. 'It means dread or sudden terror.'

'Panic,' said Jack involuntarily. He remembered his sensations by the temple earlier in the day.

'That's right. Panic, dread, sudden terror.' He shrugged. 'It's easy enough to laugh at these things, but I don't like it.'

TWELVE

I t was odd to come out of the darkness of the garden into the brightly lit drawing room.

Evie Leigh looked at them with a worried smile. 'Is Mr Wood settled in?'

'He's as comfortable as he can be,' said Frank Leigh absently, walking over to the sideboard. He poured himself a whisky and, lighting a cigar, sat down, his chin in his hands.

'I don't think I'd ever be brave enough to spend a night in the cave,' Evie said to the company in general. '*So* uncomfortable and so chilly and damp, too.'

'I can't explain what happened this evening,' said Mary Hawker dubiously, looking up from her newspaper. 'The spirits usually send messages of comfort and reassurance.'

'He will be all right, won't he, Aunt Mary?' asked Celia. She swallowed. 'There isn't anything that could happen to him, is there?'

Isabelle got up and went to sit beside her, putting her hand comfortingly on her arm. 'Come on, Celia. Mr Wood's a grown man. He can take care of himself.'

'Exactly,' said Mary Hawker gruffly. 'You mark my words, he'll be as right as rain in the morning.' She glanced at the clock. 'It's probably too late to start a game of cards now, but there's an interesting bridge problem in the paper. Celia, my dear, come and give me a hand, will you?'

Celia reluctantly joined Mary Hawker in the pool of light cast by the standard lamp by the sofa.

'Is Mr Wood okay?' muttered Isabelle to Jack.

'He was fine when we left him,' said Jack in a low voice, sitting on the arm of her chair. He flicked a glance over to Mary Hawker. 'Any reaction?' he murmured.

Isabelle shook her head. 'Nothing much. I can't make it out, Jack. Did she set it up?'

Jack shrugged. 'Maybe.'

'It beats me,' hissed Isabelle in frustration. 'She seemed really shaken by the séance. She's been talking about bridge to take our minds off things. She said as much.' She nearly smiled. 'Leonard Duggleby lit out as fast as he could. He can't stand bridge, so he's retreated to the library.'

Mary Hawker looked over the top of her glasses to Isabelle and Jack. 'Mrs Stanton? Major Haldean? You play, don't you? What d'you think of this?'

Jack and Isabelle joined Mary Hawker and Celia Leigh on the sofa. As usual in newspaper bridge problems, the players were East, West, North and South.

'East's got adequate trump support for a raise but no ace or king so he'd better bid two no trumps on the first round. West can't possibly be thinking of a slam. What about West playing a heart lead and continuation?' asked Mrs Hawker.

'It'll be awkward for West to play in spades,' said Jack, trying to drag his mind away from Wood in the cave. Could this middle-aged, tweedy, county, bazaars and committee woman really want to murder anyone? Let alone him or Wood? It seemed incredible but Wood had taken a gun with him to the cave. What on earth was he expecting? 'He should give his partner the chance to play in clubs.'

'Exactly,' said Mary Hawker triumphantly. 'That's precisely what I would do. Would you bid six here, Major Haldean?'

'It's tempting, but I don't think so,' said Jack, forcing himself to concentrate. 'Look at East's bidding pattern. He's made a series of minimum bids. I'd say he's too weak for six.'

'I'd say the slam needs more than the club finesse,' said Celia, hesitantly. 'If the defence begins with two rounds of hearts, West's trumps are shortened to the ace and queen alone.'

'Well done, dear,' said Mrs Hawker approvingly. 'Exactly right.'

'He can't pick up South's king of clubs,' commented Isabelle, looking over Mary Hawker's shoulder. 'I can't see East has anything more to contribute.'

As the discussion went on, it was clear that someone else, as well as the fictional East, had nothing to contribute.

After half an hour listening to bridge, Evie Leigh was obviously bored to tears. She picked up a magazine, flicked through it, tossed it to one side, yawned, examined her nails, added to perfection with an emery board, looked at the clock, yawned once more and then, evidently struck by an idea, sat up straight.

'Major Haldean, I don't believe you've ever seen my sapphires?'

'I have, as a matter of fact, Mrs Leigh,' Jack said with a smile. 'I went to meet Isabelle at Charing Cross station after her adventure on the train. Inspector Rackham showed them to me.'

Evie shuddered. 'Don't! I can't bear to be reminded of that horrible affair.'

'I'd like to see them again,' said Isabelle kindly. It was perfectly obvious that Evie Leigh wanted to show off her jewels. She probably wanted to do almost anything other than talk about bridge. 'I've seen them, of course, but I couldn't really say what they looked like. All I knew was that they sparkled.'

'They certainly do,' said Evie enthusiastically. 'We've had them cleaned and re-set. They arrived back from the jeweller's today and they're simply stunning.'

'Why don't you get them?' asked Mary Hawker, putting down the newspaper and bowing to the inevitable.

'What a good idea!' said Evie, as if the thought had only just occurred to her.

She went out of the room, returning shortly afterwards with a blue leather box, but, before she undid the clasp, pursed her lips in a little petulant frown. 'Where's Mr Duggleby? He saved my sapphires. I want him here to see them. He can't still be stuck in the library, can he? Go and get him, Frank.'

When they were all assembled, Evie put the box on the table and opened it with a little, happy sigh.

'Good Lord,' said Jack in involuntary admiration as he gazed at the sapphires on their ivory silk background. Gone was the heavy gold elaborately ornamented surround. Instead was a sleek, streamlined necklace where the sapphires, framed by diamond chips, shone deep blue against white gold.

'They're beautiful,' said Evie Leigh, stroking her hand over the jewels. 'Seddon and Coles have the most marvellous little man who's an absolute genius with jewels. Truly sympathetic. I told him what I wanted and he drew the most perfect design right away. I said he was a positive mind reader, didn't I, Frank?

I added a few touches of my own, and here we are.' She stroked her hand over the necklace once more and sighed happily.

With Evie's permission, Mary Hawker reached out and picked up the necklace. 'It's very fine,' she said with grudging respect. 'Remarkable. It's just a pity to think of the circumstances, though.'

Evie Leigh looked puzzled.

'Mrs Paxton,' said Mary Hawker heavily. 'To say nothing of that poor fellow on the train.'

'Sapphires are often thought to be unlucky,' said Duggleby chattily. 'I don't know why. In medieval times they were meant to protect their wearers from evil. The ancient Greeks thought the sapphire, the colour of the sky, was the gem of Apollo, the god of the sun.'

'They certainly are beautiful,' said Jack, taking them from Mary Hawker. He turned his back so the light shone on them. 'They look very different now they've been re-set.'

'The setting's made a huge difference,' said Duggleby. 'I'd have never recognised them as the same stones I found on the train.' He held out his hand and, with a nod from Evie Leigh, Jack passed them to him.

'Absolutely wonderful,' said Duggleby, but his voice was puzzled. He weighed the necklace in his hands and, as he did so, his forehead creased in a frown. 'They even feel different to the stones I saw.'

Duggleby turned to the standard lamp to look at the necklace better, his back to the room. He held the sapphires up to the light and then, very quickly, held the necklace up to his mouth. Jack saw his shoulders grow rigid. 'Mrs Leigh,' he said in a strained voice, 'these stones are fake.'

Evie gaped at him.

'Fake?' repeated Frank Leigh brusquely. 'What the devil d'you mean?'

Duggleby swallowed hard. 'They're fake.' There was no doubting his sincerity or his shock.

'Absolute poppycock!' snarled Frank Leigh.

Evie Leigh reached out to Duggleby, staring into his eyes. 'Are you sure?' He nodded dumbly. She gave a little hissing cry, then clasped her hands to her mouth, her eyes wide.

'Why do you think they're fake?' demanded Jack, raising his voice over Frank Leigh's protests.

'They feel wrong,' said Duggleby. 'They look all right but they're all wrong. They're warm when you put them to your lips. Real stones are cold. These are nothing but paste.'

'I think you're taking a dickens of a lot upon yourself, young man,' said Frank Leigh. 'Those stones aren't fake.'

Evie reached out for the necklace like someone in a trance. 'Fake?' Duggleby nodded once more. Evie was suddenly galvanised into life. '*Fake!*' she screeched. 'My necklace has been stolen! Stolen, I tell you! Stolen by somebody in this house.' She rounded on Celia. 'Was it you?'

'Evie!' protested Frank, shocked.

'I . . . I never . . .' stammered Celia.

'You wanted them. You thought they should be yours.'

'So what?' bit back Celia. 'It's the truth. That will of Aunt Constance's was *wicked*. The sapphires should be mine, but I didn't steal them.' She drew back her shoulders and met her stepmother's eyes with cold dignity. Jack had rarely admired her more than he did at that moment. 'I'm no thief. Besides that,' she added, rather spoiling the effect, 'I wouldn't know how to steal them, even if I wanted to.'

Evie looked at her icily. 'You could have arranged things with the jewellers.'

'For heaven's sake, Evie, stop this nonsense now!' roared Frank Leigh. 'Those jewels are real.' He glared at Duggleby. 'Duggleby's made a mistake, that's all. An honest mistake, I don't doubt, but a mistake all the same.'

Mary Hawker cleared her throat. 'Could Mrs Paxton have sold the originals and had paste copies made? That's easier to believe than any of us could've stolen them.'

'Sorry, Mrs Hawker,' said Jack. 'It's not a bad idea but it's a wash-out, I'm afraid. Inspector Rackham had the necklace valued after it was found on the train. Those stones were the real McCoy.'

'Of course they were,' snapped Evie, gripping the back of the chair. '*My sapphires have been stolen!* Someone's guilty.'

Celia put her hand to her mouth with a cry. 'Guilty!' She stared at Mrs Hawker. 'You said blood meant guilt, didn't you? That's what the blood meant, the blood on Mr Wood's hands.

That's what the spirit was telling us. Mr Wood's guilty. He's guilty of stealing the sapphires.'

'For heaven's sake,' thundered Frank Leigh. 'No one's guilty of stealing *anything*. I'm damned if I going to let a man be accused because of some tom-fool jiggery-pokery. Celia, you ought to be ashamed of yourself!'

Celia faced her father, her chin very determined. 'Dad, please! Who is Mr Wood? We know nothing about him.'

'He's my guest,' said Frank Leigh, speaking very stiffly. 'He might be an employee, but he's my guest and I will not have him accused in this disgraceful fashion, especially when he's not here to defend himself.'

'Then I'll go and fetch him,' said Celia.

'I'll come with you,' said Jack quickly.

'So will I,' offered Isabelle.

'No,' said Evie quickly. 'We need the police. Leave Wood exactly where he is until they arrive. Celia, stay where you are.'

'I'll go exactly where I please,' said Celia in a dangerous voice.

Evie Leigh turned to her husband. 'Frank! We need the police.'

Frank Leigh bristled with fury. 'Of course we don't. Those stones are real and that's the end of it. You go and fetch Wood if you like, Celia. I'll have no more of this damned nonsense.'

'I'm going,' said Celia abruptly. 'You say Wood locked himself in, Dad? I'll take the spare key.'

Ignoring the row that was breaking out between Evie and her father, she turned and marched out of the room, Isabelle and Jack following.

'Can you *believe* that woman?' said Celia through gritted teeth, as she seized the key from the study drawer and led the way out of the house. 'Imagine Evie telling me – me! – I took her sapphires. How dare she! It's obvious Wood's guilty.'

'Why are you so certain?' asked Jack.

'Who else can it be?' demanded Celia rhetorically, storming off across the lawn.

'She's right, you know,' said Isabelle to Jack as they hurried after her. 'There simply isn't anyone else. I don't know what Mrs Hawker's up to, but I can't see her stealing jewels. The only other stranger is Mr Duggleby and it can't be him, surely?'

'No, it can't,' agreed Jack. 'He was knocked sideways when he realised the stones were false. He wasn't pretending, I'd swear to it.'

'Jack, could Wood have arranged the séance, d'you think? He might want the time to escape.'

'Maybe,' said Jack doubtfully. 'I can't see why, though. He could've pushed off just as easily after we'd all gone to bed. Buck up, Belle. I don't want Celia facing Wood alone.'

They caught up with Celia as she reached the slope up to the temple. Celia had retreated into soundless fury. Jack and Isabelle swapped glances and decided against saying anything.

Her heels clicking on the white stone floor of the temple, Celia strode across to the cedarwood door, when Jack caught her arm.

'Wait a minute!' He sniffed the air. 'Can't you smell something?'

'It's smoke,' said Isabelle. She stepped back from the cedarwood door in alarm. 'It's coming under the door.'

'Fire!' said Celia, her voice a gasp. 'I knew it! We were warned in the séance! It's a fire!'

Jack took the key and, unlocking the door, pushed it open.

A haze of acrid wood smoke billowed out at them and, from deep within the smoky darkness, came the crackle and hiss of fire.

Jack stepped back involuntarily, coughing. Already the columns of the temple, bright in the moonlight, looked as if they were clutched by fingers of drifting mist.

He seized a torch from the tin box under the bench and shone it down the passage. The passage was full of billowing, shifting smoke, reflecting the torchlight back in grey clouds.

For a few fractions of a second, Jack hesitated. Was Wood in the cave? Could he really have stolen the sapphires and started the fire to cover his getaway? He shook his head impatiently.

'Stay there, girls,' he called and, eyes throbbing from the smoke, plunged in. If Wood isn't in here, I'll kill him, he thought grimly.

He couldn't see a thing. His torchlight showed only shifting grey masses of smoke. He reached out and found the rocky wall by touch, then groped his way forward until he reached the spring. He cupped some water in his hands and splashed his face, feeling the instant relief to his eyes. He soaked his handkerchief in the water and, tying it round his mouth and nose, stumbled forward.

A dull flicker of flame reflected on the rocky walls beyond. A few steps more, then the smoke eddied and he had a brief glimpse of the entrance to the cave. As he saw it, he felt and heard it, a wall of black and red heat, deafening him with the crackle and tear of fire.

The wooden beams at the entrance were on fire. In the smoke-filled light of the leaping flames, he saw some of the beams had collapsed. He fell back as another beam fell, sending up shrapnel of burning embers.

There was nothing he could do. The entrance was completely blocked.

He stumbled his way back along the passage, lungs bursting for air. He staggered rather than walked back out into the temple. He saw Isabelle and Celia, their faces white and frightened in the moonlight, then sank onto the marble floor, chest heaving. The open air, smoke-laden as it was, felt wonderful.

Isabelle put an arm round his shoulders. 'Jack?'

Jack shook his head wearily and slowly got to his knees. 'The entrance is gone,' he managed to say between fits of coughing. 'Can't get through.' He sat back then, with Isabelle's help, hauled himself onto one of the marble benches. 'Whew!'

He buried his face in his hands, thinking furiously. 'Celia, is there another way into the cave?'

She shook her head. 'No, there isn't.'

There had to be a way. There was something Frank Leigh had said . . . That was it!

'What about the spring? Your father said there was a well. If I climb down the well, can I get into the cave along the stream?'

Her eyes widened. 'I suppose so, but . . .'

'Jack, you can't!' protested Isabelle.

'I've got to try. Belle, get back to the house as quick as you can. We need help. Please, Belle, hurry!'

Isabelle looked at his determined face, then turned on her heel and ran.

Jack looked at Celia. 'Show me the way. Come on!'

With Celia leading, they plunged into the woods behind the temple, scrambling their way down the rough path, so the mound of Breagan Stump lay between them and the house, coming out onto a darkened, tree-shadowed lawn. The well was in the shadows of the trees, a low, circular, brick-built wall over which stood the roof, pulley and winding gear.

Holding onto the roof of the well, Jack climbed on the wall, shining the torch into the uninviting blackness. He could hear the hollow gurgle of water from far below.

'You can't do it, Jack,' said Celia. 'It's crazy.'

Jack shushed her impatiently. 'Let me think.'

He made a mental note of the direction of the cave from the well. As the stream flowed it would be what? Two hundred yards? Three? About that.

The bucket, a stout wooden construction, was attached to a hook. He glanced at the pulley. There was a ratchet – you'd need that to draw the heavy bucket full of water up from the depths – but he didn't fancy trusting himself to it. If the ratchet broke while he was descending, clinging onto the rope, he'd be hurled to his death.

No. He climbed down and released the ratchet. The spindle whirled, the rope paid out and the bucket creaked down and then splashed into the dark circle of water far below.

'You can't go down there,' said Celia, her voice wavering with fright.

He seized the rope in both hands, pulled it out to its furthest extent and grinned encouragingly at her. 'I'll be fine!'

He swung himself over the well and started to climb down.

'I'm still fine!' he called with a cheerfulness he certainly didn't feel to the anxious face peering down at him.

He wasn't fine, exactly, but the rope was thick and gave a good handhold. He only wished he was wearing rubber soled-shoes with a proper grip, not his dress shoes with their smooth leather soles.

The well must have been forty feet deep. He came to the surface of the water and looked up once more at the dim circle of starlight above his head.

'Here goes!' he shouted. Keeping firm hold of the rope, he let himself down into the water. It came over his knees and was bitterly cold, but the bed of the stream, although uneven, was firm, scoured by the swiftly flowing water.

On either side of him were the rough semicircles of the tunnel, glistening with damp in the torchlight. The passage was about four feet high and he had to go against the flow of the stream.

The water flowing past him was unbelievably cold but his main fear, that the tunnel would become too low for him to get through, was unjustified. It had been cut from the chalk, earth and clay before the Georgians had changed its course and could have taken a far greater volume of water. He had to squeeze round tree roots, over stones and cover a lot of ground crawling forward on his stomach, his torch rammed into his coat collar, but it was never impassable.

A haze of eye-stinging smoke on the rippling water told him he was nearly there. He took precious seconds to tie his handkerchief round his face before crawling forward once more, then he crawled into a bank of thick, choking smoke.

His torch, which had showed gleaming stone, dull clay and hanging roots, showed nothing but moving greyness. He shut his eyes and managed to breathe by keeping his face close to the numbing coldness of the water.

The smoke thinned and, with a surging sense of relief, he reached out to touch the roof above his head. His hand met empty air. He was out of the tunnel! In a few moments he heaved himself out into the cave and stood upright.

The heat was ferocious. At the entrance of the cave, looming through the grey shifting smoke, the fallen beams of the entrance glowed red beneath the black of the mass of charred timbers. He tried to call Wood's name but was racked by a fit of coughing.

The smoke was thinner near the ground and he dropped to his knees. With the altar behind him, he kept close to the ground, half-crouching, half-crawling into the cave. There was a creak and a crash and another roof timber split and fell, sending up showers of brilliant embers.

The smoke eddied and for a few precious seconds the torchlight picked out the huddled body of a man lying face-down, one arm outstretched.

There he was! Wood was lying at the side of the cave, near the wooden grave-markers.

Jack felt a surge of relief. He hadn't realised, until that moment, how the thought that Wood might not be in the cave had wormed away at his courage.

He flung himself across the floor of the cave, but before he could reach Wood, the smoke billowed in again and he was blinded once more. On his hands and knees and working by touch alone, he managed to find Wood's body. He reached out and, finding Wood's neck more by luck than judgement, felt the faint flutter of life in his throat. Retching for breath, he put his hands under the man's shoulders and heaved him across the floor. Above him, there was a hideous creaking and a dull haze of flame. An ominous rain of burning splinters scattered the ground. Another timber was going!

Grunting slightly, with Wood a dead weight in his arms, he came away from the wall, keeping his elbow against the rock for guidance. His knee went from under him and he fell awkwardly to one side. He'd knelt on the charred wooden covers of the old graves and they had crumbled under his weight. He jerked himself back onto the solid floor of the cave, then stopped, an ice-cold finger of fear on his spine.

There was a body in the grave.

THIRTEEN

With a yell, Jack staggered backwards. He couldn't help it but it was the worst thing he could have done. He missed his footing completely, rolling against the upright timber supporting the roof beam. The shower of brilliant embers became a rain.

With strength born of complete desperation, Jack grabbed hold of Wood. He hauled him against the rocky wall and, sheltering him with his body, flattened himself against the stones as, with a sound as if a giant had ripped a canvas sail, the beam collapsed.

The sound seemed to go on forever. With what seemed like complete detachment, Jack heard the hiss and smelt the singeing of cloth as the shards of burning timber caught at his sodden clothes.

Then, at long last, came silence. In the black, fire-speckled darkness of the cave, he wasn't sure if it was deafness or absence of noise. There was an incredible pressure on the small of his back. He moved slightly and the scrape of his shoe against rock reassured him. Other noises started to filter in. More creaking and snapping, more hissing and crackling as the fire licked lazily around what was left of the wood in the cave.

With the side of his face pressed hard against the gritty roughness of the rock, Jack really only knew he was alive. That seemed to take up all his thoughts, but he knew he must think. It seemed very hard to join ideas together. He had to get out, to get away from falling timbers. There were no timbers over the spring. He had to take Wood to the spring.

Wearily he dug his elbows into the ground, to drag himself out from under the fallen earth and timber. He couldn't move! Keeping his rising fear screwed down, he tried again. The pressure in his back jagged into white splinters of pain. Again he tried, and again the pain flared. A paroxysm of coughing shook him. Exhausted, he lay still, gulping the smoke-filled air.

There was silence, broken by the occasional sharp crack and flump of falling burnt wood, the high, cold sound of the spring and the rasp of his breathing.

With gritted teeth he tried a third time and fell back, chest heaving with the effort. He stretched his arms wide in front of him and tried to pull himself free, but even though the muscles in his arms and shoulders were rigid with effort, he couldn't move.

He craned his neck – it was horribly awkward – trying to see over his shoulder. The fire had died down, with just the odd spurt of flame flaring from the fallen timbers. The blinding whiteness of the fire faded to a steady glow of red under the blackness. The roof timber had fallen across the mound of earth and rubble, pinning him down. He could see the long streak of red, segmented into squares of blackened ash. His stomach turned over. The fire was advancing up the timber, inch by lazy, lethal, inch and there was absolutely nothing he could do. When that red streak reached him and Wood, they would be slowly burned to death. It was as simple and brutal as that.

Maybe it was the pain from his back or the despair that

gripped him, but Jack felt himself drifting away. He knew Wood lay beside him, completely unconscious, and could feel the rock and grit of the earthen floor against his face, but for what must have been minutes, he was incapable of action. He shook his head, trying to bring himself round and snatched another glance over his shoulder. The fire had advanced visibly along the beam.

The sound of the spring was tantalizingly close. He could really do with a drink. Instantly his thirst raged and he cursed himself for thinking of water, so close and yet so utterly out of reach. He couldn't think of anything but the splash and gurgle of the stream. It sounded almost human . . .

He raised his head, listening intently. It wasn't the spring! Very faintly and from far away came the distant sounds of muffled voices. He couldn't make out the words but thought he heard his name. He tried to call back but his voice cracked dismally.

Rescuers were digging their way through the blocked entrance. They'd have all the men from the estate going full tilt, trying to break through. He took another look behind him. Although the men didn't know it, they were in a race with that streak of red advancing up the wooden beam.

He didn't think they'd make it.

It was bloody ironic, to have them within calling distance and not be able to call; to have the spring so close and not be able to drink.

His eyes narrowed. There was a fleeting light on the water. He gazed at the stream, seeing the slanting light catch the dark ripples. What on earth?

Torchlight! It had to be torchlight! There was someone coming along the passage from the well!

Hope rushed through him in a tidal wave. He raised himself on his elbows, steadied himself and, with a huge effort, called out. His voice came out as a rusty croak, but it got a response.

The light steadied. 'Haldean? Is that you, Haldean?'

It was Frank Leigh. Frank Leigh, thought Jack with a jolt of fear, had talked about murder with Mary Hawker. Was that why Leigh had followed him into the cave? He desperately tried to move, but he was completely helpless.

There was a slushing sound from the spring as rocks and

pebbles were disturbed, then, torch in hand, Frank Leigh emerged into the cave.

Jack blinked, shying away from the dazzling light in his hand. Frank Leigh dropped to his knees beside him, his breath coming in great gulps. The torchlight showed Wood, slumped against the wall. Leigh reached and touched Wood's face, then dropped his head in relief as he felt the warmth of life on his skin.

'Are you all right?'

Jack couldn't answer. Frank Leigh stood up, shining the torch along the heap of rubble and wood. 'I see what the trouble is. Hold on. I think I can shift it.'

Leigh stripped off his sodden coat and, wrapping it round his hands, took one end of the beam and heaved.

The beam, weakened by the fire, splintered into two, and Jack felt the pressure on his back lighten. He reached out his hands and Frank Leigh took him under the shoulders and pulled. Jack felt himself move and, with the new freedom, dug his foot into the earth behind, adding his strength to Leigh's. Frank Leigh heaved again and this time Jack was able to scramble free.

Jack crawled to the stream and plunged his face into the icy water, taking great gulps of the shallow water. It was, perhaps, one of the very best moments of his life.

He didn't want to move, but Frank Leigh slipped his arms under his shoulders again. 'Come on. Let me get you across the spring. We'll be safe on the other side.'

With Leigh's help, Jack stumbled through the water and collapsed against the rocky wall. Beside him, Frank Leigh knelt beside the unconscious Wood, wiping his face with a handkerchief he wrung out in the stream. Wood groaned briefly, then relapsed into unconsciousness.

'He's taken quite a battering,' Leigh said. 'Thank God he's still alive.'

He stood up and shone the torch round the cave, face contorting as he saw the mound of mud, earth and fallen timbers blocking the entrance.

He laid a hand on Jack's shoulder. 'You got him out of that?' Jack nodded. Frank Leigh's hand tightened briefly on his shoulder. He felt in his pocket and brought out a hip flask, helping Jack to drink.

'We're safe now,' said Leigh. 'My men are digging their way in and the fire brigade is on its way. All we can do is wait.'

Jack felt the brandy sting his throat, then utter exhaustion claimed him and he fell asleep.

He awoke as a light shone in his face. A fireman was kneeling by him, shaking his shoulder. 'Come on, son, let's get you out of here.' He helped him stand up. 'Easy does it. Nothing broken? Good lad.'

The men had cleared a hole through the rubble at the entrance. Dimly, he heard the sound of a ragged cheer as he was helped through the rubble. It was wonderful to see their faces and hear their kindly, concerned voices as he crawled through the passage, stood upright and walked out into the open once more. It was daylight outside, the strong early morning sun blinding against the marble white of the temple.

Isabelle, her face drawn with anxiety, ran to him and buried her face into his shoulder. 'Jack! Thank God you're safe.'

He was so tired he could hardly stand.

'Leave him to us, miss,' said a fireman beside him. 'He needs to get to bed and see a doctor too, I shouldn't wonder. He'll be all right now.'

'Mr Leigh,' Jack managed to say. 'He saved us. Wood and me.' He couldn't think why, exactly, but it seemed very important that Isabelle should know what Frank Leigh had done. 'Leigh saved us. Good man.'

'Don't you worry, sir,' said the fireman comfortingly. 'He'll get the credit he's due. Let's get you back to the house.'

He had a hazy, chopped-up vision of sunlit lawns, the oak hall and staircase of the house and then, without knowing quite how he got there, there was the coolness of linen sheets next to his skin and he slept.

It was eleven o'clock in the morning. Jack, after a long sleep and a very welcome late breakfast served on a tray in bed, was submitting, with strained patience, to Doctor Sutton's ministrations.

'Hmm. There's some bruising on your back . . .'

'You're telling me!' said Jack with feeling, as the doctor's firm fingers explored the small of his back. 'Easy with that rib! I had half of Sussex fall on top of it.'

'It didn't do you any lasting harm,' said the doctor with a grin. 'You've got a good few cuts, bumps and grazes, but all in all, you'll live. Here, let me help you sit up.'

'How's Wood?' asked Jack, once he was propped up against the pillows.

'Well, like you, he'll be a bit stiff and sore for a few days, but there's nothing that won't cure. From what I've heard, it was lucky for him that you got to him in time.'

'And lucky for both of us that Mr Leigh arrived when he did.'

'Exactly,' said Doctor Sutton, fastening up his bag. 'I'll leave you to your visitors, Major Haldean. You've got some people who are very anxious to see you.'

He opened the door and ushered in Isabelle and, unexpectedly, Superintendent Edward Ashley.

'My word, Haldean,' said Ashley, 'you look a great deal better than I expected, after hearing what Mrs Stanton had to say on the telephone.'

He brought the fireside chairs over to the bed for himself and Isabelle. 'We got the report of the fire first thing. As soon as I heard what it was and where it was, I was prepared to bet my pension you'd be involved in it somehow. Then, of course, Mrs Stanton rang and told me what had happened. No sooner had I put the telephone down from you, Mrs Stanton, I had a note to call on Mrs Leigh double quick and pronto, as her sapphires had been stolen.'

'And have you seen her?'

'Of course.' He shrugged. 'I don't know if the jewels have been stolen or not. That chap Duggleby seems convinced they're fake but what the truth of the matter is, is more than I can tell, so I've called in some help. There's a jeweller in Lewes, a chap called Bloomenfield, who's helped me out a couple of times before. He owned a shop in Hatton Garden before he retired. I've sent him a wire and he's promised to call in and give us his expert opinion.'

'Well, that should clear that up, anyway,' said Jack.

'Only if the jewels are real. If they've been stolen, how the dickens was it done? Mrs Leigh looked at them when they arrived from the jewellers yesterday, then locked them away securely in the safe.'

'If it's the safe in the study, it's been bust before.'

'True. If they have been stolen, the thief has to be someone in the house. With the sole exception of Mrs Hawker, everyone who was here yesterday is still on the premises, and even she's expected to call later on, so Mrs Leigh's agreed to sit it out until Mr Bloomenfield's had his say. She's not happy, though.'

'Does Mr Leigh know about this jeweller chappie coming?'

Ashley shook his head. 'Not from me, he doesn't. They're not his sapphires. And, after hearing what Mrs Stanton had to say, I'm a bit leery of Mr Leigh.'

'I told Mr Ashley about the séance,' said Isabelle. 'And what I heard Mr Leigh and Mrs Hawker say in the gallery. I can't understand it.' She shuddered. 'I can't tell you how creepy the séance was, Mr Ashley.'

'It seems very odd altogether,' said Ashley. 'I've been asking around and there's no end of stories about Breagan Stump.' He scratched his chin distractedly. 'The local lads – and you'd say they were ordinary, sensible police officers who'd laugh at the idea of ghosts and suchlike – said to a man they wouldn't spend a night in Breagan Stump, not if you offered them a hundred pounds.'

'I just don't know,' said Jack. 'If it was a trick, it's hard to see what anyone would get out of it.'

'Come on, Jack,' said Isabelle. She glanced behind her to see that the bedroom door was firmly shut. 'After what I heard Mrs Hawker and Mr Leigh say? Mrs Hawker was out to get you and Wood as well.'

'In that case, why did Mr Leigh turn up when he did? He saved my life and Wood's, Belle. There's no two ways about that.'

'Are you sure you didn't get the wrong end of the stick, Mrs Stanton?' suggested Ashley.

Isabelle shook her head. 'I don't see how I could've done.'

Ashley sucked his cheeks in thoughtfully. 'Who suggested the séance? Mrs Hawker?'

'As a matter of fact, it wasn't,' said Isabelle. 'It was Celia, who you'd think would be the last person to suggest holding a séance.'

'Why did she do it, then?'

'I honestly thought it was because she's been making sheep's eyes at Leonard Duggleby.' She grinned. 'I suppose she's a bit too old for Postman's Knock, but it's much the same idea, isn't it? Duggleby's the resident expert on that beastly cave and everything in it and Celia wanted to call up the spirits of the cave. She couldn't give tuppence about the cave before Duggleby came along.'

Ashley raised his eyebrows. 'Leonard Duggleby? He's an odd sort for a lady like Miss Leigh to take a fancy to.'

Isabelle shook her head. 'Jack couldn't see it either, but he *is* attractive.' Jack and Ashley swapped baffled glances. 'I don't suppose it'll come to anything,' she added. 'Anyway, that's all by the way. Celia suggested the séance but Mrs Hawker was very quick to back her up.'

'Nobody really objected, Belle,' said Jack. 'Mr Leigh had to be cajoled, but he took part. The thing is, Ashley, Celia Leigh could easily have the idea of a séance suggested to her and believe it was her own idea. But as regards Mr Leigh, I'll say it again. If it wasn't for him, both Wood and I would be goners by now.'

'He was desperate when he realised that Wood was stuck in the cave,' agreed Isabelle. 'When he found out what you'd done, he was determined to follow you in case you needed help.'

'Thank God he did,' said Jack fervently. 'I was pinned down like a butterfly on a card. Like an idiot, I blundered into the prop holding up the roof and brought it all tumbling down . . .' He stopped and Isabelle saw his face change.

'Jack? What is it?' she said urgently. 'You look awful. Shall I get the doctor?'

He waved her silent. 'No, it's not that.' He struggled further upright in the bed. 'Oh, my God, Belle, I've just remembered *why* I blundered into the prop. I yelled my head off and jumped six feet. There was a body, a body in the grave.'

'*What?*' exclaimed Ashley. 'Which grave?'

'One of the graves that had human sacrifices in them.'

'*Human sacrifices?*' repeated Ashley in a stunned voice. His eyebrows crawled upwards. 'I beg your pardon? What's been going on?'

'Nothing recently,' said Jack with a laugh. Ashley looked so completely at sea he couldn't help it. 'That ghastly god had human sacrifices made to it and a Victorian vicar, who excavated the caves, found the poor beggars in shallow graves in the cave and re-buried them in the churchyard. He marked where they'd been with wooden covers. The wood must've been affected by the fire, because when I knelt on one, it crumbled underneath me. There was a body in the grave. It gave me no end of a fright, I can tell you.'

'But this is incredible,' said Ashley. 'Are you sure it was a body?'

Jack nodded. 'It was a body, certainly, but, what with one thing and another, such as having the ruddy roof cave on me, I couldn't make what you might call a thoughtful or prolonged examination of the evidence. I was rather more concerned with my own affairs at that point – and for some considerable time afterwards.'

'I'd better get onto this right away,' said Ashley. 'By the stars, Haldean, you don't half live. It's just one thing after another. Inspector Rackham's on his way. I'm going to meet him off the quarter-to-two train. If you're going to turn up unexpected bodies, it's probably just as well.'

'Why's Bill coming?' asked Jack.

'I'm not sure. He didn't want to go into details on the telephone, but it's something to do with Wood.'

'I wonder what?' asked Isabelle. 'There's something very odd about Wood. He doesn't act like a private detective.'

'You've got so much experience of private detectives, of course,' murmured Jack.

'Well, he doesn't. He acts as if he was one of the house party, not as if he was an employee at all.'

'How d'you mean, Mrs Stanton?' asked Ashley. 'You mean he acts as if he owns the place, perhaps? A bit cocky?'

'No, it's not like that at all.' Isabelle shook her head in irritation. 'He just *fits in*.' She sighed and looked at Jack for support. 'You know what I mean, don't you?'

'Yes, I do. He told me he wouldn't have done this sort of job before the war. Maybe it's that.'

'Maybe,' said Isabelle, twisting the silk of the bedspread between her fingers. 'I thought Mr Wood might be Terence Napier in disguise, but you don't think that's on the cards, do you, Jack?'

'No, I don't.'

'I can't see that's possible,' said Ashley. 'Dr and Mrs Mountford spoke to him at some length in Topfordham. Mrs Mountford told us all about it. She's a noticing sort of woman and the doctor's nobody's fool. They'd have recognised him, even if he was in disguise.' He sighed heavily. 'I wish I knew what the devil was going on. Your escapades in the cave have taken centre-stage, Haldean, but now there's a body to think about as well as those ruddy jewels. What I can't make out is this danger you're meant to be up against. Going off what Mrs Stanton overheard, it sounds as if Mrs Hawker's gunning for you, but why? What have you done to her?'

'It's because Jack's a danger to Mr Leigh,' said Isabelle promptly. 'She said Mr Leigh had committed a murder and she's scared Jack'll find out about it.' She coloured slightly. 'I know I was eavesdropping, but there was no denying how Mrs Hawker feels about Frank Leigh. She's desperate he doesn't come to harm.'

'In one way it seems to have worked out,' said Jack. 'Cue the séance, Wood goes off to spend the night in the cave, and the rest we know. Only we don't know, because Mr Leigh came to the rescue. If he'd wanted to kill me, it would have been easy enough to knock me on the head and let nature take its course. I couldn't have stopped him and Wood was unconscious. He'll never have a better chance.'

'I'm blessed if I know what to make of it,' said Ashley. 'However, the fact you've found a body, Haldean, makes the idea of murder that much more credible. Did he actually say, *I've committed a murder*, Mrs Stanton?'

'More or less. Mrs Hawker said words to the effect of, *this is murder we're talking about. I don't blame you, but this is murder*, and he sort of gulped at her and said he didn't know she knew.'

Ashley shook his head, bewildered. 'None of it makes sense. There's one thing for sure though, we need to find that body in the cave. That's solid evidence. Then, if Mrs Hawker knows so much about murder, maybe she can give us an explanation.'

'I'll get up,' said Jack. 'I can't imagine what the cave's like after the fire, but I can show you where I found the body.'

'Are you sure?' asked Ashley. 'I don't want you suffering a relapse.'

'I'll be fine,' said Jack, which was near enough the truth for his conscience not to be troubled. 'Besides that, I want to be up and doing when Bill Rackham arrives.'

FOURTEEN

The path up to the temple had been carpeted with lush green moss. Now it was rutted with churned-up ridges of mud and innumerable scars of boots, all bearing witness to the frantic struggles of the night before. The smell of damp, fire-ravaged timber hit them in a dismal wave as they went through the cedarwood door in the temple.

'I see this part of the cave is more or less untouched,' said Jack, as they splashed past the carving of Euthius weeping his tears into the stream. 'I couldn't see a thing last night, the smoke was so thick.' He shone his torch at the carvings of *dendrophori*. 'There's a fair old bit of soot, but that should clean off.'

There were lights and voices up ahead. Four men, gardeners from the estate, armed with spades, picks, buckets and a wheelbarrow, were clearing the rubble from the entrance.

'Morning,' called Jack cheerily, as they approached. 'My word, you've got your work cut out here and no mistake.' He pulled out his cigarette case and offered it round.

Nothing loath, the men rested on their spades. 'Are you the gentleman who was pulled out of the cave last night, sir? The one who climbed down the well?' asked one of the gardeners, a grizzled, older man in a moleskin waistcoat. Jack nodded.

The men exchanged looks. 'It's more'n I'd care to do, and no mistake,' said the gardener. 'I said as much to Sam, here.' He nodded at a younger man in earth-spattered corduroy who smiled bashfully. 'We never thought as our old well' ud come in so handy.'

Jack stepped back and looked at the entrance. The men had made an uneven gap about five foot high and three foot wide in the mound of earth and rubble. 'This must have taken some clearing. Have you been at it long?'

'Since nine or thereabouts. Excuse me, gentlemen, but were you wanting to go in the cave?'

'We were, actually.'

The men looked at each other dubiously. 'I don't know about that, sir. Mr Leigh said nobody was allowed in. He was worried about the roof collapsing, you see.'

'That's all right,' said Ashley. 'I'm a police officer. This is official business.'

The men looked at each other and shrugged. 'Mind your heads, then,' said the man in corduroy. 'There's a fair old bit of timber down in there.' He reached out his hand to help Isabelle over the rubble. 'Up you come, miss. Watch your step.'

With her torch as a guide, Isabelle picked her way through the entrance and into the cave, Jack and Ashley close behind.

The light of their torches showed the bulk of the damage was beside the entrance and up the far side of the cave, where the fire had burnt away the timber props of the roof and walls. Jack winced as he saw the mound of rubble he had been trapped under.

Ashley made his way across the stream and directed his torch at the soot-blackened altar. 'It's enough to give you nightmares,' he said with feeling. 'I'm not surprised there's so many tales about Breagan Stump, with that thing in the middle of it. Who the devil is it meant to be?'

'I imagine it is more or less meant to be the devil,' said Jack. 'According to Duggleby, it's a British god called Euthius from late-ish on in Roman times. The Reverend Throckmorton, the Victorian vicar he quotes endlessly, thinks Euthius was the god of an anti-Christian cult.'

'I wouldn't expect to see his picture on a Christmas card, that's for sure,' said Ashley. 'And that ghastly thing had human sacrifices made to it?'

'He nearly had a couple more chalked up to him last night.'

Isabelle shuddered and Jack squeezed her arm comfortingly. 'Come on. Let's see what we can turn up.' He shone his torch at the roof. 'I think everything that was going to fall has fallen already, but we'd better not make any sudden noises.'

They picked their way across the uneven ground. The remains

of a roof timber, charred and hollow with white ash, lay scattered across the shallow depressions of the graves.

'There were six graves in all,' said Jack. 'Six grave covers, anyway.' He crouched down and shone his torch along the ground. 'The covers have mostly burned away but there's a rim of wood round the edges.' He reached out and the wood crumbled to ashes in his hand.

'Are you sure there were six graves?' asked Isabelle. 'I can only see five.'

'One's under the rubble, Mrs Stanton,' said Ashley. 'I can see the edge of it. Haldean, where were you when you found the body?'

Jack stood up and, with his torch, picked out the broken beam which had pinned him to the ground. Looking behind him, he took a few paces backwards. 'This is the place. Which means,' he added, directing the light downwards, 'the grave in question should be . . . here!'

They crowded round. The depression in the earth was filled with ash and scattered earth, but nothing else.

'It'll be one of the others, I daresay, Haldean,' said Ashley. 'You probably mistook the place, and no wonder, on top of everything else that was going on.'

They carefully searched through the rest of the uncovered graves. They found a great deal of ash but nothing else.

Ashley rocked back on his heels. 'Haldean, you can see for yourself there's nothing here. Could you have imagined it?'

'No, I couldn't. I admit I didn't stand and gaze at the thing, but there was a body in the grave, all right.'

Ashley ran his hand round his chin. 'It wasn't a skeleton, was it? I'm wondering if it was an ancient body that this Victorian vicar overlooked somehow. If they were old bones, they might have been burned in the fire and be mixed up with all this ash.'

'It wasn't a skeleton. I knelt on the thing and it was, if you'll pardon the expression, all squishy.'

'Then where the deuce is it?' said Ashley, getting to his feet. 'It'll be difficult to get the chief constable to take any action if we haven't got any evidence to show him. He can't argue with a corpse but if we haven't got one to show him, it's going to be tricky.'

'It was here last night,' said Jack firmly. 'It's not here now. Therefore it's been moved.'

'But who could have moved it, Jack?' asked Isabelle. She stopped. 'I don't suppose Mr Leigh could have, could he?'

'He *could*,' agreed Jack. 'After he pulled me out from under that ruddy beam I was spark out until the firemen came to the rescue. He could have moved a hundred bodies and I wouldn't be any wiser. The trouble is, I know what you heard him say in the gallery all right, but he saved my life.'

'Which doesn't stop him from being guilty, more's the pity,' said Ashley.

'Let's have a word with the men clearing the rubble,' said Jack. 'They'll tell us if anyone's been in here.'

But the gardeners' account was nearly, if not quite, conclusive. There had been a succession of sightseers coming and going to the entrance all morning, which Jack could well believe. Gazing at the aftermath of a fire was such a natural human response that he wouldn't have credited it if they'd said otherwise. As far as getting into the cave itself, though, the gardeners were sure that no one, bar themselves, had done it. No, not even Mr Leigh. Quite apart from Mr Leigh's instructions, the hole hadn't been big enough to get through with any ease until an hour or so ago. Which wasn't, as Isabelle said, the same thing as saying that no one *had* got through; it was just they hadn't been spotted doing it.

'They'd have to get out again, though,' said Ashley. 'They'd be very lucky not to be seen either coming or going.'

'The body was here,' insisted Jack. 'Someone's moved it.'

'Well, where is it now, Haldean?'

'It must be in the cave somewhere,' said Isabelle. 'I still think someone could have waited their moment and sneaked in and out, but I can't see them taking a body with them.'

'That, I'd say, would be very unlikely,' agreed Ashley dryly.

After a good forty minutes, in which time they had thoroughly explored the entire cave, including both entrances to the stream and a good way along the course of the water, they had to give it up as a bad job. The body could, as Ashley said, be hidden under the rubble from the roof, but Jack could tell that Ashley's faith that there had ever been a body at all was waning fast. Not only that, but the light of his torch was growing weaker by the minute.

'I think we should give it up for the time being,' said Jack, much to everyone's relief. 'I'll come back later.'

'It's nearly lunchtime,' said Isabelle, squinting at her watch in the dim light.

'Oh hell,' said Jack. 'Are we going to be late?'

'We will be if we don't get a move on. It's only cold stuff, thank goodness, not a formal meal, but we need a wash and brush up. We must look like absolute sweeps with all this ash and mud.'

'Fair enough,' said Ashley. 'I've got to meet Rackham at the station and I've got Mr Bloomenfield, the jeweller, arriving this afternoon. I think, if you don't mind, we'd better keep what we were doing in here private for the time being.'

'Give us some credit, old thing,' muttered Jack. 'The last thing either of us is going to do is to rush up to Mr Leigh and Co. and tell them we were playing hunt the corpse. However,' he added thoughtfully, as they climbed over the earth and rocks to the entrance, 'we'd better give the gardeners some sort of story.'

Sam, the gardener, was loading up the wheelbarrow with earth as they climbed through the hole.

'Sam,' said Jack, as they scrambled clear. 'It is Sam, isn't it?' The gardener nodded. 'We've been looking for my diamond bracelet.' Sam's eyebrows rose in surprise. 'Well, not *my* diamond bracelet, of course,' said Jack with a diffident laugh. 'It's actually Miss Celia's, but that's the trouble. I was looking at it when we got the alarm about the fire and I just shoved it in my pocket without thinking. I know I had it in the cave last night, but I think I must have dropped it in the comings and goings.'

'That's a real shame, sir,' said Sam sympathetically.

Jack rubbed the side of his nose in an embarrassed sort of way. 'You're telling me. Miss Celia doesn't know it's lost yet. I was hoping to find it before she rumbled the fact it had gone, if you see what I mean.' Jack gave a man-to-man laugh. 'It might be awkward, you understand?'

'I do,' said Sam with fellow feeling.

'The thing is, if anyone else finds it, Miss Celia will know I lost it, and I'll be in the dog-house, good and proper.' Sam grinned broadly. 'So,' said Jack, taking out his wallet and handing Sam a ten-shilling note, 'if anyone else from the house comes poking round the cave, let me know who it is, will you? If I catch them before they spill the beans to Miss Celia, I might be able to get away with it, after all. I'll be back later on, but I'd be obliged if you could just keep tabs on things for me.'

'That's very generous of you,' said Sam, pocketing the note. 'Don't you worry, sir. Ladies get very attached to things, I know.'

'Don't mention it to anyone from the house, will you?' asked Jack, lowering his voice anxiously. 'I don't want anyone to know it's missing.'

'Right you are, sir,' promised Sam.

'You really are the most accomplished liar, Jack,' said Isabelle in amused disapproval, once they were out of earshot. 'Did you really think it was worth ten bob to satisfy the gardeners' curiosity with all that rigmarole?'

'I thought it was worth ten bob to know if anyone else tries to get into the cave,' said Jack. 'And to stop Sam and his pals talking about what we were doing. We don't want to put the wind up anyone unnecessarily, do we?'

'I thought it was pretty smooth,' said Ashley in approval.

'Are you going to ask Mr Leigh and Mrs Hawker about what I heard them say in the gallery?' asked Isabelle as they emerged into the temple.

Ashley shook his head. 'No, I'm not. That'd achieve nothing, apart from warning them to look out.'

Isabelle breathed a sigh of relief. 'I'm glad about that. If Mr Leigh knew I'd overheard them, it'd be very awkward.'

'Don't worry, Mrs Stanton. We'll just let sleeping dogs lie for the time being. If we'd found this blessed corpse, that'd be a very different kettle of fish but, as it is, it's hard to see what I can do.'

'I'm going to find that body,' said Jack. 'I damn well know it was there.'

'I only hope you do,' said Ashley. 'In the meantime, I want to know what Inspector Rackham's got to tell us.'

Isabelle, after a thorough wash and change of clothes, came out of her room. There was, she knew, a cold lunch in the dining room and she really should be there, but . . .

She hesitated at the head of the stairs, then continued along the corridor to the portrait gallery. The events of yesterday had been so fantastic, they had a dream-like quality to them, and they had started with Frank Leigh and Mary Hawker in the gallery.

She hadn't been mistaken about what Mrs Hawker said. *This is murder we're talking about. I don't blame you for what you've done but this is murder.* That much she was certain of. Was there anything else? Some forgotten phrase perhaps? Maybe if she stood in the gallery once more, it would come back to her.

She walked into the oak-panelled room, with its wide, dark, creaky floorboards. She shut her eyes and remembered Mary Hawker's sharp, frightened voice. *You must get rid of Major Haldean, Frank. He's dangerous.*

A sound made her snap her eyes open. She froze as the door in the middle of the gallery opened, then sighed with relief as Jack opened the door and shut it carefully behind him. 'Thank goodness it's you. You nearly gave me a heart attack.'

'I thought I'd see where the staircase in the middle of the gallery led to,' Jack said quietly. 'The first room on the floor below is Mrs Leigh's. If she was looking out, she'd have a good view of Mrs Hawker, say, coming up that staircase. It'd be easy enough for her to follow, to see why Mrs Hawker was wandering round the house.'

'Especially if she had her suspicions of an affair between her and her husband,' agreed Isabelle, softly. 'I wish I knew what it was all about, Jack. I *like* Mr Leigh.'

'After last night, so do I.' He ran his hand though his hair. 'Besides that, I'd have said he was a good sort and, of course, he's Celia's father.'

'She thinks the world of him,' said Isabelle. 'She gets exasperated with him sometimes but she really does care for him an awful lot.'

Jack nodded towards the portrait of the cavalier holding his doffed hat with its sweeping feathers. 'He's obviously an ancestor of Mr Leigh's, isn't he?'

'That's what I thought. It's amazing how the same faces crop up in a family. Do you remember that bit in *Northanger Abbey,* where Jane Austen says that once a face is painted, it's painted for all generations to come?'

'Vaguely,' said Jack. 'As I remember, she's making fun of the idea, but there's a lot to be said for it, all the same.'

He walked up the gallery, pausing to smile at the seventeenth-century incarnation of Celia Leigh. 'Here's a family face. The teeth are different, though.'

'Not really,' said Isabelle. 'Celia had to wear a brace at school. She hated it, poor girl. Still, it did the trick, otherwise she'd have ended up with rabbit teeth.'

Jack stopped. 'That rings a bell. Who've I heard of recently who had rabbit teeth . . .?' He frowned in an effort of remembrance, then clicked his fingers. 'Mrs Welbeck!'

'Who?'

'Mrs Paxton's housekeeper. Hello!' He stopped by the portrait of the Georgian clergyman that had puzzled Isabelle yesterday. 'Who the dickens is this?'

'That's Ebenezer Leigh,' said Isabelle. 'I wondered about him. He looks familiar, somehow, but it's hard to tell with that full wig.'

'Hold on,' said Jack. He pulled a chair over to the portrait, climbed up and held his hands over the painted wig. 'Does that ring a bell?'

Isabelle took a step backwards and gave a little gasp. 'Jack! It's Mr Wood! Aloysius Wood! Hold on, let me take your place so you can see.'

Jack got down. Isabelle climbed on the chair and held her hands over the wig.

Jack gave a low whistle. 'You're right! Crikey, that's him all right. You *said* he fitted in. Blimey, Isabelle, it's not surprising, is it?'

Isabelle got down from the chair. 'He must be a member of the family, Jack. He just has to be. I suppose,' she added, pausing delicately, 'he could be – er – *unacknowledged.*'

'He most certainly is,' said Jack with a grin, 'but not, I'll be bound, in that sense, so there's no need to blush.'

'Why are you so sure? From what I've heard, Mr Leigh's father had quite a reputation.'

'Yes, but why does that mean that Wood has to conceal his identity? It's not as if old Matthew Leigh was known as a pillar of virtue. Far from it. If Wood's just a stray member of the family, why not say so? Every family has odd cousins that nobody shouts about too loudly.'

'A good many families do, at any rate,' amended Isabelle. 'That's true enough.' She stepped back and looked at the portrait thoughtfully. 'D'you know, I've always wondered about Mr Wood. I think it's his Christian name, apart from anything else. *Aloysius* seems so unlikely, somehow.'

'Yep,' said Jack, nodding. 'Some poor beggar might be called *Aloysius* but I'd say it's either a family name you're saddled with or the sort of moniker you give yourself if you've got a wayward sense of humour.'

'But who is he, Jack?' asked Isabelle, as he put the chair back and dusted off the seat. 'My first thought was that he's Terence Napier, but he can't be. We know that.'

Jack braced his hands on the back of the chair. 'Yes . . .'

He stood quietly for a few moments, his eyes narrowed. 'Isabelle,' he said slowly, 'I've got the beginnings of an idea. Why did we think it was the Vicar who was out to get you?'

'Because of the things you found in the train,' said Isabelle. 'You know. There were the cards with his sign drawn on them and the books with his name written inside and so on.'

'There was also the case, a handkerchief, a hairbrush and a hand-mirror. They were old and expensive. Anyone can write a name in a book or scribble a drawing on a card but those things were *real*, Belle. Someone – someone whose initials were *A.P.* – had kept those things.'

'A.P.,' said Isabelle slowly. 'Alexander Paxton. I said as much before.'

'Yes,' said Jack thoughtfully. 'Alexander Paxton.' He stood for a few more moments, then drew a deep breath. 'I've got a rotten feeling this is going to be very awkward.'

'Is there any chance you could let me know what you're thinking?' asked Isabelle.

Jack looked up, saw Isabelle's expectant face, and grinned. 'Only when I've thought it through properly. Come on. Let's go and get something to eat, shall we?'

The first person they saw as they entered the dining room was Aloysius Wood, enthusiastically tucking into salmon mayonnaise.

Frank Leigh was chatting to Mary Hawker over the fruit salad and Celia, sausage roll in hand, was talking, in a worried sort of way, to Leonard Duggleby.

Wood turned as Jack and Isabelle came into the room, his round face creasing in a broad smile.

'Haldean!' he said warmly. 'I can't tell you how grateful I am for last night, old man.'

Celia shuddered. 'I'm so sorry I suggested the séance, Jack. I've said as much to Dad and to Mr Wood, but I want to say sorry to you, as well.'

'Never mind, Celia,' said Mary Hawker, with rather assumed heartiness. 'All's well that ends well, eh? Have a cheese straw.'

Celia absently took a cheese straw, her hand shaking slightly. She was, Jack noted warily, in the grip of a fairly strong emotion. 'I've heard séances can be dangerous but I've never believed it. I was so *scared*!' She looked at him beseechingly. 'Please say you'll forgive me.'

'Of course,' said Jack, with a reassuring gesture of his beef muffin. 'You weren't to know what would happen.'

'What gave you the idea, Celia?' asked Isabelle.

'I'm afraid I might be partly responsible,' said Mary Hawker.

'No, you weren't,' countered Celia. 'It was me. I've heard of people holding séances in Egyptian pyramids and finding wisdom and insight. I'd been so fascinated by the cave –' she shuddered once more – 'that when Len said he wished he could find out more about the people who'd built the altar, I wanted to give it a go.'

Frank Leigh gave her wrist a reassuring squeeze. 'Don't distress yourself, my dear. It's all over now. That cave is a dashed dangerous place to fool around in, though. It always was. I've a good mind to close it off altogether.'

'You mustn't do that, sir!' protested Leonard Duggleby earnestly. 'It's a very important archaeological site. I doubt if there's another like it in England.'

'I'd just as soon as forget about it,' said Wood with feeling, reaching for another helping of mayonnaise. 'I've never been so terrified in all my life.'

'What actually happened?' asked Jack.

Wood began to speak, then stopped. 'It's no use,' he said

helplessly. 'I know what I thought I saw but it must have been a dream.' He gingerly put a hand to his temple. 'I woke up with the dickens of a sore head, I do know that, but you must have some bumps and bruises of your own.'

'Duggleby, your Victorian vicar had a rum experience with a fire in the cave, didn't he?' asked Jack.

'That's putting it mildly. He said the altar was a mass of flames. According to him, Euthius himself seemed to come to life.'

Wood drew his breath in sharply but said nothing.

'That's fascinating,' said Jack, 'especially when you think of what happened at the séance. The sequence of water, blood and fire follows the sequence carved on the altar. What started the fire?'

'I suppose I got a knock on the head somehow and knocked over the oil-lamp,' said Wood reluctantly. 'I know this much. I'll never laugh at psychic whatjamacallit's ever again. There was something evil there last night. I felt it and it scared me stiff.' He took another forkful of salmon mayonnaise. 'From now on, I stay in this world and this world only. Any god, ghost or spirit can go and haunt someone else. I'm not playing.'

'Quite right, too,' said Frank Leigh approvingly. He turned as Evie Leigh came into the room. 'Ah, there you are, my dear.' He picked up a plate from the table. 'What can I get you?'

'Nothing at the moment, Frank.' There was a gleam of triumph in her eyes. 'Superintendent Ashley is here, together with Inspector Rackham from Scotland Yard. They want to see Mr Wood.'

Wood went very still.

Frank Leigh's colour rose. 'They want to see Wood? Why?'

Evie's voice was cutting. 'I would have thought that was obvious. Stay where you are, Mr Wood!' she added, as Wood backed away. She turned to the door. 'Officers! In here!'

Ashley and Rackham came into the room. 'Good afternoon, everyone,' said Ashley placidly. 'We're sorry to disturb your lunch, but we'd like a word with Mr Wood.'

Wood's shoulders went back, then he consciously relaxed. 'Me?' he said cheerily. 'What's wrong? I haven't been caught speeding, have I?'

'Nothing like that, sir. Tell me, sir, you're employed as a private detective, aren't you?'

Wood's shoulders went back again. 'I am.'

Bill Rackham spoke for the first time. 'Mr Wood, I believe you informed Mr Leigh you are employed by the Rapid Results Agency in Victoria, yes?'

Wood swallowed and said nothing.

'The thing is, Mr Wood, the Rapid Results Agency know nothing about you.'

Wood hesitated, his head to one side. 'Indeed? That's very remiss of them. Need I really tell you, inspector, that it's some-times necessary to work under a pseudonym?'

Bill's eyes narrowed. 'And need I tell you, Mr Wood, that the Rapid Results Agency is far too concerned for its own welfare to give misleading information to Scotland Yard? They know nothing about you because you are not, and never have been, employed by them.'

Evie Leigh let out her breath in a hiss. 'I knew it! You're an impostor, here to steal my sapphires. You *have* stolen my sapphires!'

Frank Leigh stepped forward, very red in the face. 'Nonsense, Evie. Inspector Rackham, Superintendent Ashley, I must insist that you stop browbeating Mr Wood in this fashion. There's been some mistake, that's all.' He turned to Wood and clapped him on the shoulder. 'Wood's a fine feller, an excellent chap. He has my complete confidence.'

'That's a very interesting attitude, sir,' said Ashley in his slow, countryman's voice. 'It strikes me that you know a bit more about Mr Wood than you're letting on.'

Frank Leigh swelled in visible fury. 'What the devil do you mean, sir? I won't have it! This interview is at an end.'

'No!' snarled Evie and would have said more, when Mary Hawker, very white, stepped forward.

'Frank, stop it!' She swallowed and spoke very rapidly. 'You've shielded this man long enough but it won't *do*! Don't you see, you're being dragged down with him? For your own sake, Frank, you have to tell the truth. This is murder we're talking about, *murder,* I tell you.'

'Mary!' said Frank Leigh in an agony of apprehension. 'Be quiet!'

'I've been quiet for long enough.' She drew a deep breath. 'You're perfectly right, Superintendent. This man's name isn't Wood. It's Terence Napier.'

FIFTEEN

E vie Leigh sprang to her feet with a shriek. 'Terence Napier!' She looked wildly at her husband. 'You *shielded* him, Frank?'

Frank Leigh buried his head in his hands.

'Arrest that man!' screeched Evie, pointing at Wood. Her eyes blazed. 'I insist you arrest him this instant!'

Frank Leigh looked up. 'Evie, please! Of course Wood isn't Terry Napier. Evie, will you *calm down*!' He took a deep breath and braced himself. 'Terry's dead. He was the man who was murdered on the train.'

Evie stared at him open mouthed. 'He can't have been. You're lying, Frank. Wood's guilty. I *know* he's guilty!'

'Napier was the man on the train?' repeated Bill Rackham in astonishment. 'When did you find that out?'

Frank rubbed his hand over his forehead. 'When he came to the house. Evie, please! Let me think. Terry had changed so much I didn't recognise him. It'd been years since I'd seen him, remember, but something about him made me feel very uncomfortable. He seemed to act as if he owned the place, you know? I couldn't wait to get rid of him. After he'd gone, I couldn't get over the idea that I knew the man. I didn't say anything, but it worried me. It wasn't until much later it struck me who he was.'

'Why on earth didn't you tell us, Mr Leigh?' asked Bill.

'What was the use?' asked Frank with a shrug. 'Terry was dead. He'd stolen the sapphires and the money from the safe, but they'd been recovered. All I really wanted was to forget about the whole wretched business.'

Ashley stared at him keenly. 'Are you prepared to swear to that, Mr Leigh?' Frank nodded. 'Are you sure, sir? You made such a point of telling everyone Napier was innocent.'

'So he is,' said Frank quickly. 'Terry couldn't possibly have murdered Aunt Constance. I admit I didn't recognise him at first, but what you have to remember is that I knew Terry, knew him well. He simply wouldn't harm an old lady. He wouldn't harm anyone.'

Bill Rackham turned to Mary Hawker. 'You seem very certain Wood is Terence Napier, Mrs Hawker. Why?'

'I recognised him,' she said. She was trembling. 'Or, at least, I thought I did. I've been beside myself with worry.' She bit her lip. 'I thought Frank was sheltering him. I hated him being here. I thought Frank would be dragged down with him.'

'Sorry, Mrs Hawker,' said Wood, recovering some of his self-possession. 'Absolutely not guilty.'

'I don't believe you,' said Evie abruptly. 'I don't believe a word of it. I always knew there was something wrong about you. You're Napier, aren't you? I don't care what Frank says. He'd say anything to get you out of trouble. You're not just a thief, you're a *murderer.*'

'No, I'm not,' said Wood. 'I'm nothing of the sort.'

'Then who the devil are you?' demanded Ashley.

'Yes, who are you, Mr Wood?' asked Jack. 'You're certainly a member of the family. There's a portrait of one of your ancestors in the gallery upstairs. It could be a portrait of you.'

Wood rolled his eyes upwards. 'Ebenezer Leigh,' he said ruefully. 'Oh, blimey.' He puffed his cheeks out in a sigh. 'I never thought of Ebenezer.' He turned his hands palm upwards in a defeated gesture. 'Never mind, Frank. Bear up. I suppose I was bound to be rumbled sooner or later.'

'You seem to be taking this remarkably calmly, I must say,' said Mary Hawker with a sort of fascinated horror.

'What's there to take?' asked Wood. 'Don't bother getting the handcuffs out, Superintendent. I'm not Terence Napier.'

'So who the devil are you?' repeated Ashley.

'Can't you guess?' Wood grinned. 'We'd better own up, Frank. I'm Sandy Paxton.'

Evie Leigh gave a little shriek. 'You're lying! I know you're lying!' She suddenly stopped, took a deep, shuddering breath, gathered herself together, then looked up, eyes bright and sharp. 'If you're Sandy Paxton, you're in big trouble. Desertion is a crime!'

Wood rubbed the side of his nose. 'It *was* a crime,' he conceded, 'but it isn't any longer. They've said as much in Parliament a few times. Forgive and forget, and all that. I admit that when the children – if I ever have any – ask me, "What did you do in the Great War, Daddy?" it's not something I'll recount with pride, but it isn't a crime.'

'There's a few other things that are crimes, though, Parliament or no Parliament,' said Ashley levelly. 'What about the jewel thefts?'

'Exactly,' breathed Evie.

Wood put his head to one side and raised his eyebrows. 'What jewel thefts would those be?'

'The ones before the war. If you are Sandy Paxton, you were an associate of the Vicar, weren't you?'

'So it's said. I don't believe it was ever proved, was it? In fact, you'll find it quite a job to work out exactly what I am meant to be guilty of.' He put his hand on Frank Leigh's shoulder. 'Come on, Frank. You've been an absolute brick but there's really nothing to worry about.' He looked at the assembled company. 'When the news broke about what happened to my mother, I got in touch with Frank. Frank wanted me to make a clean breast of things, but I preferred to hide my light under a bushel, so to speak. I wanted to see if I could dig up exactly what did happen in Topfordham. I thought my own name would attract rather too much attention.'

'You're right about that,' growled Ashley. 'If you've done nothing else, you've been withholding information from the police. Did you meet Terence Napier in Paris?'

For the first time, Wood hesitated. 'I . . . didn't. No, that's not actually true,' He stopped short. Armitage, the butler, had come into the room.

'What the devil is it?' barked Frank Leigh testily. 'Can't you see we're busy?'

Armitage, obviously deeply offended, drew himself up to his full height. 'A Mr Bloomenfield has arrived, sir.'

Frank Leigh ran an exasperated hand through his hair. 'Bloomenfield? I don't know anyone called Bloomenfield. Send him away, Armitage. I can't see anyone at the moment.'

Armitage coughed. 'He says he was asked to call on a matter of business by Mr Ashley, sir.'

'Did he, by Jove!' rapped out Frank Leigh. 'Mr Ashley, what is the meaning of this? By George, it's come to something when policemen stroll into my house and invite their own guests along into the bargain.'

'Mr Bloomenfield is an expert in precious stones,' said Ashley. 'As the question of the authenticity of the sapphires has arisen, I thought it as well to get them checked.'

'You can think again,' snarled Frank Leigh. 'There's nothing wrong with the ruddy sapphires. Damned if I know what the world's coming to. There's no earthly reason why I should let a complete stranger examine my property.'

'*My* property, Frank,' cut in Evie Leigh icily. She turned to Bill Rackham. 'I would very much appreciate Mr Bloomenfield's opinion. Armitage! Show the gentleman in. I will get my sapphires.'

Cold fury radiating from her, she stalked from the room.

Frank Leigh slumped into a chair, staring sightlessly at the lunch table. Wood dropped an encouraging hand onto his shoulder as Armitage ushered Mr Bloomenfield, a man in his sixties, in faultless morning dress and with a sharp, intelligent face, into the room.

Celia Leigh swallowed and stepped forward. 'Good afternoon.'

In what seemed like a ghastly parody of the usual social conventions, Celia rapidly introduced everyone. 'My step-mother, Mrs Leigh, has just gone to get her sapphires,' she finished. 'As you can see, we're having lunch. Would you care to join us?'

'Nothing for me, thank you, Miss Leigh,' said Mr Bloomenfield. 'Glorious weather we're having, aren't we?'

It was, thought Jack, a weirdly unreal situation. Bill, untidy and ginger-haired in his London clothes, Ashley in his dark suit and the sharp-faced jeweller stiltedly talking conventional nothings to the girls in their summer dresses and the men in blazers and flannels round the lunch table.

It was as if the conversation should centre on nothing more than a stroll through the woods, a game of tennis or a row on the lake, but Frank Leigh sat rigid and unseeing, Wood beside him, while Leonard Duggleby fussed around the table.

Mary Hawker, who was obviously regretting her outburst,

covered up her awkwardness by offering Mr Bloomenfield ham muffins, scones and sponge cake whilst talking weather, horses, dogs and crops in a flood of stultifying artificial speech.

It was a relief when Evie Leigh returned, jewel case in hand.

Mr Bloomenfield opened the case. 'My word,' he said admiringly. He took the sapphires out of the case and held them out in the sunlight streaming into the room. 'Very nice. Yes, very nice indeed.'

'Are they real?' demanded Evie Leigh.

Mr Bloomenfield took his jeweller's eyeglass from its leather case and screwed it into his eye. Holding the necklace, he turned it in his hand so the sunlight fell on it. 'Oh no,' he said absently. 'Of course not. Beautiful work, though.'

Evie Leigh gave a hiss of triumph. 'Are you *sure*?'

'Absolutely certain,' said Mr Bloomenfield, 'but they're very nicely done. The setting's completely authentic, but the stones are coloured glass.'

'Those sapphires,' said Frank Leigh, speaking for the first time since Mr Bloomenfield had arrived, 'are ancient. They're part of the Breagan Bounty. First-rate stones.' His voice was thick and he was obviously finding it a real effort to speak. 'It's not to be expected they'd look like modern jewels.'

Mr Bloomenfield tutted in disagreement. 'My dear sir, ancient or not, a first-rate sapphire will have what we call "silk". It makes an inner star within the stone. Take my eye-glass and see for yourself, if you wish. This necklace is composed of nothing more than coloured glass.' Then, just as Duggleby had done last night, he held the necklace momentarily to his lips. 'You see? It's warm to the touch. There isn't any doubt about it.'

'That's good enough for me,' said Ashley, rubbing his hands together.

'My sapphires have been stolen,' ground out Evie. 'Stolen and a copy made by an acknowledged jewel thief.' She pointed a trembling finger at Wood, then spun round to confront Bill. 'Now will you arrest him?'

'Mr Wood?' asked Bill. 'Or should that be Paxton? What have you got to say for yourself?'

Wood said nothing.

Ashley and Rackham swapped glances, then Ashley stepped forward. 'I think you'd better come down to the station with us, sir.'

Wood took a deep breath then nodded slowly. 'All right. I'll come quietly.'

Jack looked sharply at Frank Leigh, hesitated, then was silent.

'No,' said Frank desperately. 'No, you can't *do* that.'

Wood squeezed his shoulder. 'It's probably for the best, Frank.'

'No!' said Frank Leigh in a gasp. 'I can't . . .'

'I'm afraid,' said Wood, his voice cool and regretful, 'that the game's up.' He smiled very briefly. 'You could say I've got taking ways. I always did have, more's the pity. I always liked jewels. Just one of my little foibles, I'm sorry to say.'

Jack cleared his throat. 'Hold on a minute, Wood. When, exactly, did you steal the sapphires?'

'I . . . er . . .'

'Last night,' spat out Evie. 'It must have been last night.'

Jack shook his head. 'That would've been awfully tricky. Granted the safe is no great shakes, when did you see the necklace in order to copy it? Mr Bloomenfield has told us what excellent work it is. A necklace of this quality isn't produced in a matter of a half hour or so. It'd need careful planning and some considerable skill.'

'Both of which I own up to,' said Wood. 'I knew the necklace was going to be re-set, so I had a substitute necklace made. Easy, really.' He turned to Ashley. 'If you are going to arrest me, would you mind hurrying up? This isn't the easiest social situation I've ever found myself in.'

'No,' muttered Frank Leigh. 'No, I can't let that happen.' His face was ghastly. 'I stole the wretched jewels.'

'Frank, don't!' said Wood quickly, but Frank Leigh shook his head.

'No.' He stared at the fascinated, horrified faces around him, then held up his hand to ward off Wood's protests. 'I can't let you be blamed for something I did.'

Evie, her eyes fixed on her husband, groped her way to a chair. 'Why?' she breathed.

Frank shrugged. 'Can you ask? I needed the money. Celia needed the money. She and Ted Marchant wanted to buy a farm.

They could have had it. You had your necklace. You didn't know the difference. You should've been happy.'

'Happy?' repeated Evie. '*Happy!*'

Frank raised his hand feebly. 'Don't worry. The stones are safe. They're in a box in my dressing room.'

Celia gave a little cry. 'You did it for me, Dad?'

Frank nodded. 'If it wasn't for Duggleby spotting them, it would've worked.' He looked from Celia to Duggleby then back again. 'Marchant's a good man. I . . . I was worried.'

'Give me my sapphires,' said Evie. 'I want my sapphires.'

Frank Leigh sighed heavily and stood up. 'I'll get them for you.'

As soon as he had gone, an outburst of noise filled the room. Mary Hawker turned on Evie, Duggleby was stammering he hadn't meant any harm and everyone was talking at once.

Celia burst into tears. 'Dad did it for *me!*' she sobbed.

Moved by a sudden fear, Jack caught at her arm. 'Celia,' he hissed. 'I need you. Now!'

Celia dried her eyes. 'What is it?' she asked in a choky voice.

Jack didn't answer but ushered her to the door. 'Bill!' he called in a low voice. 'Come on.'

'Well?' asked Bill, once the three of them were in the hall. Frank Leigh was nowhere to be seen.

'Celia, I saw your father's face,' said Jack urgently. 'He's a desperate man.' He reached out and held her hand, speaking very quietly. 'I think he might attempt his own life.'

Celia gazed at him in horror.

'Does he keep a gun in his dressing-room?'

'He . . . He might.'

'Are there guns in the house? A gun room, perhaps?'

Celia gulped and pointed wordlessly down the hall. 'It's along there. The end of the hall.'

'Fine. He might have gone upstairs, of course.' He stared at her earnestly, willing strength into her. 'Take Bill to your father's dressing room. Go on. Quickly!'

As if suddenly galvanised, she started along the hallway to the stairs, Bill after her. Jack turned and sped off in the direction of the gun room.

At first he thought the room was empty. Three tall glass-fronted cabinets, with shotguns and sporting rifles, stood closed, the glass reflecting the dazzling sun. Over the mantelpiece, a sabre on a green baize board, with its sheath beneath, glinted in the light.

Jack turned away and caught his breath. Frank Leigh, pistol in hand, was slumped into a dark corner of the room, rigidly still.

'Mr Leigh?'

Frank Leigh shuddered. 'I hoped you wouldn't see me,' he said in a dried-up voice. 'It's over.'

'Mr Leigh, give me the gun.'

Frank Leigh looked blankly at the gun in his hand, then his face contorted. Bringing the gun up, he aimed it at Jack's chest, his finger on the trigger. 'Leave me alone! It's over, I tell you!'

Jack froze. At that moment, he didn't think Frank Leigh was completely sane. 'Mr Leigh,' he said, keeping his voice very level, 'you saved my life last night.'

Leigh made a noise like a sob.

'I'm going to reach out,' said Jack steadily, and slowly stretched out his hand, palm upmost. 'I want you to put the gun into my hand.'

Frank Leigh's eyes were fixed on Jack's. Jack dragged his eyes away, focusing on the gun in Frank Leigh's hand. The wavering black muzzle seemed huge and Jack could see Leigh's knuckles turn white.

'Get away,' said Leigh shakily. 'Get away or, by God, I'll kill you!'

For a fraction of a second, his finger tightened on the trigger.

Jack's muscles tensed, ready to spring. The silence lengthened. Jack risked another step forward, reached out and took the gun from Leigh's unresisting hand.

Leigh crumpled against the wall, his hands to his face.

As his fingers closed round the cold metal, Jack breathed a huge sigh of relief. That had been horribly dangerous. He broke open the gun, took out the bullets, and put both gun and ammunition on the table.

Leigh lowered his hands, his breath coming in huge gulps. 'You shouldn't have stopped me,' he said distantly. 'I was going to do the decent thing.'

He looked up, his eyes fixed on the sabre on the wall. 'That was won at Waterloo. There's . . . there's traditions. Family traditions. Reputation, you know? Get it wrong and pay the price.'

'Family?' repeated Jack sharply. He wanted to jolt Mr Leigh back to reality. 'You are your family. Besides that, what about your father? What about his reputation? That wasn't so hot, from what I've heard.'

Frank Leigh's eyes blazed with anger, then he suddenly relaxed. 'D'you know, you're right.' His voice had, thank God, lost that distant, dreamy note. 'He was a good man in his own way, you know? Generous to a fault, but he just couldn't keep away from the gaming tables.'

He sighed deeply. 'He wasn't a thief, though.' His mouth twisted. 'I am. It seemed such a good idea. All that money, tied up in a few sparkling stones.' He shrugged. 'I thought of them as mine.' He nearly laughed. 'That's family traditions again, I suppose.' He was quiet for a few moments. 'You knew, didn't you? I saw you look at me in the dining room.'

Jack nodded. 'I thought it was very likely.

'How? How did you guess?'

Jack shrugged. 'The way you reacted, of course. Add to that, the fact that the necklace only arrived yesterday. It could only have been copied by someone who knew the new design and had the skill to do it. Paste copies are often made to protect the original, so I thought the obvious people to produce a fake were the jewellers, working on your instructions.'

'That's it,' agreed Frank Leigh. 'I only thought of it after Evie had approved the new design. I asked Seddon and Coles to make me a paste necklace while I kept the original. They never dreamt there was anything wrong. It seemed such a simple solution. Wrong, of course. I know that.'

He heaved a deep sigh, then, shaking himself, straightened his shoulders and, walking past Jack, went to one of the glass-fronted gun cabinets. Opening it, he took down a twelve-bore shotgun.

'Rabbits, you know,' he said with the faintest of smiles, taking some cartridges from the drawer. He broke open the gun and slipped the cartridges into the breech. 'I think I'll have a crack at the rabbits.'

'Mr Leigh!' Jack's voice was firm. 'Don't do it, sir.'

'I know what I'm doing, young man.' A spark of anger showed in his eyes. 'When I need your advice, I'll ask for it.'

'Give me some more time, sir,' Jack pleaded.

'What the devil difference will more time make?'

'I need to find out what happened last night. If you had an accident, say, it would make it very awkward for me to investigate.'

Frank Leigh dropped the shotgun onto the table out of sheer surprise. 'My word, you've got some brass neck, I'll give you that. You honestly expect me to . . . to rearrange my affairs so you can go ghost hunting?'

'I hope so.'

Frank Leigh's face flushed and he was about to answer when the door was flung back on its hinges. Celia, with Bill close behind, rushed into the room. She looked from the shotgun to her father, then, with a yelp, flung herself at him.

'Dad! Oh, Dad, I've been so *worried*!' She buried her face in his shoulder, arms around his neck. 'I don't care about the money, I care about you. I don't want to marry Ted. I don't care about him. All I care about is that you're safe.'

'Everything okay, Jack?' asked Bill in a low voice.

Jack nodded at the pistol on the table. 'He nearly had a pop at me with that,' he said quietly. Bill whistled softly. 'He's not safe. We can't leave him loose. There's no saying what he'll do and he knows a great deal more than what he's told us, I'll swear to it. Will you back me up?'

'All right,' said Bill.

Jack cleared his throat loudly. Celia Leigh broke away from her father and turned to face him. 'Jack! Thank God you got here in time.'

'Don't be too grateful, Celia,' said Jack warningly. 'Your father's guilty of some serious crimes.'

'Crimes!' stuttered Frank Leigh. 'What the devil d'you mean, sir! What crimes?'

'Attempted suicide,' said Jack icily. 'That's a crime. You threatened to kill me. That's attempted murder, which is another crime.'

Frank and Celia Leigh gazed at him speechlessly. 'Jack, don't,' said Celia helplessly. 'You know Dad didn't mean to shoot you. You know it was just the heat of the moment. You can't blame him for that.'

'Oh, can't I?' said Jack.

'There's the theft of the sapphires as well,' said Bill. 'That's grand larceny.'

Jack nodded. 'Very grand, indeed, considering how much they're worth. Mr Leigh made a full confession to me of how he'd stolen the sapphires.'

'That doesn't matter,' said Celia desperately. 'You know why he did it!'

'All in all, Mr Leigh,' said Bill, 'I think it would be as well if you accompanied me to the station.'

Frank Leigh darted a glance round the room, then made a dive for the shotgun, but Bill was there before him.

'Don't do it, sir!' Bill handed the shotgun to Jack. 'And, incidentally, sir, you've just resisted arrest, which is another offence. Ring the bell, will you Jack? I could do with Ashley in here.'

SIXTEEN

Jack paused on the edge of the dining room. He could hear Celia, her voice thin with tears, giving high-pitched vent to her feelings, Mary Hawker's bass rumbles of disapproval and Evie's sharp questioning. Listeners, he reflected ruefully, never heard good of themselves.

'. . . and Jack said Dad tried to kill him. Kill him! As if Dad would do such a thing. He wouldn't hurt a fly. I think Jack was just being vindictive. It was *horrible*!'

'But your father did have a gun?' That was Isabelle, trying to pour a bit of oil on these extremely choppy waters.

'Well, what if he did? Dad was upset. He . . . He . . . Jack said Dad was going to shoot himself but he wouldn't have done, not really.'

'Dear God,' said Mary Hawker. 'So that's why Major Haldean went off like a scalded cat. He was trying to stop him.' She sighed, obviously deeply moved. 'I should have known that would be Frank's reaction once the truth was out. He's an honourable man.'

'Honourable!' yelped Evie. 'Honourable! *He stole my sapphires.*'

'Yes, well, perhaps he shouldn't have done,' conceded Mary, 'but the main thing is that Frank's all right. I think you've got to give Major Haldean credit, Celia. I know this arrest is beastly, but at least it's stopped Frank from taking the final step. Your father's a difficult man to argue with. Once he gets his teeth into something, he won't drop it.'

Jack froze. The voices in the dining room seemed suddenly faint, as if the volume on a wireless set had been turned down.

'Doesn't anyone care?' shrieked Evie from very far away. '*He stole my sapphires!*'

Teeth! *Once he gets his teeth into something, he won't drop it . . .* He'd thought about teeth in the portrait gallery before lunch. What the hell was it about teeth?

Evie had small, white, even teeth. Mrs Hawker had rather horsey teeth, Duggleby had a chipped tooth, Frank Leigh had a gold tooth, Celia had straightened teeth so they weren't rabbit teeth like the girl's in the portrait . . . Mrs Welbeck had rabbit teeth. Celia's teeth must have been like Mrs Welbeck's . . .

Teeth. Get his teeth into something. Biting off more than he could chew . . . The voices in the dining room swelled back to full volume.

Mrs Welbeck's teeth!

'Did Frank have my sapphires?' demanded Evie.

'Of course not,' bit back Celia. 'He said they were in a box in his dressing room. Is that all you care about? What about Dad?'

Evie's voice had ice in it. 'My dear girl, your father is under arrest. What's more, he only has himself to blame. In the most underhanded way he brought a man into the house who would certainly not have been welcome under his own name, told a pack of lies from start to finish and ended up by stealing from me, his own wife. I cannot be expected to be dripping with sympathy. I am going to retrieve my sapphires.'

Jack heard her heels clicking across the parquet flooring to the door. He dodged down the hallway and out of sight behind a heavy velvet tasselled curtain. The last thing he wanted at the moment was to confront the seething Mrs Leigh. He watched her march up the stairs, fury radiating from every stiff line of her body.

His mind was racing. He had an idea. Mrs Welbeck's teeth, last night's séance, the murder on the train, Evie Leigh's sapphires – everything came together and made sense.

And yet . . . an idea remained just an idea without any proof.

How on earth *could* he prove it? Dr and Mrs Mountford would know. He looked across the hall at the telephone in its cabinet. It would be easy enough to pick up the phone. Easy enough to drive over to Topfordham, to speak to the Mountfords, and then . . . Then what? Part of the mystery *might* be solved but he couldn't be certain. Besides that, it would all take time. Was there anything he could do now?

The cave. Yes. He was sure he was on the right lines with the cave. He clicked his tongue. He, Ashley and Isabelle had searched the cave very thoroughly before lunch. The cave held its secret closely. He needed a guide.

Jack drew his breath in and nearly laughed out loud. *Throckmorton's book!* Of course! That earnest Victorian vicar, that persistent antiquarian, that learned man, with his knowledge of Tacitus and Sidonius Apollinaris, probably knew more about the cave than any man ever had and the results of his labours were contained in a dumpy little volume which had sat on a library shelf for the last eighty-odd years, unread and unregarded until Duggleby picked it up.

Was it in the library or was it in Duggleby's room? He glanced up the stairs.

Mrs Leigh's footsteps had clicked away into silence. The arguments still rumbled on in the dining room. It sounded as if Celia was being comforted by Duggleby. Unlike Evie Leigh, he was being very sympathetic indeed. Now was his chance.

Keeping a wary eye on the open door of the dining room, Jack ran lightly up the stairs.

Duggleby's room wasn't far from Jack's own and, if Jack's bedroom was anything to go off, shouldn't take long to search. Bachelor guests were not expected to take up a lot of space and were given correspondingly small rooms. After trying a couple of unoccupied rooms, Jack found Duggleby's. Throckmorton's book was in plain sight on the dressing table.

Brilliant! Picking up the book – it was too big for his pocket – he closed the door quietly behind him and headed down the stairs.

This time he wasn't so lucky. As he drew level with the dining room, Isabelle, Celia and Duggleby came out of the room.

At the sight of him, Celia drew back with a sort of revolted gasp, regarding him with deep and haughty loathing. 'You! I suppose you're proud of yourself, *Major* Haldean!'

'Come on, Celia,' pleaded Jack, adjusting the book so the title on the spine wasn't visible. 'Get off your high horse. It doesn't suit you.'

'Don't you dare talk to me like that, Jack,' snarled Celia. 'How you've got the nerve to look me in the face, I don't know.'

'That's better,' said Jack cheerfully. 'What on earth should I have done? Your father was an absolute menace to himself and everyone around him, waving that gun around. Absolute danger to traffic, I tell you. I managed to stop him loosing off with a revolver and the next thing he did was grab hold of a shotgun. Blinkin' nasty weapon, a shotgun.'

'He wouldn't have harmed you,' sniffed Celia. Duggleby put an arm round her shoulders. 'You know he's good and kind and . . . and . . .'

'A bit of an idiot,' finished Jack. 'And, although I'm not looking for adulation or anything, thanks to me, still alive.'

'What's that book you're holding?' asked Duggleby over Celia's shoulder. 'Throckmorton?'

There was nothing for it but to come clean.

'That's right,' said Jack as casually as he could manage. 'I thought I'd go in the garden and read.'

'But I left it in my room. I'm sure I did.'

'This is another copy. I found it in the library.'

'Oh? I didn't realise there was another copy,' said Duggleby, his eyes glinting with sudden interest. 'Can I see? There might be some additions to the text. Marginalia, perhaps.'

Celia drew in her breath in exasperation. 'What does it matter *which* stupid book it is? I can't imagine anyone thinking of books at a time like this. Don't let us stop you, Jack. You can relax now my father's in *prison*.' She shook herself free of Duggleby's arm. 'Come on, Len. I want to go and see him.'

With a final disgusted glare at Jack, she stalked off down the hall. Duggleby shuffled from foot to foot indecisively. Halfway down the hall Celia turned and called, 'Leonard!' Duggleby shrugged and went after her.

'Whew!' said Isabelle when they had gone. 'I don't think she's too gone on you at the moment. It's so unfair, Jack.'

'Never mind about Celia,' he said, making for the door. 'Come on, let's get out of here before anyone else collars us.'

'What's all the hurry about?' asked Isabelle as they walked down the steps and away from the house.

'I want to put as much distance between myself and Duggleby as possible. If he's going down to the village with Celia, he'll probably want to go up to his room to change his jacket. He's bound to notice his book's missing.'

Isabelle's eyebrows shot up. 'So it is his copy?'

'Yes, of course it is. I nicked it from his room.'

'But why?'

'Because I wanted to read it, Isabelle. I've got an idea about the cave and I wanted to see what Throckmorton says about it. I've an idea he might prove a very illuminating guide.'

'So we're going to the cave?' asked Isabelle in dismay. 'I can't, Jack, not in these shoes.'

'Why do girls always wear such ridiculous shoes?' asked Jack in amused exasperation. 'You don't have to come at all if you'd rather not.'

'Don't be silly. I'll go and change and meet you up at the temple.'

By the time Isabelle, attired in what she described as walking shoes ('What other sort are there?' wondered Jack) reached the temple, Jack was lolling on a stone bench, cigarette in hand, deeply immersed in the works of the late Reverend Bertram Throckmorton. The temple walls were smudged with smoke and the marble floor was muddy with the marks of boots and wheelbarrow tracks from the day's work.

'Have you found anything?' she asked eagerly as she sat beside him.

'Getting there,' he replied abstractedly. He looked her up and down and grinned. 'Good grief, Belle, I thought you were only

changing your shoes. I didn't realise you were putting on an
entirely new outfit. No wonder you took so long.'

'I couldn't possibly wear these shoes with the dress I had on.
I had to change.'

'We're going to explore a cave, not go out to lunch. Why on
earth have you got your handbag?'

'This dress hasn't got any pockets. Besides, I always carry my
handbag. I had to change that, too, of course.'

Jack grinned once more and muttered something which
sounded like *girls.*

'There's one thing, at any rate,' he said, nodding to where
the gardeners were upending a wheelbarrow full of earth and
rubble onto the grass. 'My pal Sam assures me that no-one's
been in the cave all day. Not that,' he added, 'anyone's had
much opportunity, what with stolen sapphires, dissension in the
household and Mine Host being lugged off to quod. Anyway,'
he said, picking up the book again, 'let me see if I can get
anything out of Throckmorton. He's a long-winded beggar and
far too given to classical allusions and scholarly footnotes, but
informative, all the same.'

Isabelle lit a cigarette and let him read. He wasn't, she noticed,
reading the book word for word, but skipping through it with
the practised manner of an experienced reader who knew what
he was looking for. It must have been nearly quarter of an hour
later when he gave a muttered grunt, and, turning back the page,
read it again.

He looked up and took a deep breath. 'Got it,' he said quietly.
He closed the book. 'The next thing, Belle, is to see if Mr
Throckmorton's information is accurate.'

He stood up and waved at the gardeners. 'Oi! Sam! Can we
go into the cave?'

'You can, sir,' said Sam, coming towards them, wiping his
face with a large red handkerchief. 'I reckon we've just about
finished for the day. We'll have to shore up and make good
the entrance and the walls with some props, but we'll tackle
that tomorrow. It's a nuisance you can't find that diamond
bracelet, sir.'

'Mrs Stanton's come to give me a hand,' said Jack with a
smile. 'I think she's got sharper eyes than I have.'

'Especially where diamonds are concerned,' said Isabelle, a remark which made Sam grin broadly.

'Well, best of luck, sir – miss. It *should* be safe enough, I'd say, as long as you watch your footing.'

Picking their way over the uneven ground, Jack and Isabelle, torches in hand, went into the passage and scrambled through the dug-out entrance into the cave.

Instinctively keeping their voices low, they approached the altar. Isabelle couldn't repress a shudder as she looked at the snarl of jagged teeth, now blackened with smoke. She reached out her hand and touched the stone, then drew it away sharply.

'What is it?'

'I felt something,' she said shining her torch to where her hand touched the stone. 'It's a piece of string or cord, Jack,' she said puzzled. 'What's it for?'

A short piece of thin cord projected from the bottom of the altar. 'It's woven into the carving, somehow. The carvings look solid, but there's actually a bit of space behind them. The cord looks new. I don't think it's been here long.'

'There's a piece sticking out of the other side as well,' said Jack, shining his torch along the bottom of the altar. 'That's a puzzle, Belle. I've no idea what it's for.'

'This isn't what you wanted to show me, is it?'

'No,' said Jack with a grin. 'I've got something a bit more exciting up my sleeve – if Throckmorton can be relied on, that is. Let me show you.'

She followed him up the altar steps and round the back.

'Hold my torch,' said Jack, handing it to her and kneeling down. 'Keep the light steady, old thing.' He stretched out his arms wide and pressed hard into the two top corners of the altar. 'If I can just get this right . . . Throckmorton says I have to lift and pull . . .' He grunted involuntarily.

Isabelle gasped. The back of the altar, a solid block of stone, came away and slid into the ground, leaving a dark, oblong hollow.

Jack shone his torch into the darkness and visibly relaxed.

'What were you expecting?' asked Isabelle.

'A body,' said Jack, standing back. 'The body which has so

mysteriously vanished. But,' he said with a shrug, 'as you can see for yourself, it's empty.'

'I can't say I'm sorry,' said Isabelle fervently.

'No . . . It's interesting how this works,' he said, running his hand over the pulley. 'You can see the weights and levers. Throckmorton, bless his Victorian heart, restored it and wrote a very long piece about the mechanics of the thing into the bargain.'

'I wonder if that piece of cord I found has anything to do with it?'

'It might have, but I can't see what, exactly. As you can see, there's a stone slab to sit on inside and steps going down. The steps lead on to a passage, which according to the Reverend, runs right the way to the cellars of the house.'

Isabelle crouched down and looked into the blackness. 'I don't like the look of that hole. The cellars are medieval, aren't they?'

'They're at least medieval, I'd say. They stretch for a dickens of a long way, I do know that.'

'I bet they're Roman, Jack,' said Isabelle. 'After all, this is an authentic Roman altar, so they could be.'

Jack nodded. 'Yes, it's not so great a leap of the imagination to say there once was a Roman villa on the site of the house. Throckmorton says that the altar had a trick, a way for the old priests to achieve a very scary effect. Let's see if it works.'

He took back his torch. 'Go round the front and turn your torch off.'

Isabelle did so. As she turned back to look at the altar, she drew her breath in a startled gasp.

The face on the altar seemed to come to life. In the complete blackness of the cave, the eyes started out, glowing, malevolent embers above the evil snarl of teeth. It was, Isabelle knew, nothing more than a trick of the light, but the mouth and the teeth seemed to be dripping with blood.

'Good effect, is it?' said Jack, climbing out from the altar.

'It's really scary,' said Isabelle, a bit shakily. 'Here, let me hold the torch so you can have a look.'

Jack obediently gave up his place and went to the front of the altar. 'Good God!' he said involuntarily. 'That'd scare the pants off anybody, particularly if there was chanting and wailing going on.'

'And human sacrifices,' put in Isabelle. Her voice from inside the altar was oddly magnified.

Jack jumped involuntarily. 'Blimey, Belle, that was *creepy*. The altar makes your voice all huge and hollow. You sound like the Voice of Doom.'

'Do I?' boomed the Voice of Doom.

'Absolutely. It doesn't sound like you at all and to have you say *human sacrifices* is really weird. I take back all I said yesterday about the artist who made the altar being no great shakes. He knew exactly what he was doing.'

'Jack,' boomed Isabelle's voice again. 'Shall we explore the passage?'

Jack couldn't help laughing. 'Put like that, it seems like a divine command. All right, I'm game if you are.'

He returned to the back of the altar and scrambled into it beside her. 'Ladies first?' he asked with a grin.

'Let's not stand on ceremony, shall we?' said Isabelle with a smile. 'I'm more than happy for you to lead the way.'

'Okey-doke.'

He climbed carefully down the narrow steps, feeling his way along the rough chalk walls. At the bottom a passage led away into darkness. It was tall enough for them to stand upright but not quite wide enough for them both to walk side by side.

'Where are we?' asked Isabelle quietly, after a little while. 'D'you think we're still in the cave?'

'Maybe not. It's hard to judge. Whoa!' He stopped abruptly and flung his arms wide. Isabelle stopped just short of running into his back. 'The ground slips away,' he said in answer to Isabelle's indignant query. He stepped to one side so she could see. 'Look, the passage splits into two.' He shone his torch along the two paths.

'It opens onto another cave, I think, Jack,' said Isabelle after a couple of moments. 'Let's see.'

'All right, but watch your step. The ground's very uneven.'

The cave was like a high, narrow room. The path sloped steeply down and they were glad of the handholds provided by the rocky walls. Jack stopped abruptly once more.

'This is the end of the line, I think. The passage simply stops. There's just a big hole beyond. I say!'

'What is it?'

'It's the cave! The altar cave, I mean. The passage opens onto the back of the cave.'

He lay down, shining his torch out of the hole. 'Yes, that's right. We're at the back, about four or five feet above the ground. You can't see this entrance from the cave because there's this spur of rock jutting out, shielding it. My word, put this together with that beastly altar, the old boys with their ghastly cult must have had a field day, jumping out on unsuspecting worshippers. Coming to church seems to have been a very different experience years ago.'

Isabelle didn't reply but made a funny little choking noise.

He turned his head. 'Isabelle?'

'Jack,' she said in a strained whisper. 'Come here.'

She had found the body.

It was lying on a rocky ledge, away from the path, and it was easy to see how they had missed it in the flickering light of the torches and the utter darkness of the cave.

Jack ran his torch beam over the sprawled mass and hastily turned the light away. 'That,' he said tightly, 'isn't nice. She's obviously been dead for some time.'

Isabelle reached out for his hand. 'Who is it?' she managed to say.

'I think that's Florence Pargetter,' said Jack grimly.

'Poor thing,' said Isabelle softly. She focused her torch beam on the flap of fabric that covered the body's legs. 'She's wearing a new coat.' Her voice broke. 'I bet it was her best coat.'

'Come on,' said Jack gently. 'Let's get out of here. We need to get hold of Ashley and Bill as soon as possible.'

They scrambled back up into the main passage, then Jack froze, rigidly still.

'Isabelle,' he whispered urgently. 'Someone's coming!'

From far away there was a gentle murmur of voices and a faint shuffling sound.

'Back,' hissed Jack. 'Back to the altar.'

As quietly as they could they retreated back along the passage, Isabelle silently blessing the fact she had chosen shoes with noiseless rope soles.

They reached the altar. Isabelle made to climb out but Jack put his hand on her arm.

'Wait,' he said, very softly. 'Turn your torch off.'

The darkness was so complete it was like a smothering blanket. With her nerves as taut as piano wire, Isabelle waited, then she felt Jack's mouth close to her ear.

'I think they've gone the other way. We'd better stay put.'

Straining their ears, they could hear noises. He was right. The noises were coming from inside the cave. Whoever it was – and there were obviously at least two of them – had evidently gone down the other passage and climbed down into the cave.

Out of the back of the altar they could see a very faint, flickering light, high above them on the roof of the cave. Isabelle breathed a silent prayer of thanks for Jack's caution. If they had climbed out of the altar they would have been seen right away.

'What d'you think, Wood?' said a voice. It was Duggleby, his voice brimming with excitement. 'Or should I call you Paxton? That passage is a remarkable discovery, isn't it?'

'I'm not bothered about what you call me,' said Wood genially. 'It's the passage that interests me. No matter what you said back at the house, it isn't the first time you've been down that passage, is it?'

There was silence, then Duggleby laughed. 'How did you guess?'

'Footprints in the dust. Also, you weren't hesitant enough. You were far too assured about finding your way. Not that, of course, I needed you to show me. Frank was never interested, but years ago I found my way through every inch of these passages. I grew up here.' He paused for a moment. 'You see, I'm Terence Napier.'

Isabelle gave a little breath of surprise. Jack's hand tightened on hers.

There was silence in the cave, then Duggleby spoke again. 'Napier? You admit it, do you?' He drew out the words slowly. 'Terence Napier.'

'At your service. Yes, I'm Terence Napier. You rumbled me yesterday, didn't you?'

'I did, as a matter of fact. Then, of course, when Mrs Hawker had her unfortunate outburst and Frank Leigh came – very clumsily – to your rescue this afternoon, I was completely certain.'

Isabelle's eyes had become accustomed to the very faint light and she could see the outline of Jack's head. He nodded vigorously at Napier's words. He *knew*, thought Isabelle with a shock. He *knew*.

'Yes,' said Napier regretfully. 'Poor old Frank never was much of a hand at concealment and Mrs Hawker hasn't helped at all. It took her a little while to work out who I was, but ever since, she's been begging Frank to get rid of me. Funny, really. She used to be very fond of me. She worried poor old Frank to death about harbouring a murderer and I suppose you can see her point of view. Nasty thing to have around the house, a murderer. Incidentally, that is what you had in mind when you brought me down here, isn't it? Murder, I mean.'

Duggleby laughed. 'Of course. I know the light's not good in here, Napier, but you should be able to see the gun in my hand. It's pointed right at you.'

'You won't use that. How on earth will you explain a body with a bullet in it?'

'As a matter of fact, I do have something more interesting in mind, but a neat little suicide will probably do the trick. Sandy Paxton – you did own up to being Sandy Paxton, you know – is suddenly overcome with remorse on finding his past life catching up with him. And don't pretend you're armed. I know that isn't true. Once I got rid of Celia I got you from the dining room. You haven't got a gun.'

'You're absolutely right, I'm sorry to say. I'm not sure if you'll get away with suicide, though.'

'Watch me,' said Duggleby. 'Turn around and walk towards the altar.'

'Another human sacrifice?'

'Less of it. Move.'

Napier heaved a deep sigh. 'You're quite right, Duggleby, old man, I haven't got a gun. But, when you called me out of the dining room, I thought something was about to happen, so I had the foresight to pick up the *pepper*!'

An agonised scream rang out. Jack leapt up, seized hold of the top of the altar and swung himself out. 'Stay there!' he hissed to Isabelle.

By the light of the oil lamp on the floor, he could see Napier and Duggleby wrestling together. Duggleby, one hand to his eyes, was fighting like a madman. Napier must have thrown a handful of pepper in Duggleby's eyes.

Jack raced towards the two men and flung himself at them.

Duggleby went flying. He rolled over, gave a grunt and lay sprawled out on the deep shadow of the cave floor, helpless and unmoving.

Napier, on his hands and knees, drew a deep shuddering breath, picked up the fallen gun and got to his feet unsteadily.

'Haldean! Where the hell did you come from?'

Jack looked at the gun in Napier's hand.

'Never mind that. I've heard every word.'

'Did you?' said Napier, warily.

'Yes. And, like our pal over there, I'd guessed who you really were. Incidentally, would you mind pointing that gun in another direction? I've already had Frank Leigh wave a pistol in my direction and two attempts on my life within an hour of each other don't half strain the patience.'

'Frank wouldn't have harmed you.'

'No? Perhaps not, although he was pretty wound up. You're right, though. I don't believe he's a killer.' Jack paused. 'What's more, I don't believe you are, either.'

Napier stared at him for a long moment then, with a laugh, lowered the gun. 'As a matter of fact, you're right. It's a funny thing, but I've been trying to decide whether or not to tell you.' He ran a hand over the back of his neck. 'The trouble is, you're a bit too pally with the police for my liking. It's one thing knowing I'm not a murderer, it's quite another proving it to the police.'

Jack gestured towards the unconscious Duggleby. 'Once he wakes up, I think the police will be very interested to hear what our friend here has to say. I don't think you'll have any problems proving your innocence.'

Napier laughed once more. 'Nothing's ever as simple as it seems but yes, if we can persuade Mr Duggleby to talk, then a great many things will become a lot clearer.'

He walked across to Duggleby and hauled the limp man upright.

With a speed like a striking cobra, Duggleby lashed out. Taken utterly by surprise, Napier missed his footing, stumbled and fell back. Duggleby wrenched the gun out of his hand and clapped it to Napier's ribs.

'One move,' he ground out. 'One move and you're dead.

Haldean!' he called. 'Go up to the altar – slowly! Take the lamp with you. Any tricks and Napier's dead. Move!'

Jack had no choice but to obey.

'Now,' said Duggleby, when Jack reached the altar. 'Sit down with your back to the altar. That's right,' he said in approval. And you,' he said, jabbing the gun into Napier's back, 'move. Go and sit beside Haldean.'

Napier walked unwillingly to where Haldean sat. 'Sorry,' he muttered, as he sat down.

'Quiet!' snarled Duggleby.

Keeping them covered with the gun, he knelt down and felt for the piece of cord that Isabelle had found. 'I watched you and your friends searching the cave earlier,' he told Jack. 'I thought then I might have to arrange a little surprise for you. Napier here was always on the guest list, of course, but you, Mr Haldean, are an unexpected bonus.' Taking the cord in his hand, he drew it out, looped it first round Napier, then round Jack, so their hands were securely pinned to their sides.

'You're tying us up to the altar?' remarked Jack loudly. 'Why?'

'Because this is part of my little surprise,' said Duggleby.

Still with the gun fixed on them, he took the loose end of the cord to the other side of the altar and found the other piece and, without taking his eyes off them, knotted the two ends together.

'You were quite right, Napier,' he said, stepping back. 'I don't want your body to be found with a bullet in it. Or yours, Haldean.'

'Much obliged, I'm sure,' said Jack. 'I feel much the same.'

'You see, I could hide Napier's body,' said Duggleby, ignoring him, 'but why make things difficult for the police? They'd probably search rather more effectively than you did this morning and that wouldn't do at all. And – take this as a compliment, Haldean – if you went missing the police would certainly hunt for you very vigorously indeed. So we're about to have a tragic accident.'

He took a brass cigarette lighter from his pocket and, opening it, idly flicked the little wheel. The wick burnt with a steady blue and yellow flame. 'This is my lucky lighter,' he remarked. 'It's never let me down.' He closed the lighter and put it back in his pocket.

He retreated into the shadows and emerged a couple of seconds later with a jerry can. 'Petrol,' he said, his voice quivering with excitement. 'This should do the trick.'

Napier strained against the cords. 'You can't burn us to death!'

'Oh, I can,' said Duggleby. 'Don't worry. I'll arrange a land-slide afterwards, with you both artistically disposed in the rubble.'

Napier gave a funny little grunt. Jack knew why. He had felt the cord grow taut and then slacken.

Isabelle!

'Now!' Jack bellowed and the two men sprang forward.

With a deafening roar, the gun went off. The sound of the shot echoed off the cave walls in thundering reverberations.

In the darkness and the confusion it was impossible to see who was fighting who. His ears ringing from the shot, Jack's world seemed to be a grappling, scrambling struggle. Then there was a sharp cry of triumph and Duggleby, petrol can in hand, flung himself at the altar. Jack and Napier both made a leap for him, then skidded to a halt.

Duggleby unscrewed the can and upended it on the altar.

The sharp, acrid smell of petrol caught Jack's nostrils. The petrol glugged out, a sinister, hollow series of gurgles.

With a laugh, Duggleby held his cigarette lighter aloft and flipped open the lid.

'Don't be a fool!' yelled Jack desperately. 'One spark and we all go up.'

Duggleby looked insane, his eyes wide, mad with power. 'Let's do it!' His thumb quivered on the little wheel of the lighter.

'STOP!' boomed a voice from the altar, reverberating round the cave.

Duggleby gave a shriek of fear and leapt forward.

Jack caught the lighter as it sailed through the air, then, as his hand closed round it, in one fluid movement crunched his fist into the side of Duggleby's head.

Duggleby fell to one side with a grunt, then Napier was on top of him.

'It's all right,' he said shakily after a few moments, getting to his feet. 'This time he really is out cold.'

'Let's tie him up,' said Jack, catching his breath. 'We can use the cord he used on us.'

Napier moved forward then stopped, looking warily at the

altar. 'I . . . I . . . Did you hear it, Haldean? Did you hear a voice from the altar?'

'I certainly did,' said Jack cheerfully as Isabelle emerged. 'Let me introduce you to the Voice of Doom herself. Keep an eye on him,' he said briefly and went forward to Isabelle.

'You were absolutely wonderful,' he said, hugging her tightly.

'You were there all along?' Napier asked Isabelle, as, still keeping a watchful eye on Duggleby, he took the cord and tied him up securely.

'Yes, I was,' said Isabelle. 'I heard everything but I couldn't see a thing, of course. When you said, 'You're tying us up,' Jack, I knew you were telling me. I couldn't think what to do for a moment, then I remembered I had my nail scissors in my bag and managed to cut the rope.'

'Wonderful,' repeated Jack. 'I'll never laugh at your handbags again.'

'There's one thing,' she said. Her chin came up and she suddenly looked very wary. 'Mr Wood – I heard you say who you really are. You're not Sandy Paxton, are you? You're Terence Napier.'

'Of course he is, Belle,' said Jack. He indicated Duggleby, trussed up on the ground. 'Our friend here is none other than Sandy Paxton.'

'*Duggleby's* Sandy Paxton?' said Isabelle starting back. 'Jack, are you sure?'

'Certain. I knew it when we saw the portrait of old Ebenezer in the gallery before lunch. There was no one else Duggleby could be, but I couldn't prove it. Not then. I'll be able to later on, but first of all, I'd like to see if I can just bring matters to a conclusion.'

He turned to Napier, 'You know the area. There's a path, a right of way, that runs along the side of Breagan Stump. Where does it come out?'

'Not far from the village.'

'Good. Isabelle, can you go and get Bill and Ashley from the police station? I think they should be in on this.'

SEVENTEEN

Jack lay sprawled out on the hard earth of the cave floor, waiting. It was well over an hour since Isabelle had gone for Bill and Ashley. He was dressed in Sandy Paxton's jacket with his face concealed by his arm. In the dim rays of the oil lamp, he looked, he hoped, convincingly dead.

The only sound was that of the stream and the hypnotic, constant drip of water. He couldn't know for sure how much time had passed. Then he caught a sound that brought all his senses flaring into life.

It was the faintest chink of a foot against a stone but he hadn't heard the sound of anyone scrambling through the entrance. There was another scraping sound followed by a brief grunt as someone dropped to the ground. They'd come down the passage from the cellars of the house and through the concealed entrance to the cave. The footsteps hesitated behind him and he could hear quick breathing.

'Sandy?' a low voice called. 'Sandy?'

He felt a hand under his arm and another under his leg and his body was rolled over.

He dug his elbow into the earth and, with a swift movement sat up.

'Looking for Sandy Paxton, Mrs Leigh? Or should that be *Mrs Welbeck*?'

Then Bill and Ashley blew their police whistles simultaneously and the cave was full of jabbing light, pounding feet, shouting voices and, rising above it all, the sound of Evie Leigh screaming.

In the dancing light he could see the glitter of a gun in her hand. He flung himself to one side as she fired. The bullet zinged off the rock, catching his arm. He scrambled to his knees, then hurled himself at her as she raised the gun again.

His arm was numbed from the shot. If it hadn't been for that, he would have reached her in time.

'Jack!' yelled Bill over the noise of the shot. 'Are you all right?'

Jack caught the beautiful woman in his arms and laid her reverently on the ground. He felt suddenly sick. 'It's all over, Bill,' he said quietly. 'She's dead.'

Lady Alice Rivers took the glass of sherry Arthur gave her and sank back in her chair. 'I'm glad to have you back in one piece, Isabelle. I thought you'd be safe at Breagan Grange.'

'So did I,' said Arthur with feeling. It was a couple of days after the events at Breagan Grange. Arthur had arrived that afternoon, heartily relieved to see his wife again. 'If I'd had any idea what that little rat, Paxton, was up to . . .' He stopped and swallowed.

'I still can't make head or tail of it,' said Sir Philip forlornly.

'It's very puzzling, dear,' said his wife kindly. 'That's why we're waiting for Jack. He'll be able to explain everything.'

Jack, who had spent the day at Scotland Yard, had telegrammed to say he would be back for dinner and was bringing Terence Napier with him.

'Terence Napier, hmm?' had said Sir Philip doubtfully. 'Dash it, Alice, I know you said he was all right, but are you sure he's all right? I'm not one to make a fuss, as you know. Least said, soonest mended and all that, but the man was wanted by the police.'

'He was innocent, Philip,' said Lady Rivers patiently. 'Jack proved it.'

Sir Philip hunched his shoulders disconsolately. 'Dashed if I know why he couldn't say as much in the first place, then.'

The door opened and Jack poked his head round the door.

''Ullo,' ullo,' ullo,' he said cheerily. 'Sherry? We've timed our arrival well.'

'Come on in,' said Sir Philip, getting to his feet. 'Nice to see you, m'boy.' He stopped as he saw the man behind Jack. Sir Philip's eyebrows rose but he recovered himself manfully. 'Terence Napier, eh? Er . . . Pleased to meet you. Absolutely. Yes. How d'you do?'

'Very well, thank you, sir,' said Napier, taking the sherry Arthur poured for him. 'All the better for having run across Haldean, here.' He raised his glass in a toast. 'If it hadn't had been for you, old man, I don't know if we'd have ever got to the bottom of it.'

'Don't be so modest, Jack,' said Aunt Alice, seeing he was about to protest. 'Isabelle's given us some idea of what happened, and I couldn't agree more. For one thing, I can scarcely credit that Evie Leigh was really Mrs Welbeck. It sounds incredible.'

'It *sounds* incredible,' said Jack, taking a cigarette from the box beside him, 'but, like all good tricks, it depends on what went on behind the scenes.'

'I didn't tumble to it,' said Napier. 'It never crossed my mind that Mrs Welbeck was anything other than what she seemed. If anything, I thought she'd been killed to keep her quiet. I suspected Evie, of course, as she benefited from the whole scheme, but it never occurred to me that she was Mrs Welbeck.'

'Why didn't you come clean and tell us who you were right away?' asked Arthur.

'Absolutely,' agreed Sir Philip. 'Why pretend, eh? If you'd faced up to things, it would all have been a great deal easier for all of us.'

Napier hesitated, sipping his sherry. 'Frank,' he said eventually. 'Because I knew Frank, I simply couldn't own up.'

Sir Philip exchanged puzzled glances with Arthur.

'You see,' continued Napier, 'When Aunt Constance – Mrs Paxton – was murdered and it looked for all the world as if I was guilty, I was in Australia. The first I knew about it was what I read in the newspapers in Sydney. I came hotfooting back and immediately looked up Frank. He believed I was innocent of course, and was all for going to the police. He couldn't understand why I hesitated. At the time, I couldn't explain it to him, but I can tell you.'

He leaned forward and took a cigarette from the box. 'The reason was Evie. I *knew*, absolutely *knew,* that there'd been some jiggery-pokery at Topfordham and, as Evie was the chief beneficiary I thought she had to be behind it somehow or other. However, it only took a few minutes conversation with Frank for me to realise he'd never believe Evie was involved unless there was proof positive. Frank's a terrific chap, you know. Very loyal and loath to see the worst in anyone. I think he was beginning to realise his marriage was a mistake, but he's a stubborn beggar. He'd never admit it and he'd certainly never countenance the idea Evie could be anything other than what she seemed. Poor old Frank,' he added. 'It's really knocked him for six and no mistake.'

'Poor devil,' muttered Sir Philip.

'Yes,' agreed Napier. 'If there's one good thing to come out of the whole business, it's that Frank's free of a very dangerous woman. It took me a dickens of a lot of persuasion to convince Frank to keep my identity secret but I insisted. I not only thought Evie was in it up to her neck, I had a fairly good idea that the man who'd impersonated me at Topfordham was none other than my cousin, Sandy. I wanted to find out the truth but, if Evie tumbled to who I was, I'd be in real danger.' He gave a wry grin. 'It took me a while to suspect who Duggleby was. I should have guessed right away.'

'Had Evie really known Mrs Paxton, in the war?' asked Arthur.

Jack shook his head. 'No, of course not. She made that up to scrape an acquaintance with Frank Leigh.' He lit his cigarette and blew out a thoughtful cloud of smoke. 'I'd guessed most of this, by the way, but Sandy Paxton's – Duggleby's – evidence confirmed it. We knew, because Dr Mountford told us, that Sandy Paxton had married an actress. What we didn't know, of course, was that the actress he married was one Daisy Price, known to us as Evie Leigh.'

'Good Lord!' exclaimed Sir Philip. 'That feller Duggleby and Evie Leigh were *married*?'

'Yes, that's right. They were also members of the Vicar's gang. Paxton was very valuable to the Vicar. From all accounts, Parsons, the Vicar, was a real thug, but Paxton had genuine charm and was admitted to a class of society closed to the Vicar.'

'He did have charm,' said Isabelle. 'Real charm, I mean. He had a way of making you feel sorry for him. I thought he was a complete pet and, of course, once you'd thought that, it was only a short step to realising he was actually a very attractive man.'

'I'll have to take your word for it,' said Arthur with a baffled shrug. 'I thought he was a weedy sort of beggar.'

'Not so weedy,' countered Isabelle. 'He gave that impression but it wasn't actually true. And, as for his charm . . . well, Celia certainly fell for it.' She gave a sly grin. 'She stopped making eyes at you, Jack, when he came along.'

'Isabelle!' said her father, shocked. 'Celia's engaged to be married.'

'I entertained very warm feelings of gratitude towards Duggleby for a while,' said Jack with a grin. 'Don't look so disapproving, Uncle Phil.'

'I'm glad to say that Celia's patched things up nicely with Ted Marchant,' said Napier. 'Not that, from what I can gather, young Marchant ever realised there was anything wrong.'

'He probably didn't,' agreed Jack. 'Anyway, charm or no charm, the wheel came off Paxton's wagon in 1915. Parsons, the Vicar, was killed in a warehouse theft that went wrong. That left Paxton and his wife in a bit of a spot.'

'Wait a moment,' interrupted Lady Rivers, putting down her sherry. 'I thought the Vicar – Parsons – murdered the man Isabelle found on the train.'

'So did we, Aunt Alice,' said Jack with a rueful smile. 'I'll come to that in a minute. Anyway, with the death of the Vicar, the gang was broken up and Paxton's livelihood was gone. At this point, Frank Leigh, of all people, threw Paxton a lifeline.'

'That was typical of Frank,' sighed Napier. 'He thought he was giving Paxton a chance to make a new start, to put his past behind him. He more or less bribed Aunt Constance to get Sandy to join the army.'

'He deserted, didn't he?' said Arthur.

'Absolutely, he did. I imagine he always intended to.'

Jack nodded. 'I'd say so. For the next few years, Paxton and Evie laid low in France. I'm not sure when the idea of stealing the sapphires came to them.'

'I bet they always wanted them,' said Isabelle. 'After all, they were jewel thieves. The idea of the Breagan Bounty sapphires lying shut up in a bank and out of reach must have really got to them.'

'You're right,' agreed Jack. 'And, of course, they knew Frank Leigh was going to inherit the sapphires. Marrying Mr Leigh must've seemed like a big step forwards.'

Lady Rivers looked at Jack quizzically. 'What would've happened if Mr Leigh hadn't been so obliging as to fall for Evie?'

'I don't know,' said Jack, taking a cigarette. 'Our precious pair would've certainly done *something* but, as it was, Frank Leigh was hooked.'

'She was a very striking woman,' said Aunt Alice thoughtfully. 'He must've been flattered, poor man. He was probably lonely, as well. Wasn't there a danger, though, that Frank Leigh would introduce his wife to Mrs Paxton? After all, she was his aunt and Evie Leigh was meant to have been an old friend.'

'None whatsoever,' said Napier, shaking his head. 'Aunt Constance blamed Frank for Sandy's supposed death. She wouldn't have anything to do with him. You think Sandy let his mother know he was alive though, don't you, Haldean?'

'That's certain. She went from believing him dead to believing him to be a deserter, and the obvious person to tell her that is Sandy himself. Anyway, there we are. Evie's now secure as Frank Leigh's wife and Paxton's waiting on the sidelines.'

'What were they waiting for, eh?' demanded Sir Philip.

'For the right opportunity to crop up, Uncle Phil. Paxton came to London, established his identity as Leonard Duggleby, the down-at-heel journalist, and Evie had something approximating to the life of Riley at Frank Leigh's expense. As Frank's wife, she could afford to wait. They probably had a few schemes in mind but an absolute corker became possible when Mrs Paxton's housekeeper retired.'

Jack blew a smoke ring and studied it for a few moments. 'The fact that the plan meant murdering Paxton's mother didn't seem to bother them at all.'

Lady Rivers and Isabelle gave a little cry.

'That's revolting,' said Arthur, standing up. 'Here, let me refill your glass, Jack.'

'Thanks, Arthur. Well, Evie, with, no doubt, forged references, got the job and created the personality of Mrs Welbeck.'

'She couldn't have kept it up for long,' objected Isabelle. 'Someone would have cottoned on to her. Besides, even Evie Leigh couldn't stay away from home forever.'

'She didn't have to keep it up for long,' said Jack. 'Just long enough to convince everyone that she was Mrs Welbeck, the housekeeper, a plain, conscientious woman who kept herself to herself and whose ambition was to go back to the north of England. With Evie in place, it was time for Sandy Paxton to appear on the scene. And this,' he added, leaning forward and flicking the ash off his cigarette, 'is where it gets clever. Imagine an old lady – an old lady alone with her servants – is murdered. Who's the first person or group of people the police question?'

'The servants, of course,' replied Aunt Alice promptly. 'They know more than anyone about what goes on in a house. And, of course, a newly arrived servant would be open to suspicion.'

'Absolutely,' agreed Jack. 'And that would never do.' He nodded towards Napier. 'So Evie and Paxton arranged things so suspicion would immediately fall on you.'

'Don't I know it,' said Napier, ruefully.

'Why on earth did Mrs Paxton agree to introduce her son as you, Napier?' asked Arthur.

'Aunt Constance was always soft on Sandy,' said Napier. 'At a guess, he wrote to his mother, saying he wanted to return to the fold but couldn't come back openly as he'd been a deserter.'

'There's a general amnesty for deserters,' said Arthur.

Jack wrinkled his nose. 'More or less, but only if there's no other charge against the man in question. As we know, Paxton's record was distinctly spotty. Paxton probably said he could only come home if his mother told everyone he was her nephew, Terence Napier.'

'Why did Paxton take his mother off to Paris, Jack?' asked Isabelle.

Jack thoughtfully swirled his sherry round in his glass. 'There's a few reasons. Both Paxton and Evie wanted Terence Napier to make as big an impact as possible and this was the perfect way to ensure that Terence Napier was talked about endlessly in the village without actually having to face a battery of questions from inquisitive neighbours. Again, although Mrs Paxton wasn't a chatty woman, she might very well have let something slip if they stayed put. As far as his mother was concerned, Paxton could have told her he was taking her for a holiday or, more probably, that she had to sign documents in Paris that would prove that he really was Alexander Paxton, her son, so he could return openly to England. It'd be easy enough for Paxton, who had lived in France for years, to hire an office and get a couple of old pals to pretend to be French officials. Nothing he signed would be examined, you see. All he had to do was convince his mother.'

'And she, poor woman, would want to be convinced,' said Lady Rivers softly.

'Exactly,' agreed Jack. 'The second part of the plan was put into effect when Mrs Paxton and her son returned home. The interesting thing is that our account of what happened next rests solely on Mrs Welbeck's evidence.'

'And Mrs Welbeck is our old friend, Evie,' said Arthur slowly. 'My God!'

'I should've seen that,' said Napier. 'It never occurred to me that Mrs Welbeck was a phoney.'

'She's a good actress,' said Jack. 'She asked Dr Mountford for a fresh bottle of sulphonal and asked him to call the following morning. The whole story of the quarrel between Mrs Paxton and Terence Napier rests on her say-so. Dr Mountford – and, I may say, all of Topfordham – believed that Terence Napier was out for what he could get. It seemed only too believable that Mrs Paxton had tumbled to the fact Terence Napier was up to no good and thrown him out. That gives Terence Napier the reason, as was thought, to act quickly, to forge a will, to poison the brandy decanter and to disappear, hoping for the best. The thing is, though,' he added, reaching for another cigarette, 'we were meant to see through that will.'

'Were we?' asked Aunt Alice. 'I thought the doctor was very bright to spot it.'

'He was bright,' agreed Jack, 'but it was bound to be spotted soon enough. Evie, in her incarnation as Mrs Welbeck, had learned enough about Topfordham to use two obviously false witnesses. And, once that will had been discounted, it also seemed obvious that the second will was the real one, the one that left everything to a Mrs Evangeline Farley or, to put it another way, to Evie.'

'I guessed both wills were false, of course,' said Napier. 'And I still didn't suspect Mrs Welbeck.'

'She was helped along by Dr Mountford,' said Jack. 'He's so obviously honest that he's a perfect witness. Evie wanted him to find the body. She knew he'd spot the discrepancy about the bottles of sulphonal and she was on hand to point out the brandy decanter laced with sulphonal, if he happened to miss it. For all the world it looked as if Terence Napier had murdered Mrs Paxton and dressed it up as suicide. That was very important, of course, because otherwise the police were bound to suspect Mrs Welbeck. She was the one who gave Mrs Paxton her sleeping draught, you see.'

'So was the sulphonal – the fatal dose – in the brandy decanter?' asked Isabelle.

'I doubt it. I imagine Mrs Welbeck slipped the fatal dose into the glass and laced the brandy decanter afterwards.'

Isabelle shook her head. 'It's so simple.'

'Absolutely,' said Jack gravely. 'And that very simple crime should have been it. Evie Leigh produced evidence to show she had been Mrs Evangeline Farley – which, unless she'd been bigamously married to a Mr Farley, she couldn't have been – and the bank handed over the sapphires, no doubt reassured by the fact that, by a happy coincidence, the Mrs Farley of the will was actually Mrs Leigh and therefore the jewels were returning to their old home. But, as we know, they were very definitely Evie's and not the property of the Leigh family.'

'Did she want the sapphires for themselves?' asked Aunt Alice. 'Or was it the money she was interested in?'

Jack shrugged. 'The money, I think. In either case, I don't imagine Frank Leigh would have lived for much longer to worry about it.'

'I told him so,' said Napier. 'I don't know if he believed me.'

'So what happened next?' asked Isabelle. 'Where did the poor man on the train come into it?'

'Who the devil *was* the man on the train?' demanded her father. 'I can't work it out at all.'

Jack laughed. 'D'you know, I very nearly guessed it when I was with Ashley at the Mountfords'. The man on the train was John Bright.'

Sir Philip continued to look baffled. 'Who the dickens is John Bright?'

'John Bright,' said Jack, 'was a Topfordham man born and bred, a bit of a local Lothario—'

'Raffish,' put in Isabelle.

'As you say, raffish, and Mrs Paxton's outdoor man.'

Sir Philip's frown deepened. 'So how on earth does he fit into it?'

'He fits in,' said Jack, 'because of the poor girl Belle and I found murdered in the cave. She was Florence Pargetter, Mrs Paxton's maid, and a sharp, observant girl. I don't think Florence suspected Mrs Welbeck was anything other than a housekeeper while she was at Mrs Paxton's. Certainly she never said as much to her bosom chum, one Mavis Stainburn. However, she did notice Mrs Welbeck had false teeth. John Bright must've noticed them too.' Jack coughed delicately. 'John Bright had – er – tried his luck with Mrs Welbeck and her false teeth had shifted to one side.'

'So what if they had?' questioned his uncle. 'It sounds a sordid little episode but that's all.'

'It didn't strike me until later. Mrs Welbeck was described as having rabbit teeth. You see?'

'No,' said Uncle Philip, after some thought. 'I can't see that I do.'

'Of course!' said Aunt Alice. 'False teeth – real false teeth, if you know what I mean, – are straight! That's why they often look so unnatural, because they're perfect. No one would have false teeth that stuck out, unless they were in disguise.'

'Exactly,' said Jack. 'Mrs Welbeck was someone in disguise. As soon as I twigged that, I realised just how much our ideas depended on Mrs Welbeck's evidence, the mysterious Mrs Welbeck who disappeared so abruptly after Mrs Paxton's death. So who the devil was she? And the answer to that, incredible as it seemed at first sight, was obvious. The woman who'd benefited from the crime, of course.'

'Evie Leigh,' said Isabelle. 'Jack, when we discovered Florence Pargetter's body, you knew who she was right away. How?'

Jack leaned forward and tapped his cigarette on the ashtray. 'Evie Leigh had been photographed wearing the sapphires. That photo was published in *Joy, Love and Laughter,* a relentlessly wholesome publication, which Florence, according to her friend, Mavis, was excited about. Now, at this point I'm guessing, but I think I'm right. I think Florence Pargetter let slip to John Bright she thought the woman in the magazine was none other than Mrs

Welbeck. I'm not sure if John Bright stumbled upon the magazine in Florence's hands or if Florence asked him outright if he knew who the woman was, but John Bright certainly did know, because we found the torn-out page from the magazine in his jacket pocket.'

'That was much later on though, Jack,' objected Aunt Alice.

'Yes it was. What I think happened is that Florence went off under her own steam to beard Evie Leigh. And, as Isabelle and I found her body in the cave, we know how that interview turned out. John Bright hung about, waiting for Florence to return and, when she didn't, decided to have a crack at Evie Leigh himself.'

'So John Bright was the man who turned up at the Leighs'?' asked Arthur.

Jack nodded. 'Yes, that's right. I think, because of the way that things worked out, Bright must've written to Evie, asking for an interview, so Evie knew what time he was coming, and warned Paxton to be ready.'

'So did Bright rob the safe?' asked Aunt Alice.

'Of course not. Bright was a gardener, not a safe-cracker. No, Evie Leigh gave him the fifty quid that was in the safe to buy him off and put the marked card in the safe to make it look like the Vicar's work.'

'Why did they bring this Vicar into it?' asked Sir Philip.

'They simply couldn't allow Bright to live,' said Jack. 'He was far too dangerous. At the same time, they wanted, at all costs to avoid the link being made with Mrs Paxton's household. Now the police will try very hard to identify a body, even a headless one, so Evie and Paxton did their level best to give us an identity, that of their old, safely dead, boss, the Vicar. They used his trademark cards, and enough French bits and pieces, including the dagger and the gloves, to suggest it was a French crime, which tied up with the Vicar. Sandy – Alexander – Paxton also put some of his own things in the compartment, to add a bit of depth to a character supposedly called Andrew Parsons.'

'Did Evie Leigh give John Bright the sapphires?' asked Lady Rivers.

Jack shook his head. 'I doubt it, Aunt Alice. What I think is actually far more likely is that she gave them to Sandy Paxton. Because, you see, what must've happened is that Sandy Paxton trailed Bright from the Leighs'.'

He turned to Isabelle. 'You were on the train. You felt the shock of the impact as Bright's body hit the bridge. You came across Paxton – Duggleby – standing beside the compartment with Bright's body in it, and yet you didn't suspect him. Why?'

'The same reasons that you didn't, Jack,' said Isabelle with a shrug. 'He looked so pathetic for one thing, and, for another, I couldn't see that anyone would commit a murder then hang around in the corridor to tell people about it. The main reason was the sapphires, though. He told me they were there. That alone seemed to prove he was innocent.'

'We all thought the same, didn't we, Jack?' said Arthur.

'Of course we did. It was a brilliant move. From Evie and Paxton's point of view, it worked perfectly. Paxton murdered Bright, planted the sapphires, and no one suspected him. Paxton kept guard outside the compartment to yell blue murder at the first passer-by and ensure that same passer-by didn't nick the sapphires. Evie got her jewels back and the evidence Paxton planted on the train sent us hurtling off in the wrong direction, hunting for the Vicar.'

'But we knew it wasn't the Vicar,' said Isabelle. 'I'd heard Bright speak and he couldn't speak French.'

'Exactly,' said Jack. 'Evie and Paxton must've realised that you could disprove that Bright was the Vicar early on, so that's why they shadowed you to the Criterion and why they tried to kill you. As soon as Paxton realised you weren't dead, he staged his own accident and was careful to tell us his accident was linked to yours.'

'Did it really matter that much?' demanded Arthur. 'That we should believe the man on the train was the Vicar? After all, even when we worked out he couldn't be the Vicar, we weren't much wiser.'

'That's true,' agreed Jack. 'However, we thought that the *murderer* was the Vicar, which, from Evie and Paxton's point of view was nearly as good.'

'There's something I want to ask,' said Napier. 'When you and Mrs Stanton saw the resemblance between me and the portrait of Ebenezer Leigh in the portrait gallery, you knew who I was. Why were you so sure?'

'Because of Mr Leigh,' said Jack. 'Granted you were a member of the family, you more or less had to be Terence Napier because that's who Mr Leigh would protect. He wouldn't shield Sandy Paxton. That gave me a bit of a problem though. It seemed impossible you could be Napier, because you'd been to Topfordham and, what's more, had a long talk to Dr Mountford. That meant, you *couldn't* be Terence Napier – unless the Terence Napier accused of murdering Mrs Paxton wasn't actually Napier but an impostor. And, granted that Mrs Paxton had been party to the deception, I knew who the impostor must be.'

'I guessed Paxton was behind it,' said Napier. 'I wanted proof, though. That's why I wanted a photo of him. I wanted to show it to Dr Mountford.'

'Evie must've destroyed it,' said Jack. 'She had ample opportunity to get rid of it.'

'How did Evie and Sandy get onto me?' asked Napier. 'They obviously did.' He grinned. 'I knew that séance was a set-up.'

'You were simply too much at home,' said Isabelle. 'I noticed that. You fitted in too well and Mr Leigh treated you very warmly.' She sighed. 'Poor Celia. Sandy Paxton must've got her to suggest a séance. She'd never believe it, but she's a very suggestible person.' She turned to her mother. 'The séance was really creepy. It was the noise of the water that got to me. It sounded just like the cave. Jack told me how they'd done it.'

'And how was that, dear?' asked her mother.

'I'll show you.' Isabelle reached out her hand to Arthur. 'Now, you're on one side. Jack, bring that low table over to the sofa and sit on my other side. We're pretending,' she explained to her mother, 'that we're at a séance, you see? Now, everyone put their hands on the table.'

'You're doing this very well,' murmured Jack.

'I'm only doing what you showed me. From now on, this is going to be one of my party tricks.'

She laid her hands flat on the table, so she touched Jack's fingertips with her left hand and Arthur's with her right. 'You can see we're touching each other's fingertips, yes? It would be dark, of course, so you can't actually see, but you can feel the other person's fingers. Arthur, close your eyes, darling. Jack, close your eyes as well.' Isabelle wriggled and moved her hand. 'Sorry, I just need to get comfortable.' She readjusted her position. 'Arthur, without opening your eyes, tell me. Am I touching your fingertips?'

'Yes, I can feel them.'

'Have a look.'

Arthur opened his eyes and gave an astonished laugh. Isabelle's left arm was draped across the back of the sofa. Her hand, the hand that was touching his, was also touching Jack's.

'You see?' said Isabelle. 'When we rejoined hands, you assumed you were holding the same hand as you'd been before, but you can see for yourself I've now got a free hand.'

'And with that free hand,' said Jack, 'you can drop liquid into a glass and, with the right atmosphere, it sounds exactly like the drip of water in the cave. Good, eh?'

Sir Philip laughed incredulously. 'By George, I always thought that séance nonsense was a load of trickery, but it's remarkable to see how simple the trick is.'

'It really is remarkable,' said Lady Rivers. 'Obviously the blood on Mr Napier's hands was a trick too, but how did that work?'

'Again, it's simple,' said Jack. 'Any boy who's ever played with a chemistry set can make magic blood.'

Arthur smacked his hand on his thigh. 'I know! I've done it! Years ago now, but I've done it. What are the chemicals, Jack? Potassium something or other and iron nitrate, aren't they?'

'That's right,' said Jack. 'Potassium thiocyanate.'

'What do you do with potassium thingy?' asked Isabelle.

Jack held out his hands. 'If I put potassium thiocyanate, which is colourless, on one palm and iron nitrate, which is also colourless, on the other palm and bring them together, the chemicals mix and produce what looks like deep red blood. Napier was sitting between Evie and Paxton. Evie, say, put a few drops of potassium thiocyanate on her hand and Paxton put iron nitrate on his and, when they touched Napier's hand, the chemicals mixed and Napier looked as if he were dripping with blood. Wonderful, eh?'

'Remarkable,' repeated Aunt Alice.

'I was really shaken by it,' said Napier. 'I'd presumed the séance was a trick but when I saw what I honestly thought was blood on my hands, I'm ashamed to say I wondered if it was a real message from a spirit in the cave, after all.'

'You haven't been in the cave, Dad,' said Isabelle, sensing his scepticism. 'It's a lot easier to believe there really was something there, once you'd seen that ghastly altar.'

'Real or not,' said Napier, 'I thought the easiest thing to do was to go along with the game. I was on my guard and hoped I could catch Evie up to no good. Once I'd got some sort of proof, I could convince Frank that Evie was a wrong' un. All I can say is that I was taken completely unawares. Despite being, as I thought, sceptical, this awful whispering started.' He nodded towards Isabelle. 'You know how the altar amplified sound. I couldn't catch the words but it felt *evil*.' He shook his head. 'You'd have to know the cave to appreciate the effect. Then, without warning, the altar became a white-hot glowing mass of flame, with that ghastly face in the middle of it. You think they used a magnesium flare, don't you Haldean?'

'Magnesium fits the bill, certainly.'

'Sandy must've have lit the flare, then got into the cave by the tunnel under the altar. I was gazing thunderstruck at the altar when I sensed something behind me. He must've walloped me with a cosh and set the place on fire. And, as I'd firmly stated I was going to be in the cave all night, that should've been it.'

'It should, shouldn't it?' agreed Jack. 'However, when Paxton got back to the house something happened that neither he nor Evie expected.'

'And that was?' asked Uncle Philip.

'Frank Leigh had stolen the sapphires,' said Jack. 'Evie was beside herself.' He grinned. 'I was standing next to Paxton when he rumbled the sapphires were false and, believe you me, he wasn't acting.'

'Neither was Evie,' said Isabelle with a laugh. 'She went up like a rocket.'

'You can see their point of view,' said Jack, reaching for another cigarette. 'They'd been to a dickens of a lot of trouble to get those sapphires and they weren't going to let them go lightly.'

'Poor Mr Leigh,' said Isabelle. 'I'm just glad you were able to stop him coming to harm, Jack, even if Celia didn't thank you for it at the time.' She paused, putting her head to one side. 'He will be all right, won't he?' she asked hesitantly.

'Frank?' questioned Napier. 'He will, if I've got anything to do with it. I'm not going anywhere until Frank's sorted out. I've already roped Celia in on this.' He grinned. 'Frank's not up to making decisions at the moment but now the Breagan Bounty's back where it belongs, Celia can have her farm and Ted Marchant and stay in England, which is what she wanted. As for Frank . . . Well, once the dust has settled, we're going to point out to him what's blindingly obvious to everyone, and that's Mary Hawker is perfect for him. I want to see Frank safely married.'

'It seems a little high-handed,' said Lady Rivers. 'I presume Mrs Hawker has a say in it?'

'There's no problem there, Lady Rivers. Mary Hawker has thought Frank's the bee's knees for ages.'

'You'll like her, Aunt Alice,' said Jack. 'She's a very sound, trustworthy sort of woman and devoted to Mr Leigh. She's scrupulously honest, too. Uncomfortably so, on occasions,' he added with a smile. 'Celia thinks the world of her. The pair of them will be very, very happy.'

Aunt Alice beamed and picked up her sherry. 'Now that,' she said, 'really is good news.'